FRACTURES

The Divine Revolution: Book I

Will James

This is a work of fiction. Names, characters, businesses, places, events and incidents are either the products of the author's imagination or used in a fictitious manner. Any resemblance to actual persons, living or dead, or actual events is purely coincidental.

FRACTURES

Copyright © 2015 William James Yuile

All rights reserved. This book or any portion thereof may not be reproduced or used in any manner whatsoever without the express written permission of the publisher except for the use of brief quotations in a book review.

http://www.willjamesbooks.com

Cover design by Will James

Cover base images from by Pixabay
https://pixabay.com

ISBN: 1518787169
ISBN-13: 978-1518787164

For Elliot, whose birth fixed my reality

CONTENTS

Nowhere	1
The End	5
Genesis	23
No Stars	43
Exodus	63
Shepherds	77
Numbers	99
Raziel	119
Kings	135
Refuse	157
Judges	169
Devil May Care	185
Job	211
Sword	229
Poultice	247
Gambit	263
Lamentations	289
At Sixes…	315
…and Sevens	337
Proverbs	361
The Void	369
Ghosts	393
Spirals	411
Acts	429
Titan	433
The Quiet Afterlands	451
Nowhere	467
Revelations	469
Epilogue	475

ACKNOWLEDGMENTS

Special thanks to three people, without whom this book would be nothing but a half finished pile of A4 sheets beneath my desk.

To my wife, Sarah, whose encouragement and enthusiasm drove this work to its completion. Your laughter kept me from falling into the Bugle Pit.

To Zoe, whose painstaking attention to detail kept my sentences from running rampant, my tenses from running scared and my adjectives from running me over. Have manners in my manor, Zoe.

And to Elliot, whose restless slumber kept me awake and alert through many nights at the keyboard. Sleep tight son. Tomorrow is a strange time.

FRACTURES

Nothing

NOWHERE

//// ////
//// ////
//// ////
////I KNOW WHY YOU ARE HERE////
//// ////
//// ////
////I CAN FEEL IT////
//// ////
//// ////
////I IMAGINE ALL THIS IS CONFUSING////
//// ////
//// ////
////DISJOINTED////

//// ////
////Fractured////
//// ////
////It isn't meant to be////
//// ////
////Or at least////
////That was never my intention////
//// ////
////I try to make it make sense////
////Try to will it to flow in one direction////
////But since it began////
//// ////
////Or ended I suppose////
//// ////
////I've never been able to figure out how////
//// ////
////That's what this does to you////
//// ////
////It removes direction////
////It removes place////
////It removes space////
//// ////
////Once those are gone////
////It's that much harder to hold on to the rest////
//// ////
//// ////
////Where did it begin for me?////
//// ////
////They would tell you I was destined for it////
////That it began at the moment I began////

FRACTURES

//// ////
////I DOUBT THAT////
//// ////
////I DOUBT THAT ANYONE IS BORN TO ANYTHING////
//// ////
////EVEN NOW////
////AFTER ALL I'VE SEEN////
////AFTER ALL I'VE BEEN THROUGH////
//// ////
////I DON'T BELIEVE IT'S ALL FATE////
//// ////
////NOT ALL OF IT////
//// ////
////IT MIGHT HAVE STARTED WITH THE FIRST URGE////
////IT MIGHT HAVE STARTED WITH THE FIRST FLIGHT////
////IT MIGHT HAVE STARTED WITH THE FIRST KILL////
//// ////
////BUT I DON'T THINK SO////
//// ////
////LOOKING BACK////
////NOTHING WAS INEVITABLE THEN////
//// ////
////NOTHING SET IN MOTION////
//// ////
////THERE WERE DOMINOES////
////ONE AND TWO AND THREE////
////ALL LINED AND READY////
//// ////
////BUT NOTHING TO TIP THEM////
//// ////

//// ////
////THE TIPPING POINT CAME LATER////
//// ////
//// ////
////I THINK////
//// ////
//// ////
////I THINK IT STARTED THE FIRST TIME I DIED////

Chapter One

THE END

Deborah was not new to this.

People have an idea of what an assassin is. They have a notion. A child will picture a nightmare type, silent and haunting. Historic, otherworldly. A cloak and dagger, a vague sense of honour. As the child grows, their idea might refine to fit a modern context. Sophisticated and suave. A man of steely nerve. Taking care of the government's business with a cigarette and a silenced pistol. James Bond. The adult most likely rewrites this archetype again. A military man, black ops. Trained and lethal, operating with stealthy precision.

Deborah was blonde. She was slight. She looked young for thirty, and her baby-blues would look most fitting behind a pair of bright, plastic ray-bans. Her cherry lips most at home around a plastic take-away coffee cup lid, and her fingers most fitting clutching a smartphone, or perhaps a little designer handbag. Maybe even with a little designer dog perched in it.

Deborah was not who anyone would picture. But we don't really choose what we look like.

As she lay prone upon the manicured lawn, grass blades tempered sharp in the icy cold, she glanced up at the statues. Creepy things, she thought. They stood over her with stoney, scornful gazes. Watching.

One would think this place the set of a movie. Some grand old-Hollywood film. The estate of a wealthy old dame, an ageing actress living in the lap of luxury. Or perhaps a gothic horror, the mansion of some reclusive figure of lore. The Wolf-man's manor.

Deborah had been many places on business, but none quite so ostentatiously grand. Statues in the grounds. Not a garden - little council houses had gardens - this place had *grounds*. Statues in the grounds meant something. Not just money, but *old* money. Not just richness, but *wealth*.

Wealth made sense of course. Whoever wanted rid of the owner of this place, they knew about wealth too. This would certainly be her most profitable job, in a career comprised of profitable jobs. The rich conduct their affairs with the rich. And their affairs turn ugly just as often as everyone else's. Probably more often. This job, it might have been hastily planned, but done right, it could be the beginning of a whole new level, Deborah mused. A higher tier. Higher pay. Retire earlier maybe. Try her hand at living real-life, with the rest of the world. Try her hand at the smartphones and the coffee cups and the ray-bans and the designer handbags. Full-time. Not just playing at it. Probably still pass on the little dog though. If she could give it up, that was. If she could break the hold it had on her.

She slipped out her scope and raised it to her eye, scanning the perimeter. In the distance, through her misting breath caught in the air, she saw the gatehouse. There was light - for sure someone was in there - but it pulsed dully, blue-tinged. A television set. Across the rear of the building she couldn't see a soul.

"There's no security," she whispered softly.

"No one?" asked Eli in her earpiece, incredulous.

"Someone in the gatehouse, but no one on the grounds. It's deserted."

"That's good. Should be simpler."

"Hmm," she exhaled in the affirmative, but she wasn't so sure. This place was huge. Why no security on the grounds? Unusual. At least she assumed it was. Without any real context she could only conjecture, but with the wealth and status the grand mansion suggested, she had expected *something* more.

She shifted her focus. A couple of rooms had soft glows behind their curtains. Ground floor, though. Not the target. This late, the man of the house wouldn't be on the ground floor. Not at the rear of the building anyway. That was staff. Housemaids, a chef maybe, security of some description for sure. A guy with a house like this lived very well, and living well meant staff.

It was dark. Dusk had given way to icy black over an hour ago, but no clouds hung in the cold air. The starlight glinted, dancing across the facade, highlighting its cracks and crevices as though guiding her eye. There was something up there - one, two, three, four of them. Cameras? No. No lens reflection, and wrongly positioned. Too widely spaced.

"Floodlights. Motion sensitive," she whispered. "I can see four. Looks like a clear route west-side."

"No, hang on." A little urgency crept into his voice. *"Hang on, there should be five at the rear. That's what I have here. Keep looking."*

Where... are... you...? she asked the night, scanning the area. Hedges, balconies, fountain, tennis court... *tennis court.* Her eyes narrowed. There you are. One, two, three – she scanned back across the building, taking note of their direction – four, and five. She wouldn't need to damage anything. There was a clear path from her position. Easy to spot when you knew what to look for. That's how it always was though. All security had a weakness. It was simple to beat when its design was revealed.

"Got it."

"Ya' welcome," he drawled. Deborah's face hinted at a smile. Eli was never quite serious. Even when he was serious.

She scanned across the grounds one last time. Still no one. Stillness but for the twinkling of the stars and the soft flicker of the guardhouse television reflected on its walls. She compressed the scope and slid it into her pocket, feeling at her side to ensure the little pistol she carried was ready for action. That was a last resort, of course. That would negate her contract, and her pay. It was only for use in a pinch, to get the hell out if things went bad. This guy was supposed to look like it was just one of those things. An accident or a natural death. But better safe than sorry.

"I'm moving up," she breathed.

"There's a camera at one of the windows, can you see it?"

"No."

"Okay. Don't worry about it, I'll be able to see you in a minute."

"You in all of them?"

"No, but the feeds are all looping, you're fine. Just watch the motion lights. They're not on the grid."

Deborah hopped up onto her haunches beside the sullen statue. The dewy cold clung to her, but the adrenaline sparks were kicking in, the thrill of the job heating her from within. Control it right and its engine warmed better than any jacket.

She moved with silent speed. Not running, but briskly and with purpose. Round the corner and, across the grounds to the edge of the tennis court. She didn't need to look towards the motion detectors, she knew where they were, and where their monolithic stares focussed. Once committed to memory the path was set. You don't second guess once you've started. That's how you mess up. That's how amateurs fail.

Stepping around the fenced section to where a wooden enclosure housed an automatic ball server, she stopped. She crouched down and crept across the path of the motion detector's gaze, obscured by the screen and the wooden kick plate. Round the next corner and across the lawn, down the hedge line and round, she moved with a fluid, feline precision, stopping at the path's edge. This is the spot, she thought. No second guessing. Here goes.

She stood. No click. No light. Deborah breathed a small sigh of relief and stepped across the path to the perimeter of the building, glancing at the guardhouse window. It was close now, close enough to make out a pair of shoes, crisscrossed. The toes slightly obscuring the light from the television. Whoever was in there wasn't paying attention to anything outside.

"Hey there pretty girl," Eli said casually. Turning, she spotted a camera pointing down at her from within the nook of the architectural detailing. Looking into its eye for a moment she gave Eli the briefest of nods.

"Hey Gorgeous."

She turned back to the window frame. Old style, as expected. No magnets, no alarms, and best of all, no decent lock. Just a mechanical latch. Deborah quickly unfolded her little set of tools, locating the one she wanted without so much as a glance. She fitted its flat hooking end at the base of the window frame, worked it left then right, and felt it slip under the base. Darkness remained, inside and out. Sliding it along the base of the frame she located the resistance of the latch, and, with a quick twist, heard it ping. She stood silent a few seconds as the sound faded. Nothing left in the air but the ghostly hum of frozen air across open ground. All clear.

Placing her hands firmly on the frame, she lifted. It slid upwards with a low creak, quieting as she eased off, leaving a gap a foot or so wide.

"I'm heading in."

"See you in there."

Deborah swung her leg over the sill, stepping onto a polished floor within.

She was in some kind of game room. A full sized snooker table took centre stage. Set for a new game, the green felt immaculate. Either rarely used or meticulously maintained. Along the ornate, panelled walls were dark, heavy oil paintings. Nautical themed, seascapes mostly. Majestic old ships, their sails billowing. The minutiae of games were dotted all around the room: a dart board, several card tables of varying shapes, what looked to be a mah-jong game laid and ready to begin. Along the back wall of the room ran an extensive bar, each bottle perfectly placed and perfectly full. Unused. *Nothing* seemed used. The room functioned not as entertainment, but as a status symbol, thought Deborah. The grand fireplace was stacked with wood, but there was no sign or scent of ash. Like a film set. The place had the trappings of character, but it was skin deep.

"I'm in a leisure room," she whispered.

"Yeah. No visual in there, I'll see you in the hallway."

"Something weird about this place, Eli."

"Weird?"

"I..." She thought for a second, and came up with nothing. Her unease was palpable, but its basis inarticulable. "I don't know. Forget it." She crossed the room, towards the exit.

"Hold up, got someone approaching."

She flattened against the wood panelling next to the entrance. An echoey *clack, clack, clack* of footsteps outside the room rose from the stillness. She held her breath a moment, hand falling to rest on the pistol at her side. *Clack, clack, clack*. Heels. A woman. Walking steadily, but not hastily. Footfalls of nonchalance, not of investigation. Deborah breathed slowly. *Clack, clack, clack*. The steps gained volume, peaked, then began to dull as their source passed the room and moved on their way.

"Staff?"

"Looks like it," replied Eli. *"You're good to go. Should be a left, down the corridor to the stairs."*

Deborah tested the door handle, which swung down with ease. Cracking the door a fraction, she eyed the hallway beyond. Paintings lined the walls, oils again, but portraits this time. Stern looking men, serious men. Men of purpose throughout the ages, chillingly similar in their features. An eerie green tinge shone from an old fashioned desk lamp on a credenza a few feet down the hall from the door. Odd place for it, she thought as she slipped through.

Closing the door behind her, she took care to let the latch catch its mark with as little sound as possible. Turning and heading down the hallway she once again felt her hand drift to her pistol. The metal felt good. Comforting.

"I have you," Eli said.

The enclosed hallway had opened up, giving way to a wider space. An ornate set of stairs swept round the corner of the room, heading up to a balcony at her back. Deborah's eyes followed the bannister round, spying a security camera mounted just below the upper floor balcony, pointed down at her.

"Better move, someone coming up the other hall."

Deborah trusted Eli. She always had, and he had always earned it. She strode across the expanse to the foot of the stairs. As she passed the arched frame of the adjoining hallway she felt a slight movement at her feet, and one of the old floorboards let out a creak of discomfort. Shit. She darted to the carpeted stairs, dropping to all fours and scaling them nimbly. This was an old trick. Distribute the weight. Don't anger the floorboards further. Treat them with respect, and they'll let you pass without grumbling.

A soft sound clicked below her. A door opening. Deborah crossed to the balcony and peered down. Above the camera, still in the darkness, she perched like an owl spying prey as a man in a suit passed under the archway. He scanned the room with a flashlight across the ground floor, shifting the beam slowly from one end to the other, then back again. As he began to trace the bannister up the steps Deborah drew back and down, her view obscured, her face hidden from the light. She felt the beam pass above her and paused a moment until it passed back. As its glow dissipated she peered down, watching as the guard took a second, half-hearted pass across the ground floor of the room. He paused, seeming to question what he had heard, or thought he heard, and then passed underneath her, heading to the rear of the old building.

"Okay," Eli said. *"Head up. Second floor."*

Deborah pulled back from the balcony, and headed round to another flight of ornate stairs. Creeping up another floor, she felt more comfortable. There was less light here; intricate wall mounted lamps hung at intervals around the stairs and along the hallways, but not lit. The old place seemed somehow more normal, more inhabited in the inky darkness. Illuminating it highlighted its fakery - the hint of desperation in the grand facade showed less in the gloom. Deborah didn't come from any wealth, but she had paid a visit to a few wealthy men in her time, and while they did live in some degree of detachment, the homes they actually inhabited didn't seem quite as... cold? Sterile? No, that wasn't what this place was. Not sterile, but... lifeless.

"I'm on the second floor," she whispered. Dusty silence all around her.

"It's too dark. The camera aren't scotopic. You'll be on your own for a bit."

"No lights anywhere?"

"At a doorframe at the south east corner. Should be our guy, but no camera in there."

"Okay, moving up."

"Head down the south hall, you should hit a big room. A ballroom maybe? In there and across, should put you right outside target's room."

"Copy."

Deborah moved silently along the wooden hallway, keeping to the walls as much as possible. Avoiding creaking floorboards. *Fool me once...*, she thought wryly.

The air up here was heavier. Musty and old. There was a hint of leather, of wood, and a thick scent of books. The dusty aroma of bookshop silence. She passed more portraits on the walls of the halls, more stern looking men. Each one indistinguishable from the last. Just how long was this guy's lineage? How old was his money?

At the end of the hall a great oak door stood ajar, its wrought-iron handle dangling slightly askew. Deborah stilled, checking through the doorway. A great library lay on the other side, shelves reaching to the ceiling, stacked meticulously with leather-bound volumes.

"It's a library. Big one."

"Guy must have a lot of time on his hands."

Pulling the door slightly it let out a wheeze, and dust clouded at its rear. This room, like so much of the manor, had not seen visitors for some time. Guess the old guy isn't as into reading as he likes to think he is – or, she thought, as he likes other people to think he is. Another put-on. Another gesture of sophistication without the substance to back it up.

She squeezed through the gap. The mildewy fragrance of old paper filled her nose, thick and stifling. Crossing the room, she peered round at the book-lined shelves. The library was palatial. The books were perfectly arranged, not one out of place. Dusty chandeliers hung, adorned with cobwebs above her head. She guessed the maid service didn't extend to this wing.

Peering across the darkness, Deborah identified her exit - a door just like the one she had entered, this one closed at the east side of the room. She ran a finger across the spines of the books as she traversed the library. They felt weighty. Ancient, but untouched. At the door she took a long, slow breath and pulled on the handle. The door creaked as she had expected, but dully. Just one of a dozen creaks in an old place like this. Everything was going well. Considering how quickly this job was pulled together, Deborah mused, everything was going exceptionally well.

The hallway on the other side of the door was just like the others, remarkable only for the trace of light emanating from the skirt of a door ahead. The orange flicker of a hearth fire, lapping at the dark. Now things got real. That door was the precipice. Every job had one, and here, that door was it. Once through, going back was not an option.

"I see it. We're in business," she breathed.

"Okay. Get in, get out, get paid." Eli's little catchphrase hadn't changed in fifteen years, in thirty seven jobs. It wasn't changing now. Deborah inched toward the light.

Breath control was the key. She knew that. The excitement, the adrenaline and the fear, the dopamine rush of the job, those were the enemies. They were the traitors that lived inside you, that seduced you. Convinced you to strike too quickly. Recklessly. To rush to the finish; to abandon prior restraint. To give in to the roar of the blood rushing through your ears and the life bursting through your fingers. To fuck up. Deborah was not new to this. She steeled her breath and her nerves, and stalled at the entrance to the room.

Those glowing flickers of orange beneath the door? *They* were her real friends. They were gonna help her get this done right. Pulling a small dental mirror from her belt, she lay prostrate at the edge of the doorframe. She slid it into the crack between the door and the wooden floor, twisting it around methodically. The reflections offered only the smallest glimpse of her destination, but to her trained eye gave a good sense of the space. A fireplace, built of exposed stone with a dancing flame in its mouth. A mantle, devoid of ornamentation but for a carriage clock and an old metal cigar box. A gun rack above, sporting various old rifles. Vintage, well kept, but unlikely to be in working order. Decorative. For investment purposes only. Like everything else. Tilting the mirror further revealed the corner of a heavy oak four-poster bed. Ornate and beautiful, exquisitely carved, adorned with a heavy green quilt. And feet. Bare feet. This was her guy, asleep, lying uncovered atop the silk sheets, draped in a gold-hemmed night robe. Perfect. Easy money.

Deborah lifted herself once again and did her final check. She removed her pistol, ensured the safety was off and twisted the silencer, checking it was locked in place. She placed it back in the holster, flipped the mirror back into its slipcase at her waist and removed the syringe from her strap-pack. Holding it up she tilted it gently, seeing the clear, viscous liquid shift in the dull light. A dose big enough to ensure a rapid death in seconds, but without leaving traces in the blood. Just the puncture mark could give it away. Had to be hidden. Between the toes was best. Or the ball of the foot if need be.

Breathe.

In a single, fluid motion she pressed the door handle, slipped through the doorway and paced across the room, straight as an arrow towards the sleeping figure, long legs striding. It was all about speed, but not hurry. Purpose, but not haste. Like lightning, she flipped one leg up onto the bed, flipped her second leg up over its occupant, kneeling on all fours above his body, syringe in hand. The old man stirred, his slumber broken by the shift of the mattress, or perhaps simply by her body's proximity.

"Where…" he began, panic gripping his voice through dazed waking.

All at once she flattened her crotch and hips over his face, clamping his airways firmly. She pulled his leg, hooking under his boney knee with one hand, drawing it to her and pressed the needle between his two largest toes with the other. She felt a twist beneath her hips as he stirred violently, kicking his foot out, but late, too late to help himself. It was done. Deborah kept pressure on his head, keeping him restrained beneath her as his frantic strains became spasms, spasms became twitches, twitches became still.

The sensation rippled through her, that now familiar rush. It was impossible to describe to anyone who had never felt it, the endorphin blast that accompanied the snuffing out of a life. Deborah had once read that the French referred to orgasm as 'la petite mort' - the little death. The euphemism was apt. She had wondered if whatever Parisian writer had coined it had ever killed a man. She suspected so. It was too perfect an analogy, as the converse was so very true also. The act of killing, the moment of it, could well be described as 'le petit orgasme.'

Deborah had never killed for pleasure, but deep down it was not hard for her to understand how serial killers and sadists could find themselves unable to stop. Addicted. That seduction, the desire to chase that sinister dragon down into the depths; it was the most dangerous aspect of her profession. The hunger had claimed a few operatives she had know. In one case, it had been Deborah herself who had been tasked with ending their particular extra-curricular activities. Lucille. Lucy. The perverse look of pleasure that had passed behind her eyes as the life left them, coupled with Deborah's own petit orgasme - that moment had never truly left her. In the small hours it would come back and battle with her slumber, and it would win more often than not.

A moment of calm passed before she pressed a gentle finger to his wrist, searching for the throb of a pulse. She felt nothing but papery skin, dry and lifeless.

"Thirty nine," she whispered.

"Thirty nine," breathed Eli. Cautious, but tinged with relief. *"Now get out of there."*

Despite the fire, Deborah felt the air crisp in the room. Familiar cold descended, and the hush. The hum of life, audible only by its absence, stilled. The killing floor quiet. She steeled herself and turned to leave the room.

"Deb, there's something going on." Deborah stilled. Eli sounded different now. Anxious. *"There's too much movement down there. Security is getting active."*

"How many?"

"Four I think, maybe five in your wing? There're so many fucking black spots in their system." He was brusque now. *"I can see four for sure. You need to move. The way you came is clear for now. Not seen anyone head upstairs yet."*

"En route."

Deborah slipped out of the room, sliding the door shut behind her and hurried down the hallway to the library door. Cracking it open she saw it was empty, as before, and entered, striding in silence. She followed the perimeter wall this time, out of sight of the entrances. Better safe than sorry.

Crossing the room she heard a creak and a squeak of shoe leather. She froze. Someone was there. Passing the central corridor of the library. Nothing but the rows of bookshelves between them and her. Nothing but silence and old paper. Got to keep moving, her inner self scolded. Can't get rooted here. Got to keep going.

She headed towards the east side of the room, crossing between rows of bookshelves. How many were there? Keeping track was difficult. The gaps between rows were staggered and followed no logical pattern, but, weaving in and out, she made her way towards the centre of the east wall as best she could tell in the gloom. Passing between yet another set of polished wooden shelves she spied her exit, looming in the darkness. She cast a glance back over her shoulder, seeing only the faint outline of the squeaky-shoed man, his back to her now. She breathed an inaudible breath and turned back to the door.

Not to the door. The door was open. To a man. He stood silent and suited. His arm fully extended. The barrel of a pistol glimmering in the darkness. Aimed steady, straight at her chest.

Time slowed to a crawl as Deborah's eyes locked with his. Cold and purposeful and terribly, terribly dark. Her mind raced, blood-streaked and shrieking across her life, relentlessly storming through the years in search of guidance, for an answer to this impossible equation. How do we get out of this one? it screamed. Panic blazed behind her eyes. Deborah was not new to this, but no answer was forthcoming.

The bullet punched her in the heart. Warm, screaming pain burst through her in a wave, subsiding into nothing as she fell back through the darkness of the library. In slow motion she heard a muted thud as her rag-doll body crashed into a bookshelf, her head lolling to one side, no longer hers to control. The darkness surrounding her and her killer began to lighten in blooms of white, bursting forth through tiny pinholes in reality. Books fell from above and cascaded to the floor, their pirouettes beautiful in the glacial slow-time. Their pages flapped with otherworldly lightness; they seemed blank to her dulling eyes, the scene all the more unreal for it. Everything of movement was lent an impossible grace in its impossible slowness.

Deborah strained to hold on to the image as the blossoming white slowly, relentlessly filled her vision to a blinding singularity.

Eli stared blankly at the readout on the screen in the back of the van. The awful spike and then the awful nothing. No pulse. No sound. Nothing. He lowered his head silently.

Fracture one
GENESIS

The first time Deborah felt the urge to kill, she was nine years old.

"Nah, that's okay," Deborah said.

"Aww, c'mon, I got lots of good ones!"

"No you don't. You have, like, *four* that are worth trading, and I have them already."

"What about this?" asked Mikey, holding up a Penguin card, trying valiantly to mask his dumb, pleading look with one of shrewd salesmanship. "It's worth more."

"I have it already."

"But it's *worth* more. You could trade it for something else."

"So why don't *you?*"

Deborah knew she was smarter than Mikey. She had heard many times that girls mature faster than boys, and had always assumed grown-ups said so because she was tall. Taller than the boys in her class anyway. By her second year in school she had consistently had an inch or two on even the taller boys, and, in Mikey's case, her blonde hair fell at least three inches before it would meet the crown of his round little head. She had thought it a strange benchmark for maturity given her slender frame. There were plenty of boys in the class who could run faster or jump higher or play harder. Now though, she realised, that might not be what they meant after all. She was *smarter*. Smarter, at least, than Mikey Porter. Maybe that was what they meant.

"I *could*," replied Mikey, with transparent affectation, "but I'm doing you a *favour*. You give me that Joker one, and I'll give you this aaaaand..." he shuffled around in his pencil case, "and this Catwoman. It's the *rarest* Catwoman there is."

"I have it. I only need a number nineteen and a number six. You said you had them."

"But..." Mikey stalled. This was a kid used to getting his own way. He didn't like being told no – not by the teachers, not by his peers, and especially not, Deborah realised, by a girl.

"Well, I'm not trading for those," she said firmly. "You lied. You're not supposed to lie. You're supposed to trade properly, that way it's more fun."

Mikey's chubby face contorted, first into frustration, then into a snarl.

"Why do you even *want* them anyways, *Debbie*?! Batman is for *boys*. Not stupid *girls*. Why don't you just collect the *Barbie* ones?"

"Shuttup," Deborah snapped, angry less at being called stupid than at being told what she should like. "You're just jealous 'cause I got almost *all* of them, and you're missing *loads*."

She started sweeping her cards off the top of the wooden bench, in to the tin cigar box she kept them in.

"You're a *bitch*," Mikey snapped. "I'm gonna tell on you."

Deborah stifled a laugh. "Tell on me for what?" she asked, bemused.

"You're not supposed to do trades in school - I'll tell on you and say you were trading and we'll both get in trouble, but *my* dad won't mind cause I'm a boy, and *your* dad will cause you're a girl and girls are supposed to not get into trouble and be nice and DO GIRL THINGS!" Mikey raised his voice in angry triumph. He had talked himself round to his own logic, almost by accident.

"Okay, go," she replied calmly. Calling this fat idiot's bluff was the easiest thing in the world. Mikey was a spoiled little creature, she knew, but his dad would very much mind. She had seen how he acted around his father on the days he came to the gates to pick Mikey up in his fancy car. Mikey came from good stock, as the grown-ups said. He was posh. Posher than most of her classmates anyway. Neither his mother, nor his father looked the 'won't-mind' type. She carried on shuffling her cards into the musty scented tin.

"I'm *going*," snapped Mikey, standing up from the bench and taking a couple of half-hearted steps away from the picnic bench towards the school entrance. A couple of other kids looked his way, but not for long. Mikey Porter didn't have many friends, and it was not difficult to understand why.

"'Kay," breezed Deborah, exaggerating her disinterest to a sharpened point. Mikey wasn't going anywhere but the other side of the playground to sulk. Or to find some other kid to sucker with his low-rent cards. It wouldn't matter anyway. Even if he did decide to tell Ms Taylor, Deborah knew he'd get it worse than her. She knew fine well that little punks like Mikey Porter were just as ill-liked by the grown-ups as they were by her, and she knew how to talk her way out of trouble. Teachers were easy to talk to. Teachers followed the rules.

Mikey huffed and disappeared round the corner of the school building as Deborah closed her card tin and sighed. She had wanted Mikey to be telling the truth. If he *had* had the cards she needed, that would have been a complete collection. Deborah liked complete collections. She liked to complete things. Sure, the fun is in the collecting, not in the collection itself, she knew that, but finishing one still felt good. It felt right. Everything in its place. Ordered. Sorted. On to a new challenge.

Oh well, what can you do. Dad would tell her she could always send off for the last few - the companies that make them will let you order the specific cards you need, and when it's just a few left that's okay. But it wasn't. That wasn't how you were *supposed* to do it. You were supposed to hunt around for trades. Do it properly. Win by the rules.

The clear air and murmur of mingled conversation was cut by the sound of the school bell, followed by a stereoscopic sigh of deflation from the students dotted around the break tables. Monday morning. Deborah stuck her trading card tin into her backpack, slung the pack over her shoulder and headed round the corner towards the entrance.

Class was boring. Ms Taylor was okay Deborah guessed, she seemed nice enough. Just like any other teacher. But Mondays? Ugh. Monday morning was spelling and showing your homework from the weekend. Deborah had no problem completing *her* homework, but had no love for the predictable litany of tedious, often outlandishly elaborate reasons her classmates had for their failure to do likewise. Why not just get it done on a Friday, like she did? That way you still have pretty much your whole weekend to yourself. Plus the added bonus of not having to hear Ms Taylor rehash her patented 'diligence' speech.

As she half listened to the laborious cavalcade of excuses from the front of the class she glanced around the room. There was Suzanne, one braided pigtail in her mouth, as usual. There was David, not so surreptitiously inspecting the contents of his nose, also as usual. In front of him sat Mikey Porter, hunched over his desk, picking at its scabby corner.

What a liar he was, thought Deborah. Lied about his cards, then lied about telling on her. Well, at least she had been firm with him. That's what Dad would have told her to do. Be fair but firm. That's how grown-ups behave, and if you want to get anywhere in this world Deborah, you need to know how to deal with difficult people. That's how Dad would describe Mikey. Difficult. He wouldn't call him mean, or fat, or any bad words; he would just say he was difficult, and that she shouldn't sink to his level.

Mikey must have felt her watching him, because he turned and met her glance. His eyes narrowed in his chubby face, lending him an uncanny similarity to one of those little waving cats they had in the Chinese takeaway. The thought almost made her smile, but she caught herself. She didn't want Mikey to mistake her smile for an olive branch. She was still annoyed. Mikey took a quick glance around to confirm Ms Taylor's back was turned, turned back to Deborah and stuck two fingers up at her, mouthing words silently. "F.U.C.K Y.O.U."

He's *difficult*, her Dad's voice said.

Yup, you're right Dad. He is difficult. And a fat idiot. And a liar. Why couldn't people just be nice? Just be themselves, tell the truth, obey the rules? Everything would be so much easier. Deborah sighed.

The day plodded on, through homework, through spelling, via maths to lunch break. Deborah had brought her lunch from home as always. Juice, a sandwich, whatever piece of fruit Dad had included. An apple today. Never very imaginative, but Deborah didn't care. Her Dad worked hard. He took care of her and he always took time for her and he never grumbled about anything. Deborah wondered what her mother had been like, and her father had never shied from answering her occasional questions, but even at the youngest age Deborah had understood what that faraway look in his eyes was when he talked about her mother. She knew that it made him sad. Terribly, deeply sad. She didn't ask too often. He was her Dad, and she wouldn't make him any more sad just so she could hear his soft words on the subject. It wasn't like she could ever meet her and know for herself, and besides, she had died too early for Deborah to really miss her. She knew that deep down. She knew she really just missed the idea of her. The concept.

Sitting on the hard packed ground beneath the old oak tree that stood guard in the corner of the school grounds, she ate her sandwich, watching the other kids. She had always preferred to watch the other children from a distance. Teachers like Ms Taylor this year, and Mrs Wilson last, they never seemed to understand that it wasn't because she didn't like the other kids, or that they didn't like her - Deborah got on well with most of her classmates - but rather because she simply never felt at ease in a group. She *chose* solitude, it wasn't thrust upon her. Once, last year, Mrs Wilson had requested to speak with her Dad on the matter. Deborah had not been privy to the conversation of course – teachers always talked *about* her, never *with* her. That night her Dad had sat down in her room. He had asked her about her school, about the other kids and what and whom she liked. Not prying, but more inquisitive than usual. She had simply told him the truth: the other kids were fine, but she liked to think on her own. He had nodded and listened, and finally had looked her right in the eyes and smiled.

"You're a smart girl Debbie. You do what you want to do. I know you'll do the right thing," he had said warmly. And that had been that. The end of it.

Her mind was meandering lazily when she felt someone approach. To her side she heard two sets of feet step off the soft grass onto the worn dirt that encircled the tree. She looked round and saw the little round face of Mikey Porter emerge from behind it, and with him a taller boy. Just as round in the face, with the same loose, irritated look that was Mikey's calling card, though it cast less comically without the round-rimmed spectacles to dampen it.

"That's her," Mikey remarked to his consort as they sidled towards her. "She promised to trade me a Joker, but then she welched."

Deborah looked at him pointedly. "No I *didn't*, Mikey. I didn't *promise* you anything."

Mikey glared at her then turned to the other boy again. "She's lying. Everyone knows she's a liar, that's why she's got no friends."

Deborah didn't like this new twist. She shot a quick glance behind the pair, scanning the playground to see who was around. There was a disorganised football game going on by the bushes and few girls gossiping and giggling by the benches, but all out of earshot. No help there.

"Make her give it to me Danny."

Daniel Porter was in his seventh year at the school, two years older than Mikey and Deborah. In a few months he'd be heading off to the fabled 'Big School'. Secondary. To reset his status as a small fish in a big pond. For the moment though, he was one of the big kids. A big fish in Deborah's pond.

"Just leave me alone Mikey." Deborah made a point to address Mikey alone. No need to bring his brother into this unless he involved himself, and so far Daniel hadn't spoken. He hadn't thrown his lot in with either side yet. For all she knew, Danny might have just as low an opinion of Mikey as she, and most of her classmates, did.

"Danny! Make her give it to me!" Mikey repeated. He wasn't speaking to her. He knew from their earlier encounter that wouldn't do anything for him. Most likely it would just make him look stupid. He spoke to Daniel, as if she wasn't there at all.

"Look, just give him the cards he wants, okay?" Daniel said wearily. His tone conveyed volumes about his relationship with his brother, Deborah realised. There was more to it than she would glean from this exchange, but for sure Mikey was calling the shots. Daniel was going to cause her hassle. He was Mikey's muscle, despite whatever objection he seemed to have to what he was doing. He would back his brother regardless.

"I'm not going to just *give* him anything." Deborah worked to keep her voice flat. To keep it from betraying her growing disquiet. Most of the boys in her class would not hit a girl, but she was pretty sure Mikey was the exception to that rule. Who knew where his brother stood on such schoolyard taboos?

"I *was* going to trade, 'cause he said he had cards I needed, but he was lying. I'm not giving him anything."

Daniel glanced at his brother with a look Deborah recognised. She had seen it on her Dad's face many times. Mostly when he was listening to one of Aunt Trisha's stories - about how bitchy her colleagues were, or how they were all jealous of her looks, or how she was not getting a promotion, because 'it's all office politics.' Resignation. The look said, *yeah, you and I both know you're full of it, but we're family. So I'm stuck here on your side. The wrong side.* She almost felt sorry for Danny. Having to go through life with a scheming little shit like Mikey Porter for a brother must be pretty rough.

"That true?" Danny asked his brother.

"Nuh-uh. I already *told* you she's a liar. You said you'd help me. You better, or I'll tell mum and dad."

Glumly, Deborah wondered what family feud she was planted in the middle of here. Mikey was obviously the aggressive one at home too. She wondered for a moment whether there were any Porter sisters. She doubted it. She hoped not at least.

Daniel let out an audible sigh and turned to face her once more. "Just give him the fucking card, okay lass? 'Else I gotta to take it. I don't wanna be smackin' a wee girl."

Deborah stood, bracing against her own nerves, and looked right into Danny Porter's eyes.

"You'll have to," she said, as cold and measured as she was able. It sounded pretty good out loud, she thought. It sounded like she was tough. It didn't hint that she was well on her way from anxious to flat-out scared. Deborah didn't want to get hit, but she wasn't going to just let herself get bullied. That wasn't how things were supposed to go. Bullies were supposed to be stood up too. Bad guys were meant to be vanquished. Those were, as far as she had gleaned from her considerable library of teen-fiction, the universal rules.

"She keeps them in a wee metal box." Mikey smirked at her as he gestured towards her backpack. "In there."

Daniel reached half-heartedly towards the pack and Deborah sidestepped, blocking him. She felt the jitters rising. However this was going to play out, she didn't like her chances. Smarts might win in the long run, but brawn was the safe bet in this particular exchange.

"How you doing Michael? Daniel?" A man's voice, gruff but amiable, rose from behind the boys. They whipped around, startled cats caught playing with their mouse. "You lads aren't giving this young lady a hard time I hope?"

Deborah felt a wave of relief as she saw the rough face of Mr Gilmour rise over the boys.

"No sir," Mikey stated innocently, in a tone well practiced. Daniel said nothing, but adopted a distant, hang-dog demeanor. Less practiced, but, Deborah suspected, oft employed.

"Well, that's good to hear. Deborah? You just having a chat?" Mr Gilmour was nice. He had been the janitor and handyman at the school since long before she began her tenure; he was as much a part of the scholastic furniture as the oak tree she stood by. His gravelly voice and good-natured ways reminded her often of her Dad.

"Hi Mr Gilmour. Yes, we were just... talking. About trading cards."

"Oh, well, that's good. Best head back up though. I think your Ms Taylor is doing rounds, and she'll not want to hear about those cards in school again, eh?"

Deborah smiled appreciatively. Mr Gilmour could often seem distant, oblivious even, but she suspected his presence around the schoolyard all these years had given him an insight into playground life and law that far outstripped the other grown-ups. Even the teachers.

"Yes sir," she said, retrieving her backpack from the ground and slinging it over her shoulder. The jitters were subsiding. She doubted either boy would detect the little tremor she felt in her arm as she did. As she headed towards the main building, she heard Mr Gilmour address the Porter boys behind her.

"You lads just wait here a minute or two, okay? I need a couple of strong, young men to help me move some bags round to the gym. Darn nice of you lads to volunteer to help. I appreciate it."

"But..." Mikey began to protest weakly.

"Yup, real good of you lads. On you come now."

Safe for now, Deborah thought, a relieved smile pulling at her lips. Thanks Mr Gilmour.

All through afternoon class Deborah felt Mikey's pique glowing like a fire from his seat at the front of the class. She tried to focus her attention elsewhere, but found herself unable to ignore his bitter glances. Mikey was not going to let this go. Twice now he had tried getting what he wanted from this wee blonde bitch, and twice he had been foiled. Once by her nasty girl smart-mouth, and once by that stupid fucking janitor. She knew he wouldn't let things lie there. He wouldn't be able to. He wasn't the type. Deborah knew there was a word for what Mikey was, a grown-up word - she had read it in one of her novels. Misorjist? Something like that. It meant he hated girls especially. Anyhow, she knew this silly altercation was going to come to a head. Probably sooner rather than later. Probably right after school. Guys like Mikey could never wait and think about things. They always had to keep on and on and on until everything was blown way out of proportion, and more than that - Mikey knew he had her beat. With his brother in tow there was nothing she could do to stop him, short of being rescued, like before, or just running away. The thought squatted on her mind, refusing to budge. Every time she tried to ignore it, to think around the side of it, it would shift right into the path of her train of thought. Derail it.

She mapped out the route home, over and over. Was there an alternate route? Where was best to outrun the Porter boys? Where would most likely have people around? And where, if it came to it, would be a smart hiding spot? The whole incident had her far more nervous than she wanted to admit. That damn clock on the wall didn't seem to care much for her plight though. It ticked on regardless.

The end of day bell had barely ceased its dissonant clangor as Deborah passed through the classroom door and headed down the corridor towards the front entrance. It wasn't a run - that would call attention and give away the only currency she had left - but it was as brisk a pace as her long legs could muster without breaking into one. She wasn't going to glance around to see whether Mikey was following. No sense in that; the last thing she wanted to do was invite him to follow. Besides, she thought, Mikey on his own was not the problem. It would take him time to rendezvous with his brother. Probably a good amount of time, given that Daniel didn't seem particularly fond of his current role as Mikey's enforcer. Maybe he would just leave. Avoid his younger brother, just as she was. That would be a relief. One more victory for the good guys.

She swung open the school doors and squinted. The sunny midday had given way to a hazy orange-tinted late afternoon, the closeness of the air drawing the scents of the plants and enriching them. The whole playground was alive with the sweet vanilla of gorse bushes and the live green of cut grass. Deborah's mood was lifted a little along with them as she crossed the playground and passed through the side gates. She could hear the din of her peers piling out of the school building behind her, muffled, as if the lazy warmth had cast a quilt over them. Looks like I'm okay, she thought to herself. No Mikey, no Danny, just a sunny walk home. Tomorrow was tomorrow, and that was years from now.

She kept her stride at first, but as she passed a block, then another, then a third without sight or sound of the Porters, she began to ease to a saunter, and admire the day around her. Afternoons this nice were rare, especially in Glasgow. Not to take some pleasure in it would be such a waste.

Passing the old, derelict chapel that marked her halfway point, the day's unpleasantness truly lifted. The fear that had sat in her mind like a tumour relented, allowing thoughts of the evening to flow freely. She'd help Dad make their supper and maybe sit in the garden, read a book. Maybe he'd continue her chess lessons. Her Dad was a good player. He prided himself on it in his quiet way, and Deborah liked when he taught her. She wasn't much good, she had trouble seeing more than a few moves ahead, but she was getting better. He had told her many times she had the makings of a grand master. He always winked after he said so, which probably meant it wasn't true, but she didn't care. The lessons were fun anyways. Or maybe she'd just watch the wilting sun with him out back. Deborah's father had worked as an auto mechanic at Carmichael's for as long as she could recall. It was a job he seemed to like and he was friendly with Mr Carmichael, but it meant he was usually pretty tired by the time he got home. During the summer holidays, Deborah would sometimes go to see him for lunch, and she could not remember ever turning up and finding him less than busy. Yeah, he'd probably be tired, but he liked to sit out in the back yard when it got nice like this. The little house he and Deborah shared was modest, but her Dad took great pleasure in that little patch of green.

She turned and crossed to the top of her street. Still feeling a million miles from her troubles, she noticed some business down the road. There were figures standing around at her neighbour's house, chatting in the sun. No doubt just remarking on the weather, she thought, but as she covered the distance they seemed more animated than that would warrant. Their gesticulation more frenetic.

Was something going on with old Mrs Brooks? Maybe she had had another fall? Poor lady had fallen last year, and had spent a week in the hospital, and Deborah and her Dad had done her weekly shopping for her for a good few months after that.

Closer now, she noticed the white and blue and yellow of a police car parked by the kerb. Uh-oh. Whatever the old lady had done this time must be serious, Deborah thought. Although… wouldn't that mean an ambulance? Not the police, surely? Wait. Those figures weren't neighbours. That was Aunt Trisha. Aunt Trisha talking with a policeman and a man. Mr Carmichael. She felt her stomach lurch. Not Mrs Brook's house. *Her* house. She broke into a run.

"Oh Debbie! Oh Debbie, come here!" Aunt Trisha's eyeliner was smeared and had left soft grey streaks across her face where she had wiped it. Deborah aimed to pass Trisha and head straight to the policeman to ask what was going on, but was caught in her forced embrace. "Debbie there's been an accident, your dad…"

Deborah's stomach lurched again, this time seeming to push up through her chest, drawing blood up with it. Her throat felt swollen and coppery. No one ever started with *'there's been an accident'* if things were going to be okay. They started by saying *'now, your Dad is going to be fine but…'* or *'everything is okay, but…'* Whatever this was, it was not a *'but'* situation. It was an *'and'* situation. Those were much worse.

She pulled her face from where Trisha had planted it between the base of her neck and shoulder and stepped back, wide-eyed, a hint of a tremble in her face.

"What…?" she began before Trisha cut her off.

"Oh Debbie, he was fixing a car in the shop and it fell! That stupid machine…" Trisha shot a vicious glare at Mr Carmichael. He stood by the policeman, a terrible, fraught expression on his face. "It dropped it right on him!"

The tremor that had fluttered into Deborah's lip took a grip of her whole body. She felt an itchy heat flood her face.

"Is he…" she began, only to be cut off by her aunt once again.

"They took him to the hospital…" Trisha paused to take a deep breath. It caught several times in her throat as she did, but she managed a lungful after what seemed an eternity. "He didn't make it, Debbie."

She backed up a step further in stunned disbelief. Looking from Trisha to the policeman, standing sombre and dutiful, to Mr Carmichael. Nice Mr Carmichael, who was always jovial. Always happy to see her. Always had some old groaner of a joke for her, and a chuckle reserved for when she rolled her eyes at it. The horrible disconnect of the man she knew, now wearing this sorrowful, broken look - that sealed it. Tears came, pooling in her eyes at first as she stood rooted and staring, then running in great, hot trails down her face, catching at her lips.

She wanted to say something – anything – but she couldn't. She had numbed to the outside world, her private misery enveloping her in a Novocain bubble. She could see her surroundings, but the sound had dropped out. The whole world had flipped the treble right down and the bass up. She thought Aunt Trisha had hugged her again, and she knew there was discussion happening around her, between the policeman and Trisha. Discussion about where she would stay that night, among other things. None of that penetrated the curtain that had dropped around her. Deborah couldn't think in the present. Not with all the past that was flickering behind her eyes. All the times she and Dad had laughed. All the times he had taken her to the park or the zoo or the library, or when they had just lounged together on the sofa. Watching his documentaries or her sitcoms. All the times she had needed a hug and he had delivered, or needed a joke and he had one, or needed to talk and he had just *known*. Made the time.

All of that was gone, and with it most of her identity. So much of herself was her father. With no one else in that house, their world had only had two main characters. Everyone else had been just an extra.

Well, now it's just me, she thought. The weight of that thought was crushing.

As she stood in silent despair, the back and forth between the adults playing out in muted animation before her glassy eyes, something familiar drifted into view. Deborah was drawn back to the world. Across the street, closing the distance on a BMX bike, was the podgy form of Mikey Porter. With a glance around at the scene he spied Deborah, her shaky vulnerability on show for all the world to see. For a brief, teary moment her eyes locked with his in the squinting midday sun. Then with the grotesque disinterest reserved solely for the wilfully oblivious, he stuck his middle finger up at her and passed by on his way.

Deborah didn't respond. She didn't move an inch, but behind her eyes her mind exploded with hatred. Anger filled her. An anger she had never felt before. Rage.

That fat fucking shit. That gross little cunt. That shit-eating, dimwitted, callow, fuck-headed, craven little demon. With one action Mikey Porter had channeled all of her, every inch of her sorrow, into bitter, searing fury. She imagined roaring. She imagined smashing his face, over and over, grabbing him off that bike and ripping the skin from his fat head. She imagined sticking knives in his chest, burning him with cigarettes, cutting his limbs apart with scissors. She imagined tearing the flesh from his bones with her bare hands. She imagined destroying him. For the first time in Deborah's young life she imagined killing.

It felt good. It felt *right*. In a battle between disbelieving grief and fury, the fury felt better. She would hang onto that. The day Deborah's father died was the day she realised, for the first time, the truths that would come to define her.

The world was not fair. The universe didn't care. And the urge to kill could be a blanket in the darkness.

Chapter Two

NO STARS

It felt like falling. With nothing around but white, with no context she might have been floating, but it did not feel so. It was not peaceful.

The whiteness around her was endless, featureless. Deborah had no idea how long it had lasted. A second? An hour? A year? Time seemed not just impossible to measure, but irreconcilable with the *concept* of measurement. It was simply irrelevant here.

As she stared into the infinite nothing, she became aware of something appearing in it. Some shapes. Distant geometric blocks rising from an invisible horizon, as colourless and bright as the space around them. Forms betrayed only by the twisting parallax of her falling perspective. Up and up they rose, hundreds and hundreds of them. A skyline. A great city skyline, pure as snow, behind which rose an aurora.

A sunrise. A golden sunrise, unlike any she had ever seen. Its light glittered as if projected through airborne diamonds, dancing between the buildings as it rose behind them. As the light shone higher and higher, gilding the city, it broke across the top of one tower, then the next, then the next, divulging their height. One by one by one by one the light outpaced them, until only one kept pace. Higher and higher it rose, the golden light chasing it ever upwards as it dwarfed its peers. Deborah gazed at it in wonder, her eyes tearing in the beauty and the uncanny brightness. Higher and higher and higher and higher and just at the point that she began to believe there was no top to this shape, no end to its splendour, the light cut across a spire, revealing a new source. A dark-gold light, shining out from a void that seemed suspended in space at the pinnacle.

She stared into the vortex, mesmerised. The rest of the city seemed to melt away. A rush of dark-gold light came tearing outwards. A pulse, engulfing the white skyline and streaking out across the infinite. Behind it darkness, the first darkness she had seen here, swallowing the white in its wake. It rushed towards her as she fell, transfixed. The wave approached and she closed her eyes, feeling an overwhelming force clawing at her free-falling form.

Right as the wave hit, she felt a rumble. A great and terrible voice. The voice of earthquakes and shattering worlds. A Univoice. The voice of the universe itself. It

spoke one word, low and long and with crushing resonance.
//// SIX ////
it said.
She convulsed, woken from the dream.

❦

Had it been a dream? All of it? Deborah looked around, disorientated. She was in a room. A hospital room? The bed she lay on was cold. The mattress was pristine, but the metal frame dark and rusted. She rolled slightly and felt her arm press against something clammy. Something living. A second person lay in the bed beside her. Shocked, she sat up, and stared. It was a girl, sickly looking, young. Dark stains around her sleeping eyes. She had no hair - not on her head, nor above her eyes. The patented look of chemotherapy - of the late-stage cancer patient. Despite Deborah's sudden movements, she lay perfectly, peacefully still in the bed. Whatever was going on, this mystery girl was unaware.

The walls around were grey and empty, with a floor and ceiling to match. A single, unadorned bulb hung from above, casting a pale glow. There was no furniture save the bed and a single tall stand, metal also, set in the centre of the room.

"What the *fuck*?" Deborah whispered, her voice cracking. Her slumbering companion did not stir. Where was she? How did she get here? She remembered a mansion. A job? Yes! Yes, her latest job, that one that had come in out of nowhere. Too fast for the usual scrutiny, but a job all the same. She had been in a mansion; there was… there was a library, and… and a bed… She strained to focus, to grab at the spectral ribbons of her memories. They were hazy, out of focus. Yes, there was a bed, and her target had been on it. She had done the deed, she remembered that. He had relinquished his life to her without incident, and then… library…

Deborah's eyes widened as it came back to her. The door, the man, the gun. The shot. The memory seemed to fire a second ghostly bullet through her. She could almost feel it punch through her heart once again and she shot a hand to her breast. Nothing there, she thought. No wound, no blood, no nothing. It *had* been a dream, though more vivid than any dream she had ever had. She lifted herself up further in the bed, feeling around her body for sign of injury. She found none. She was *dressed* for a job, that was for sure. Her tight black trousers, black vest and top and her light leather boots. Her gun and belt were missing though.

Was she under arrest? It was possible, she supposed. The law would certainly take her tools of the trade and her weapons from her, and the room was bare, as it would be in a government facility. But it didn't seem right. Why would she share a bed with the sleeping stranger?

Maybe this was The Orchard's doing? Didn't seem their style either, though even after so many years as one of their contractors, there were aspects of their methods she would never understand. Aspects operatives like her were not meant to know.

Standing from the bed, she reached out to the wall and touched it. Cold, like stone. She stepped lightly, tracing her fingers and gaze around the wall, corner to corner, until she spotted something at the far side of the wall. A small keyhole, set in the smooth stone. Looking around, she saw it lying on the stand. A heavy, golden key, old-fashioned and ornate. Well, not much choice here, she thought. She plucked it from its pedestal and slid it into the waiting keyhole.

It would not budge an inch. She frowned. Scanning around again, she sought a second keyhole. She saw none, but did see something else. Lying at the foot of the bed, tucked beside one of its legs was a second key. This one not so ornate, and of dull iron, not gold. She stooped and grasped it, and replaced its golden counterpart on its stand. She tried the new, less ostentatious key in the lock this time. It turned with a soft click, and the outline of a door seemed to peel across the wall in front of her eyes. Inhaling gently, she held a moment as she gathered what she could of herself. Then she pushed.

What she had expected Deborah could not really identify - a corridor of grey, like the room she had occupied? A hospital waiting room? A government building of some kind? Whatever she had expected, this was not it. Her foot fell on a metallic floor. Rusted and discoloured, like that of an abandoned tanker. At either side she observed long expanses, narrow and claustrophobic, all metal and concrete. A ramshackle patchwork of rusted steel walls, intermingled with crumbling stone and rotting, wooden barricades. It stretched in every direction, with levels and ceilings to match. There were platforms above and below, some of grate steel, some corrugated, some broken and crumbling. All around and as far as she could see there were thrown-together partitions and half-walls and floors. All decrepit, all failing. The detritus of decades and decades of half-hearted repair and rebuild and modification and expansion. An endless jungle of rust. An industrial nightmare.

There were people too - everywhere it seemed. Pockets of bedraggled beggars and throngs of sad-looking civilians, milling slowly or sitting, apparently waiting. The diversity of clothing and ethnicities was endless, as was the variety of tongues that made up the low, ever-present din. A few passers-by glanced her way as she stood in shock, catching her eye briefly. They were grimy, uniformly dishevelled. Their eyes betrayed horrifying sadness, but what struck Deborah most about them was not the misery but the pathetic hope. The pleading in their wretchedness. Deborah knew something of that look. She knew the awful desperation of the homeless and loveless, but whenever she had seen it prior, it was in contrast to the bustle of a thriving city. The sad pathos of the abandoned a skewed reflection of the happy indifference of the content. Here, pathos seemed the norm. The few souls who noticed her moved on without comment. They seemed all too familiar with her dumbstruck look.

Instinctively Deborah reached back behind her. Whatever this was she needed to think, and doing so from the confines of the hospital room would be simpler than out in this maddening throng. Turning to push at the door, her mind slid a little as it tried to reconcile what she felt with what she saw. The door was gone, replaced with nothing. Another long expanse of steel and makeshift engineering stretched out in front of her. The spot where the door had been, a mere step behind, was an empty space. Wherever she had been, she wasn't returning. And the rules of the world she knew were dissipating like so much smoke in the air.

This is still the dream, she thought. This is *all* the dream. The bullet pushed me into a coma. I'm lying in a hospital. Police, or Interpol standing guard. Machines ticking and whirring, keeping my body alive as my brain rides this fucked-up rollercoaster, trying to make sense of it. Or *none* of it was real, she thought with a glimmer of hope. I'm asleep in my apartment, and my mind has conjured up this whole thing - the mansion, the bullet, the visions and now this… this nightmarescape. It's trying to warn me. Warn me not to go ahead with the quick job. Not to be seduced by the easy money.

There was a part of her that could latch onto this, that would will it, by force if necessary, to be true. But not the best part. The best part of her didn't believe it. Don't be so fucking naive, it told her. Deborah was not given to flights of optimism. A doggedly pragmatic outlook had always been her guide, and it had served her well in the past. She had, since early childhood, only truly believed in what she could see and feel, touch and smell, and this? This was *real*. She was here all right. And she had better get her bearings, because wherever she was, it sure as fuck didn't look forgiving.

She inhaled sharply and began to walk in one direction. One was as good as the other. What did it matter? she thought with grim resignation. Dream or not, I'm nowhere right now, with nothing to guide me. I can't stay here, so I go somewhere. Anywhere. *Outside.* Got to try and get outside. See the sky, see the horizon. Work from there.

Wherever she turned, the industrial trappings of the slum continued. There were sections with particular slants, different mimeses of real world counterparts. A spot to her left predominantly of plasterboard and old creaky timber. Another to her right of rough concrete blocks. Left, an area built of the rusting innards of a ship, riveted metal and circular port-hole windows caked in filth. Right, a precarious concoction of matchstick grey girders, endlessly crisscrossing, reaching towards patchwork walls in the distant gloom.

On and on and on she trudged, sometimes along thoroughfares, sometimes up or down ladders and stairways. Left and right, up and down, the scenery ever different though never truly changing. Pockets of variation served only to create a chaotic, broken whole.

Everywhere the people shuffled in quiet misery. Some milled around with a semblance of purpose, slow, wretched, but about some grim business. More often though they leaned or sat. Some in silence, some muttering to themselves like drunks, or madmen in a wretched asylum.

Once, as she made her sorry way, Deborah had bumped right into one. A young girl, no older than twenty. She had stood facing a solid wall, right around a blind corner. Deborah had stumbled back, falling on her hand which had scraped painfully on the rough ground. As she had stood and turned, to apologise, or simply to speak out loud to someone, what she beheld had rendered her silent.

The girl's eyes had been live, electric and darting. They twitched and convulsed, their direction not always uniform. Madness and sickness in them, and above, a great blotchy red. Her forehead was a mass of blood and shattered bone, the tissue smashed and ground in to the pulp within her skull. As Deborah locked wide eyes with the girl's mad ones, a great, insane grin had painted across her face. The fissures and cracks of her head-wound shifted grotesquely as her facial muscles contorted. Clenched in her mouth, between shattered teeth, was a string of wooden beads. Rosaries. They forced her lips open at uneven angles and, where they did, long strings of viscous spittle and sticky, congealing blood trailed down across her face, hanging erratically from her chin.

Deborah had stared, frozen. Queasy horror sunk through her stomach, but the girl had simply turned to the wall and resumed her insane business. Her smile fixed, she had carefully drawn her body back and then violently smashed at the wall with her head. Then again, and again, and again. The hollow splash of her wound, wet against the splattered stone was rhythmic and hideous. A fleshy metronome. That sound alone was enough to make Deborah retch, but the humming was somehow worse. All the while, she sang through her bead-filled mouth in a reedy whine. Deborah couldn't be sure - the girl's mind had shattered and her voice had strained to breaking - but she had thought she recognised a tune. It had sounded like a guttural arrangement of Ave Maria.

The fascinating repugnance of the scene was still with Deborah now. She imagined it would follow her for quite some time. She *hoped* so, in fact. The only circumstance she could imagine in which it would not, was one in which such grotesqueries were commonplace. Here, she could not yet be sure that they weren't.

༺ ༻

She felt she had been moving for many hours, perhaps a day, perhaps longer, when it first occurred to her that she had not eaten or drunk anything since waking in the strange nowhere-room. Her belly did not feel empty, nor her throat parched. Another physical rule she could check off the list. Wherever, *whenever* she was, sustenance seemed not a priority. Or at least, food and drink were not. There *was* hunger. She felt it within her, swelling, but not hunger for any victuals. It was a deeper hunger, more primal than that. It seemed to cry out not from her stomach, but her chest. A craving undeniable yet incomprehensible. It gnawed at her.

As she passed another doorway, cobbled together from chipboard and what looked to be wrought-iron fixtures, an odd luminescence in the air ahead caught her eye. It hung in space, eight feet or so above the ground. A blade of light, cast seemingly from nowhere. It cut across the air and began to extend, and as it did Deborah realised with a flash what she was seeing. It's a door, her mind exclaimed. She was witnessing a new victim being born into this slum. Just as she had been.

The air swung open at a right-angle to itself. A static feel ran through the air, slight but perceptible. A figure stepped out of the empty void and onto the concrete ground, several yards ahead. The woman was older, grey haired. She wore a stout cardigan and a long pleated skirt, sensible shoes and a look of utter disorientation. She looked to Deborah like a Sunday school teacher, or a chapter head of the Woman's Institute. She'd know her way round a community hall bake-sale, that was for sure. As she stared timidly at the nightmare that surrounded her, bafflement melted into dread. Her mousey eyes darted this way and that, until, meeting Deborah's, she locked her gaze and approached.

"This is it, isn't it?" she stammered.

"I don't..." Deborah wasn't sure what to say. She had nothing to offer the woman. No knowledge to sate her, no wisdom to comfort her.

"This is it. This is..." The woman, nodding, inhaled a sharp, shallow breath. "*Hell.*"

Deborah said nothing. The idea had occurred to her certainly, but hearing someone else say it was solidifying. The bake-sale woman was probably right. In the face of her mute solemnity, the woman closed her eyes. Tears pushed from the brink of her lids to trickle down her face.

"I died. I *died*. It was that infection... it just... I died..." She would glance around periodically, coming back to meet Deborah in fearful desperation. "I'm in Hell. *Why?* I tried so hard... I tried to live well, nothing

I did… I never… Even when they tried to…" She was rambling now, her voice descending to a mutter. No longer directed at Deborah, but at the world in general.

She shuffled aimlessly towards a makeshift doorway and collapsed on her haunches, murmuring and sobbing. Another voice added to the dim cacophony. A new singer in the miserable choir, singing the hollow song that rattled through the whispering spaces of this world.

Deborah moved on. There was nothing else to do.

⁂

Many hours later, her aimless quest for something, anything to illuminate her situation, brought Deborah to a vista. The ground beneath her had, over time, morphed from grating to solid steel and then to hard stone, which now yielded to craggy, fissured rock crops at a cliff edge. It seemed to Deborah, her mind still clinging to the world she knew, that the landscape below would open to an ocean, a beachfront. The rock was porous and pitted, like that found in oceanside climes. This could be it, she thought. An edge to this madness finally. Somewhere with a view to whatever lay beyond.

As she stepped to the edge in anticipation, her hopes were dashed. The area was reminiscent of a seafront certainly, but where the sea should lie, there was only more chaotic, labyrinthine constructs. In place of a beach, stretching around in a great arc, was a solid rock wall. A sheer face of grey, littered with openings and ladders and metal containers cut and built into it, fading to murky black as it rose.

More, she thought wearily. More of the everlasting nightmare. For the first time since she had stepped through the nothing-door, she hunched and sat on the ground. Pulling her long legs up towards her face, she hugged her knees and pressed her face into the pit between them. She tried to steel herself against the anguish. The deep hunger in her breast was sharpening. It cried to be sated, but by what it didn't know. Like an infant it wailed at the world, lost and pained, without any comprehension of its needs.

She couldn't let herself give in. She *wouldn't*. That was what this place wanted. The despair of its inhabitants was testament to that. She forced her head back up and looked, *really looked* around her. What *did* she know?

She knew the place was enormous. That much was obvious. She knew that it was built. It had been constructed - slap-dash and ramshackle to be sure - but engineered. Or at least, not naturally occurring. Though underneath… The vista she sat at did betray one thing - this was the first area she had seen where the construction appeared to follow a preexisting terrain. This had been a landscape prior to the years of erection and rebuild and modification and addition. There was natural topography buried beneath.

Above though? Above was pure black. No clouds, no visible ceiling to the expanse, and no stars. Nothing to guide anyone. Was this a cave? Was she underground? Deborah thought not, the air felt wrong, but she would not rule out the possibility. To accept her place in a world without stars? Without hope? That would turn her into that woman she had seen at the doorway. Into another member of the anguished choir. To accept that, she might as well stand smashing her head against a wall. No. Instead, she resolved to keep walking. In the absence of stars above, she surveyed the bay below for some marker to follow.

At first glance it was all chaos, just more thoughtless, hodgepodge apocalypse, but if she stared down long enough, there did appear to be some crazy order to it. Over to one side, out into the not-sea, it had the high-stacked look of a burned out city. It was hard to articulate why, but it certainly seemed more… residential. In contrast, the space below, at the base of the great wall, was more open. Flatter. There was more movement there too. The pinprick people shuffled around more, and in straighter lines. A little more purpose to their back-and-forth. That was her destination. Where there was purpose there was, most likely, interaction. Where there was interaction there might be hustle. Hustle was where wits could get you by. At this point, wits were all she had left. If she gave up? If she gave in to the darkness? Then she wouldn't even have those. She stood, surveyed the cliff edge, traced a precarious descent and stepped down.

꘎

The area that had appeared open from the cliff was anything but once Deborah was within its throng. Certainly there was less above her. The mishmash of platforms were scattered more infrequently here, but the makeshift walls and partitions at ground level were, if anything, denser than she had seen prior. A maze of doorways and arches with facades of metal and wood filled every crevice. They split the space one way then the other with no discernible pattern. The whole place brought to Deborah's mind images she had seen of the aftermath of a hurricane. Pieces of half-buildings within other buildings. Parts of rusted machinery serving as structure. Fractured shipping containers and concrete tunnelling and sections of once-were-vehicles littered all around. Like a great beast had swallowed a city and then vomited it back up across a dead and desolate land.

Here, unlike above, there did exist some semblance of life. There were pockets of huddled people crowding in alcoves, engaged in hushed parley. A few lone figures slunk around in apparent circles, pausing occasionally for whispered words with passers-by. Sometimes dismissed, but more often leading to muted exchanges of sorts. Some kind of wheelings and dealings. Queues of dirty faces lined walls, snaking from squalid establishments, disquieting desperation their only unifying trait. Deborah recalled the old westerns she had seen as a girl, on Sunday afternoons with her father. The dangerous little border towns they took place in. Magnify those, view them through a kaleidoscope so they're all jumbled and upside down and back to front, douse it all in filth and rust and here you go, she thought grimly. Your very own hellscape town centre.

She approached the nearest of the queues, glancing in at the doorway. Suspicious eyes surveyed her from the front of the line. Its members did not look accepting of some neophyte blonde worming her way to the front. After a moment or two, the door swung open and a doe-eyed young man scuttled in and handed something to a brutish bouncer. He inspected it with scrutiny before nodding him through. Over his shoulder lay a wretched looking dive. Upturned cable spools served as tables. A long, sheet-metal bar stood at the far side, behind which a bald, ghoulishly thin barman stood in a stained apron. He smiled a toothy, craven grin at his new customer over the bowed heads of maybe two dozen patrons.

The door swung closed once more, rattling as it bounced against the rotten frame. Deborah turned to an older man at the front of the queue. His skin was black as molasses, his face a mosaic of cracks and fissures. Beneath the ever-present filth, his attire was a dated remnant of US army fatigues.

"What's in there?" she asked. As calm as she tried to keep her voice, it had not been used in some time. It pitched higher than she had planned, and was cracking worse than before. Desperation was taking hold.

The man smiled a despondent, knowing smile. "The love, little girl. The love." His voice a deep, soulful drawl. What the fuck did that mean? The *love*? She frowned.

"How do I get in?"

"You wait, little girl. You wait and you wait. Then you hand over yo' paper."

"Money?" She had not thought about money, but now that she did, she knew right away she had none. She always carried money - a sizeable roll of local currency on every job she took for The Orchard. Eli had always insisted. Just in case. Best to have and not need than need and not have. Her last job had been no different - she had brought money. It was neatly stuffed in the belt she no longer possessed. Fuck.

"*Money...*" The soldier repeated with a faraway look in his eyes. He smiled again. "Not money little girl. Just yo' paper."

Everything here was riddles and traces. Deborah's wits clamoured to find footing. "I don't understand," she began, "where do I get..."

The soldier pressed a huge, weather-beaten finger to broad, cracked lips and she trailed off. "*Hush* little girl. It don't do to talk here. And 'sides, I ain't got none o' what answers you seek."

Deborah looked into the milky pockets of his eyes. He sounded remorseful, but his look was resolute. "Who does? Who does have... the answers I seek?"

"Ain't for me to know little girl." The soldier's voice descended to a wispy lilt. "Ain't for me to know."

"You! Hey you!" snapped a voice from behind the soldier. Deborah turned. A mean-looking young woman glowered at her. Her hair was long but patchy - she seemed to be losing it in spots - and her skin was sallow, waxy. Purple blotches traced up her arms. Deborah knew that look. She had seen it many times in her younger days. The gauntness of the heroin junkie. "Yeah slut! I'm talkin' to you! Get your bitch ass back to the end of the fuckin' line!" She spat her words with a sharp, nasal whine.

Deborah glanced back behind her. The queue stretched the length of the facade, running round a corner out of sight. She sighed. What did it matter? She had no *paper*, whatever that meant. She had no idea what this place offered, no concept of where she should be or what she should do. She had no one to guide her, no Eli quipping to cut the tension. Worst of all, she had no idea how to sate the intense hunger. She had nothing.

Stepping back across the thoroughfare and looking around, she caught sight of a man. He sat alone at the edge of a sheet-metal wall across the open space. Smiling. Cradling something in his lap. Deborah, desperate now for any kind of guidance, began to approach. Hoping beyond hope for something, anything to cut the desperate sadness that hung everywhere around her. Any respite at all. He was smiling. Maybe he knew something. Please. Let him know *something*, she pleaded.

As she stepped close, she saw with rising horror the object of the man's affection. Piled in his lap were the torn remains of a book, the pages ripped and the spine twisted apart. The etched cross on the cover and the pile of shredded pages were crimson with blood. His arms, set in his lap, ended in bloody stumps, all digits missing save the thumbs. Piled in a sticky mess among the pages were his fingers, gnawed and pulled from his hands. Something else was in there too. Something clear and white and gelatinous. Looking down at his face, close now, she saw his grinning, bared teeth, coated in clotting blood, below two bruised sockets that had once housed eyes. His appalling smile was horror incarnate. She fell back. There would be no respite. No. There was nothing but madness here.

The despair claimed her. She felt the truth crushing down, driving her body into the dirt. This was Hell. It had all been real. The job, the suited man, the bullet. She had died, and in her Hell she was homeless and lost. No documents, no money, no hope. Again. This time though? This time it would be endless. Her punishment. Her guilt manifest. She stumbled towards an unoccupied spot by the edge of a crumbling wall and slumped to her seat. She stared out across the makeshift square with vacant, hollow eyes.

Fracture Two

EXODUS

"Debbie!"

Deborah lay in silence.

"Debbie, I know you're in there!"

She sighed and glanced towards her bedroom door.

"Debbie, I don't like locked doors in my house! Now get out here!" Trisha was particularly shrill today. Guess she was having more trouble than usual slapping the makeup on and coaxing her straw hair into place. Every fucking Friday, thought Deborah, rolling her eyes to the empty room and pulling her earphones out. She slid off the bed and traipsed to the door, turned the key and opened it a crack.

On the other side, Aunt Trisha was waiting, fiddling at her ear with an ostentatious diamanté earring. Her dried-out, peroxide birds-nest was half askew on her head.

"Stop locking that door," she said flatly. "Where are my straighteners?"

"I don't know," Deborah replied pointedly. "Ask Gregor." She started to close the door but Trisha pushed it back.

"Your uncle won't know where they are. He wouldn't know *what* they are. Don't get smart with me." Deborah narrowed her eyes.

"*Don't* call him my uncle. You living with someone doesn't make them related to me. I don't have your straighteners, okay?" She stepped back and swung the door fully open. "You want to check for yourself?"

"Oh don't fucking start with me Debbie. I'm in a hurry, the girls will be waiting." Trisha waltzed past into Deborah's little room, casting her eyes around suspiciously. "I *choose* to have him live with me Debbie, I'm *stuck* with you and your smart-mouth."

"It'd be hard not to have a smarter mouth than his," Deborah muttered, deliberately audibly. Trisha took a moment from her fruitless half-search to fire a glare at her, before turning her back once again.

"Doesn't seem like you have such a problem with him being here," she mused with an airy, highfalutin tone, "the way you flirt with him."

Deborah baulked. The idea of anyone flirting with Gregor was enough to make her queasy, but the idea that *she* would? That was positively grotesque.

"Are you kidding me? Why the fuck would I want to flirt with that manky old drunk?"

Trisha spun around and raised her index finger in Deborah's face. The same supercilious posture she always adopted in these conflicts of her own making. One of these days, I'm going to grab that finger and snap it right the fuck off, thought Deborah.

"That *manky old drunk* is my boyfriend, and he pays half the rent, which is more than I can say for you, young lady."

"I'm fourteen! What do you want me to do? Quit school and work down a fucking mine?"

"Not everyone can spend all their free time sitting in their room reading and listening to that bloody racket you call music," Trisha raised an eyebrow, "and only coming out to parade themselves in front of other people's boyfriends."

"Parade myself how?" Deborah asked, practically choking on incredulity. Trisha sucked in a deep breath, they way she always did when she was gearing up to impart one of her condescending little life-lessons.

"I was young once Deborah," she began.

Oh, thought Deborah, how droll. I'm getting a full-name this time. She must be ready to drop some real pearl of wisdom.

"…And I pretended *I* didn't know what effect I was having on men then too. But the way you dress…"

"I'm wearing jeans and a fucking T-shirt," Deborah began, but it didn't matter. Trisha was rolling now. She wasn't going to let her uppity niece – or logical sense for that matter – get in the way of the point she thought she was making.

"The way you dress… the way you flaunt that little body of yours… It's so easy for you isn't it? Well someday you'll get older and some young thing will come along that turns heads faster than you…" Trisha tailed off. Deborah rolled her eyes again. It was patently clear her aunt was losing track of her own convoluted point.

Her ramblings, of course, served only to highlight her own insecurities. Even before living with her, Deborah had known full well that Trisha was virtually unable to have a conversation about anything without turning it into something about herself. Her egocentricity was borderline pathological. Now, as Deborah was growing up and Trisha's looks were fading fast, that self-centred vanity more often than not twisted into bitter resentment.

"Get out of my room," sighed Deborah, planting a hand on the door. Trisha glared at her once again but relented and stepped towards the door.

"It's *my* room Debbie. You want to call it *your* room then you pay the rent." She pulled the key from the lock and pocketed it. "And until then, young lady, I don't like locked doors in my house."

Trisha stepped out into the hall and Deborah slammed the door behind her. It rattled in the frame, loosening a corner of her prized Siamese Dream poster. She flopped back down on her bed and watched as it peeled over limply and crumpled to the ground, leaving dirty blobs of blu-tack behind on the door. No matter how hard she tried to plaster her own life onto this house, it always seemed to reject her. She pushed her earbuds back in. Fuck it. Cobain may have been a junkie, but his heroin-fuelled lyrics still made more sense than any of the extras in her young life.

As she listened, staring into the dead space above her bed, Deborah wondered. Did the fact that she shared so little of Trisha's preoccupation with looks make her aunt more aggressive towards her? She'd probably have an easier time if she acted more like the vapid, air-headed disco-tarts that seemed to rule her school. Deborah certainly had the looks for it, she couldn't help that. What had once been called 'tall-for-her-age' was blossoming into 'statuesque'. Her chest was flatter than some, but her slender frame could easily make the slutty dress-code of the popular girls shine, and her legs went all the way down to the ground. She could peroxide lighten her blonde hair, she mused, and slap on the make-up – play right into Trisha's fears. Be the younger version of her ageing self. The idea brought a smirk to Deborah's face.

She'd never pull it off of course. There was a reason she could never be like those girls. You can't fake oblivious stupidity. You have to come by it naturally. You could try and force yourself to care about the current fashions, the popular music and the slew of newly interested and ever-horny boys, but eventually intelligence would make itself known. Hide your smarts as much as you like, but they'll always betray you in the end. Deborah knew her aunt didn't hate her for being more attractive. She hated her for being more attractive and *not caring*. Deborah having the looks was one thing, but having the looks and not needing to rely on them? That was what really stoked the engine of her resentment.

Trisha had never wanted children, Deborah knew that. She had known it back before her father had died. But it was only after awful circumstance had forced the two under the same roof that she had really seen, first hand, why her aunt *shouldn't* have children. Trisha may have aged, but she had never grown. She still thought of herself as the young blonde bombshell she strived to emulate and had, at one time at least, approximated. There wasn't a parental bone in her body. She acted the way she thought a parent should of course, publicly, but inside she saw Deborah as nothing more than a rival in her relentless quest for attention. And to Trisha, attention was most evident in the interest of men.

Knowing all of this on an intellectual level didn't make it any easier to live with her though. For years now Deborah had felt trapped. She longed to break away from her aunt and her string of shit-heel boyfriends. To escape this house and her school and Edinburgh – this fucking city that she felt no connection to – and…

And what? Go where? That part of the plan never quite came together in her head. It would, she was sure. Eventually. She was only fourteen. There was still time. She was counting on that. But in the meantime she simply withdrew. Into her books, into her music, into this pokey little room with its pokey little bed. Into her thoughts.

Deborah skipped her CD Walkman on to a track she liked better and lay still, letting the music take her away.

An album and a half later, Deborah glanced around. The daylight had slowly melted into dusk outside the high window. She wondered what was in the fridge downstairs; she was getting hungry. She turned and checked the clock by her bed. Ten past eight. Trisha must have left a while ago. Friday night out with the 'girls'. They were pushing the definition of 'girls' to breaking point at this stage, Deborah thought. Not one of the painted faced strumpets Trisha consorted with was under forty, but whatever. That was ever the Friday night plan for Trisha. The unimaginative highlight of her unimaginative week. Out with the girls.

Gregor would be halfway through his twelve-pack by now, staring vacantly at whatever football game was on. Half-cut by this point, no doubt. With any luck he'd be half asleep and she wouldn't have to deal with his lecherous looks or moronic comments. Lifting herself up from the bed, she padded on bare feet over to the door, swung it open and stepped out, down the stairs towards the kitchen.

Sure enough, the living room door sat ajar. The dull pulse of light from the television set illuminated the hallway sporadically. Deborah could hear the monotone drone of sports commentary. Why do they always speak in that same exact cadence? she wondered disinterestedly. No one ever talks like that in any other circumstance.

She passed the door and headed into the kitchen. No smell of cooking, but that was pretty normal. Trisha wasn't much of a chef. She generally only cooked a meal when there was someone to impress. Someone to whom she could say 'Oh *this*? Oh I just threw this together.' Trisha never missed an opportunity for false modesty. It was a trait unbecoming in a woman whose talents were, in fact, so very modest.

Swinging the refrigerator door open, she surveyed its contents. A few trays of congealing takeaway remnants, milk, some half-empty jam jars. A couple of sad looking condiment bottles. The lower two shelves were entirely devoted to vacuum wrapped packs of beer. Some full, most in various states of unpacking. She wrinkled her nose in displeasure and closed the door. Surveying the kitchen, she spotted an open loaf of bread on the counter. It was close to stale - that idiot Gregor never thought to wrap shit up after himself - but it was free of mould. That'll do, she thought. She grabbed a couple of slices and dropped them in the toaster.

As she stood waiting for the pop, she heard the drone of the television fall as the living room door swung closed. She grimaced. Gregor stepped onto the linoleum with a sway in his gait. He eyed Deborah for a second.

"When's your ma gettin' home?" he asked with a hint of a slur. Not blind drunk yet, but working on it.

Deborah turned to stare into the orange glow of the toaster. Anywhere but at his unshaven, gormless face.

"My *ma* is dead," she stated flatly.

Gregor paused for a second as his boozy brain caught up to the conversation. He tried again. "When's *Trish* gettin' home?"

"I don't know Gregor," she replied wearily. "Late I suppose." Talking to him in this state was as dreary as it was futile. She doubted he was taking much, if any, of it in. "She's usually late on a Friday isn't she? Did she not tell you?"

"Nah," he slurred as he stepped past her and pulled open the refrigerator door with more force than it required. The jars rattled in the door as he did. "Always out with those lassies," he muttered.

"Yup, every Friday," Deborah replied, disinterested and distant. She kept looking down at the toaster, as if to will the bread to heat faster. Get her out of this depressing back and forth.

"Seems like more often." Gregor pulled a tin of beer out of the plastic wrap and closed the fridge door beside her back. "Always leaving us here together, eh?"

Christ, Deborah thought, here we go. She could feel him eyeing her from behind and hear his shallow breath rattle in his throat. "She should be more careful, eh? Leaving her man with a tidy young lassie, alone on a Friday night?"

Jesus. Just stare at the toaster. Don't make eye contact, don't engage. Let him stagger off back to the sofa to pass out. Gregor had made comments like this before, and they always revolted her. She knew by now to just avoid him where she could and ignore him where she couldn't. Let Trisha come home with her vodka-and-gossip induced high spirits and deal with the horny old fucker's urges. The worst she would have to do was stick her earbuds in to avoid hearing them fumble about drunkenly in their bedroom. Drown out his grunts and her donkey-bray guffaws.

She flinched as a pop-fizz reverberated around the little kitchen, followed by a wet slugging as Gregor chugged beer from the can.

"Never know what might happen," he murmured. As he did, Deborah felt her stomach lurch. Gregor was running a finger up the exposed part of her torso, from behind. She whipped around to face him.

"Get the *fuck* off me!" she blurted, caught off guard by his brazenness. This was worse than usual. Gregor fired a grin her way, perhaps intended to be boyish, but through his inebriation the result was menacing.

"Oh? How come? It's a sin, y'know. Seein' a tidy wee thing going to waste on a Friday night…"

He stepped in close. Deborah recoiled back against the kitchen counter. She could taste his rancid beer and cigarette stink hanging in the air. She tried to twist to her side to get away, but he clamped a heavy hand around her arm.

"Where you going?" he asked, seeming genuinely hurt at first, though this quickly slipped into a snarl. "We're just having some fun you and me."

Deborah looked in his eyes and saw only glassy emptiness as they scanned up and down her body, coming to rest aimed square at her midriff. "A bit of fun's what we *need*."

Oh no, she thought. Oh God. Oh No. His free hand grabbed at the top of her jeans, four fingers inside the waistband, groping down at her underwear. She twisted against his grip, but it was no use. Gregor was built big, and the alcohol fuelled a single-minded madness in his eyes. Deborah wriggled and squirmed in panic, her eyes darting around the little room for help.

She found nothing but fluorescent light and cold white counters. This was it, she thought with panicky anguish. The gross old fuck was going to do what he was going to do. What she had always known he thought about, but until now had never dared. She was powerless to stop it. Her eyes pressed closed in dread.

Right then she heard a springing snap, and Gregor whipped his head up with drunken, stuporous surprise. The toaster. With the half-second between her sober and his drunken comprehension, she twisted again, forcefully. She slid in his hand this time, his alarm loosening his grasp momentarily. Grabbing the toaster with her free hand, her fingers deep in the slot where the elements still glowed, she slammed it against the side of his head. Searing pain flooded through her hand and up her arm as both the toaster and Gregor crashed to the plastic floor. For a moment, she stood rooted to the spot.

"Mmm*FUCK*!" Gregor spat, kneeling up onto all fours and turning his head to her like an animal. Little strings of blood and spittle leapt, cartwheeling from behind nicotine-stained teeth and catching in his greying ginger stubble. "Ya wee fuckin' *CUNT*!" he bellowed.

His bark was a starting gun, snapping her out of her daze. She bolted from the kitchen, almost slipping as she scrambled round the door and into the hallway. Past the living room door, and up the stairs, her mind racing. She could hear Gregor's rage as he stumbled to his feet. At the top of the stairs, she turned, darted into her room and slammed the door. Throwing her hand down instinctively to turn the key, she found only air.

No, she groaned in panic, No! Trisha you dumb fucking bitch! She had taken her only defence against this madman, her only hope of enduring until help came.

She stared around the room for anything that could help her. Nowhere to hide in here, the room was too small. There was nothing but the bed and her little chest of drawers among the posters and scattered CD boxes and books. Back out the room? her panic asked. Nope. She heard the familiar squeak of the floorboard at the bottom of the steps. Gregor was coming.

"Get back here ya wee bitch!" His voice was slurred far worse than before. Perhaps the booze, perhaps the blow to the head. It didn't matter. His blood was up. Among other things. And he wouldn't be denied.

Deborah rescanned the room, this time in search of a weapon. She didn't fancy her chances much even with one; Gregor was 240 pound of sheet-metal plater and she was a slim fourteen year old, 110 pounds soaking wet. But with a weapon was better than without. Regardless, she came up with nothing. What was she going to do? Throw a little plastic CD rack at him? Hit him with a coat hanger? For a second, she wished she *had* had Trisha's hair straighteners. The thought almost made her cry. That exchange felt like a very long time ago.

The pounding footsteps rose and rose, reaching an apex right outside. Deborah grabbed the heaviest object she could - the decorative piggybank her father had bought her years ago. Across its side the lettering she herself had emblazoned with her father in happy times, a thousand years before, in blobby glitter-paint. 'GOING AWAY FUND'.

The door burst open. Gregor stood in its frame, his swaying head inches from the lintel, his bloodied teeth bared. He glanced at the piggybank in shaking hands. A horrible smirk drew across his pale lips.

"What the fuck you gonna do with that?" he snarled, "Pay me?" He snorted - a disgusting liquid gargle - wiping at the bloody mucus on his chin. "Dinnae bother hen. I fuck for free."

Deborah knew she only had one option. She spun around and with both hands she flung the piggybank at the high bedroom window. It arced through the air and smashed through the old wooden frame, sending fractured glass and splintered wood careening out into the cold dusk. A flash of genuine confusion ran across Gregor's face and Deborah bolted across the room towards the window. She planted a bare foot on the ledge and, tucking her arms in close to herself, hurled herself through the shattered remains and out into the gloom.

The cold hit her first. The ground hit soon after. The impact of her body on the grass below knocked the wind from her, but she struggled not to writhe. The glass would still be lying splintered beneath her.

Gingerly, she lifted herself. The pain in her side was deep, but dull. The throb of bruising, not the stab of glass rending flesh. Standing, she ran her hands across herself, feeling for any splinters or cuts. The fingers of her left hand throbbed where the toaster had burned them, but through her jeans and her t-shirt she felt no anomalies.

The air was cold, and her bare feet were colder. Casting a look back up at the remains of the window, she saw Gregor standing staring out into the night. A stupid, confused animal that had lost its prey along with its mind. She turned away from the house, nursing her burned fingers.

Deborah was cold. She was alone, barefoot and pained. But she was free. She was free and she was never coming back here. Shaking and shivering she stepped out into the night.

Chapter Three

SHEPHERDS

"Deborah?"
"Is it her? Might not be her."
"It's her, moron."
"Don't call me that. How do you know?"
"What's that say?"

Deborah opened her eyes. She saw only the crook between her own knees where her bowed head lay, but stayed motionless for now, listening.

"...with her head in her knees."
"Yeah, this girl with her head in her knees."
"Lot of girls here Zote. Most of 'em got knees."
"But this one is *this* one. Excuse me!"

Deborah felt a hand jostle her knee. She raised her head and squinted. Two faces stared down at her, both heads cocked comically in opposite directions.

"We're terribly sorry to interrupt your little rest in this delightful… um…," the one on the left glanced around, scrutinizing the area as he spoke, "…shit-hole here m'dear, but might you by any chance be Deborah?" He looked to be in his thirties, with a shaven face below unkempt, dirty-blonde hair. He sported a pair of worn blue-jeans and a simple white t-shirt, and spoke with a broad Irish accent.

"Who are you?" Deborah asked. Her voice sounded groggy to her. Had she slept? She didn't think so, though she couldn't be sure. She felt no more rested than she had when she sat, and the hunger still snarled within her.

"Begging your pardon m'dear, but I do believe our inquiry came first." His counterpart nodded at this. He was eerily similar in looks to his vocal companion, though perhaps a little more boyish in his face. A tad more sedate in his smile.

"Deborah *is* my name…" she replied warily. These two acted friendly enough, but nothing she had seen since arriving in this forsaken place disposed her to trust anything it presented.

"Well then!" The left of the duo beamed triumphantly. He turned and nudged his companion with a smirk. "Well met m'dear. You've certainly travelled some way since you arrived, haven't you? Most folks tend to stay put for a good long while before they decide to get themselves lost!" His tone was jovially conversational.

"Allow me to present myself. I am Zotiel. At your service of course." He dipped in exaggerated genuflection. "And this doubtful Thomas is my compatriot Zephon." The boyish one bowed his head. More stilted than his companion, but still comically formal in this dismal setting.

"Okay..." Deborah replied. She was confused, and more than a little curious, for sure, but she was well practiced at keeping such things hidden. Keeping her cards close to her chest was not just a requirement of her profession. It was ingrained in her through long experience.

"Okay indeed!" beamed Zotiel, his affected grandeur unswayed by her apparent disinterest. "Well. As lovely as this spot you have chosen for yourself is, we would be much obliged if you would accompany us."

"Why would I do that?" she asked pointedly. He frowned.

"You'd rather stay here?"

Deborah looked around at the dismal thoroughfare. Claustrophobic gloom remained, coating all she saw.

"Where to?"

"Oh, just a stroll to take in the beautiful sights," Zotiel answered, wilfully flippant.

"Fantastic," Deborah sighed leaning against the corrugated sheet wall at her back. "I'm in Hell, being courted by a couple of comedians."

The two glanced at each other, sharing a look of perplexed amusement. Zotiel knelt down to meet Deborah face to face and stared for the first time directly into her eyes.

"My dear, if you were in *Hell*," he winced as he said the word and leaned in close, "believe me. You'd fucking *know* it."

Deborah stared back at him. She thought she detected a glimmer of what lay beneath those piercing eyes. A deep well of sorrow behind his jester mask, but it lasted only a moment before he backed up. His smile seemed genuine once more. He extended an oddly smooth, white hand towards her.

"There's someone who requests an audience with you m'love, that's all. Someone you should meet. We humbly request that you accompany us to meet him."

"I have a choice then?"

Zotiel frowned curiously.

"Of course. You could stay here. Your will is free."

Deborah stared back at him. She was lost, she was alone, and she didn't have shit to her name. She had searched long and hard for anything of guidance. Now here came *something* at least. Still though, her instincts troubled her. What instincts she had left, at least. The gnawing in her chest was stealing her thoughts from her like a mental leech.

Zephon spoke, quieter than his partner. "She's probably got the hunger by now, sure?" His lilting cadence was similar to Zotiel's, though missing the overblown theatrics.

"Ah! Where are my manners? Of course!" Zotiel's intonation reached a crescendo, and began, mercifully, to subside a little. "Of course. You've been here a while and, as my esteemed compatriot so eloquently articulates, you probably have a rather unpleasant craving about you, eh m'love?"

Deborah looked up at the pair, steady now. Her face was no longer able to disguise her curiosity. Keeping one's inquisitiveness discrete was easier before there was promise in the offing.

"Yes?" asked Zotiel knowingly.

"Yes," she replied. The hunger seemed to scrabble around more wildly inside her as it heard itself discussed.

Zotiel turned to his partner, who swung a leather messenger bag round to his front. Lifting the flap, he rustled around inside, removed something and handed it to him. Zotiel then presented it to Deborah with a showbiz flourish. A small, cut-glass vial, the size of an apricot. Not overly decorative, but exquisitely fashioned. Inside, there was a vibrant, golden liquid.

"This will take care of that in short order m'love."

Deborah accepted the vial in her hand. It was heavier than she had expected, and warm to the touch. She stared at the liquid inside for a moment, tipping the vial from side to side. It shifted within the container, but with an airy lightness incongruous with the receptacle's weight. It seemed more vapour than liquid.

"What is it?"

"It's your *saviour*," replied Zotiel, smiling enigmatically.

Wrapping her fingers around the little cork at its top, she looked back up at him and paused.

"If we wanted to do you harm, why would we come and find you m'dear? You weren't exactly having the most pleasant of times alone. What've you got to lose?"

She frowned. The weird Irishman had a point. She twisted the cork from the bottle. Gaseous vapours clung to the rim of the vial, whispering over the lip and down its neck to gather in the crevices between her fingers. They sparkled where they pooled. She lifted it to her mouth, tipped its contents and swallowed. There was no discernible taste, just a pleasant warmth running down her throat and into her belly. She waited in silence and, as she did, a glorious feeling coursed through her. It began in her stomach and ran down her legs, up through her breast and down her arms, snaking a trail to her fingertips. It climbed up, through her neck and into her troubled mind, soothing as it went. A milky white serenity, calming every nerve and staying every tremor. Her whole body sighed. This must be what it feels like for an infant to be pulled into its mother's embrace, she thought. Or for a junkie to feel that sweet morphine kiss, shooting up after a long dry spell.

As the euphoric wave dissipated, the hunger melted with it. She felt right again. The yearning had been consuming, but only in its sudden absence did she realise just how debilitating it had been. She felt she could think for the first time in days. Zephon and Zotiel exchanged knowing glances and turned to her expectantly.

"Okay then?"

"...Okay then," she said. Pulling herself to her feet and brushing flecks of rust and grey dust from herself, she added, "Fuck it. Let's go."

"Excellent!" Zotiel replied, turning out towards the makeshift streets, his extravagant fervour returned.

She rolled her eyes but couldn't quite suppress a tiny smile. Whatever Deborah thought of this odd pair and their blithe speech and manner, at least they seemed alive. In this land of crushing sadness, that was something she supposed.

~~~

"So what is it?"

They had been walking for hours now, weaving in and out of alleys and passages as she followed. She had tried at the outset to maintain a mental map of their route. Long years working for The Orchard had made the skill second nature, but nothing she had ever encountered had prepared her for this maze. Mapping was futile. She would have no idea at this point what direction to head in if she wished to get back to her miserable alley.

"What's what m'love?" asked Zotiel. He certainly was the talkative one of the two.

"I thought this place was Hell. Suspected, at least. You say it's not. So what is it?"

Zotiel turned his head back over his shoulder and offered her a wry smile.

"My dear, you are now a proud resident of The Purgs. One of a great and growing number, I might add."

Deborah scoured her memory. She had not been raised to any religion. Her father had never been overtly staunch in his atheism, but he had been a man of practical things. A mechanic by trade, and a pragmatist by spirit. A man of metal and earth. Concepts and theories of religion were not something she ever remembered him discussing one way or the other with her. And Trisha? Trisha had fancied herself a catholic, but that notion only extended as far as wearing a little gold cross around her neck when it suited her outfit. Deborah doubted she would have been able to name a book of the Bible, let alone read one. To recall anything of religious dogma she had to reach awfully far back, to her limited exposure during early schooling. 'The Purgs' he had said.

"Purgatory?"

"Well, call it what you will m'darling. It's had a lot of names over the years," he replied off-handedly.

"That's one of them though?"

"That is, as you say, one of them." Zotiel had an archaic rhythm to his speech that seemed at odds with his Irish brogue, though she found its lack of economy oddly comforting. Every person she had conversed with since awakening here spoke in nothing but compact riddles, snapping jibes or anguished moans. Hearing a voice with anything more than dejection behind it was a welcome relief. Fuck brevity.

"So this is like, what? Heaven's waiting room? Hang about until you get waved on in?"

"Used to be," Zephon muttered, and Zotiel nodded in agreement.

"That was once its purpose, yes. This was the nexus, where the good paid penance for their sins as they waited for the call to the gates. Still is - in a manner of speaking. Though the *definition* of sin has…" Zotiel trailed off a little, clearly choosing his words carefully, "…broadened somewhat. As has the list of possible… destinations."

"Destinations?" Deborah asked.

"Where once was a corridor, now lies a crossroad," Zephon added. He lent voice to thought more sporadically than Zotiel, and when he did was more succinct. It was Zotiel who elaborated further.

"There was a time that those souls who arrived here were just waitin'. Biding their time. Punishment yes, to be sure, but with the promise of *eventual* absolution, and, with it, Paradise. That's not..." He trailed off with melancholy in his voice. The first time Deborah had heard him adopt such a tone. "That's not how it works any longer. There are other paths this place can lead now. *Lower* paths."

"You mean, H..." Zephon whipped his head around, and Zotiel stopped in his tracks, silencing her.

"Yes. Though if you'll forgive us m'dear, we've no love for hearing the name spoken aloud."

"Okay," Deborah nodded. They began walking again. She followed a half-step behind.

The areas where Deborah could see pockets of the starless black above were becoming less and less frequent as they traversed the oppressive chaos. The footing undulated as they marched, but she had, over time, become aware that they were trending down more than up. Deeper into the hive. The feeling of claustrophobia was thickening, and the environs seemed older, more established. There were fewer of the spindly, spider-web steelworks and more stone and hewn rock. In some spots, ancient looking brickwork began to show.

Still everywhere there were people. The endless hordes of the pitiful, milling around despairingly. Wherever she turned, the souls were there, ubiquitous and awful and pathetic and alone. All together and all alone.

⁂

The trio had been walking for many more hours before Deborah broke the silence once more.

"How far is…" She paused and thought for a moment. How far was what? She had not actually asked where the meeting with her mysterious host would take place. She hadn't seen the point, given that she didn't have the slightest clue what or where *anything* was in this place.

"How far is wherever we are going?"

"We're gettin' there m'darlin'. We're gettin' there. Don't you worry about that," replied Zotiel. An answer, Deborah noted, entirely devoid of information.

After a minute or two more Deborah asked, "How big is The Purgs?"

"Ever-expanding m'love. An answer as to size requires a context, and context don't really exist here. It's as big as it needs to be."

"In comparison to a city though?" Deborah persevered. The cryptic nature of the answers she was receiving vexed her. Deborah was, among other things, a practical woman.

"In comparison to an *Earth* city?" Zotiel and Zephon shared a look. "What size is the air in comparison to an elephant? The two can't be *compared*. Both're pretty big by some scale, pretty small by another m'dear."

Deborah sighed in resignation. Whatever answers these two had, this line of questioning wasn't leading to any useful ones. She tried a new line.

"Everyone here, all these people," she cast a surveying glance across the collection of dispirited souls, "they're all dead?"

"They all *died*," Zotiel corrected emphatically. "They're not *dead*. You can see them walkin' about right in front of you, can't you?"

"They all *died*." Deborah corrected herself thoughtfully. "And they all woke in a hospital bed? In a room made of nothing? Some patient beside them and a couple of keys?"

At the mention of her sleeping companion, Zephon shot a brief glance at Zotiel. Beckoning, or perhaps permitting his partner to explain, she assumed. Maybe Zephon was the one in charge?

"Well, in a manner of speaking m'love. Not all rooms are the same, I don't think. A hospital bed is something *you* understand. Something familiar to you. It wouldn't be to a medieval knight or a slave who built the pyramids. It likely wont be to a spaceport denizen of the thirtieth century either. But the *construct* remains. There's always a room, and always a key. It is simply the way to pass. The room is a vessel, the key is a shibboleth."

Deborah had heard the word shibboleth only once before.

"A password?"

"Um, well, yeah. Sort of."

"And they all have other people in them?"

"That," Zotiel paused. "That I don't know."

Deborah peered at him, scrutinising his pale features. He didn't have much of a tell, but there was something there.

"Yes, you do."

Zotiel tilted his head, screwing his features uncomfortably. "Well, look. That may well become apparent." He was selecting his words carefully again. "Not our place though."

Deborah frowned, but relented. Where Zotiel was vague, pushing further only seemed to encourage more vagueness.

They walked on for a while longer in silence. Deborah tried to order her thoughts, to gain a mental foothold in the conversation. The terrain was pretty loose.

"So how did you two die?" she asked.

At this the pair both looked around at her, bemused.

"What?" Zotiel asked.

"I thought all of us, all of these people died?"

"*They* did. You did. We are not the same as you."

"You didn't die?"

"We aren't people."

Deborah slowed a little, prompting the pair to tarry in turn. Zotiel smiled.

"You'll get all the explanations and whys and wherefores you seek m'love. Soon."

She picked up her pace and followed onwards.

☙◦❧

Deborah had suspected as she followed her guides that their path was descending; now there was no doubt. As the haphazard steelwork had given way to rock, the trio's route now weaved through purposeful stonework. Sets of stairways and stone arches became the dominant features, and beneath the ever-prevalent wooden boards and sheet metal, cobbled walkways and medieval architecture appeared. Under the chaotic additions there was a gothic city. It was ancient and labyrinthine and convoluted, but it was definitely there beneath the ramshackle adornments.

"This place is older isn't it?" Deborah asked.

"Nothing gets by you m'love." Zotiel's playful tone was unrelenting. "We're in the oldest parts of The Purgs. At one point this place actually had a nice view, of sorts anyways. Sadness of course, and so much longing and praying and repenting, but there was a kind of beauty to it."

"What changed?"

"*Everything*," replied Zephon.

"Indeed," added Zotiel. "The *rules* changed m'love. The purpose of the place was… warped. Manipulated. The infrastructure couldn't cope with it. It was never designed to house so many folks for so long. And so…"

"What you see above." Zephon finished the thought.

"Yup," agreed Zotiel. "Chaos. Madness. Nothing much left of the search for absolution. For penance. Just a bunch of poor sods milling about, crying in self pity and fear."

"The whole place went mad just from overpopulation?" Deborah asked. It sounded more incredulous than she had wanted it to, though Zotiel did not seem to pay heed to her tone.

"*Just* from overpopulation? No. Imprison a man and tell him he'll get out in a decade and he'll hate his incarceration for sure, but he'll get through it. He might even feel it's justified if he knows his own guilt, and most here in the old days did. The fact that he knows *one day* he'll be free will help him stay sane. But imprison a man and tell him that in ten years he *might* be freed or on the other hand, maybe he'll, say, be flayed and burned alive? It's the waiting that'll drive him over the edge. Come back in ten years and free him, or don't, but the odds are you're looking at an unhinged mess."

Deborah considered this analogy as she followed the pair down another narrow set of stairs. She was about to pry further, but as they descended and she peered beyond the great black archway at the foot, her train of thought was taken from her, along with her breath.

The space beyond was uncannily vast. An enormous square of cobbled ground, intercut at regular intervals by towering pillars. Between each, a great semicircle of brick arched, like the underside of a victorian bridge. Blackened grey stone, scorched by smoke and ash and industry she assumed, though none was apparent. Beneath every one was set some kind of establishment. Some had brick facades, unbowed by time, others were crumbling and haphazardly repaired. Some were thrown together with loose timber and nails in the gaps where the brickwork had all but disappeared, or never existed at all. All were buzzing with people.

People. Everywhere. It seemed to Deborah's Earthborn eyes like the market districts of Constantinople, but set in gloomy Dickensian London, and viewed through a hundred angled mirrors. This, Deborah realised with wonder, was what the place she had arrived at below the vista had been approximating. The comparison was laughable. The outer areas of The Purgs were mere suburbs in comparison to this convoluted metropolis. The slum markets above, a mere pop-up paper cutting of this subterranean bazaar.

"Oh my God," Deborah breathed.

"Not even close," Zotiel responded, raising a single acerbic eyebrow. She considered her choice of expression. Words formed by habit rather than thought. She decided, rather than address it, she would simply outpace her faux pas.

"What are they all buying? What are they *selling*?"

"Whaddaya need?" asked Zotiel, adopting a theatrical snake-oil salesman persona. "Cures for what ails ya'?" Zephon seemed somewhat amused by his partner's antics this time.

"They are selling everything, m'dear. Information, trinkets, *themselves*." As Zotiel said this he nodded casually towards an area in a darker corner, where a group of young men and women stood. Whether in the living world or the lands beyond, it seemed, the comportment of those selling their bodies was ubiquitous. It seemed somehow more grotesque here than what she recalled of her contact with the trade in her youth. Here, both the sellers *and* the buyers she saw engaging their service acted without any care to disguise the empty sorrow in their eyes. Loveless transactions in a joyless world.

"They sell papers and scrolls, books and scraps, and things to stave off the hunger."

Upon hearing this last item, Deborah noticed a familiar sight across the way. A queue filled with hopeful eyes, trailing back from one of the oldest looking facades. Just like she had seen above. Making the connection she scanned around. This was not the only one. At least a third of the building fronts she could see had a similar set-up, and the clientele to match.

"Like the stuff you gave me?"

"*Like* the stuff we gave you, sure. Not as effective though. You got the prime juice m'darlin'." Zotiel cocked his head back at her as they walked. "The real deal. The true Word of God, distilled. Most of what these poor sods will queue for days for is nothing but imitation piss. Brewed-in-a-bathtub moonshine. Most of them that have been here long enough? They'd kill you dead a few times over just for a sniff of what you got."

Deborah frowned, confused once more.

"What good would that do? I'm dead already."

"Don't you listen m'love? You *died* already. Dyin' isn't a virus. Dyin' once don't make you immune to dyin' again."

"I always kind of figured you were either one or the other. Alive or dead, I mean."

"Spoken like a true child of the twentieth century. Everything's digital to you kids." Zotiel smiled. "Once you've been here a while I think you will find, m'dear, that the whole concept of life and death are a lot more analogue than you think."

Deborah frowned again, considering this.

"So I would, what? Wake up in a room again? With another key? Another poor, sick fucker sleeping next to me?"

"If you died here? Maybe. But like I said, there are other possible destinations. Nothing's an exact science anymore."

"Amen," Zephon muttered. His grimace hung sourly on his boyish face.

※

They had weaved in and out of the brickwork and pillars many times, without any direction apparent to Deborah, but as they turned now past another opening, she saw they had traversed the great market area. She stood facing one of its outer edges.

"We're here," Zotiel told her.

Surprised by their journey's sudden end, Deborah looked around. Between the cobbled stone floors, the high brick walls and the milling crowd, the scenery had completed its slow metamorphosis from razed hurricane apocalypse to dark gothic burg. It might as well have been a moonless night in victorian London.

Her guides, their backs to her now, stepped towards a small set of steps that led up to a doorway. An old-fashioned sign hung precariously from a wrought-iron sconce above. Its gold-on-green lettering, faded and almost lost to time, read 'SHEPHERDS.' Beneath it, a pair of suited men stood stone faced and imposing.

Security if Deborah had ever seen it. A shudder tickled up her spine as she flashed back to the library. The deep, dark stare of her killer was chillingly similar to those worn by these two.

Zotiel stepped up first and nodded to one, who nodded back in familiarity. They stepped apart, granting single file passage. Zephon hung back a little and extended his arm, beckoning Deborah to step in front of him. She complied, slipping between the bouncers at Zotiel's back.

⁂

Inside the doorway she saw the first sign since meeting her guides of anything conforming to their accents. She was standing in the entrance of an old Irish pub. Wooden tables dotted around the room were encircled by patrons. Most drank from glass tankards - beer of some description it looked like - and engaged in quiet, or not so quiet, conversation. The mood in here, unlike anywhere outside, contained more than sadness. Downcast, oppressively pessimistic to be sure, but there was life to it. Boisterousness even. It made the interior seem more real than anywhere Deborah had encountered since her demise.

As she followed Zotiel between tables towards the bar, she noted the frequency with which members of the clientele would pause their drinking or exchange to glance her way. Sizing her up. She wondered if this interest stemmed solely from her status as stranger in this land, or from the company she kept. Or perhaps simply her gender. Between the attention she drew and the unfamiliarity of the interior she had instinctually adopted a more discrete posture, but flicking her eyes as covertly as she could, she saw very few, if any, female patrons. Shepherds was, apparently, quite the boy's club.

Whether Zotiel noticed the general interest in his ward or not, he paid it no mind. As he approached the bar, he nodded once more, this time in greeting. A silver-haired Barman nodded back and, continuing to polish an empty glass pitcher with a yellowing cloth, spoke.

"How goes it Zote?" His accent had a hint of Irish to it also, but only slight among a medley of other slants. Deborah could not place him. He seemed from everywhere. That kind of accent she had heard before - usually from the mouths of mercenaries. International operatives. The nowhere and everywhere tongue of those who live their lives everywhere and nowhere.

"Can't complain Auggie, can't complain." Zotiel was cordial but reserved as he twisted and perched on a barstool.

"Who's your friend?" The Barman glanced at Deborah with the practiced nonchalance of a lifetime spent in carefully nonjudgemental service.

"Just an Earth girl. Can't be all business all the time." Zotiel winked at him, adopting a lecherous look. Deborah said nothing, feigning coquettish timidity. She wasn't sure of the play here - best to acquiesce and remain silent.

The Barman maintained his level tone, but a cocked eyebrow betrayed skepticism beneath his nod.

"True that, Zote, true that." He raised his head, looking past Deborah. "Zeph," he greeted, then shifted his focus back.

"You and your little lady want a drink? Or," he glanced at Deborah, "a room?"

"Maybe later." Zotiel replied. "He in the back?"

"To whom do you refer oh Zotiel of The Guides, Shepherd of the Lost, Cicerone of…"

"Cut the shit, Augustine." Zotiel paused as the barman smiled to himself and finally finished polishing the pitcher. He set it down on the bar. "Is he down there or not?"

"I believe he is waiting for you."

Zotiel stood. "Why didn't you fucking say so?"

"Oh," the Barman replied airily, "you know, I just enjoy your company is all."

Deborah could feel Zotiel roll his eyes, even through the back of his head.

"We're going down. Open the damn door."

"As you wish sir, as you wish," the Barman replied. He reached under the bar, did something Deborah could not see, and smiled at her.

"You have fun little miss," he told her with an enigmatic grin. "Don't let them talk you to death." Deborah said nothing, but followed Zotiel as he headed along the bar towards a door at its end.

"What was that about?" Deborah whispered as they approached the door, judging that she was out of earshot.

"Don't worry about it m'dear," sighed Zotiel. "Old irritations build up, that's all. They *last* when eternity is the timescale."

He pushed the door. The three slipped through into a storage area filled with wooden casks and shelves stacked with bottles. Tables and stools more scuffed and broken than those in the bar lay upturned or stacked around the room. Zotiel walked through with familiarity, approaching a single upturned table at the rear - unremarkable, save for its segregation from its broken brethren. Stooping, he lifted its flat top. As it rose the two back legs collapsed in on themselves neatly, and Deborah saw that the 'top' was hinged underneath. The table formed the lid of a covert trapdoor. An impressive decoy, she thought with a measure of respect. She had seen some smartly disguised panic rooms and safes in her career, but couldn't say with certainty that she would have detected this one had she encountered it in a professional capacity.

Lifted to its fullest extent, the table-door revealed the top of a wooden ladder, which Zotiel twisted onto and began to step down. Deborah followed, Zephon behind.

As they descended Deborah asked, "The drinkers in the bar... They were like you? Right? Not... *people*. Not like me?"

"Right," Zotiel replied.

They reached the base of the ladder and she found herself in an underground tunnel. Wooden beams had been built into the cut earth as supports. It looked like a mineshaft.

"But the Barman, *he* was. He was..." She pondered her wording, then settled for the best she could muster. "Human?"

Zotiel turned to her, seeming genuinely surprised for the first time in their long journey. "Right! How did you know?"

"I... don't really know. He seemed too... Something. Too real?"

"Ha!" Zotiel chortled. "Believe me m'dear, my kind are a lot *realer* than you, but if that's what you want to call it, then so be it." He wore a look of puzzled amusement, adding, "You certainly have an eye to you."

They walked the only path available, stooping occasionally to avoid low beams and hanging lamps strung along the way. A short distance ahead, the outline of a door emerged in the gloom. Their destination.

"So what *is* your kind?" she asked as they approached.

"That'll all be made apparent in just a moment m'dear, but suffice to say, we've been around a lot longer than you lot. Longer than your world, longer than *this* world. Longer than the planets and the stars. Longer than anything *you* could name."

He pushed on the door. It clicked and swung inwards.

"What about God?" she asked coyly. More playing with him than seeking an actual answer.

As the door creaked open, a deep, sombre voice resonated from within.

"God is gone."

Fracture Three
NUMBERS

Glasgow was less than fifty miles from Edinburgh, but Deborah's situation there and here were a million miles apart.

It had been seven days now since she had fled into the cold, barefoot and alone, and huddled, freezing, in an open garden shed she had stumbled across as she traversed the suburbs.

It had been five days since she had pilfered these oversized boots and this mangy-smelling hoodie from the Salvation Army collection bins down by the supermarket. They *were* for the homeless, she had told herself, and that was what she was now. She wasn't really stealing. All she was doing was cutting out the middle man. Unfortunately, as her olfactory sense made her now keenly aware, the middle man was the one that did the laundry. It didn't really matter though, she supposed. A few more nights and her clothes would all smell. Worse probably.

It had been three days since she had tried to bed down in an unfamiliar alley out of the wind, only to be forced to outrun a couple of vicious junkies whose spot she had unwittingly taken. Two days since she had fled some greasy looking, goateed man who had, with a lecherous smirk, offered her twenty pounds in exchange for 'Just a little help. Some *lip* service, kiddo.' Between those two exchanges, Deborah's conviction that she was now well and truly alone had cemented. It scared her more than she had ever imagined it could.

It had been one day since she had resolved to leave that city behind. Get the fuck out of Edinburgh, her home for the past five years. Head back to where she had shared her *real* home - with her father. Deborah was smart enough to know that homelessness in one city was the same as another, certainly in two cities of the same clime, but Glasgow pulled at her nonetheless. With nothing but her drive to escape Gregor and Trisha, coupled with her memories of happier times, the west coast had a gravity that the east didn't.

Besides, her aunt would almost certainly report her runaway to the authorities. That was what a good parent-slash-guardian would do, thought Deborah bitterly. Aunt Trisha would definitely do exactly what a good parent-slash-guardian would do. Publicly. A *real* guardian would have helped her, defended her from that perverted old fuck after seeing all the warning signs. A real parent-slash-guardian would see him punished. Deborah was less confident Trisha would go that far. She'd go far enough to ensure *she* was beyond reproach, to ensure she looked to be the caring protector of her ward. Not so far as to make sure her ward was actually protected though. That would cost *her*. Who would stick it in her and make her feel young then? She'd have to start over with some new man. Too much effort there. Too many oh-so-visible indications of spinsterhood. Trisha couldn't have that.

Getting to Glasgow without any money had been time consuming, but not difficult. There were only eight stops on that line, but she had needed to vacate the train and wait for the next one at five of them. Forced either by the conductors' presence or, in a couple of cases, by their monotone order. Exactly zero shits had been given in regard to her clear need for help. The grimy hoodie and the stench of vodka didn't help, she supposed. The makeshift bandage she had fashioned - a strip of t-shirt, doused in the contents of a stolen quarter bottle - would likely shield her burned fingers against infection, but it carried a stench that couldn't be disguised. Still though. The total lack of concern for her obvious plight had been a rude awakening to the harsh reality of street life. Have money, or fuck off. That's how it was. So the trains had taken all day.

Stepping from the fifth and final train carriage onto the platform in Glasgow's Central Station, she was famished. Hungry to the point of tears. She peered around. The crowd of commuters ebbed and flowed, swirling around the platforms and little shops that flanked the open space. She gravitated towards a newsagent near the gated entrance to the streets, noting in particular the open plan refrigerators filled with little triangular sandwich packs. Couldn't be too difficult to swipe one of those, she thought hopefully. Right?

As she sidled towards her prize however, she glanced around, as nonchalantly as she could, and spotted her foil. The shopkeepers might be oblivious to the easy pickings of their stock, but the various transport police dotted around the station no longer seemed oblivious to her. Seven days on the streets and the only attention she invited was the unwanted scrutiny of the authorities. The raggedy hoodie, coupled with her unwashed hair and face were projecting her sorry status admirably.

No joy here, she thought miserably. She pulled her hood up and adjusted her direction. Casting her eyes to the ground she passed by the closest officer, through the open gates to the street beyond.

The early evening streets were a hodgepodge mix. Smartly dressed nine-to-fivers strode purposefully this way and that, heading to busses and trains and the tube stations. Mingled with them, the first wave of fancy-dressed bar hoppers, night-outers and clubbers laughed and joked in little troupes. Deborah carried her empty, growling stomach along the pavement, weaving between them. Even with her head down, she could feel the indifference around her. The more downtrodden you looked the more people strained not to see you. The more care they took not to care. She knew that, she had been guilty of it herself. No one wants to accidentally lock eyes with someone in need. It reminds them of the help they aren't giving.

Approaching the end of a street, Deborah spotted a convenience store. It was well lit, glass fronted. Through frosted lettering she could see the shelves of chocolate bars and little packeted cakes. Right by the entrance. Waiting for her. She slowed. Squinting up and down the street under her hood, she saw nothing but disinterested faces, all wrapped up in their own affairs. No one noticed her, as far as she could tell. Inside, there were no customers at the tills, the sole cashier busying herself pushing cigarette packs into the little spring-loaded tobacco dispensers. Her back to the entrance.

Deborah considered her options. This seemed easy plunder, but she'd have to be fast. Grab and dash. Maybe she should wander some more? Find a more subtle way to fill her stomach? At that thought, her stomach let her know its opinion on the matter, grumbling hard and twisting inside her. That made up her mind pretty quick.

With a nimble motion she pushed the door open and grabbed a handful of the chocolate bars. As she did, an electronic *BUH-BUHRRR* echoed through the shop, startling her. An entry chime set off by the door. The cashier turned.

Deborah spun, jammed her prize into the pocket of her hoodie and sprinted out of the shop and up the street. A confused "Hey!" from the store followed, but she was ten feet from the entrance already, with a running start. She ran on, keeping her pace as she weaved between irked and tutting pedestrians, until, after a minute or so, she turned off the main street into a side alley. She stood, panting, obscured from the street by a couple of large steel bins.

No one's going to follow, she thought, calming herself. Not over a measly couple of chocolate bars. Especially not some minimum wage cashier just looking to finish her shift. I'm perfectly safe. She pulled her modest haul from the hoodie pocket and surveyed it. Two Mars Bars and a Twix. Hardly the cornerstone of a nutritious supper, but enough to keep her going for a night. She raised one of the bars to her teeth to bite open the wrapper.

"That was ballsy," said a voice from behind one of the rubbish containers. Deborah stood frozen and wide-eyed. "Pretty stupid though."

What awful business was this now? Another junkie? Another would-be-pimp? Some grizzled old hobo, looking to stick her with a knife, or something worse? The voice's owner stepped around into view. Deborah stared apprehensively.

He didn't look much older than her. He was slim, bordering on skinny, with dark, curly hair above a youthful face. He was dressed in layered clothing, dirty and scuffed. All the hallmarks of street living. But his eyes were honest.

She fought to regain her composure, and was modestly successful.

"It worked didn't it?" she replied faux-casually.

"Yeah, it worked." The boy shrugged. "But that place is a franchise, it's part of a chain. Chains like to prosecute. For their image. To make a point. And they got cameras. You want to rip them off, you should be smarter about it."

He spoke softly, thoughtful and disarming. Deborah wondered if that was for real, or practiced. She could very easily be being hustled here, but what would this stranger be able to get? A few sweets? He was not much bigger than she was, not a physical threat, and his demeanour did seem genuine.

Deborah opened the chocolate and bit off a sizeable chunk. The sweetness was exquisite after her long famine.

"Smarter how?" she asked through a full mouth.

"Girl like you? You tidy yourself up a bit, take off the sweater. Go in there and ask to use the phone. Say it's an emergency, someone got hit by a car or something."

"And?"

"Little place like that'll only have a phone in the back, and they'll only have a couple of staff at the most. Odds are they leave the counter to go back to the office. There'll be a good twenty seconds before they get to the other side of the one-way mirror thing and can see you again. Makes for easy pickings. They probably won't even bother to check the camera - if you don't get too greedy."

"Hmm," Deborah nodded. Whoever this guy was, he certainly didn't seem to mean her harm. He spoke like he knew what he was talking about.

"What if they take me back? To the phone, I mean?"

"Well, then you go. Your friend steps in and grabs some stuff. You play along until they leave you alone and you head out and share your haul. Easy."

Deborah swallowed a too-large chunk of chocolate and drew a sullen grimace.

"I don't have a friend."

The boy pulled off a green, woollen mitt with his teeth and extended a hand. "Mark."

Her grimace slipped to an amused grin at this roguish introduction. She looked at his hand for a second then shook it with her free one.

"Deborah."

"The main thing is keeping warm, obviously. You want to find somewhere out of the wind. Away from other street folks if you don't know them. Not everyone's nice."

"Far as I've seen, no one is," Deborah muttered.

"Hey! I'm positively delightful." He put on theatrical airs as he gestured to himself. She smirked.

"We'll see."

"We will."

Deborah walked side by side with Mark through another back alley. He certainly seemed well versed in these lanes and paths off the main thoroughfares. The hidden city. In their brief time together, already he had bade her, twice, to cast her eyes down as they passed some more nefarious looking street-people. Both encounters passed without incident. Despite his awkward charm, he clearly had the street-smarts to back up his advice.

"Some folks go to the shelters at night, but I don't and I'm guessing you can't?" He looked around at Deborah with perceptive inquiry. "You're, what? Sixteen?"

"…Fourteen," she replied after a pause. Mark looked surprised, but did not comment directly.

"Okay. So someone is looking for you?"

"…Probably." There was no sense in being coy. She had nothing to lose at this point.

"And you don't want them finding you. So the shelters are out. They have to report minors." He was matter-of-fact, but affably so.

"How old are *you*?" Deborah asked Mark. He certainly looked young, but he spoke like he had been living rough for some time.

"I'm six… no…" He squinted and thought for a second, then corrected himself. "I'm seventeen now."

"How long have you been living like this?"

"Not that long. A couple of years now." His tone was casual, but what he said hit Deborah like a hammer. A couple of *years*?! And that was 'not that long?' The enormity of her own situation rushed at her. When she had fled her aunt's house she had envisioned no goal beyond immediate escape, and since then her plans had not stretched further than to the next day. The dawning realisation that this way of life might not be a journey but a destination, frightened her immensely.

"You..." She stumbled over her thoughts as they came too fast. "How did you end up here?"

Mark smiled at her. "I walked with you."

Deborah cocked her head and shot him an 'oh-please' look.

"Maybe when we know each other a bit longer." A hint of melancholy peppered his words.

"Okay," she replied, nodding. Understandable, she supposed. In her young mind, she could imagine a variety of circumstances that could lead to his current situation, none of which would make for happy conversation.

Adopting a sage-like tone once more, Mark continued.

"Food is the next thing. There you got some options. End of the day, there's usually good pickings behind any of the bigger supermarkets. They chuck old rolls and pastries, that kinda stuff out back - stuff they don't sell and can't keep. Most of 'em got high fences and such, but you can go that route. Just avoid anything that can make you sick. No meat or fish, obviously."

"Obviously."

"You *could* pull a grab and run," he cocked an eyebrow at her, "but you're taking a risk there."

"Sounds ballsy," Deborah said shaking her head and adopting a serious face. "But pretty stupid..." She turned to him and smirked. "You want half my Twix?"

Mark laughed. He had an impish giggle that amplified his youth. He seemed younger than her for a moment.

"Yes I do."

Deborah pulled the wrapper from her pocket as he continued, raising it to her teeth.

"What happened to your hand?" Mark glanced at the wrapped cloth around her fingers as she tore the packet open.

She glanced at the cloth. Her fingers were still tender underneath, but had scabbed over, dulling the pain.

"Maybe when we know each other a bit longer." She sighed. He nodded. "Or?"

Mark took a beat, then picked up his train of thought.

"*Or* you can be smart about it. Play on the main asset both you and I have."

She handed him one of the sticks of chocolate and bit the end off the other. "What's that?" she asked as she chewed.

"Youth," he replied. "Believe it or not, there is a bunch of stuff you and I can get away with that most of the other street folks can't. You especially."

"Me especially?"

"You're young, you're blonde, you look how you look. People trust a pretty face."

That he mentioned her looks did not escape her notice. A part of her instinctively baulked at the potential come-on, but she believed that Mark was genuine. Imparting wisdom, not snaking his way in some ulterior direction. It didn't feel lecherous, the way comments concerning her appearance so often had. The observation made her wary certainly, but to her surprise it also made her something else. Flattered she supposed. Since she met Mark, mere hours ago, she had seen either a threat, a guide or a chaperone. For the first time, she looked at him as a boy. He was good looking in a gawkish way, handsome even, beneath the veneer of grime that clung to his hair and face.

"So what, I get all sexy up in folks' faces and you grab all their stuff while they're staring at my ass?" She tried to pitch this as playful jest, but it sailed wide and landed sarcastic. Caustic even.

"What? No, I didn't mean…" Mark stammered a little, thrown off guard by her sudden change in demeanour. He seemed so very much younger when he was caught off his game.

"Mark. I'm kidding. I know what you meant." Deborah threw him the conversational lifeline he needed. Just as he grabbed at it though, she tugged a little. "So. You think I'm pretty?"

"Uh, look, I don't want… I mean, you're young and…" The hole Mark found himself in was slippery. After a brief struggle to climb out, he seemed to give up and let himself fall. "Yes. You're very pretty."

"Uh-*huh*," Deborah nodded with astute inflection. She liked this. Mark was clearly shy when it came to these matters, and Deborah's newfound upper-hand was empowering. She was out alone in the world for the first time. Not a world of her choosing, but a world all the same. Taking some power back for herself felt good. It felt a bit like freedom.

"Is that why you talked to me? Why you followed me?"

"I didn't *follow* you. You made quite a spectacle of yourself."

"Okay, is that why you *talked* to me?" Deborah knew she was toying with him. A little mean, sure, but she wanted an answer all the same.

"Yeah. I guess. You were obviously new though. I guess I figured you were too new to have gotten mean, and too healthy looking to have gotten strung out. It does get pretty lonely out here."

"I can imagine," she nodded. "Mark?" He turned. "Where are we going?"

"You can't stay in the shelters, and, trust me, you don't want to try roughing it in the centre of town. If the polis don't pick you up, someone will."

He was right she was sure, but he hadn't answered the question. "Right, so, where *are* we going?" she repeated calmly, but more emphatically this time.

"Up this way, about a mile now. Past the Trongate. You'll see. It's a good place. I swear."

Mark had been true to his word. As the daylight failed, he had walked her to a large tenement block beyond the edge of the city centre. Its entire ground floor was occupied by a nightclub. A painstakingly crafted-to-look-uncrafted sign above the door declared 'GOMMORAH' in silver, lightning-bolt script. The scuzzy, dissonant riffs of some local metal band tore from within, interspersed with indecipherably grunted lyrics. The upper floors, however, had metal panels affixed across every window. No one had occupied those floors in quite some time. Not in any *official* capacity anyway.

She had followed him round the building to the rear where scraggly shrubs and overgrown grass strewn with broken bottles and trash formed a long-abandoned garden area. Deborah's skepticism had been plainly visible, but Mark had answered it only with a smile. He pulled a wheeled refuse bin round from the side of the building, following a track worn in the grass. He had beckoned her to climb up onto it, and on up to a fire escape ladder hanging from the building's edge. The pair had shimmied up and ascended two flights of metal stairs to the top level. She had watched as he pulled on one of the metal sheets, lifting the corner and holding it, allowing her to crouch and climb in.

Stepping forward a few paces in the darkness, she heard a thud as Mark hopped through behind her. As she stood peering into the gloom, a light flickered to life. He had lit a small travel-lamp in the corner, bathing the dilapidated surrounds in a flat, yellow tint.

She stood in Mark's den. There was dust everywhere. Hanging loose from the ceiling were the remains of light fixtures and wiring, long since pulled and discarded. Short lengths of copper piping lay around the bare wooden floorboards and, in one corner, a broken toilet and sink stood, flanked by nothing where a wall was conspicuously absent. Kicked in by vandals, she assumed. The mono-drone of the band below growled and reverberated around the echoey space, and the whole place smelled vaguely of rotted plaster - stale and musty. But it was dry. It was sheltered. It was warm - warmer than outside, at least. And it was free of any prying eyes that might seek to do her harm. Or worse, to return her to the life she had fled.

"Home sweet home," Mark proclaimed. "Shall I put the supper on?"

Deborah turned to return his joke, then silenced herself when she saw, with amazement, that he was dead serious. Next to the lamp, he had a small camping stove set up, and various unopened tins of food were stacked neatly along the skirting board, next to a small rollaway mattress and a pile of sheets. In comparison to the cold nights she had spent this past week, it might as well have been a five star resort. How could this all have happened to her? So quickly? It seemed impossible, how her luck had changed in just a few short hours. When tides had turned this quickly for her before, it was always in the wrong direction. Her eyes welled.

"Mark this is… why are you doing this for me?"

Mark shrugged.

"I told you. It's lonely. And I'm not an asshole. You could freeze to death out there. Get caught or get killed. I remember how it was for me in the beginning. I don't know what you're running from, but I remember running. It's not fun."

"Sure, but…" Deborah tried hard to control the swelling in her throat. This kind of kindness - if this was genuine, and please, please let it be - this kind of kindness she had never seen coming. She had been homeless only seven nights, but every one had been a cold, pained, fearful eternity.

"I mean, there must be other people you could have… what I mean is, you must have met…" She paused. "Why *me*?"

"You seemed nice," he replied, shrugging again.

In that moment, that was all she needed. Deborah smiled wide as a couple of tears rolled down her grubby cheeks.

Tinned sausage and beans never tasted so good. As she shoveled the warm, chunky goop from the can Deborah doubted *anything* had ever tasted so good. Mark kept quiet as they ate. Seeing her ravenously attack the first hot meal she'd had in a week, he elected to give gustation precedence over discourse. When the silence was finally broken, it was Deborah who broke it.

"How long have you slept here?"

"While now," he replied, through a full mouth. "Six months or so? Since the start of winter."

"Where did all the stuff come from? The little cooker? And the bed things?"

"It's mostly camping stuff. You can get it all in the outdoors shops. In the mall."

Deborah nodded, fishing another glob of meat from the can. "How'd you get it out? Of the store I mean. Don't they have a bunch of security guys in the gallery?"

"Oh, you can't steal that stuff. Too difficult, too bulky."

"But you can steal the money to buy it," Deborah answered her own question this time.

"Yup. Just gotta pick the right pockets is all."

"Right. Which are?"

"Hmm?"

"Which pockets are the right pockets?"

"Well, the easy ones. You'll see. I'll show you."

"Tomorrow?" Deborah asked through an involuntary yawn. As her hunger had subsided so too had her energy. The drive to fill her belly and the nervy adrenaline of the streets had been all that had sustained her until now. Both quelled, exhaustion took a firm grip.

Mark smiled and tipped his can, slurping down the dregs of its contents. He set it down in a polythene bag and extended an arm out towards her. Deborah eyed the inside of hers and, seeing nothing but liquid dregs within, passed it to him. He threw it in the bag and tied the top neatly.

"Got to make sure you keep this stuff wrapped. Don't want rats or pigeons in here thinking this is their spot now." He was quiet, distracted.

Deborah persevered. "Tomorrow you'll show me?"

Mark stood.

"Yeah," he replied. He paced off towards his makeshift bed and pulled apart some sheets and the camping mattress. *His* mattress. He inspected them assiduously, frowning as he selected the least grubby of them, then walked around to the corner opposite his and began to lay out a second bed. The care with which he did so almost brought fresh tears to her eyes.

"There. Not exactly the Ritz, but it beats sleeping out there." He nodded towards the shutter. The hiss and howl of the wind behind it loud enough now to compete with the din from below. Deborah stepped towards him. Mark may have been older, but she noticed now they were the exact same height. Their eye-lines perfectly level. She looked straight into his.

"*Thank you* Mark," she said simply, embracing him through her thick hoodie and his thicker coat.

Mark lay awake, staring up at the cracked cornicing. What a weird day it had been. This girl, Deborah? At first he had just meant to warn her. Teach her that grab-and-dash was amateur shit. To be more careful. But then? Then he had started acting all big-shot. Like, what? Like he was king of the streets? Gonna teach the new girl how to live like he did? Sure. Because he lived so well in his broken down shit-hole kingdom. Fucking idiot.

She was nice though. Nicer than any of the users and abusers he usually encountered. She still remembered how to think about more than pure survival. He could talk to her - actually talk - without worrying she was going to stick a blade or a needle in him. He hadn't had that in quite some time.

Maybe she would stick around? Maybe. She might not think he was a total loser. Might even be a friend. Might not be fixing to rob him in the night. Even if she was, he thought, at least he would remember today. More than the hundred lonely days that preceded it. At least something *happened* today. He had spoken aloud to someone. That had felt good.

The wind whistled past the steel panelling at the window above him. He listened. The cacophony below had reached its crescendo and faded some time ago. The murmur of the audience ebbed away into the night. Must be well after two now. Why was he awake? He turned restlessly to his side and froze. There was something by his side in the dark. Feet.

The girl was there. She was standing in the dark by his side, clutching a bed sheet in her good hand. Queasy panic tickled up through him. 'Oh God. This is it,' he thought. 'I've been played. Something *bad* is about to happen.' No sooner had the thought occurred than another followed in its wake. A bleaker one. 'I don't care,' he thought. 'I'm not fighting back.'

It had been so long living like this. So long eking out an existence against this harsh reality. If this - *especially* this - if this had all been a horrible set-up? Then he was resigned. Fuck it. Let the world win. Let it take him.

He rolled his head. A sad, plaintive look crossed his eyes as they locked with hers. She stared back down at him for an inscrutable moment in the musty quiet. Then she bent and carefully lay down beside him. She pressed the back of her body into his and draped the sheet across them both. Gingerly, she pulled his arm across her. She held his hand in hers, under her shirt, pressed gently into the flesh at her stomach. Then she closed her eyes and lay still.

Mark lay a while in silence. He wondered how long it had been since he touched the skin of another person, and drew a blank. He could smell her unwashed hair at his face and feel her body warm against his. He listened to her breathing as it steadied from a staccato into a smooth, rhythmic slumber. Then he drifted into sleep himself.

Chapter Four

RAZIEL

Three words. 'God is gone.'

Deborah stepped through the door and beheld the orator. He sat at the far side of the room in a tattered leather wingback, his arms resting along its sides, feet planted firmly on the ground. Like Lincoln on his memorial.

The room was sparsely decorated, gloom its most prominent trapping. It looked to Deborah as she imagined a captain's quarters of an old ship, though that may have owed more to the lack of natural light than the decor. There were no windows. Two dark green couches, their leather cracked and scarred, sat at right angles to each other in its centre, next to a polished mahogany table. A poorly maintained antique.

The walls were dark wood, devoid of frames or adornments save some decorative panelling. A couple of high, wooden bookshelves stood guard at either side of the wingback, flanking the mouth of a corridor that stretched endlessly into the distance behind. Its sides were lined with similar shelves, every one overstuffed with books and parchments and dust. Dim amber glowed from a flickering fireplace, giving the whole room a haunting, otherworldly ambiance.

Deborah stepped further into the room and heard a soft click as Zotiel and Zephon followed and closed the door behind her. Her eyes never strayed from the chair's occupant. His age was impossible to determine from his appearance. His skin was smooth and impossibly white - not sickly looking, far from it - but radiating and pure, like unfinished marble. His frame was imposing. Sitting, she could not judge his height with certainty, but she would have guessed that he stood at least seven feet tall. Beneath the simple, white shirt he wore, a sculpted, muscular frame was readily apparent. Golden-grey hair cascaded down behind his shoulders, and his eyes… His eyes were solid black. No iris, no white, just globes of pure obsidian set in the milky pool of his face. Black voids in white snow. He was a grand sight. A terrifying adonis, set in judgement of his domain.

Deborah was speechless. The figure said nothing. He simply watched her with curiosity as she stared back into his black eyes. The moment seemed to span a lifetime, until finally the silence and her trance were broken by a familiar voice behind her.

"Deborah, may I present His Eternity, The Archangel Raziel," Zotiel stated. Palpable, if muted, occasion in his voice.

Deborah stood in silence as the figure lifted himself from his chair and stepped forward. Her estimation of his height had been, if anything, conservative. Approaching, he towered above her. A rush of fearful adrenaline kicked within her, and she fought a terrible urge to flee. A feeling not rational, but primal. Primeval. He stopped a few feet in front of her, biceps level with her face. As she watched in awe, he stooped to one knee. Taking her compliant hand in his, he raised it to his lips and kissed it. Then, lifting his head once more, he looked directly at her and spoke.

"Honoured."

When he stood back up he seemed strangely less intimidating. As if he had lost some of his grandeur. He still was tall, incredibly so, but appeared somehow less than before. Deborah wondered for a moment if it was the firelight toying with her, but she was not convinced. It seemed his authority was amplified then diminished by choice, not circumstance. Whatever the reason, the change granted her some licence to gather herself. When he bade her to sit, she had the wherewithal at least to do so, and to survey the actions of her travelling companions. There was plenty of space for Zotiel and Zephon to sit alongside, but both refrained. Instead they moved to opposite sides of the room, standing just behind her periphery. Ensuring she saw only her host. She wondered whether this was a sign of respect to him, or of standoffish contempt. Either way, she now sat in a one-on-one, face to face with her great and terrible black-eyed host.

"What do you mean gone?" she asked. Every ounce of herself fought to regain a sense of composure. She had no notion of where this conversation would lead, but she did know she wished to be as sober and level-headed as she could throughout.

"God is gone," Raziel repeated, solemnly. "The True God. He is... departed."

"To where?"

"Indeed. To where indeed? To *else*where."

"I don't understand."

"I know," he replied, pausing momentarily. He seemed contemplative. His tone became thoughtful. "Have you read scriptures Deborah?"

Deborah shook her head slowly. "No. I don't..." She paused for a second to look into his face. Bracing herself, she continued, "...I *didn't* believe in God."

The walls did not crash down. The roof did not cave in. Her interlocutor did not stand and strike her down where she sat. He simply nodded thoughtfully.

"Many don't. But now? After what you have seen?"

"I..." She tried to answer as honestly as she could, but her instinctual reserve kicked back. "I don't *know* what I've seen. The substance I can look at, but not the truth behind it. I *think* I know... that I died."

She looked round at Zotiel, recalling his cryptic explanations, but he kept his stoic gaze cast at middle distance. She was to engage in this parley alone.

"I know that I'm here now, in what *they* say is Purgatory. I know that I probably belong here... or worse…" Raziel's features twitched at this, but he remained in solemn silence, letting her continue.

"And I also know…" She stared at him with more composure now; "you wouldn't have summoned me, you wouldn't have sent your footmen to find me… Unless you *want* something from me."

Raziel stared, each eye a pensive abyss. She could feel his gaze pierce right through her.

"I want some real answers first though," she added.

Her host tilted his head and raised a beckoning hand, inviting her to proceed.

Okay then, she thought, you got your chance Deborah. Where the fuck to start?

"How can God be missing? I'm a far cry from religious, but I know what omnipresence means."

Raziel stared forward inscrutably for a moment, then spoke.

"There was a time, not terribly long ago Deborah, when the rudimentary understanding even a heathen such as you has of our world was largely accurate. The Almighty sat atop The Throne in the Kingdom of Heaven. His Angels sat at His side; your kind below. There was beautiful order. Your brethren sinned, or not, and their actions in life decreed their destination in death. Here, Glory, or the Depths. It was ever thus."

His cadence was oddly rhythmic. A weighty recitative.

"The individual sins and paths of your kind were not, however, the only influence your world had on mine. There is a quote in the scriptures you would do well to keep in your mind. It has certainly been burned into mine. Burned into my brethren's. The Son, speaking unto Matthew: *'Truly I say to you, whatever you bind on Earth shall be bound in Heaven, and whatever you loose on Earth shall be loosed in Heaven.'* Those words were not mere metaphor. They tied the fabric of my world inextricably to the whims of yours."

Raziel's demeanour was stoic, but harboured a sorrow deep within. At certain words he betrayed the distain beneath his calm exterior. *'Burned.' 'Whims.'* His anger was deep, but visible through the cracks.

"What did we bind?" Deborah asked.

"What you bound is not important. What you loosed is."

"Okay, so what did we loose?"

With the first sign of true emotion Deborah had seen on his colourless face, Raziel growled; "Democracy."

Deborah's face tightened in puzzlement.

"Wait… what?"

Her eyes darted to Zotiel then Zephon then back to Raziel, incredulity plastered across her face. "You *voted out* God?"

"Don't be ridiculous." Raziel's face was iron. Deborah slipped back into silence.

"When monarchies and principalities were the norm on Earth the old order of the divine stood in glory. A fitting facsimile of your world. As above so below. What you bound below in your fashion we bound above in ours. The Great City of Eden stood in splendour.

"But one by one your nations changed. Elected governments replaced the existing orders. As democracy spread across your world the symbiosis with ours began to falter. The mass conscience of your kind no longer recognised hereditary right. Divine right. You all wanted a shot at the top. To *choose* who rose and who fell. The... s*eepage* of that change ran like a torrent through the streets of the Great City. The beautiful order began to waver. The foundations, the bedrock of our world, shifting. The balance wavered.

"Eventually the tipping point came. The time arrived that the majority of religious establishments on earth existed within the confines of democratic nations. Our hands were forced. Change *had* to come. The Prophecies had to be maintained. The word of God *had* to remain infallible."

"As below, so above. Okay," Deborah said somewhat flippantly. "So you go democratic. Can't you and all your Angel friends just vote for God? I can't imagine there was anyone else on the ballot? Who'd compete?"

"*We* can't vote for *anyone*," Raziel spat with venom in his voice once again. He reined it back in quickly, but not quick enough.

"The Angelic do not have free-will. Not truly, not like your kind do. Even the lower of us. Divine Democracy could not be predicated on *our* desires. That would not fulfil the tenets of the prophecy. It had to come from you."

"From *us*?" she asked, incredulous again. "I don't remember receiving my postal vote..."

Deborah could not help being facetious. The conversation was surreal. Despite her tone though, Raziel continued. Either unfazed by, or oblivious to her impudence.

"Spiritual Consensus. The Divinity need not *poll* a human to understand what is in his heart; it is apparent. The consensus of man's truest nature, across all establishments of religion, of theology and of spirit was gathered. That provided the mandate. All that was needed was a vessel. A being who represented all the aspects the consensus sought. An embodiment."

Deborah squinted for a second and then interjected.

"Wait a minute, stop. The *true* nature of man provided the mandate? Without warning? Without consent?"

Raziel, seeing perhaps that she was beginning to put the pieces together herself, sat silent. Expectant.

"That's fucking lunacy."

"Indeed," he replied gravely.

"People don't choose well. Even when they *know* they're making a choice, they don't choose well. And people who aren't even aware of the choice..." Deborah sighed. "I've seen a lot less altruism in my life than I'd like to have."

"The Chosen One, the New God, He *was* the consensus choice of Man. He embodied *all* aspects of pious Man. The good, and the bad. And having been a man in life these aspects were in his nature. Ingrained."

Deborah squinted once more.

"So you get a bad egg. All democracies have had them, haven't they? They get voted out. Next time round?"

Raziel grimaced.

"There was no 'next time round'." Grief and anguish danced through his voice now.

"With your ideals of Democracy, like your ideals of Man, came both the good and the bad. Negative elements, in a land unaccustomed to swift change. Ill equipped to respond to concepts like corruption. Self interest. Fearful megalomania and skittish paranoia in its ruler. The power of the Throne was, *had always been*, absolute. The idea of democratic safeguards against tyranny unthinkable."

Realisation dawned on Deborah, the real-world analogy completing in her head.

"And so dictatorship. The New God declared himself supreme leader?"

Raziel bowed his head, and as Deborah glance round she saw Zotiel and Zephon had done likewise. The trio may as well have been just three more nameless faces out there in The Purgs.

"Any and all future elections were suspended. The Throne of God was gone, The Office of God consolidated its power. The autonomous Angels, we of the Lower Spheres, we were cast out of the Monolith. Out of The Great City. Stripped of all but our names and ranks. To serve of course, all must swear fealty to The Office, but not in the sanctum. Our ability to think, to think and to *remember*, without constant connection to the All-Mind? That threatened the Almighty. Your kind, the most pious and acidic among you, you replaced us. Judgmental and embittered in life, tyrannical in death. Those were the new officers of the Divinity."

"Can't humans think for themselves also?" Deborah asked.

"Oh yes," Raziel replied sadly. "Yes they can. But to the Office of God the choice between autonomous entities with pure hearts and memories, and free, but servile soldiers who know only judgment, tyranny and ceaseless, fearful loyalty to The Office? That was no choice at all. They rule the occupied City with a golden fist."

Raziel took a moment, his history lesson winding to its conclusion.

"And so it was. The Monarchy fell. The Old God usurped. The Office reigned supreme."

"And you?" she asked inquisitively.

"The expulsion fractured our order. Splintered it. All remain loyal to the Office of course, officially. Some fiercely, vehemently so. But there are some. Some who, like us, remember the glory of the Old Order with more than mere nostalgia. Who would seek to… return. To the halcyon days."

Deborah sat silent for a full minute, maybe two, digesting the conversation. It was outrageous. Ridiculous. Yet here she sat. Talking to an Angel with obsidian eyes, telling her how Heaven, a place she had never believed in, fell to tyranny.

"You know…" she muttered, breaking the long silence finally, "anyone on Earth with two brain cells to rub together could have told you that would happen." Her voice began to rise as she spoke.

"I mean, what the fuck were you all thinking? You let humans take control of your whole world? The 'Divine' world? The promise that's supposed to get people through their shitty, miserable lives on Earth?"

Deborah was unsure exactly where her anger was coming from. She could remember no instance in her life when she had allowed her emotions to roar like this. Mere days ago she would have dismissed any mention of Heaven or Angels or God as superstitious, dogmatic tripe. But nevertheless, fury came. Rage.

"Humans are idiots! We can't take care of our own fucking world! Most of us can't even take care of our own fucking *lives* without it all turning to piss and shit and blood! Trust me, I know all about that!"

Raziel seemed entirely unfazed by her anger. He observed patiently as she vented it to its crescendo, and as her words hung and faded in the flickering light of the fire he replied with soft malevolence.

"Oh yes, Assassin. We know you do."

※

Deborah was beginning to see where the conversation was leading. It was unthinkable. Unbelievable. She could spot the conversational markers, and had dismissed them until now - the concept of the conclusion they mapped was too ridiculous. But she had to know. She *wanted* to know. She wondered if they would say it. If they even could.

"Why me?" she asked, with grim curiosity.

Raziel seemed to ponder this, though Deborah was certain she didn't know why. Her host did not seem the type to have sent for her on a whim.

"There were a number of factors that fell into place with your... demise."

"Well I'd like to hear them." Deborah was finding her feet in the best way she knew. She was taking control back.

"Well of course your profession, for one."

"Uh-huh," she replied flatly. "A lot of assassins in my world. A lot more in yours. We have a limited lifespan. Even by the standards of *my kind*."

"That is true," he replied. "However, very few could ever enter the gates without arousing *overwhelming* suspicion or *catastrophic* destruction. Your soul may be stained - horribly so - but it is purer than most who wallow in your particular... career. Under normal circumstances, under the old regime, you would have spent a *very* long time in this place." Raziel gestured towards the door she had entered, to The Purgs.

"A very long time indeed. But you would have had a chance. A slim one, yes, but a *chance* at redemption. Enough of a chance, at least, that your presence in the Great City will not violate the Laws of God. Bend them a little perhaps, but not shatter them as others might."

"Okay... sure. I'm the hitman with the fucking heart-of-gold." Deborah felt a creak in her conversational footing, but she wasn't going to let herself slip.

"Let's assume for a minute that's true - it's not, but let's assume - that's not all, right? Literature is filled with virtuous assassins. There has to be more than just little-old-me in the non-fiction section?"

"There are other factors. Less... tangible ones. You are thirty years old."

"What does that matter?"

"The age of thirty has significance to my kind and yours. At thirty, David became a king. At thirty, John the Baptist paved the way for the Messiah. At thirty, Joseph ascended to his command under the Pharaoh, and at thirty, Ezekiel was called as a prophet. The Son, he began his ministry at the age of thirty."

"What does any of that matter?" Deborah asked, visibly vexed. Her atheism may have been put through the wringer these past days and nights, but her aversion to superstitious clap-trap still stood firm. She had little tolerance for this kind of alogical correlation.

Raziel, ignoring her obvious skepticism for now, continued.

"Then we can turn to your professional accolades. You keep count, do you not, of your… quarry?"

"I know how many jobs I've taken if that's what you mean."

"It is. And what, pray tell, is the current toll?"

Deborah had no idea how this factored into Raziel's thinking, but played along begrudgingly. "Thirty Nine."

"Aren't you prolific," he commented humourlessly. "Forty is a good number. A *complete* number. Moses sat forty days on Sinai Mount. The rains fell forty days and forty nights. The Son fasted forty nights in the wilderness, and remained forty nights after the resurrection. Solomon, Saul, David, all reigned for forty years. Eli sat in judgment of Israel forty years. Your kind, your kind at your closest to God, in pregnancy, last forty weeks. Forty is a good number."

Deborah sat stoic. That was it? That was how this came about? A bunch of fucking superficial, numerological bullshit? It was too much to bear.

With a cold, dry stare into Raziel's abyss-eyes she summoned all the conviction within her. All the cold detachment she could muster.

"Well, I'm at thirty nine," she growled. "And I'm not doing it."

Raziel returned her stare softly.

"Doing what?"

"I'm not doing what I know you want me to do. What you won't say, except in your hints and your fucking riddles. It's ludicrous, it's impossible, and it's not my fucking problem."

She stood up slowly, not yet releasing him from her knife glare.

"Kill Him yourself."

She turned her back to stride towards the door through which she had entered. At the edge of her vision she could see Zephon and Zotiel standing, heads lowered and still. She did not - she *would* not - turn to face them. This whole conversation had been preposterous. A hustle. Preamble to an impossible task, predicated on an inconceivable premise. She had reached her limit. Fuck them.

She grabbed for a door handle, but found there was none. Pushing at the door yielded nothing but solid wall pushing back.

"You are making a mistake, Assassin." Raziel's voice sounded rather more sinister to her now, as she realised she was trapped.

"Then I bet I'd fit in nicely with your lot," she replied coldly. She gave up on the door and turned back to Raziel. He had not moved from his chair.

"Let me out of this room."

"I'm offering you a chance to wipe your slate clean. To atone for your sins in the way most natural to you."

Deborah stared back at Raziel with blades in her eyes.

"Let me *out* of this room."

"You could change the fate of all of us. You and all your kind, me and all of mine." He kept his tone level, but little cracks of desperation were forming in the facade now. She could almost see them splinter.

"*Let me the fuck out of this room!*"

Raziel stared in silence for a moment, deep into her eyes. Then, barely perceptibly, he wilted.

He stood, seeming much smaller than before. Frail even. He extended an arm towards the empty corner of the room behind him and Deborah watched as a familiar prick of light appeared from nowhere and sliced across the air like a knife. The staticky feeling she had felt in The Purgs buzzed through her once more, and she saw the rippling glow of the firelight fold in on itself as a nothing-door opened in the empty space.

"You are no prisoner. Free-will remains, as ever." He sounded haunted. Deflated.

Deborah stepped towards the door and as she reached it she turned her head to her host and his footmen. All three pairs of eyes watched her intently.

"Maybe it's true. Maybe everything you say is real, maybe it's all bullshit. I don't know. But I do know one thing. If it *is*? If it *is* all how you say it is? You brought it on yourselves. Fuck you."

She stepped through the nothing-door.

Deborah sat perched on a stone wall at the edge of a rampart, staring vacantly out across the stained gothic vista. Out here, outside the confines of Raziel's meeting room, the enormity of the conversation seemed all the more outlandish the more and more it danced around her mind.

She did not know what awaited her in this awful, hollow place, but if her host had been truthful? Then the consequences of falling in with his brand of clandestine resistance would certainly be worse.

Eternal hustle in an endless, hopeless, starless city; that was a hell she could at least understand. Perhaps even a hell she could survive. She didn't want to risk finding out how a *true* Hell might compare.

Fracture Four

KINGS

Jim Huke sipped his whisky and cast a glance around the hotel bar. These lobby bars were pretty much all the same, but this one at least had good scotch. Lagavulin, no less. An Islay malt. Jim prided himself on his knowledge of the world. The fact he knew to pronounce it 'eye-la' where his less well-travelled countrymen would say 'izz-lay' pleased him. If you were going to enjoy the finer things, you should take the care to know them. He folded his cash neatly into his wallet and returned it to his briefcase.

"You all set here sir?"

"Hmm?" He snapped out of dreamy jet-lag and looked up at the barmaid.

"Are you all set here sir?" she repeated with a genial smile. Pleasant and good-natured.

"Oh yes, thank you." He smiled back.

"Okay, just give it a ring if you need," she said, nodding to the 'for-service' bell at the edge of the bar as she stepped away. Jim allowed himself a brief peek at her posterior as she crossed the lobby. She was young, but it was just a quick look. He was a long way from home after all.

It was early in the day, not too many drinkers yet. Most of the staff still multi-tasking. Pity, he thought. He liked the company of hotel staff. Sweet young things, always cordial. Helped to pass the time.

This was problem with red-eye flights – you were invariably too early for check-in. Turned you into a hotel lobby nomad, for a few hours at least. Jim was used to it by now though. He didn't really mind. The scotch could be expensed along with the room, and he enjoyed the UK on the occasions his work brought him there. There were plenty of things he missed when away from the good old U S of A, but Scotland certainly had the good drink, and for a man who enjoyed the fleeting company and conversation of strangers, there were far worse places. Folks here took pride in their convivial 'patter' as they called it. Pity about the climate. It was a bit too close to the pacific-northwest for his taste, all this mist and rain and whatnot, but maybe it'd clear up before he headed back to the airport and on to the next meeting in the next country. 'Might even manage a round of golf,' he thought, eyeing his club bag. 'If I'm lucky and the meeting don't run long.'

As he pondered the possibility, a young man in a smart shirt and tie perched two stools down from his. He waited.

"She's headed off for something," Jim told him after a moment or two. "Need to give that there bell a ring."

"Cheers," the guy replied. A local for sure. That Scottish accent sure was a kicker, Jim thought with an internal chuckle. One word was all you needed. "I'm just waiting for someone."

"Ah." Jim nodded and turned back to his drink.

It had been a long flight. Jim didn't sleep terribly well on the overnights. Those dang chairs didn't fold back far enough for his considerable girth to find comfort, and with everyone asleep around him there had been no opportunity for discourse to pass the time. His itch for conversation needed a scratch.

"Are you a student son?" he asked the young man genially.

"Sorry?"

"I say are you a student? You're dressed very sharp for a young fella."

The young man smiled. "Oh. No, I work at the bank over there." He gestured nebulously towards the hotel entrance. "On my lunch break."

"Ah." Jim nodded approvingly again. "Are you from around here originally?"

"Born and bred," the young man replied. He seemed a quiet type, but affable enough. Jim could carry this conversation just fine on his own broad shoulders.

"Me, I'm just in from the United States. Chicago. Sorry," he extended a hand across his broad stomach. "James T Huke, but my friends call me Jim."

The young fella smiled politely and shook his hand. "Dan McDonald."

"Pleasure to meet you young Dan McDonald." Jim smiled his patented 'Big Jim' folksy smile.

"You too," the young man replied.

"Yep," Jim said casually, "just in from the windy city this morning. Got some meetings to go to, sure."

"You a salesman?" Dan asked.

"Sure am," Jim replied, "I work for an outfit across the pond, selling mechanical fittings. For construction projects and whatnot. Good work it is, and steady. Been at it a good long time too. Made it my name so it were. Good salesman has to get the clients' attention, get them to buy in, Huke, line and sinker!" Jim nudged Dan and guffawed at his own well practiced and oft-employed joke. Good old icebreaker that one. Had served him well some thirty years now. He settled his tone a little as he continued.

"Get to see a lot of fine spots around the world too. Like this one." He smiled again and raised his whisky in a miniature salute to the hotel lobby.

"You like Glasgow?"

"Oh yes my boy, yes." He nodded emphatically. "Great folks here, great folks. Lot of good courses too." He winked at the young man and tapped his club bag at his side.

Dan leaned back and glanced over his shoulder past the few staff and travellers at the entrance.

"Well, hope you get the weather for it," he said skeptically. "You travel by yourself, Jim?"

"Yup-yup," Jim replied, pleased. The young man was beginning to chat a little more freely. "Yessir, just me and the world, making our acquaintance."

"Must get a little lonely?"

"Oh well, you know. Sure, at times. But it has its perks too, you know. Rough with the smooth as they say son, rough with the smooth. I have two boys back in the States, and my wife of course. They're grown up now though." Jim cast a curious eye at the young man beside him. Very young, he seemed, for that outfit.

"Older'n you I'd reckon son. They're off to college next year, so I might try and be home a little more. Don't want the wife rattling around the house alone for too long - she'll spend too much, eh?" Jim chortled and nudged Dan with his elbow. Dan smiled back.

Jim turned with some surprise as he the rustle of a newspaper close at his side. He had been rambling and had not even noticed the slim, rather fetching young woman slide into the stool next to his. She wore a black dress - unusual this early in the day, Jim thought - but she wore it well.

'Must be losing your touch there, Jim boy' he thought to himself. 'In your younger days a pretty young thing like that wouldn't have slipped your radar.'

"Well hello there Miss. A good morning to you." He made a little cap-doffing gesture.

Jim knew his folksy charm had always been his strongest asset, and it had only ripened with age. The young woman smiled distractedly, but her eyes remained fixed on the newspaper. After a moment she muttered a scornful "Hmmm" to it.

"Something troubling you in there Miss?" Jim asked.

"Hmm. My horoscope. Not so good today. What are you?" She looked up at Jim and Dan.

Jim didn't care much for astrology, though his wife gave the cryptic little predictions in the Sunday papers a glance once in a while. Must be a woman thing.

He poised to shoot a knowing eye-roll at Dan when, to his surprise, Dan responded eagerly.

"I'm a Virgo," he told the girl, seeming far more interested than Jim had expected. Well, there you go, he thought. Not just a woman thing after all.

"Let's see…" The girl scanned down the page. "Virgo, hmm, oh this is good. Looks like you'll be coming into some money."

Jim played along, not wanting to be left out of the conversation.

"Hey, that's swell, eh?" He nudged Dan with his elbow once more. "I'm a Sagittarius myself."

"Sagittarius, Sagittarius…" The girl scanned the paper once more. "Yes, here we go. Ah. You're going to engage in new activities, ones that could spark a surge in your love life."

Jim chuckled heartily, "Oh, well, been married coming on twenty four years now, hope my wife doesn't read that!"

"Well, maybe it means her," Dan added. "What sign is she?"

"Oh erm… let me think…" Jim was caught off guard, but pleased. Talking to youngsters was a fine pleasure. Kept you young yourself. "She would be... She's an Aquarius. Yes. Aquarius."

"Hmm," the girl scanned the page, deep in thought. "Are you two the same age?" she asked, offhand.

"No... no, she's five years younger than I am," Jim replied with some pride. "Quite a looker in her day too, I might add." He chuckled merrily.

"Well *this* is interesting..." Still deep in thought the girl asked, "you're about forty right?"

"Ha!" Jim guffawed, flattered by her underestimation. "I *wish,* young lady. I'm fifty six!"

"Ahah!" The girl perked up and beamed at him lifting the paper triumphantly. Sliding it across the bar she knocked his drink, emptying it straight into his lap.

"Oh!" she exclaimed, dropping the paper to her side, "Oh I'm sorry!" She seemed flustered and glanced around for something to clean up with.

Jim stood from the stool, surveying the damage to his suit. He was careful not to seem overly annoyed. He was enjoying this most unusual conversation with these two youngsters.

"Not to worry little miss, not to worry. No harm done, I'm sure." He wiped at the stain forming across the crotch. It said otherwise, but the girl was just a young thing, and awful apologetic.

"Not your fault dear. I best visit the little boy's room though. Sort this out. Dan m'boy, would you mind keeping an eye on my clubs and such?"

"Sure Jim, go ahead."

He paced across the lobby to the bathrooms, hiding the stain as best he could manage without calling further attention to it.

Grabbing a handful of paper towels from the dispenser, he cleaned himself up. The stain on his pants was now larger, but lighter in hue. Hopefully it would dry clean, but, if it didn't, he would still have time to change after check-in and make his meeting. No harm done. Nice couple of kids he had met. Good talking to youngsters.

He stepped back out to the lobby and his smile dissolved as he cast his eyes to the empty bar. There were his clubs, there was his suitcase. Sitting unguarded by the stool. But where was Dan? Where was the young lady?

Where was his briefcase?

Jim Huke's heart sank.

"Aw *Shit*," he muttered to the lobby.

"It's not his," Mark called across the building floor. "What'd he say his wife was, Aries?"

"Aquarius," Deborah called back. She hung the shirt on their makeshift washing line, strung between two of broken light fixtures on the walls.

"That's January?"

"Yeah, twentieth, to February… eighteenth? And she's five years younger."

Mark spun the dials until they read 200-143 and tried the lock. Nothing. He flipped to the next date and tried, then the next, and the next.

"It's getting colder now," Deborah called across the space. She finished hanging his good clothes next to her little black dress, emptied the suds from the plastic hand basin down the sink and paced over to where Mark sat fiddling with their latest score. Frowning. He hadn't heard her. She stooped and touched the top of his head gently, sitting on the floor beside him.

"I said it's getting colder now. We need to maybe think about getting another heater?"

Six months had passed since Mark had first brought Deborah to his little palace above the Gomorrah, and a new winter was beginning its slow creep across the city.

"Yeah, maybe. Means we use more canisters though," Mark replied distractedly. The lock wasn't budging. Might end up having to bust it open, he thought with irritation. That always came with a risk. Might damage any valuable contents. Waste a potential score.

"Nope," he said defeated, letting the case fall in his lap. "Guy wasn't as thick as he looked. Not his wife's either. Maybe his kids?"

"Lemme see." Deborah took the briefcase from him and began to fiddle with the combinations.

"At the very least we should get more sheets," she said as she worked, "Stick some under the windows to keep the wind out. The frames are coming away at the back."

Mark looked around at the place they now shared. "Yeah, that's a good idea," he replied. "Or maybe it's about time…" His train of thought derailed as he heard a springing click. The briefcase lock popped open and he looked at her in surprise.

Deborah leaned over, pulled his face to hers and kissed him gently. Still with one hand on his cheek she smiled at him close. "He's a Yank, genius. They put the month before the day."

She passed the open briefcase back to him.

"Humph," Mark grunted through a sheepish sideways smile. "Perverts."

As he began to file through the contents of their score Deborah stood once again. She retrieved a weather-beaten copy of the Yellow Pages directory from beneath their mattress. Seating herself beside him again, she flipped it opened. The worn spine split the pages naturally - to the section marked HOTELS AND INNS - and she retrieved the tooth-marked biro from between the pages. Wearing a furrow on her brow and the pen in her mouth, she assiduously perused the list. Little blue checkmarks accompanied more than two thirds of the entries.

"We're getting through the hotels now. Mostly just the proper high-end ones left." Deborah mused.

"Well, more cash there," Mark replied with detachment, preoccupied with the briefcase's contents. "More security too. We'll need to be on form."

"I'm *always* on form," she quipped precociously and watched his bowed head as a smile broke across his lips.

"Maybe here next?" Deborah held the Yellow Pages up for him to see, her finger indicating her selection. 'MAISON NOIRE.'

Mark looked at the page, then to her.

"Classy."

"You've been there?"

"Oh yes, I stay there *every* time I visit the city for cocktails. You really *must* see it dahling, it is the *only* place to summer…"

Deborah laughed and slapped him with the book. "All right Dickhead, I was just asking."

She adored Mark. They lived in what could only generously be referred to as a dive, one she had to sneak in and out of to grift for survival. On a good day, she ate food cooked over a camp stove in the tin it came in. At night, the wind snarled at the windows, rattling steel plates the city council had erected to keep her out, and the blaring drone from the nightclub below kept her tossing and turning into the small hours. It didn't matter. She was happier than she ever remembered being. She had him, he had her, and fuck the rest of the world. As long as those two truths held? Fuck 'em all.

"What were you going to say?" she asked Mark.

"Hmm?"

"Before my, y'know, *awesome* super-sleuth powers solved the Mystery of the Yankee Briefcase? Maybe it's time for what?"

"Got the wallet, but not much else worth anything." He held a shiny brochure with pictures of steel pipes and smiling construction workers. Lifting it to the side of his face, he beamed vacantly in a mocking impersonation of the happy, hard-hatted mascot. Deborah smiled. The remaining contents of the briefcase appeared to consist primarily of technical documents - little lists of numbers and graphs that may as well have been hieroglyphics. For all she and Mark knew, they might be valuable to someone, but to anyone they knew, they were worthless. A few pens and other stationary, stamped with a company logo she didn't recognise. An unbent copy of the latest Grisham, airport shop receipt stuck to its cover, and a well thumbed golfing magazine. A zip-lock bag of miniature toiletries. A passport and set of travel documents.

"That's a pity," Mark said genuinely. "Big Jim'll have to go to the embassy." He looked up and curled a smile. "Maybe he'll make some new friends there."

"*Mark?*" Deborah dragged his attention from the briefcase.

"Deb?"

"Maybe it's time for *what?*"

"Yeah. Well…" He paused and gathered himself.

"We got a decent little stash going…" He picked up Jim's wallet. "A little more now. Maybe it's time we started thinking about, y'know, leaving here. Renting an actual place?"

Deborah was stunned, though she couldn't put her finger on exactly why. She had been living with, *sleeping* with Mark in their broke-down palace for half a year. Logically, the notion of renting a home – a real home – was an entirely natural progression. But still, the suggestion – and that it came unsolicited from him – set butterflies in her stomach. It felt like he was asking her to move in with him. Which, of course, he was.

"Mark, I… I'm still fifteen. How do we do that?"

"Well… *I* would have to rent it, I suppose. But I think all you need is two months' rent. One for the first month and one for the… the thing…" His face screwed in the boyish way that so endeared him to her.

"The deposit," she added neatly, distant with thought.

"Right. And we must have more than that by now, right? About four or five hundred?"

Deborah's thoughts were flooding. Frenetic vivacity bubbled within as she spoke. "We have six hundred and forty seven. Plus whatever the Big Jim Huke Foundation generously contributed."

"Okay." He was clearly nervous. "So, we *could* do it. I mean, you get bills and stuff, taxes and all that shit, but if we have a real address then I could get a job - a real job I mean - and that should pay for those. Right?"

He looked to her for validation, his puppy-dog eyes shaving a couple years off his face once more.

"Yes." Deborah beamed. "Yes! We can do that!" Deborah pulled his face into hers with both hands and kissed him hard. A warm flush ran through her body, excitement rising. Her elation recalling the first time she had kissed him. The first time she had kissed anyone.

With effort she forced her speeding brain to focus. To think about the practicalities for a moment. She had to - if she let it run wild she'd be mentally picking out curtains by nightfall.

"I... I won't be able to work a real job though. Not yet."

He shrugged, nodding.

"And Mark..." She pulled away a little and looked at him earnestly. "We need to be careful. Seriously. Out there, people... they won't understand. You would need..." She thought for a second then continued: "You need to tell people I'm your sister. In a year it won't matter, but until then you could get in big trouble. Real trouble. *Prison* trouble. You understand, right?"

"Yeah, I know," he replied glumly. "But you *want* to though, right?" He looked sheepish now. Visibly vulnerable. She kissed him again, soft and sweet this time.

"Yes. Of *course* I do."

He grinned and picked the Yellow Pages up, rereading the entry.

"Then let's make the next one count."

Deborah stood across the street from the Maison Noire, fiddling absent-mindedly with a packet of Marlboro as she waited. She didn't like to smoke. Deborah never saw the appeal in the sour taste and the sickly film it left on her lips, but it made for the simplest way to stand in observation without inviting unwanted attention. A youth loitering in front of a fancy hotel was suspicious. A young waitress enjoying a quick cigarette break was not.

She shifted a little, watching her breath dance in the wintery air as she discretely re-tucked the back of her shirt. It was big on her, but, folded at the back behind the little black waistcoat and tucked into the skirt, you couldn't really tell. She had lucked out with the outfit. Deborah didn't like to part with any of her and Mark's hard won cash unless she had to, but the black skirt and waistcoat had been on sale in the department store, and the heels she already owned. Souvenirs from hustles past. With her blonde hair pulled up into a bun and some modestly applied lipstick and eyeliner, the outfit afforded a reasonable facsimile of what she had observed on the bar and restaurant staff this past week. The little gold pin with the hotel's logo that Mark had palmed from an unobserved check-in area provided the icing on the cake. Not perfect perhaps, but you'd need to pay pretty close attention to tell the difference, and no one ever really looked at the nameless, faceless staff in these joints. The fancier the establishment, the more anonymous the service.

The subject of her and Mark's attention would be arriving soon. Mr Briefcase. He was a creature of habit for sure. Each of the past seven evenings, she had observed him step out of the back of the same black Lexus limousine. Not one of those crazy long limo-for-hire jobs she had seen drunken students or giddy hen parties pile into or, more often, collapse out of. It was smaller. More dignified. It reminded her of pictures she had seen of presidential motorcades, minus the motorcade.

Mr Briefcase would step out, eponymous case in hand, and stride into the hotel. Each evening, he would approach the bar and signal the barman. Each evening, the barman would pour his drink without conversation or question - a 'rusty nail' she had discovered it was called. Each evening, standing, never sitting, he would place his briefcase down by his feet as he sipped. Once, twice, three times. Then he would tip the glass, downing the remains. Each evening, he would stoop and retrieve his case and would head directly to the elevator.

Tonight, she was sure, would be no different. Well, until *they* made it different.

Mark itched. He didn't like wearing a suit. It felt to him like wearing a little jail, all constricting. A tie always felt a little to close to a noose for his liking. He supposed he could loosen it a little, but he didn't want to mess it up. He might not be able to right it if he pulled too far. Deborah had tied it for him. Mark was adept at many things, but the ability to consistently tie a satisfying Windsor, much to his embarrassed chagrin, eluded him. He always seemed to end up with either the big end so long he looked like a toddler playing dress-up, or so short he looked like a skinny Oliver Hardy. Best just to leave it as it was, he thought with vexation.

He glanced up at the clock above the bar. Ten past six. He'd be here soon. Five minutes or so. Mark toyed with the glass rim of the drink he had ordered, resisting any urge to gulp it down too fast. Don't want to actually finish, he reminded himself. Then he'd require a new prop. The prices at the bar had made him baulk.

He occupied the second to last stool at the bar. Their mark – Mr Briefcase as they had come to know him – seemed always to approach the left side, so they had calculated this was the best spot. All things going smoothly, it would place him right beside their prey as he stood with his drink.

Twelve past six. Mark slid the briefcase from his lap and placed it, discreetly but precisely, on the floor by the stool.

Deborah was smarter than he was, he thought with affectionate admiration. It wouldn't have occurred to him to keep the cases from their prior scores. He would have tossed or burned them along with the valueless parts of their contents. Destroyed all evidence of their work. She had insisted though, and so they had stacked them carefully in a corner of their den. It had take quite a while for a use to become apparent to Mark. After they had scoped the hotel a few times and selected Mr Briefcase, she had carefully sorted through the stack and pulled out this brown leather one with her loveable 'told-you-so' grin. She had been right. It was a dead ringer for the one he carried, and, with a couple of books inside, had the weight and feel of authenticity.

Quarter past six. Any time now. Mark waited.

There it was.

Deborah lit a cigarette and stood as casually and disinterestedly as she could, maintaining a watchful eye on the Lexus. It glid down the main road, turned and snaked around the hotel grounds towards the entrance.

As the car pulled up she toyed with the packet, her head bowed. Just one of the staff on her break. Nothing to see here. In her periphery, the man stepped out of the rear driver side door, case in hand. He did not, today, head for the hotel at his usual clip. Instead, he glanced around for a moment or two at the building facade then turned. For a sinking second, Deborah began to worry that this was not going to be the day –

that they would need to alter the plan, or abort it entirely. Stepping to the driver's window, he leaned down. The black-tinted glass rolled down a few inches with electronic smoothness, and he spoke into it briefly. Deborah could discern no words, but noted the top of a chauffeur's cap bobbing up and down in a nod. Then he turned, resuming his routine with a stride to the entrance.

All good. No problem. Just having a word with his driver, she thought, relieved. Sending him on his next assignment probably, or arranging his morning pickup.

It always felt like this. No matter how well they planned out a caper. When the time came, every innocuous little thing was imbued with unwarranted significant. Deborah steadied herself. She had learned a lot these past six months. She knew the plays and she knew the pitfalls. She knew the ways to avoid them. The trick was forcing her adrenaline mind to act the way her sober mind would. Not to hit the panic switch. To remember that *she* was the one that was different, not the mark. To be cool.

As his car pulled away, the same as always, Deborah dropped the cigarette - glad to be rid of its stink - and twisted it under the ball of her patent leather shoe. She finished her mental ten-count and stepped inside.

The man was signalling the barman, standing exactly where she and Mark had hoped. Mark sat hunched over the bar to his right. Just another besuited businessman, nursing his drink and his thoughts.

Deborah moved with brisk fluidity, adopting the flustered-yet-industrious comportment she had practiced to perfection. Move with purpose, make eye-contact with no one, look like you belong. No one looks twice at overworked staff.

Keeping Mark and Mr Briefcase in her view as long as she could, she marched to the restaurant entrance and, without stopping, picked up one of the circular trays and a couple of the complimentary glasses of champagne, placing them neatly on the tray as she walked. She looped back around towards the main lobby.

As Mark and Mr Briefcase came back into view, she noted, with relief, the barman place a napkin on the bar and a drink on the napkin. Like a Swiss watch, she thought triumphantly. All in perfect sync.

Mark glanced out the corner of his eye as the barman picked a glass, poured whisky and Drambuie over ice, dropped in the twist and placed it on its napkin. The figure at his side was motionless for a moment. For a brief, horrible second, he thought that the guy was altering his metronomic routine. Drinking single handed this time. A beat passed though, and sure enough, he felt the air shift as he stooped. He watched through his legs as the target relinquished the briefcase, placing it neatly next to theirs. Perfect.

He remained hunched over as he felt movement. The man turned and stood, and Mark could hear the dry sound of his sips. One. Two. Three… Mark braced a little in anticipation.

Crash.

"Oh, I'm sorry sir!" Deborah exclaimed with perfect shocked surprise. The tinkle of the shattered glasses on the tiles floor reverberated around the lobby.

"I'm such a *klutz*! I'm sorry, I didn't even see you there!"

Mark suppressed a smile. The ditzy, kittenish voice Deborah pulled for these particular capers was Oscar-worthy. It was no wonder she could get away with so much, he thought - what man couldn't be melted by that girlish charm?

As he leaned forward, poised to, by happenstance of course, pick up the wrong briefcase and walk out, he heard the response.

"Oh, I think you *did* princess." Cold and menacing.

That wasn't right.

He whipped his head around, and saw Deborah's eyes, wide and startled. The man, champagne dripping from his front, had her wrist clamped in his hand and was looking directly into her eyes with a calculating stare.

"I think you saw me just *fine*. I think you saw me *coming*."

Shit, thought Mark. Shit shit *shit*. Where do we go from here? Shit! He was rattled, queasy. But he had to help. Had to try and roll with it.

"Mister, I don't think the girl was…" he began, but the man turned to him with his eyes like ice.

"Why don't you just sit the fuck down, kid. Leave *both* those cases where they are."

Mark felt his stomach knot and plummet as the elevator of the world dropped too quick. Deborah tugged her arm with some force and looked almost set to free herself, before the champagne man grabbed her other wrist and forced both her hands to her sides.

He was menacing for sure, Mark thought through his frantic state, but there was something more than anger in his businessman face. Something that made his stare all the more sinister. In his panic, Mark could not put a finger on what it was. Curiosity perhaps? It was enough to root both Deborah and him to the spot.

"Well now," said a new voice from behind. "Seems we have a problem."

Mark and Deborah turned their heads in slow, miserable unison.

The lobby was silent and heavy, the dozen or so well to do patrons watching with anticipation as the strange scene unfolded before them. By the entrance stood two uniformed police officers, and a suited man with a gold pin on his navy blazer. Hotel security. Between the officers stood a burly man, arms crossed in a black suit. He wore a disapproving scowl on his face and chauffeur cap on his head.

Chapter Five

REFUSE

As he climbed up and gently sat beside her, Deborah stared silently across the gothic ghetto below.

She had known someone would come. Of course someone would follow; Raziel's business was too grand, his cause too important to him to simply let it lie. She had expected Zotiel. Given Raziel's verbosity, she had assumed he would consider Zotiel's theatrically archaic manner the more suited to plead his case. Nevertheless, here sat Zephon, joining her silent vigil atop the wall. They sat unspeaking for a long time.

"There's no shame in it you know." His voice was quiet and unassuming.

Deborah did not turn; she simply stared out at the dismal dark of the city below.

"In what?"

"The tears," he replied softly. Without looking at her, he produced a white handkerchief from his denim pocket and extended it.

Deborah stared at it for a second. She hadn't realised she was crying. She had not cried in fifteen years. Had hardly believed she was still capable. After so much of her life spent in the shadows, in the murky corners of the world, detached stoicism had evolved from professional necessity to instinctual immutability.

She did not take the cloth, opting instead to wipe at her face with her dirty hand. Zephon noted this without comment and pocketed it. The pair sat in silence longer before he spoke again.

"You're wrong you know."

Deborah didn't react.

"About it not being your problem." He pulled a little brown packet from his hip pocket and produced a plain unfiltered cigarette. "Not your fault? Sure. No one can blame you, or any of your kind." He paused to place it in his lips and lit the tip with a gold lighter. "But it *is* your problem. It's *everyone's* problem."

"You smoke?" Deborah watched as he inhaled. "Why? Does that even do anything for *your kind*?" She stuck a caustic flourish on the 'your kind.' She was sick of hearing about everyone's 'kind.'

He offered the pack. She pulled one from it and placed it between her lips, accepting a light from him.

"Does it do anything for yours?"

"Yeah. It kills us." She took a long drag, exhaling out into the abyss. "I doubt that matters anymore."

They sat silent once more.

"He sent you? Your boss?"

"He didn't have to."

She bobbed her head in a slow nod.

"To force me. Or beg me?"

Zephon paused.

"Yes."

Deborah nodded again. He had been honest at least. She took a moment more for herself, gazing out across the expanse.

"I never believed in any of this you know," she said with misty distance. "Not what he - your boss, or whatever the fuck he is to you - not what he was talking about, obviously. I mean I never believed in *any* of this." She gestured to the expanse of slum below and up to the inky blackness above. "Heaven. Angels. God. Any of it."

"You were an atheist." He shrugged. "There are worse things to be."

"I *am* worse things."

"We know."

She glowered bitterly across the horizon.

"Doesn't that makes me the wrong choice for his… I don't know what to call it. His coup d'état?"

"The right choice isn't always found in the obvious place."

Deborah looked round at Zephon with cynical contempt.

"Great. More penny-ante, fortune-cookie philosophy. He taught you well."

Zephon smiled wistfully.

"You've seen all these souls," he nodded down towards the slums. "You saw plenty as we walked. You saw what they are like?"

"Yes. They're all the same. All fucked up. Broken and miserable."

"They are all broken and miserable, but they're not all the same. Some are worse. More broken than others."

Deborah thought back. To the girl she had seen with her guttural song and her rosary bead smile. To the awful, eyeless man she had seen by the square, grinning his terrible grin and cradling his terrible handiwork.

"Yes. Okay," she conceded. "So?"

"Most of them, most of the worst? The *most* broken, the *most* hollow? In many cases they were also the most faithful. What has happened to this place - to all places, but especially to this place - it's the truly faithful in life who have the hardest time in death."

Deborah cocked a cynical eyebrow. "You think my lack of belief makes it easier to accept *this*?"

"Yes," he said flatly. "Your atheism was an inoculation. You expected nothing when you awoke here. Imagine what it would do, to expect Paradise and get this shit-hole instead?"

Deborah took a few more draws in silence.

"So he would have me be the knife in his great revolution, knowing full well that I don't" – she paused – "or *didn't* anyways… Knowing I didn't believe in any of it?"

"What does belief matter now?" Zephon asked. The question was rhetorical but he asked it with genuine puzzlement. "You *know* now. You don't need to *believe*."

"He asks that I believe *him* though."

"He speaks the truth Deborah. All he *can* do is ask. Humans have free will. We can't make you do it. None of us can. Not me or Zote, not Raziel or any of the resistance. All we can do is ask."

Deborah stubbed out the cigarette on the stone at her side. The smoke felt good, sobering, but with dismay she could feel the need returning inside her. The longing she had felt before imbibing Zotiel's vial. The empty hunger.

"All he can do is ask," she repeated. "All he can do is ask me to do what has to be the most outrageous fucking thing I've ever heard."

Zephon stubbed his cigarette now and stood. He leaned on the stone rampart, gazing out into the black distance above.

"This used to be a skyline," he said. "Didn't look that much different than now I guess, the stars never shone in The Purgs even then, but this was the skyline. The edge. None of that mess we found you in above. Less need for expansion back then."

He was quiet, thoughtful. Nostalgic sounding. In contrast to Raziel's blatantly self-serving history lessons, he seemed to be genuinely reminiscing. Deborah found, in spite of herself, she was warming a little to Zephon. His unassuming manner was less abrasive than Zotiel's flippancy, and certainly less corrosive to her sensibilities than Raziel's grandiose bloviation.

"I flew here once. A very long time ago." His small, sad voice made him seem young.

Deborah, not for the first time, found herself sizing him up with curiosity. The image she had of what an Angel *should* look like was nebulous at best - informed primarily by childhood fairy-tale and the theological lip-service paid by her early schooling; and latterly by occasional portrayal in popular media. Not much was specific in any of these interpretations, but the one aspect they all agreed on was the wings. Her new acquaintances could quite neatly be slotted into the abstract notion of what she did know of Angels without much cognitive dissonance, were it not for their lack of them.

"You did have wings then? I had wondered..." she began, but drifted as Zephon shifted his posture. He stood tall now.

"I was Zephon of the Malachim, Messenger of the glory of God, Solider of the Ninth Choir, Watcher of the world and Herald of the Word. I served faithfully the Divine, under the stewardship of my captain, His Eternity, Archangel Raziel."

He spoke with weight and pride. Reminiscent, Deborah realised, of seasoned military men - name, rank and serial number. There was melancholy in his tone though, and the pride faded to meek sorrow as he continued. "Yes. I had my wings then."

"So they what? Fell off?" Deborah asked glibly.

Zephon seemed for a moment to consider his words, then with wilting resignation, opted instead for silent demonstration. Turning his back he pulled at his shirt, lifting it high at the back, up to the base of his neck.

Beginning above his shoulder blades, tracing his spine and running across the breadth of his pale back were two great lesions. They ran almost his full height, the flesh warped and malformed. No surgical precision here. These awful abrasions had been forged in agony. The twisted scar tissue spoke volumes of the suffering inflicted in their creation.

"Oh my God..." Deborah's unguarded voice dropped to a horrified whisper. Without conscious thought, she reached out a hand, touching a few gentle fingertips to the protrusions. She expected him to recoil, but Zephon remained motionless as she traced the warped tissue. The wounds were old.

"In a manner of speaking," he replied sadly.

"They... they were *torn* off?"

Zephon pulled his shirt back down, but Deborah could not pull her eyes from the creases of the garment above them. Now she knew the lesions were there, they became impossible to miss, even beneath the cloth.

"Zotiel's too?"

Zephon nodded.

"And your boss?"

"He... I don't know. He may still have his. Some of the Archangels do. Only where The Office deem them necessary. For their duties, for..." He sighed. "For show mostly. To keep the masses in line. But I don't know for sure. To ask would..." He trailed off.

"He's your boss. I understand." She would not press him on this. Not after seeing his scars. Not now.

"Those of us in the lower spheres, our connection to the All-Mind is not absolute. We lower Angels especially. We're not the Seraphim, not the Cherubim, not like any of the top-brass. We can think some guarded thoughts. We may not be completely free - not like you are - but neither are we purely gestalt. The New God... to Him, that autonomy was reason enough to... *curtail* us. No sense in allowing any possible dissenters more power than they needed."

He turned back to face her, seeing the stunned revulsion in her eyes.

"Than you needed for what?" she asked.

"Well, to carry out His will," he replied.

"You still serve Him?"

"Oh yes. Of course. All do."

"How?" Deborah could not get the image of his scars from her mind. The deformation of that pristine skin was somehow worse, more abhorrent than anything she had seen here. More than the hollow sadness and the sallow madness of The Purgs. More than the destitute fear of the woman she had seen birthed through the nothing-door, more than the perversely joyless transactions of the whoring young. More even than the metallic insanity she tasted as she witnessed the eyeless grin of the fingerless man.

"Zotiel and I, we are Malachim. Messengers. The gist of which still stands, though the duties have changed a bit. We're a bit more... hands on now."

"You deliver messages? Divine Postmen?" she asked. Her grim facetiousness was returning. She still couldn't help her nature. Flippancy of tongue came as natural to her as breath, and in the face of the horror, she felt it provided a strange comfort. A piece of herself retained despite it all.

"We deliver *souls*" he replied.

"The Purgs are massive. Larger than anything you could imagine, and larger than they have ever been. Growing all the time. The checkpoints can't be relied on alone. Just because someone has finished their time here, doesn't mean they know it. None of your cell phones and pagers here. Folks need to be tracked down. Transported."

"So you wander The Purgs until you come across them?" Skepticism ran through her voice once more.

"We have our ways. We have our orders."

Deborah thought for a moment about the implications of this.

"So you two never leave The Purgs? You never go home?"

"We leave here, sure. Part of the job. We drive the trucks sometimes."

Okay, Deborah thought. That definitely required an explanation.

"The trucks? You mean *trucks* trucks? Like our trucks?"

"The Checkpoints, the Gates? They lead out of The Purgs, but it's not like you just wander through straight into Paradise. It's a long journey even to the outermost parts of Heaven proper. Souls could get lost. Waylaid. They need guidance."

"So you're like the bus drivers of Paradise?"

"Sure, I guess. Though it's been a while since I drove the, um, *good* bus. Not everyone who leaves The Purgs is going... up."

Comprehension drew across her face.

"You've been to…"

"No." Zephon cut her off abruptly, categorically. His face drawn and tense.

"No. Just to outposts. I'm just the delivery man. The garbage man. Hauling the refuse from the landfill. I don't visit the… incinerator."

"Human souls are refuse…" Deborah said, one eyebrow cocked grimly. More statement than question.

"We're *all* refuse here," he replied mistily. He sat again at her side.

"Anyways. That's one part of the job. There are other parts but they'll be more apparent later."

"If I sign on. If I agree? Join his revolution?"

"Well," Zephon sighed. He seemed reluctant to further belabour the point. "Yes."

Deborah knew the game that was being played. Maybe Raziel *was* astute enough to have known to send Zephon in his place, or maybe Zephon himself had concluded that his more softly-softly, boyish approach was their best play. It was possible even that the whole encounter was genuine, the conversation natural, and the manipulation incidental. Whatever the circumstance, she could see the play unfolding. She recognised this sinking feeling. The ghoulish spectre of inevitability. It stood impassively and immovably before her, awaiting her next move. She knew what it wanted. Her curiosity was piquing. And her needs rising.

"You got more of those smokes?"

He produced the packet once more, lit two side by side between his lips and passed her one.

"He knows it's insane right? I mean, he has to know on some level that it can't possibly work? That the idea is ridiculous?"

"It's not him alone. The Revolution is more than Raziel. And I can't speak for him. I don't know his every thought. But no, I don't think so. I think he believes it can work. *Because* it's insane. *Because* it's ridiculous. Because it's so outlandish that no one would try it. Because it's so audacious that the Powers? They would never and will never, expect it."

He drew deep and exhaled long and slow.

"And because it has to. Because the way things are? They can't continue like this forever. In his heart, in all our hearts, we believe it's possible because it simply can't not be. The balance can't have been so horribly skewed in *perpetuity*. The pendulum has to swing back. If not…" He trailed off.

"So it all comes back to faith then," Deborah mused.

"Yes, I suppose. *Our* faith. That the current way can't possibly be the *final* way. That it can be changed. That we are *supposed* to change it."

"By force?"

"Most regime change happens that way on Earth, doesn't it?"

"Some," she conceded.

"We know about you Deborah. We know your career, and more than that we know your… desires."

Deborah whipped her head to him with a glare, and while he did not back down, he did not press that particular line any further. Electing instead to skirt round the edges.

"You're a professional. You've done political jobs before."

"Ha!" Deborah scoffed loudly at this. She couldn't help herself this time. "That's your analogy!? *Seriously*? Fucking hell, you think a two-term congressman or a minister in some tin-pot dictatorship is the same as... I don't even know what the hell you would call this..."

"*Deicide*," Zephon said softly.

"Right."

Zephon looked pensively out across the void once more.

"I think that you are capable of killing a leader. A powerful, well protected leader. Without caring about their politics."

"You guys *want* me to care about your politics. Why else would you show me what they did to you?" Deborah nodded to his back.

Zephon stood a little, then turned to her.

"Well... imagine what you'd be capable of if you did?"

Deborah shook her head in quiet disbelief. Partly at the request of course, but more and more at herself. At her own inability to flatly deny it. She could not lie to herself. She could not entirely ignore her morbid and awful curiosity. She had never been able to.

She finished her cigarette in silence. Stubbing it out she turned to Zephon once more.

"And if I fail?"

"Then we *all* fail."

"Add another piece of shit to the incinerator?"

"Many, many pieces," he replied softly.

Fracture Five

JUDGES

Deborah sat alone in the holding cell. Just her, her thoughts, this bed and a seatless, steel toilet.

She had imagined the place differently, though she wasn't quite sure from where those expectations had formed. Television, she supposed. She had imagined being frogmarched in to some big holding pen. A daunting lattice of steel cage in the middle of a bustling precinct, filled to bursting with recidivists and vagabonds of every stripe. She had imagined them all pushing and shoving and yelling at the passing police, about their phone calls and about their lawyers and about how they didn't do nothin'. She had expected to be fearful – maybe have to fend off some unwanted attention or threat. Perhaps end up in some awkward-yet-genial conversation with a couple of tough, street-smart working-girls.

Nonsense of course. That was just the TV shows. Law and order didn't actually resemble Law and Order. Homicide may be a *part* of life on the street, but it didn't end neatly after fifty five minutes. In the end, she really didn't know anything about how the justice system worked. Certainly not on the inside. She was figuring it out now though. That was for sure. It didn't have bars, it didn't have yelling, it didn't have a colourful collection of criminals tossed in a crazy melting pot of iniquity. It had a small, off-white room. A normal looking bed. A normal looking door with a normal looking lock. And a seatless steel toilet.

She and Mark had been escorted from the lobby of the Maison Noire and ushered into the backs of separate police cars. They must have been waiting, just out of sight. Had to have been – there had been, what? Maybe six minutes? Between the time she watched Mr Briefcase leave his car and their abrupt exit through the lobby? No sirens, no fuss, they were just there.

The policemen in the car had been cordial. She guessed that, again, was probably not that strange in reality. Just different from the TV shows that were her only basis for comparison. After her arrest proper, they had acted more like stern chaperones than the arm of the law. They had explained what would be waiting for her and what to expect. She had acted tough, acted like she didn't give a shit, but deep down she had been glad of it. This all would have played out the same whether she was informed or not, she supposed, but the knowledge had been a small comfort.

The genial nature of her captors had not lasted long though. She had been led into the booking area and to a desk where an older, uniformed policeman sat. When he had asked her for her name, she had refused, point-blank, to tell him. Deborah was not sure exactly how information was shared around different districts and departments. She was not sure if a missing persons report with her name even existed. She was sure of one thing though - she didn't want anyone coming to claim her. The general atmosphere of 'aw-shucks' affability had ended then, and a cold, clinically bureaucratic system had taken its place.

Some considerable fuss had been made while an 'appropriate female witness' was found. The requirement apparently irked the officers considerably. Eventually, a sour-faced female – an administrative type – had been wrangled from somewhere in the building, and had stood disinterestedly, arms crossed, as an officer searched her for identification. Finding none, of course, they had finally entered her in their big book simply as #121-51624-F and moved on.

When asked her age she had flatly stated 'Eighteen.' This had invited more than a few skeptical glances, but she had stuck to her guns. The outfit had helped. Of course they knew she didn't really work at the hotel, but she did look the part at least.

The way she had seen it in that moment, the lie *might* cause her more problems on the legal side, might get her tried as an adult. A risk, sure, but better that than admitting the truth and ending up with some well-meaning social worker prying into her affairs. Or worse, looking to place her in some foster home in the absence of information concerning her past.

Deborah still remembered social workers. There had been one who visited with her and Trisha a few times after her father had died. During what they termed, with saccharine euphemism, her *'home-life transitional period.'* Elspeth. At nine years old Deborah had thought it odd for an adult, particularly one she met in a professional capacity, to introduce herself only by her first name. She had found it condescending, though she had never said so. She had simply given the answers she felt the well-intentioned busybody was looking for. Elspeth's tedious concern with her *'emotional wellbeing'* had rung false to Deborah's ear, even then. If a person needs to discuss their *'emotional wellbeing'*, she had thought, then their emotions were certainly not *'being-well'*. The input of some faux-bohemian in too many textiles, cycling through trite buzzwords with a mawkish, doe-eyed demeanor was unlikely to help in that case.

So no, she concluded. Say you're an adult. It was better to roll the dice and hope Mark did the same. If they both played their cards right, and got *very* lucky, they might still have a shot at their life together.

She had been photographed and fingerprinted. That much had fit her expectations. It was also the part that scared her the most in a way. She had never been fingerprinted before, so no problem, nothing to tie her to there, but the photos were another thing. Who knew what Trisha might have given them? Could be only a matter of time before they decided to run her nice new mug-shots through one of their databases.

They'd have the time. En route to the holding cell, the uniform that led her had informed her of her court appointment. The following Tuesday. Officer Dickhead – as she had come to name him – had taken obvious, sleazy pleasure in pointing out what an error she had made in her timing. Getting arrested on a Friday was, apparently, a rookie mistake. It meant spending a weekend in the cells was a virtual guarantee. When Deborah had, rather acerbically, pointed out that she had not been *trying* to get arrested at all, he had simply sneered and hurried her along the corridor.

Inside the little room her cuffs had finally been unlocked and the door shut and bolted with a metallic clunk.

Now here she sat. Her and that damn seatless steel toilet.

The *clank-swish* of the opening door jolted her awake. The night had been long and restless, dark in view and darker in spirit. She must have drifted off eventually though, and upon waking she saw nauseating fluorescent light had replaced the gloom, illuminating the sparse cell around her. She twisted, bleary eyed to face the door, and saw Officer Dickhead standing, officious and sullen, in its frame.

"Rise and shine Blondie. Time to go," he said with dispassionate irritation.

She frowned. Tuesday he had said, right? So what was this now? She stood, fixing her now rather grimy shirt and skirt as best she could.

"Where am I going?"

"Wherever the hell you want, apparently." His authoritative demeanour seemed a little curtailed since their previous encounter. "Charges are being dropped. How the fuck that happened I don't know. You and your wee pal must have some fancy friends."

Fancy friends? she thought, puzzled. She and Mark had each other. That was *all* they had. All they had needed – until now anyway. They didn't have friends, and certainly didn't have, as Officer Dickhead so eloquently put it, *fancy* friends.

She was tempted to press further, to ask what he was talking about, but thought better of it. Why look this gift horse in the mouth? Instead, she followed, silent, trying as best she could to seem unfazed. If this *was* some mistake, some bizarre confluence of administrative error, she sure as shit didn't want to be the one to shine a light on it.

The walk back from the cells to the main precinct seemed unfamiliar in the daylight that now streamed through the skylights above. As she walked, Deborah glanced around at the other cells, hoping to catch some glimpse of Mark. The last time she had seen him, as he was pushed into the police car behind hers, he had looked as timid and fearful as she. More so perhaps. She worried for him. He must have been in one of these cells last night too, she thought. His own sparse room with his own bed and his own seatless toilet. It had occurred to her as she lay back alone on the too-thin mattress, feeling the poke and prod of the rusting springs beneath, that in the six months since she arrived in Glasgow she had not once slept apart from him. The dark had felt darker coupled with the lonely cold. She saw no evidence of his whereabouts.

She was led, shackle-free this time, back through the corridors and partitions of the precinct, to the place where they had taken her personal items from her the night before.

"Five, Sixteen, Twenty four."

Officer Dickhead's tone was formal as he addressed the duty officer. No *'one-two-one'* and no *'F'* thought Deborah. The *'F'* must be 'female'. Maybe the *'one-two-one'* was the district? The duty officer spent an inordinate amount of time shuffling about in the little room behind the desk, before finally returning with her belongings. Belongings indeed. A packet of Marlboro and a cheap plastic lighter. Hardly worth the effort, she thought grimly. I don't even smoke.

As he extended a sheet for her to sign, a moment of panic rose. She frantically considered what to write. Picking up the pen, she elected to simply draw an 'X' and date it appropriately. That was something she had seen in movies; she had no idea if it would be accepted in real-life. The officer looked down at it for a second and pulled the clipboard back to him.

"Alright Little Miss Anonymous," he told her with weary resignation. "Off you trot."

Maybe this kind of thing was more common than she thought? Common enough, seemingly, to give rise to vexation rather than anger. She expected to have more bureaucracy to navigate, more pieces of paper to sign at least, but instead Officer Dickhead simply marched her to the main entrance and out to the steps in front of the precinct building.

"Right. Fuck off then, Anonymous," he said flatly, as he turned and strode back into the building. Deborah stood for a moment, stunned. What the *hell* had just happened?

She wondered what she would do now. The whole thing was done, apparently. She had no idea why, or how, but it was done. Where was Mark? Was he still in there? Wait, no. *'You and your wee pal must have some fancy friends,'* he had said. *'You* and *your wee pal.'*

She glanced around hopefully. There was no one in front of the building. She took a few tentative steps towards the concrete stairs that led down to the road. She half expected to hear someone call her name. Grab her. Tell her 'Hey Blondie! Hey Anonymous! What are you, stupid? We were just fucking around with you! Get back in that cell!' But no. Nothing. No shouts, no approach. She really was free to go.

She began down the steps, the stupid patent leather heels *click-clack*ing on the concrete, when she noticed a familiar vehicle parked at their foot. A black Lexus limousine. A rush of panic ran the length of her, and she began to turn instinctually. Back towards the building. Back towards *anything*. As she did so the rear passenger door swung open and she stopped in her tracks.

Sitting in the car was Mr Briefcase, a steely look on his sinister face. Beside him sat Mark, looking drawn. Drawn and frightfully young. She stood frozen for a second, trying to process the scene, but drew a blank.

"Get in Deborah," Mr Briefcase said. Calm but stern. She glanced around at the empty street for a moment. "Don't be stupid now Princess. Just get in. We need to talk."

She shot a frantic, questioning look at Mark. He nodded silently at her - a reassuring nod. It's okay, it's okay, it said, though his face was pale. He cocked his head, beckoning her to join them in the car. Deborah hesitated a moment then, trusting Mark as she always had, she took a deep, steadying breath and stepped towards the vehicle.

"You two certainly have something about you." Mr Briefcase spoke softly.

Deborah sat next to Mark, Mr Briefcase opposite. She imagined, after the fact, that she should have tried to hide her and Mark's connection in this uncertain situation, but as she had sunk into the soft leather her hand had, almost involuntarily, found his and clenched. She couldn't help it. The stress and anxiety of last night's events and the trepidation this bizarre new twist instilled had her rattled. From his look, she could tell it had Mark rattled too. They both needed a little comfort.

Mr Briefcase eyed the pair of them. He looked no different now than he had all the long week they had surveilled him. Nothing but a suit and a pair of spectacles. Nothing distinguishing. Nothing to pick him out of a crowd. He was every middle-aged businessman. Up close though, the intense focus in his gaze unnerved her. The way he sized them up. Reading their faces with the curiosity of a scientist observing an experiment in motion. Interested, but clinically so. Without emotion. He opened his briefcase and shuffled the contents, looking for something.

"You scoped the place five days?" he asked offhandedly. His accent was American, but peppered with occasional British inflections. He had the unaffected manner of someone who knows the answers before posing the questions.

Both Deborah and Mark said nothing. Mr Briefcase looked up, and with a slight raise in his brows added, "I arranged for all the charges to be dropped against you. That doesn't mean I can't have them reinstated. You're not talking to some cop here. I've had enough of the silent treatment from this one." He glanced at Mark, who stared back with as cold a glare as he could muster. After his night in the cells and his confounding release, it wasn't much to speak of.

"You scoped the hotel, The Maison Noire, five days?"

"Six," Deborah replied.

There's no point in fighting this, she thought. Whoever this guy is, he has all the cards. He's in control. She felt more though, deep down. More than mere resignation. She *wanted* to know where this was going.

"Beginning on Saturday?" Mr Briefcase glanced up from his shuffling once more.

"Sunday."

"Then you scoped the place for five days. The sixth day was the job. Your little switcheroo. *Attempted* switcheroo." He spoke in scholarly matter-of-fact. A teacher, pointing out where a pupil made the error in their formula.

"Okay, yes, then five days."

He nodded and produced a document from the briefcase, which he opened in his lap.

"Deborah Sinclair. Born December first, nineteen-eighty three, Glasgow Royal Maternity hospital. Mother, Gilda Grace-Sinclair died of ovarian cancer, nineteen-eighty seven; father, Frederick Sinclair, nineteen-ninety four. Industrial accident."

Deborah felt herself falling through the seat of the limousine. Mr Briefcase continued.

"Residence changed to Edinburgh. Patricia Anne Sinclair, paternal aunt. School enrolment... Garmount High School... Ah. Here we go. Missing child report. Filed April twelfth, nineteen-ninety seven. No further information available."

He observed her with a blank look. No questions. He hadn't been asking, he had just been stating the facts. Letting her know that he knew it all already. Deborah turned with numb shock to Mark and saw nothing but sullen disquiet in his face.

"He knows all about me too," he told her, his voice uneven.

Deborah sat in suspense a few moments. Taking stock, and searching for bearings. She found none.

"Who are you? You're not the police..."

"I am not the police," he stated flatly. "My name is Rust."

"Rust...?" Mark asked. "Rust what?"

Rust turned to him coldly and with an almost violent calm he replied, "*Mr* Rust."

Deborah and Mark glanced at each other.

"Okay. You know all about us. You're threatening us? Or blackmailing us?" Deborah asked pointedly.

"I'm just letting you know, Princess," Mr Rust replied, "that while you two might be used to being in control, keeping your small-time marks in your small-time hustles dancing to your tune – you're in *my* car now. I'm not small-time."

He shuffled his various documents together and placed them back into the case.

"I admire your little hustle," he told them. Deborah noted that he tended to speak to her primarily, glancing only occasionally across at Mark.

"The pair of you are young. You are clearly pretty good at this. My guess is you've been at it a while, but it can't be that long. You're not old enough."

Mark opened his mouth to speak but Mr Rust simply raised a finger and closed his eyes for a moment, hushing him.

"I don't care kid. Let me finish." A little malice crept through his measured tone.

"My point is, you appear to have something about you. Talent, for want of a better word. You picked the wrong mark – that's for damn sure – but don't let that get you down. Operatives with long histories and star-studded careers have tried and failed to get the better of me. Spotting a couple of kids scope me out? I could do that with both eyes closed and a bullet in my gut. But you do have the skills. It would have worked on some civilian, I'm sure. You were patient. You picked your moment. You made sure you had your little plan down. You even got all dolled up." He gestured to her faded and smeared makeup and her now crumpled outfit. "And given that shit-hole apartment you squat in, that must have taken some effort."

Oh my god, thought Deborah. This was no joke. This guy knew everything. They must have been tailed. Probably for days. Her stomach twisted painfully inside her.

"I admire raw skills. I think they need a hell of a lot of honing, but you have something. Not just talent. *Promise*."

"Okay." Deborah nodded, disguising her horror as impatience. "So what do you *want*?"

Mr Rust pulled out a smaller paper this time and set the case by his side. He smiled, pulling his tone up to faux-lightness and handed it to her. It was a photograph.

"I want this." He smiled a crocodile smile.

Deborah eyed the photo dubiously. It was grainy and blurred, seemingly taken from a great distance. It showed an office window. Inside, two suited businessmen stood in conversation beside a filing cabinet. One man had his arm resting on it, and clutched in his hand was a stack of papers. She looked to Mark, who shrugged. She turned back to Mr Rust.

"You want a filing cabinet? I think you can buy them at Staples."

Rust smiled humourlessly. "Well, aren't you quite the little pistol, Princess." He pointed to the document in the businessman's hand.

"I want *that*."

"Deborah stared at the blurry photo once more, but could make out no further detail.

"What is it?" she asked.

"It is a thing I want," he replied. "That's really all that matters to you."

"No," Deborah replied, "that's all that matters to *you*. It doesn't matter to *us* at all."

"Oh I think it does," he replied with a smile, and unfolded the file once more.

"Maybe you don't care about going to prison. I suspect that you do, more than you let on, but that's immaterial. What you definitely *do* care about is keeping away from..." he glanced down through the spectacles perched on the tip of his nose. "Your aunt Patricia. Poor dear must be worried sick. Don't worry, I'm sure this guy, Mr McTavish? I'm sure he's consoling her."

Deborah's guts constricted once again. Mr McTavish. Gregor.

"Seems his mail still goes to the same address. He must have time too, he's been collecting unemployment benefits for quite a few months now. The plating game in another dry spell, I suppose." Rust glanced up at her with menacing calm.

"He'll have a lot of time to rattle around that house. A lot of his expenditure appears to be on alcohol though. Maybe he's lonely? Maybe he needs more company?"

A horrible, queasy feeling sank through Deborah. Bitter bile rose in her throat. Mark turned to her with concern in his eyes. She hated that concern. She never had explained to him the circumstances of her flight from the home she had in Edinburgh; she had never felt the need. Why discuss the awful past when stealing moments of happiness in the present was against such odds? She had never wanted to relive that night. She never wanted to spend a waking second reminded of that drunken animal. His yellowed fingers at her waistband. His grotesque, stinking breath in her face.

It was more than that though. In truth, she had never wanted Mark to see her that way. As a victim. As helpless. As young as she *really* was. Their six happy months together had been based as much on mutual respect for the secrecy of their individual pasts as it was with mutual desire for a combined future.

"And you, Mr Greene." Rust turned now to Mark. Deborah had never known his surname. It sounded wrong to her somehow, though she couldn't think why. It was just a name. He had to have had one.

"I don't think I need to tell you that *your* father would be *most* interested in your whereabouts these past few years."

"Fine," Mark replied, cutting Rust off. "I'll do what you want. Leave her out of it though. One person can steal a piece of paper."

Mr Rust shook his head emphatically.

"No no no. This is a task for both of you."

"Why?" asked Mark haughtily.

"Because I fucking said so, kid," he replied flatly. He turned to Deborah with an expectant look.

"Well, Miss Sinclair?"

Deborah paused, glowering as she sized up her sinister inquisitor. Nothing about him conveyed his status. Nothing betrayed his emotions, save perhaps his intense, probing eyes. She wondered who this guy was, really. She wondered how he had the ability to have all charges against them dropped. She wondered how she and Mark could have been so unlucky as to pick this shady character for a target, and how long he had been researching and tailing them. She wondered if she would ever be able to recover her dreams of a normal life with Mark.

She wondered what was in those documents.

"Fine," she relinquished. "I'm in. But I'm Deborah. That's it. I don't want to hear *Sinclair* from your lips - or anyone's fucking lips - *ever* again. You got that?"

Mr Rust smiled his crocodile grin once more and leaned back. He tapped the black-tinted glass separating them from the driver.

"Whatever you say Deborah. Whatever you say."

The engine hummed smoothly to life and they pulled away from the police station.

Chapter Six

DEVIL MAY CARE

It had been a longer walk than Deborah had expected, back to the room under Shepherds. Passage through the bar had been quick this time, the stilted conversation of earlier replaced by a perfunctory nod from Zephon to Augustine the bartender, who opened the back door once again with a knowing smirk.

Upon arrival in the subterranean office of the resistance, Deborah had been greeted by Zotiel. He had smiled – warmly at her, and with respectful acknowledgement at her escort. Zephon had returned a familial nod. She wondered if they really were brothers. They certainly acted so. The comfortable familiarity of long years together was plainly apparent. Raziel was nowhere to be seen.

"You're back," Zotiel had said simply. No admonishment or judgement. "Ready to accept that you're special then?"

"I'm not special," Deborah scolded. Not the way they meant anyway, she thought to herself.

Zotiel glanced at her with amused curiosity. "Deborah, you saw a few new folks out there, didn't you? As they arrived?"

She stared at him hard for a moment then relented, nodding.

"How long did it take for them to fall apart? Not too long, right? Hours? Minutes?"

"I suppose," she replied.

"In the course of a day or two, you've died, been contacted by Angels, had an audience with an Archangel, witnessed a great breadth of The Purgs and…" he paused for a moment, glancing at Zephon, "…and beheld scars inflicted by a God."

She stood defiant, staring him down. He held steady.

"Don't you think it's odd that you can handle it? That it has not broken you?"

Maybe, she thought. Maybe her ability to accept it all at face value was strange. But, on some level, she *always* had. Deborah's reality had never been of her choosing. She had coped because *acceptance* of it had been on her own terms. This, she realised, was no different. She knew the reason she had been sought out. It wasn't because they were helping her. It was because they *needed* her. Once that was apparent, it didn't matter how grandiose the language and how outlandish the concept. It was a hit. That was what she did. Now all she had to do was figure out how.

"If we're going to do this insane fucking nonsense then we're going to need to talk it through," she told Zotiel. Her eyes were like ice.

He grinned.

"Follow me," he replied and turned towards the bookshelf-lined corridor. Deborah followed.

The corridor was not endless, despite how it had appeared from the office behind. The illusory optics stemmed not from any mystical source, not from some magical spell, but simply from a long slow dip in elevation. As they walked its course, it gradated slowly down and then back up, the dip invisible to her eye but apparent in her footfalls. After some considerable time in silent march alongside dusty, overstuffed shelves, the trio approached a door very much like that of the entrance to the office.

"Don't be intimidated," Zotiel told her ominously, as he pushed the handle down. "Remember. They *chose* you." He swung the door open.

Like the corridor, the room was thick with dust. Books and scrolls and shelves and dust. Tables and wooden chairs were dotted around, in nooks and crannies and amid the shelves. Piles of texts and papers adorned them, scattered or piled haphazardly - perused and subsequently discarded. The small comforts of the front room were not present here. No leather couches or fireplaces; no wingbacks to be seen. This room was not home to relaxation. This was a place of business.

To the left, staring back at her, was Raziel. His grandeur was diminished to that of a man, though his deep black eyes remained a conspicuous reminder of his otherworldliness. At his side were four other figures. Every one with the same obsidian void in their eyes. Seeing them stand, silent and watchful as she entered, *was* intimidating. Their collective, penetrative gaze discomforting.

Deborah, pulling slow, dusty breath into her lungs, stepped towards them. She maintained her composure as best she could, forcing herself forward through viscid unease. If she was going to engage in this outrageous affair, she would not do so in subservience. This, she thought with resolve, would be on *her* terms.

"Deborah," Raziel acknowledged. "Thank you for returning." He extended a pale hand in a gesture to his companions.

"Welcome to the Revolution."

⁂

"First things first," she told the collective. "*If* I'm on board? I want some answers."

"Ask, child." Cassiel replied.

He looked the oldest, though Deborah doubted that the true age of the conspirators was betrayed by their appearance. To them, age was merely a costume to be worn. Garb, as opposed to blemish. Nevertheless, the form he took was one of an aged, wizened man. His hair was a shock of pure white, long and straight, pulled back in a high tail at his crown. He sat on a wooden stool, arms resting at his knees, draped in a simple white tunic.

To his right, forming the first part of the loose semi circle, was Raziel. To his left, Raphael. The slimmest figure in the assembly, his blonde hair was cropped short and he wore a white linen suit. Kindness radiated from his gentle half-smile, and that, more than anything, contributed to him appearing the youngest.

Next to him, standing, was Yahoel, and to Yahoel's left, Raguel. Both shared flowing, dark hair and chiselled jawlines, high cheekbones and sombre grace. They looked like statues. Both grand figures were draped in white cloaks, beneath which vests of mail were visible. Glinting silver links under Yahoel's robes; tempered red steel beneath Raguel's. Both brooded with intense, powerful threat. Their frames were gladiatorial, their stoney faces those of seasoned soldiers. Where they differed was solely in their hands. Where Yahoel's smooth white fingers matched the rest of his exposed skin, Raguel's were black and charred. He seemed, to Deborah, to wear gloves of black ash.

Standing as they had before, flanking the group, Zotiel and Zephon watched on in respectful silence. Unlike before though, she was keenly aware of periodic glances from Zephon. Mindful concern in his eyes.

After introductions had been made, Deborah's head had swum. Not from this new set of names and faces - that much she could deal with now. The bizarre and unusual was fast losing shock value in this world. Rather, her dizziness seemed to stem simply from her proximity to the group. Being in their presence gave rise to a cloudy, dreamlike haze. Now, with an opportunity before her to get some real answers, she was forced to work to maintain a sober mind and a level head. To keep her poise. The second yellow vial Zephon had provided kept the hunger at bay, but did nothing to alleviate the dizziness that had ensued. She steadied her voice against it.

"How many of you are there?"

"How many in the Resistance?" asked Cassiel gently. She nodded.

"That depends on your definition," Raziel replied. "The five of us, we have worked many years to find a solution. To find you. There are a few others who know of our... desire. A few of our Sphere. One in particular, above others. But those who, while unaware, *may* support the cause, are a myriad. The Office of God has been a curse to many."

"One above?" Deborah asked.

"The leader of our cause. His Eternal Divinity, Lord Gabriel," Cassiel replied.

"With the trumpet?" she asked. She made no direct attempt at flippancy, but her unfamiliarity with the theological made its avoidance virtually impossible. Besides, she was not interested in being coy. She wanted answers.

A brief exchange of glances flickered around her before Cassiel replied.

"Yes. With the trumpet."

"Where is he?" she asked. "He doesn't get his hands dirty?"

"His position is... precarious. High in the Divinity. Still high within The Office. To risk His exposure by coming here would be... unwise." Cassiel spoke with soft authority.

"Okay," she replied, working through her thoughts methodically. "And how many of you are there out there?"

"You are asking how many Angels *exist?*"

"I'm asking what we're up against," she replied. "I'm asking who – and how many – *will* be loyal to The Office?"

"Immeasurable," growled Yahoel. His voice, quiet in volume, was thunderous in timbre.

Raziel, nodding, added, "You may as well ask how many stars are in the sky."

"None," she replied. "I was just out there." This time she was aiming for sarcasm. She was in no mood for more of Raziel's indirect riddling. Cassiel smiled a little.

"In *your* sky," he corrected.

"Okay. That's nice and specific. That'll help."

Cassiel, noting her irritation, elaborated.

"The Angelic Choirs are vast in number. They consist of many, many more than the Archangels. From the Office on down. At the top of The Monolith, The Sanctum of God. The Office.

"Below, the First Sphere. The Seraphim, the Cherubim and the Orphanium. The most powerful of our race. They are gestalt - individual entities, yes, but their minds are merely cells - nerve endings within a single, all-powerful cerebrum. The All-Mind. Lacking any autonomous thought, their loyalty is absolute."

At the mention of the 'All-Mind' a rumble of discomfort ran through the assembly. Cassiel, with a shudder, continued.

"They form the guard of the Monolith. They are it's sentinels, serving within. They are the keepers of the Evergaze.

"Below them, the Second Sphere. The Virtues and the Dominions, and below them, the Principalities. They walk the Great City and beyond. As guards of the Glory."

"The All-Mind runs to them also," Raphael interjected.

"Indeed," Cassiel nodded grimly. "Their loyalty does not err. It cannot. Their minds are not theirs alone. It is only we, of the Third Sphere, whose thoughts can be shielded."

"Who can think and feel for ourselves," Raziel added.

"And *remember*," growled Yahoel.

The way the Archangels bounced their conversation around was vexing. Deborah fought to keep focus, to take it all in.

"Shielded. Not disconnected?" she asked.

"No Celestial is entirely free of the All-Mind. But it does not consider us... important. Not enough for perpetual oversight. Full control would not be possible though, even if it did. We were not created so. Our duties – our *true* duties – they included business in your world."

"On Earth?"

"Yes. On occasion."

Deborah paused.

"So?"

"The All-Mind has no power there. Free will is maintained pure on Earth. By the will of its Creator. Only those with autonomous thought may walk the human plains. The Third Sphere are, therefore, the only fitting Celestial messengers to your world. We can report to the All-Mind of course – by mere thought if necessary – but on *our* terms. For the most part."

"You can't be forced, you mean?"

Cassiel glanced to the others, who returned his trepidatious air. They were reticent to look at her directly.

"We can... shield," he replied eventually. Deborah nodded. They *can* be forced, she thought. They won't say it, but they can't deny it.

"So... the Third Sphere, that's you? That's the Archangels?"

"We are of the Third, as are the lower Angels," Raziel answered, gesturing to Zephon and Zotiel.

"But not all of your... sphere are *with* you. Not many in fact. Right?"

"No," conceded Cassiel. "But they might be... persuaded."

"*Some* may," one of the group added. She was not sure who this time.

"Others may opt for safety in the current regime," said another.

"They may find it safe, but none would choose it over the old ways," said yet another.

"Of course, but to challenge and fail?"

"Failure is possible in any endeavour."

"Failure in this regard though? That would be the final failure. For all involved, Brother."

"Of course."

"No one wishes to challenge and fail. We all remember the Morning Star."

"It is not the same."

"He did not challenge The Office, he challenged the True God. He had no just cause."

"He believed he did. Others too."

"The petty jealousy of the fallen is of no concern here."

"Surely you cannot deny the parallel."

"Parallel, perhaps, but it is dissimilar in impetus."

"Motive aside, the penalty for failure remains, Brother."

"No. It is worse. The Office is less forgiving."

The conversation was disintegrating. Deborah raised her voice, attempting to refocus it.

"*Possible* help is no good to us now," she stated. Cold and pragmatic. It met with silence, which she accepted as agreement. She took a beat.

"What would happen if I succeeded? How would the True God be... reinstated?" The Archangels exchanged a few more surreptitious glances. Not encouraging, Deborah thought. Either they don't trust me, or...

"You don't know, do you?" She peered incredulously at Cassiel.

"Lord Gabriel does. You need concern yourself solely with the demise of The Office. He will see to the rest."

"Do you? Do you know?"

"Lord Gabriel does," he repeated with defiant solemnity. She sat for a moment in contemplation. This question did not really make a difference, she supposed. That was the politics. Her concern was the hit.

"What is the All-Mind?" she asked.

"What *is* it?" asked Yahoel.

"How does it work?"

"Very, very well."

She shot back a withering look. The way the answers were coming back at her, couched in knowing riddles and hifalutin rhetoric was galling. Cassiel, once again detecting her distaste, interjected.

"The All-Mind *is* the Divinity. The Divinity *is* the All-Mind. They are one and the same."

"Uh-huh," she coaxed with some irritation.

"You are a human; you have free-will. Imagine that free-will as the extreme end of a scale. The All-Mind sits at the other. The First Sphere? They know only that end. They do not think, not independently. The Second sit beside them. They may think independently, but they have no ability – and no desire - to hide their thoughts. The All-Mind's oversight is continual. Unbroken."

"They think, but do not *feel*," Raphael added. "The First Sphere *think* as one."

"They do not *think* as one," Raziel contradicted now. "Their thoughts are imposed. They are *vessels* for thought."

"For the All-Thought." Yahoel joined the fray.

"The point," Cassiel tried now to right the conversational path, "is that the Will of The Office is *all* they know."

"All they *can* know," Raziel added.

"Yes. To engage with one is to be witnessed by all. They are a hive-mind. The Divinity rules every thought of its legion. It ensures the compliance of those outside its own influence through the actions of those within. And by way of the Evergaze, of course."

Deborah struggled once again to keep up with the incessantly circling pool of agreement, addition and discord.

"What is the Evergaze?" she asked.

"A beacon," Raphael replied. "It watches across the Great City. A beam of light…"

"Of *truth*…" interjected Raziel.

"The lantern *of* truth. It watches all." Cassiel spoke with ominous portent.

"So it's security?" she asked doubtfully. "A floodlight?"

"In a manner of speaking, but it is much more. It is a manifestation of the light of God. The *will*. Repurposed, manipulated by The Office, but with all the power of the Glory. To be caught in its gaze, to be *known*? It is to be imprisoned. Laid bare."

"The Glory…?" Deborah spoke in a puzzled hush.

"The City thrives on the Glory of God. Now on the Glory of The Office." Raphael now. "The Great City has no need of electricity or steam or any of the methods Earth cities use to breath their life. The Glory grants life."

"The City lives. It *feels,* in and of itself," added Raziel.

"The All-Mind *is* the Divinity and *is* the Glory. It *is* the Evergaze and *is* the City itself."

"Independent entities also though, Brother."

"In some manner, perhaps…"

"But one, of course."

The conversation was spiralling loose. Dismay crept through Deborah. She wondered how this group had ever managed to come to a consensus on anything.

"What about the people?" she asked, raising her voice again. Cassiel turned back from their pontificating to address her question.

"The human souls you mean?"

"Yes," she replied, with a modicum of relief. That he had even heard her in the rising din was gratifying. "What threat do they pose? What do they do?"

"Well… they live. The City is theirs as much as ours," he replied.

"More so," Raziel added. "It was created for them."

"Initially, yes, though The Great City is far more than Eden's Gardens ever were," Raphael interjected.

"What is built on the bones retains the spirit, Brother," Raziel chimed back.

"Not always," Yahoel growled.

"Perhaps, but in this case…"

"The human souls retain their free-will. They could help."

"Some perhaps. But hindrance is equally possible, my Brother."

"That is true."

"Malevolent free-will is a danger as great as the All-Mind."

"Greater perhaps."

"Indeed. The human souls who have entered the City of late? They have no love for their own kind."

"*Some* do not."

"I have witnessed them, my Brother. They fight and scrape to secure their place."

"Indeed. They would not help their fellows, save to be *seen* to do so. Their loyalty to The Office is outshone only by their loyalty to themselves."

"Some are just. Many are not."

"Well…"

Cassiel joined the fracas now, and Deborah heard no more.

This was going nowhere. The information she could glean was as mindlessly vague as it was stupefyingly contradictory. It made her crazy. What had she been thinking? There was no helping these foolish beings with their foolish plans. Angels or not, she could spot a bad client – and this group? It had 'bad bet' written all over it. This was a mistake, she thought grimly. She should have trusted her instincts. She had refused when there was a single voice chattering in vagaries. With five now, it was farcical.

Four, a little voice in her head corrected. She frowned, thinking back. Yes. *Four* voices. One had not spoken. One had remained silent through all the meandering conversation and the ensuing cacophony. She turned. Even now he stood silent and sombre, surveying the scene. His charred hands clasped at his waist. Watching. Or… waiting?

She glanced at Zephon over the jabbering fandango, distressed. He returned her look with one of sad agreement. Understanding the futility she felt, clearly. Deborah considered standing and walking out. Leaving these clucking hens to their pointless sermonising. But she couldn't. The memory of Zephon's scars came back to her. The grotesque twist of flesh and the suffering it conveyed. Try as she might, she could not wholly detach from this endeavour. Her revulsion had been real. Whatever else she felt, she still desired to avenge such suffering. It was her catalyst. And the silent figure, Raguel? He might be her key.

She glanced to him and back to Zephon, questioning with her eyes. Comprehension swept across Zephon's face and he gave a slight but perceptible nod. Conciliatory.

Deborah stood. There was no hiatus in the din, no acknowledgement of her movement at all. These ancient brothers were consumed entirely with each other. She stepped forward gingerly, approaching Raguel. He turned and gazed down at her. She reached out and took his charred hand, lifted it and clasped it between hers.

"Is it even possible?" she asked quietly.

He stood what seemed a long time, his black gaze on her.

"Yes," he replied in a voice like a distant, rumbling flame. "But you will hurt."

The chatter around her continued unabated.

"I've hurt before."

"Not like this." His voice was like a dormant volcano.

"Is it worth it?" she asked.

He smiled softly. "Oh yes."

She stood a moment longer.

"Then help me," she told him.

Raguel said nothing for a moment, then nodded his head once, slowly. He glanced back at the chair she had occupied.

Taking his cue, she stepped back to it, though this time she stood. Something was about to happen. Something which, she had a hunch, she would not want to be seated for. She looked back to Raguel and watched in awe as he pulled in a breath. As he did, he seemed to grow, in size and in splendor. The change was hard to define, but impossible to ignore. It was as if the room around him shrunk and lost contrast, its energy drawn. Focussed into him. With an almighty explosion he bellowed.

"*BROTHERS!*"

The walls shook. The floor flexed. Timber bookshelves arched and groaned in the shockwave and long undisturbed dust clouded all around them. All conversation ended in an instant and four heads whipped around to look his way. Two others bowed. Deborah noticed, with some amusement, that both Zephon and Zotiel's mouths peeled in poorly suppressed smiles. They must have put up with this shit a lot, she thought. Poor fuckers must have been bored to frustration more times than they could count.

Raguel tempered the flame of his voice, but maintained his enhanced stature for a moment. Addressing his now attentive brethren, he added: "We have spent long years searching for our Assassin. Perhaps we should hear what *she* has to say?"

Deborah fought to hide her own puckish smile. She did not succeed.

⁂

"The way I see it, we can't have a plan." Deborah addressed Cassiel primarily. Prior to the earlier conversation's descent into asininity, he had seemed both the wisest and the most direct. If she could keep him focussed and uninterrupted, she might actually make some progress.

"Nothing concrete. There are too many variables. Besides, I have a hunch that part of the reason you approached me is that you already know that. Right? Because of this… All-Mind."

Cassiel took his time, scrutinising her. For a moment, Deborah worried that the others would take this lull as a cue to jump in, to reignite the cacophony, but none did. They remained, for now at least, dutifully silent.

"There is danger inherent in our knowledge, yes. We can shield our thoughts. We can shield them well, as you can imagine – we have *had* to. Being here, far from Heaven, makes it easier. But yes. Danger exists. The All-Mind is pervasive."

"There's a chance one of you could be compromised. Reveal details. Without intention." Deborah framed this as statement, not query. She wished to provide no opportunity to return to a free-for-all. She was determined to ask nothing but direct, simple questions from now on.

"A chance," Cassiel conceded.

Good, she thought. Not the content of his answer of course, that was hardly good news, but he answered plainly. That, at least, was welcome.

"So we can't have a detailed plan. Okay. That actually works out just fine – for another reason." She focussed closely on his pale features as she continued.

"You *can't*."

There. There it was. These Archangels - they seemed inscrutable, but they were not infallible. They *did* have tells. There were minute twitches, subtle clues in their facial movements. They could be read. Not as easily as people, but they could be read, and on Cassiel's face was written one thing. Shame.

"That's what I thought. You *need* a human. Because you worry about your ability to keep secrets? Sure. Because you know that a human assassin will be unanticipated? Probably. But it's more than that, isn't it? I need you to say it."

Cassiel stared back at her with his nothing-stare, but it would do him no good. Deborah had tuned into his facial language now. He was humbled. She could see it.

"Yes," he relented.

"It's because you *can't* do it. You've tried – for decades, I expect. You've come up with nothing."

"That's not entirely true."

"How so?"

"We came up with *you*."

Deborah paused a moment as she tried to figure out if he was being churlish. It didn't appear so. He truly believed that was progress. Maybe it was.

"No plan will *ever* make sense anyway. The job is too... vast. That doesn't mean we know nothing though. We know what the key will be. The one ability I have that you don't. Everything I've seen and everything I've been told about you points to one weakness. I suspect you know what it is too..."

The group watched her expectantly. The room fell silent, as if holding its breath. Then with a rumble, the answer came.

"Predictability."

Deborah turned to Raguel.

"Right." She smiled in thanks. He remained stoic, but returned a slow nod.

"You came to a human because free-will makes us what you aren't. Unpredictable. We can improvise. You can't, right? Not easily?"

They stood in affirmative silence.

"To tackle a hit so incredible, we *need* to be unpredictable. We need to be impulsive, we need to be... whatever the proper term is. There's no angle you could come up with that your 'Office' will not have considered and guarded against. We can't think our way to victory, not from here. To succeed, we need to be reckless, rash and erratic. We need to be foolhardy. We need to be *planless*."

Cassiel and the others stared back at her.

"Those are negative qualities..." he stated.

"How are your positive ones working out for you?"

He cast his eyes to the floor in answer.

"Without a plan – *especially* when there's no plan – a team needs to be assembled. We're..." she corrected herself, "*I'm* going to need people."

"Yes," Cassiel replied. "This was considered."

"This thing will take time. It will involve a hell of a journey from what I understand. Hard work and extreme danger."

Cassiel nodded, along with the others.

"So I need people. For a start, I'm going to need a..."

She paused. How would she frame her request? Which words fit? In her real life – her *old* life – she would have said a soldier. A commando. One of the ex-special forces guys, ex-PMC maybe. Or one of those old Soviet-Block tactical guys The Orchard would use on occasion. Sitting in *this* room though? That was not the world these beings understood.

"A warrior," she said. The word fell from her lips almost involuntarily. Upon hearing it aloud it seemed all at once ridiculous and entirely correct. A warrior. A warrior was what she needed.

"Yes," Cassiel nodded in approval.

Well, Deborah thought to herself. You're speaking their language now. Hope you're happy girl. 'Cause that sounds an awful lot like acceptance.

"I'll need someone who knows medicine too. Someone who can keep us alive, or whatever alive is where we're going. We can still be injured here, so I assume the same goes there?" Deborah recalled the scrape she had sustained on her hand when she first arrived. It had bled.

"Yes."

"Injury means the possibility of death… I assume we can die too?"

"Indeed."

"So what happens? We can't go up… do we come back here?"

Cassiel's face turned sour as he shook it.

"There are multiple exits to this forsaken place, but there is but one entrance. Purgatory is a land built on penance for *Earthly* sin. To commit sins of this nature in Paradise… there is no atonement."

"The only way is south?" Deborah asked rhetorically.

"*All* the way south," Raziel answered. It was the first time he had spoken since Raguel's outburst. Deborah, noticing the way the others turned to him, hid a smile. She might be beginning to talk the way they talked, but apparently her manner was rubbing off on them too. That answer didn't sound like something they would say. It sounded like something *she* would say.

"A healer," Cassiel confirmed.

"Right. A healer. And we'll need someone with game. A tactician. Someone who can help strategise on the fly."

"That is not your role?" Yahoel asked.

"What are you, the union rep?" His brow furrowed as her knee-jerk sarcasm fell flat on the dusty floor.

"I worked with a partner, in a world I understood. I need someone who thinks differently than I do. Someone I can work with. Who can consider the long game, while I deal with the immediate."

"All of these can be found," Cassiel replied.

"I'm not done. The City - it's filled with, what are for all intents and purposes, humans? Right?"

"Primarily, yes."

"Then I need someone with a good slight-of-hand. Someone who can talk their way out of a tight spot. A con-artist."

"This was anticipated."

"Okay. Lastly, I'm going to need someone that knows the City. The area beyond too. Who knows the rules of the place. We'll be learning as we go."

"My footmen can help," Raziel said, gesturing to Zotiel and Zephon.

"No," Deborah replied flatly. An injured look crossed Zephon's face. "I'm sorry," she told him, truthfully. "I'll need you guys for sure – to get us out of The Purgs and on our way. But that's it. You can't come with us."

"She is correct," Cassiel told the pair. "The guide has to be a human soul. Someone already blessed. Someone unimpeachable, who can walk the streets with other human souls, head held high. Free of suspicion."

"Right," Deborah confirmed.

Cassiel remained in contemplative silence a while. Finally he turned his void-eyes to her once more and spoke with a rhythmic cadence.

"A Warrior, a Healer, a Mage, a Rogue, a Guide."

Deborah almost laughed. Why not? A bullet had punched through her heart and she had woken in a hospital room with a sleeping cancer patient for a bed-mate. She had stepped through a door made of nothing into a city made of decay and filled with the shuffling, insane dead. She had drunk yellow vials of God's own

Word, had descended into Victorian London by way of an Irish theme pub and stood in the subterranean sanctuary of rebel Archangels. Now she was going to Heaven to kill a concept. So, what the hell? She'd use their antiquated, Dungeon-and-Dragon's-ass parlance. If the shoe fits? Wear the fucking thing.

"And an Assassin," she added.

Cassiel nodded.

"We will convene and consult."

Deborah held up a finger for a moment, drawing his attention back. "Before you do, I have one final question. Kind of a big one."

Cassiel waited expectantly as she mustered herself. Bracing, though against what she wasn't quite sure.

"Hasn't this been tried before?"

The air in the room became thick, stifling.

"You already said it, I think. I'm no theologian, but even I know what Morning Star means."

The dead silence was unbroken a long time.

"This is not the same," Cassiel said finally.

"Maybe so, but my question is... would *he* say that? Would *he* say it was different?"

"We cannot presume to know."

Bullshit, thought Deborah.

"You knew him, right? He was one of you? Once upon a time?" *In a galaxy far far away*, she almost added, but this time suppressed her ingrained desire to puncture solemnity with sarcasm.

"He was a Seraph. High council. Of the First Sphere."

Deborah frowned. "So, he was... enslaved? Part of the All-Mind? How did he..."

"There was no All-Mind. Not then. His rebellion… The All-Mind is but one of the curses it birthed."

"The All-Mind was created in response?"

Cassiel nodded. "A safeguard, to prevent…"

"Another revolution," Deborah sighed. "To prevent *us*."

Cassiel squinted in consideration. "In a manner of speaking. It was created to prevent the rebellion of those powerful enough to be perceived as a threat. The high Spheres."

"By your God. The True God?"

Seeing where she was going, Cassiel spoke up.

"The All-Mind was not always an enslaving force. At one time it was merely a steadying hand. A loving caress. The malevolence of The Office is insidious though. The tools of God remain, but the spirit is warped. Bastardised and weaponised." He paused.

"It is immaterial to us. We are too… small. Too inconsequential. Little interest is paid to our sphere. We are not threat enough for continual oversight."

"That's what you're counting on?"

Cassiel tilted his head and smiled.

"Yes."

She nodded again.

"And so? What would He say about your plan? The D… The Morning Star?"

"Before, you mean? Before his fall?"

"Okay… sure. Before." She would allow him that much skirting, for now. Cassiel waited long enough that she began to wonder if he would answer at all. Was he considering, or simply trying to wait her out? When he did finally offer some response, it was in a soft, small voice.

"I... don't know what he would *say*... but I think the Revolution might have two leaders."

She nodded.

"And now? After the fall?"

Cassiel answered in a bleak whisper.

"Who could know the mind of Lucifer now? Whatever remains of it."

Deborah opened her mouth, then closed it. She knew this was no answer, but for the first time she chose not to press further. On this particular subject – on this *one* – she would settle for the riddles. In part because she could see the terrible strain the topic instilled on her hosts, but there was another reason. In her heart, she knew she didn't really want an answer. One-time atheist or not, she was afraid of what it might be.

Instead she would heed her own advice. Reckless was the only way to do this. With grim irony, she recalled the phrase that had eluded her. Devil-may-care. They would need to be devil-may-care. She stifled a cheerless grunt. How apt.

Looking straight into Cassiel's black eyes, she spoke with resolve.

"Do your convening. Do your consulting. Don't take too long," she told him. Turning to the group she added; "We've got work to do."

The Archangels stared back at her, deep in sombre thought. Raguel nodded once, slowly, with solemn approval. His black-ash fists were clenched, but the sides of his mouth had curled in the ghost of a grim smile. A war smile.

Fracture Six

JOB

The financial district of Glasgow was an almost perfectly even amalgam of the old and the new. For every shiny, mirrored-glass tower protruding like an incisor, there was a historic, renovated tenement squatting like a sandstone molar below.

Deborah had gleaned little detail from Mr Rust's grainy photograph, but the trim of the window it showed had been stone. No mirrored glass there. The polyurethane frames and venetian blinds stood in contrast to black-stained terracotta - the pollution of old industry and new traffic on sandstone.

Standing now, at the side of the building, rain beating down from a black sky above, she eyed that same window. The right blinds, the right frame, the right pattern in the soot-stains. No light from within.

The rain was good. At this time of year 9pm might as well have been midnight, and foot traffic on this side of town was sparse. The hum of vibrant nightlife rumbled in the distance – the collective bassline of a hundred clubs and pubs – but here, the buzz of street lamps and the static crackle of rain on pavement was their only music. That, and Mr Rust of course. In their ears.

Three days prior, their parley concluded, he had dropped them off, several blocks from their brokedown palace above the Gomorrah. After taking such pains to demonstrate that he knew exactly where they laid their heads at night it had seemed a perfunctory gesture. Perhaps a nod to politeness – paying some token towards their, apparently fruitless, attempts at secrecy – but Deborah hadn't thought so. To her it felt more like a power play. Making them walk the last distance to further assert his authority. To make it plain he was in control. It hadn't mattered either way. The damage had been done the moment he had lent voice to his knowledge. Their private world had crumbled as they sat in that limousine. Their home was no longer a home. It was just the squat they slept in. Their hiding spot from the world was now nothing but a creaky, abandoned floor above a shitty nightclub.

The days since had fumbled by, both she and Mark in a kind of glum trance. Sleepwalking through the motions of their lives in a state of suspended fear, awaiting Rust's promised phone call. Nothing had tasted or sounded or looked right. Nothing felt good.

Life wasn't life, it was all just paper cut-outs and dust. They drifted through the time, numb. Waiting.

Finally the call had come. The hummingbird buzz of the cheap prepaid phone a sinister siren. They had been given an address. Nothing else. Upon arriving, Mr Rust, alone, had ushered them inside, where he provided them with the new tools of their trade. The little metal beans were oddly heavy. Deborah had thought they would feel strange, or would be hard to keep secure, but, placing one in her ear, she found it sat snug. Perfectly comfortable. The lipstick cameras were another thing. Once secured at her temple the headband fit fine, but was difficult to ignore. It felt like a tension headache imposed from without. To accompany the one growing within.

Rust had spoken softly. *Testing. Testing. One-two. One-two.* Like he was about to break into a fucking song, Deborah had thought. He had ensured he could see what they saw, hear what they heard. Then, all preparations made, a second address had been given. A street Mark knew vaguely – in the financial district. Now they stood in the pouring rain. Below a familiar window.

"*That's the one*," Rust's voice said, cold and detached.

"So now what?" Mark asked.

"*For fuck's sake kid, if I was planning on telling you exactly how to do this, I'd just do it myself.*" Rust's disdain was cutting.

"My people took care of the alarms. The rest is up to you two."

"Alright. Fuck you, Mr Mystery," Mark replied sullenly.

Deborah paid no mind. She was busy. Scanning the building's face, she tried to establish how many separate offices there were. Three rows of windows. Four floors including the ground. The main entrance up a set of steps, flanked by stone trellising, next to which an electronic entry buzzer sported two labelled buttons. The lower showed a logo and the words 'WALKEN DESIGNS LTD'; above, another, stating 'SWINTON LEGAL' in plain text. So at least two of the floors would likely have their own internal stairs, she calculated.

There were three side windows stacked above the alley. Third, second and first floor. None at ground level. These were different though. The frames were dark – painted wood. Not like the double glazed plastic at the front. Those were the key. Those were the weak point.

She indicated the lowest of the three to Mark, keeping quiet. She wasn't entirely comfortable with her new friend in her ear, though it hardly mattered. He was watching too. He saw what she saw. Mark looked up and nodded in comprehension. She glanced up and down the dark street. Not a soul. No one braving the weather. Mark stepped deeper into the darkness of the alley, and she heard a metallic creak. When he returned, he was pulling a large rubbish container. In an instant she flashed back – to the first day they met. Her standing lost and suspicious in the waste-grounds behind the Gomorrah, him pulling their makeshift step to the fire escape. That had been the end of a terrible chapter in her life – a time she had been more than happy to leave heaped in that trash container below her. She could not escape the feeling that this was the end of another. She wondered, with creeping sadness, what she might be leaving behind in this one.

The container wobbled and bumped across the slippery cobbles until he brought it to a still beneath the window. She hopped up nimbly – a move well practiced these past six months – and rested her hands on the base of the frame, steadying herself neatly.

"I need the thing," she told Mark.

He fished out the small crowbar from his backpack and handed it to her. More camping supplies. That shop in the gallery – it may have been handy for the outdoorsman, but it was a godsend for the street-lifer and the petty criminal.

Jamming the curled end under the old frame was easy, and pushing down against the leverage offered by the stone sill took little effort. A dull crunch of splintering wood, the ping of the latch straining, then relenting, and the frame was free to slide with ease. No alarm. Rust had not been lying about that at least.

As she slid the window open, Mark hopped up beside her, retrieved the crowbar and placed his hands around her hips. At her nod, he lifted, holding her steady as she swung a leg inside. He didn't really need to. Deborah knew she could have climbed, and suspected he knew that too. But he liked to help her – to be gallant in his way – and she liked to let him. He *was* gallant in his way. He was gallant in a lot of ways. She slipped inside.

⁂

Deborah wasn't sure of the specific business of 'Walken Designs Limited', but it apparently involved meetings. As she had stepped through the open window, she had felt the wooden floor oddly high, mere inches from the base of the sill. There was a strange electronic device on the floor in front of her feet. A squat, three legged dome with a red light, blinking at her. For a horrible moment she had thought it some kind of security – infrared beams or some form of sound based detection. Whatever the management of Walken Designs required to protect their valuable work. As her eyes adjusted to the gloom and comprehension dawned, she let out a slow sigh of relief. She stood on a large conference table, sturdy and polished. The device sat central. In white lettering, she could only just make out the text. 'VOICESTATION 500 CONFERENCE CALLER'.

She hopped down, pausing as Mark slid the window down behind him and followed her. With amusement, she watched as he made the same error she had. His reaction was the same, beat for beat. As he hopped down beside her, he indicated the speakerphone with a nod and mimed an exaggerated *'whew'*. Deborah pressed a hand to her lips, suppressing a giggle. The tension lifted an inch.

They made their way through the maze of the office. The meeting room was one of only a few solid-walled sections, but the main floor was partitioned off in a network of blue, felt screens, forming a lattice of workspaces. Each cubicle sported a chair and a computer on a desk, every one adorned with papers and drawings and trinkets. And photographs.

Smiling couples and bouncing babies. Children grinning through messy fingers. Fish that, Deborah assumed, must be bigger than other fish, held aloft by proud fisherman. Sports-days and holidays and birthdays. Real life. For some reason now, more than ever before, the contrast between that oh-so-photogenic world and the cold, clandestine one she occupied, made her ache.

Across the expanse of the office, there was a door. Heavy wood and thick frosted glass, leading to what must at one point have been the main stairwell, in the building's residential days. In front of this though, newer than the rest of the structure and cut in at an angle, ran a narrow metal stairway protruding up through the ceiling. Following it revealed the second floor, much the same as the first, but that was as far as it ran. Pity, Deborah thought. That meant the next ascent would be by way of lock and key. Walken Designs Limited must be a good concern; they had the first three floors of the building. Poor old Swinton Legal just had the one. They were about to lose a prized document from their files too. Some folks just couldn't catch a break.

"*Main stairwell.*"

Mr Rust's voice was as measured as before. He sounded almost bored over the earpiece, though, having spoken with him in person, Deborah knew better than to believe that. What sounded like disinterest was the same calculating cadence she remembered from the limousine. It was not lethargy, but malevolent objectivism that stilted his words.

"We know," Mark replied, keenly mirroring his tone.

Deborah might have grinned at this earlier, but her pulse was beginning to quicken. Adrenaline pumped around her body, heightening sense and diminishing emotion.

Mark knelt at the door and slung the backpack from his shoulder. From a side pocket, he produced his set of silversmith screwdrivers and the nail-file he used as a turnkey. Deborah had seen him employ this skill before. It predated her entry into his life. It wasn't one he required often any more – the jobs they pulled together were predicated more on slight of hand than skill of touch – but he had kept it sharp. The lock was a simple one, a single cylinder deadbolt. After the few lessons Mark had given, she was pretty confident she could pick it herself, but he would be faster.

As he hunched, one little flathead working the lock, a second on hand and the nail-file clenched in his teeth, a beam of light streaked behind the glass. Instinctively, Deborah dropped to the floor. Mark ducked his head with a panicked look in his eyes. The light intensified slowly, sweeping the shadows across the office. It peaked, then whipped to one side and disappeared.

Deborah felt her heart pound against her ribcage.

"*What was that?*" asked Rust, sounding almost interested.

"Nothing. A car turning. The front door's glass too," Deborah replied, as calmly as she could, forcing the tension from her voice. As much for Mark as for Rust.

"Chrithst" breathed Mark quietly, the screwdriver still clenched in his teeth. He had not stalled his progress an inch. He really is fucking good at this, she thought, smirking with affectionate pride.

With a *click,* the lock admitted defeat, and Mark pulled the door. Deborah stepped through ahead of him, into a concrete close beyond. A glance down through the well of the spiral stairway revealed only more gloom. It had just been headlights, animating the shadows for a moment as they swept past, leaving the dark to settle once more in their wake. Mark followed her, clutching his implements of trespass in a fist as they crept their way up. Every footfall echoed, try as they might to suppress them. Their attempts at silence slowed their progress considerably. Deborah's chest was pounding hard, her pulse loud in her ears. She wondered if it might echo too. Reverberate right into the earpiece and through the invisible radio waves. Right into Rust's head. Through his ears, behind his dead eyes and into his empty heart.

Upon reaching the top floor, they were met with a new door. The same construction, the same design. The same lock as below. The whole building must have been renovated at the same time, she thought with relief. Mark's handiwork was quicker this time round. The lock clearly understood. Realised that Mark had already bested its brother downstairs and accepted the fruitlessness of resistance. It clicked open softly, granting passage.

Inside, the offices of Swinton Legal were significantly more old fashioned than the open-plan layout of their downstairs neighbours. Beyond the door, a hallway ran the length of the building, doors lining either side at regular intervals. No nameplates. Just numbers. That struck Deborah as odd, but then again, what did she know? The place didn't seem particularly conducive to entertaining clients. This was more likely a place of pure business. The meetings happened elsewhere. Maybe the only people coming and going to these offices were the occupants themselves. They already knew their names.

"*Three oh-three*," Rust stated.

Deborah gave a thumbs up in front of the camera. She didn't want to speak out loud. If she had, in that moment, been asked to explain why, she wasn't sure she would have had an answer. At least, an answer beyond 'it just felt right.' It *did* feel right. It felt right because it felt like they were being watched. Of course they *were* being watched, she thought. Rust was watching them, or rather watching them watching other things. But this was something more. This floor just felt… occupied.

Padding quietly down the hall, she passed 301 on her left, then 302 on her right. As she closed in on 303, Mark strode up to her side. Was he feeling it too? This haunting feeling? Or was she merely projecting her nerves onto his actions? They turned in unison to face the door, and Mark nodded to her as he reached for the knob. She nodded back and he opened the door, letting her pass in front of him. Ever the gentleman, she thought. It was the last unfrenzied thought she had.

As the door swung open Deborah found herself face to face with a man sat at a desk. He stared back at her. A pen fell from his hand to the desk as he raised his hands in a meek surrender, his features ghoulish in the green light of a desk lamp.

She might have recognised his balding head and bushy eyebrows then. She might have identified him as the man from Rust's photograph. Possibly. Thinking back on that moment with hindsight, the specifics would elude her. What she would remember was the look in his eyes. It was a look she would come to be familiar with, but this was the first time, and it was awful. The look of dreadful expectancy. The look of gallows fear.

"I'm dealing with it, I'm dealing with it!" he cried. The pitch of his voice danced erratically. Deborah snapped her head around. Mark stood, dumbfounded, beside her. He clearly didn't know whether to turn and run or stay and address the man's ramblings.

"*That's your target.*" Mr Rust's voice was filled with sudden, violent urgency. "*Kill him.*"

"What!?" Mark blurted, staring stricken at the hapless businessman.

"I'm dealing with it I said! You don't have to do this!" he screeched.

"*This guy might be a trapped rat now, but in a moment he's going to realise you don't know what the fuck you're doing. He'll call the cops. Or worse, he'll fight back."* Rust's serpentine hiss accelerated to an unnerving tempo.

"You two better decide what you're doing. Quickly. Deal with this business or deal with your incarceration. The decision is yours."

"This wasn't the deal!" Mark yelled.

"What?!" The man's face flustered in confusion.

"The decision is yours, but if you're caught I can ensure all the charges are brought against both of you. Not just the ones they know about. Not just the breaking and entering and the shoplifting and the con games you play – that dive you live in is full of briefcases, you think I don't know about that? Not to mention…"

Deborah, rooted to the spot as this frantic exchange played out around her, watched the businessman's demeanour slowly change. His dread remained, but the immediacy of his panic seemed to subside somewhat, making room for confusion.

"Wait… What the fuck are you, *children*? Who…? Who are you?" As the seconds ticked by, his wits were gathering.

"They sent fucking *children*!?"

From where she stood, Deborah could see him fumbling at the drawer of his desk. Mark can't see, she thought with rising alarm. Mark can't see what he's doing. The fucking lamp's in the way. Staring in his eyes she realised – he was counting on that. He didn't care what *she* saw. He cared what *Mark* saw. Mark was the threat, in his eyes.

"Not to mention your particular crimes Mr Greene," Rust's voice continued unabated, filled with menace now.

"Statutory rape is a serious crime kid. Who knows when you'll get out. You know what they do to rapists inside?"

Deborah strode forward.

"Shut the fuck up!" she heard Mark yell, but it was muted now, along with the rest of the world. Like she was listening underwater. The only clear sound was the impossibly sharp, *clack, clack, clack* of her footsteps on the polished wooden floor. The office dropped to slow motion, a bubble enveloping the three of them.

Clack.

The man stared at Mark, his panic shifting, giving way to animalistic survival.

Clack.

Mark's wide eyes flicked around in chaotic anxiety. The pandemonium in his mind had rooted him to the spot. Indecision like glue on his feet.

Clack.

She approached the desk. The man, noticing her, began to turn. His hand still fished in the desk drawer. She saw now the object he sought – visible beneath a stack of clean white envelopes. A wooden stock. The grip of a revolver. She saw it all. The whole room. Clear and pristine. The bubble they inhabited was crystallising, slowing time to a tectonic crawl.

Clack.

As he turned towards her she watched him hook a shaky finger in the trigger guard and begin to draw the gun from the drawer. She reached a hand out towards the desk.

Clack.

She would do this. She would do this for Mark, to protect him. She would do it for herself. For them both. To keep the dream alive. She thought of their plans, she thought of apartments. She thought of picking out curtains. She grabbed the fountain pen as he turned his head fully to face her. With slow, dreamy clarity, she came to a horrible realisation. She wasn't going to make it. He had the drop. She might be fast, but he was faster. This was it.

Clack.

The man's face contorted. His attention pulled down in dismay. The hammer and butt had caught, jammed against the lip of the drawer and the desk top. Deborah inhaled.

With a tunnel-visioned whoosh, the world burst back to full speed and she plunged the pen deep into the side of his neck. Warm red gushed from him, spurting across her face, the coppery taste immediate and visceral as it sprayed across clenched teeth. He spun violently in his chair, relinquishing his grip on the revolver and groping instead at her blood-soaked hands. Deborah wrapped her free arm around his head, flipping her body around to his back as she pulled the pen out, and plunged it back in. Out and back in. Out and back in. Again and again and again.

Every bit of anger in her, that had *ever* been in her, channelled into this one moment. Into this one man. Every disaster that had befallen her, from the greatest to the most mundane, came flooding through her. Every cut and scrape and stab and slash that had brought down her chance at a normal life. At a *photogenic* life. For her mere fifteen years on this earth, there was a remarkable well to draw from.

He was Gregor, the monster who had tried to rape her. He was Aunt Trisha, the stupid, oblivious bitch that had permitted it. He was Elspeth, the dumb, hippy social worker with her 'emotional wellbeing' bullshit and her fucking scarves. He was Officer Dickhead, the smart-ass turnkey, making fun of her en route to the holding cells. He was the cancer that had claimed her mother. He was that sad, stupid fuck Mr Carmichael, with his shitty garage that had taken her father, and he was the car that had crushed him too.

He was Mikey fucking Porter.

The blood flew.

His groping withered to meek flopping of arms and sporadic convulsing. Warm blood spurted over and over with each downward stab, and, beneath her gripping arm, a sodden patch was oozing down his shirt. A red-black puddle of life, spilling out of him, soaking them both. A stink began to rise through the metallic, bloody haze as his limp body surrendered the content of his bowels, leaking piss and shit through his cotton trousers and onto the leather chair.

The stress and terror of the whole affair culminated within her, releasing all at once. The rush was as bizarre and unfamiliar as it was euphoric. Sensual. Sexual. A frightful orgasm of fury, topping the tension that had begun its slow build as they slipped from the rain and into the office below. Deborah felt like a god. Immortal. Not a bringer of death, but Death himself. She felt *alive*.

She stood embracing the former businessman and current corpse for what was probably seconds, but might as well have been years. She breathed a long slow breath as the tingling wave, the rapture, made its course through her body and earthed itself in the floor below. She shuddered. Then she saw Mark's face.

He stood, slack-jawed and wide-eyed, staring at her. Not at the corpse, not at the pen. Just at her. At her eyes. She was cold now, silent. Dark maroon had soaked through her sweater and run down into the crevices of her waistband. The sticky taste of blood coated her teeth, causing her mouth to over-salivate as she panted. She stared back at him and hated that look. She had never seen him horrified. She had never really seen anyone horrified; not at her, anyway. That look was more than just revulsion at the brutality he had witnessed. It was not just shock. It was re-evaluation. His image of her, his knowledge of her, it was reshaping before her eyes.

Realisation dawned, as the red mist faded, leaving only her, Mark and the leaking sack of meat slumped in the chair. She was never going to get the dream back. Her future with Mark had ended before it had even begun. He was never going to be able to see her the way he once had, all those thousands of years ago, before they entered this room. The sinking dismay that filled her was enough to drive every other thought from her head. All thoughts but one. All but her second realisation of this night - the one that burned in her mind like magnesium flame. That she was *good* at this.

"What... the..." Mark stammered, then drifted back to silence.

"*Good job.*"

Rust's voice was low and measured once more.

"Head back out the way you came. Don't leave any more mess. There will be a car waiting at the corner."

"What…" Mark stammered a little more, then shook his head, trying to regain some semblance of composure. His stare was fixed on Deborah.

"What about your document?" he asked meekly.

"*What document?*" asked Mr Rust.

Chapter Seven

SWORD

Deborah had trouble with the passage of time in The Purgs. It didn't appear to follow the rules. Perhaps it was the endless, starless night that plagued this place, perhaps something more. She suspected something more. She suspected that time, like every other living thing here, existed in suspended lethargy. It passed as it cared to pass, no longer bound to its steady schedule.

By her estimation, it had been around a week that she had waited in the odd little room above Shepherds Bar, though without the need for food, the desire for sleep or the rising and setting of a sun, the passage of time was rather academic. The only metronome she had was the ebb and flow of the hunger within her, sated periodically by the yellow vials of the Word provided by the barman, Augustine. Around every two days, she thought.

She had tried to sleep – often in fact – not out of requirement but out of simple boredom, but never was able. Exhaustion beckoned, but rest never came. The long hours of wakefulness did, however, give rise to some kind of bizarre dreams. Daydreams of sorts. Images of grand, white towers and flat, green plains, wheels of eyes and beams of light pursuing her across them. The visions were as vivid as any dream she had ever had, but, upon snapping back to reality, they faded quickly, leaving nothing but a sense of foreboding.

Cassiel had told her that the Archangels of the Revolution would convene and discuss her requirements, and convene and discuss they had. Long and hard and animated their deliberations had been, continuing long after Zephon and Zotiel had been tasked with showing her to her room and seeing her situated in it. Deborah had considered refusing, on insisting she be present for all of the discussion; she would be the one leading this team after all. In the end though, she had concluded that there was little to gain from her presence. The Archangels could do the legwork. Let them bring her the people she needed. In the end, she would have the final word on their inclusion. Besides, she thought, this was no different to how The Orchard operated. She had never had any choice in her accomplices in life. Why change things in death? So she had followed the boys upstairs.

The room above the bar was strange only in its lack of strangeness. In this abnormal place, normalcy was bizarre. The whole upper floor of Shepherds had the look of a cheap bed and breakfast in some parochial town.

The room was a loft-space, accessed via a pull-down ladder from below. The ceiling sloped at either side, with a single small, circular window high at the apex of the eaves of the roof. A wooden bed, made up, though apparently unused, sat central and a small table with two wooden stools squatted at the window end. An old fashioned standard lamp stood in one corner and a bookshelf at the other – devoid of literature save for a single, leather-bound text. Deborah had laughed aloud when she read the gold-on-red text at its foot, under a familiar amphora symbol. 'PLACED BY THE GIDEONS.' She couldn't tell if it was a joke for her benefit, or a joke at all.

She had spent quite a bit of time attempting to read through it. Despite her current situational understanding of certain parts, she found it difficult still. Where in the past her atheism had prevented any serious appreciation of the subject matter, now rudimentary knowledge was her barrier. Before, it had been an account of a land she thought she'd never visit; now it was a travellers' guide to a country she lived in, written by someone who had been relayed the information second hand. She had gone from too detached to too involved overnight. In the end, she elected not to consult it at all. Better to be unprepared than ill-prepared. Better to expect the unexpected than to expect the specific and have that confounded.

Instead she had spent the week with her thoughts, occasionally venturing down into the bar itself, when boredom or anxious anticipation became burdensome. When she did, she was fully aware of the glances cast her way, but she had been assured by Cassiel – and by the boys – that no one with malicious intent towards her or their cause would be found within these walls. Certainly no one of consequence. Any curiosity was simply the result of *what* she was, not *who* she was. Human souls were rarely permitted entry. So, on occasion, she would sit at the bar and play with Augustine, on a little wooden chessboard he kept behind the bar. She would lose most matches, and the few she won she suspected he had thrown – keeping her coming back for more, most likely. But who cared? At least it let her flex her mind against the atrophying boredom. The challenge was welcome. It had become rare enough over her life as her skills were honed.

Augustine had been human. Well, he still was, she supposed. He had been born in Thagase, Numidia – which, he had informed her, was now somewhere around Algeria – sometime in the fourth century. He couldn't quite remember the year. He had been a bishop, though when he had mentioned this he had been quick to point how little it meant little back then.

"A bishop indeed," he had said, chuckling through cigarette ash as he took a pawn with his rook.

"Sure, I wrote a few things about the church and what have you, and could speak a little. But really being a publican now and a Bishop then are about the same deal. Mostly all I did was brew beer and get my congregation rat-arsed. It's no wonder they sainted me. Checkmate."

He was likely being modest. Something about the way the old man carried himself betrayed a past of some status, though what did it matter? He was here now. The way he had said 'rat-arsed' had made her smile. His accent wasn't Irish - wasn't anything really – but the colloquialisms of his clientele had rubbed off on him over the years. The accents of the lower Angels that frequented the bar certainly gave rise to questions, but when she had enquired about them to Auggie, his answers had been vague.

"Got to sound like something, I suppose. Maybe they sound Irish. Maybe Irish sounds like them?"

So the days and nights and nights and days crawled by. Nothing but waiting and playing and reading and thinking. And waiting.

※

After possibly-a-week had passed – four yellow vials and counting – she was beginning to feel stir crazy. The knock at the underside of the floor-shutter door of her room, followed by the *creak-jolt* of the ladder being pulled, was a welcome relief from the dreary silence.

Zotiel poked his head up through the floor and glanced around the room. Upon locking eyes with her, he grinned an exaggerated smile. The sight of his beaming face, down at her feet, was comical.

"Well, the grown ups have picked out a few candidates for your band of merry men," he told her.

"About time," Deborah remarked as she stood from the bed. "Where are they?"

"Still out and about m'love. Zeph and I'll take you to meet them now. Grab yer things." Deborah looked around for a moment, then turned back to him with a cocked eyebrow.

"What things?"

"Oh, em, well. Yes. Just an expression I suppose. Won't you join us m'dear?" He beamed again.

Deborah rolled her eyes and, with a smirk, she headed for the ladder.

⁜

"Your sword'll be first," Zephon told her.

Zotiel walked a little ahead, leading the way as he had before, but this time Zephon walked side by side with her. They had been walking for some time now, but were still within the dank, victorian sections of The old Purgs. The starless dark remained above, the endless, joyless proletariat below.

"My sword?" she asked.

"Your Warrior." Zephon smiled a little at her as he said it. "That was smart calling him that. With the Archs. Using our words, I mean."

Zotiel was quiet. He was consulting what looked to be a moleskin notebook. He held it in his hand, reading as he walked.

"Well, sure. It felt right. I hope it doesn't mean I'm going to be meeting some old-school knight in a suit of armour though. Or a samurai or something? I'm not much good in Japanese." She spoke with a playful cynicism, but around a serious point. For all the international work Deborah had undertaken, languages had never been her strong suit. A little French, some Spanish for sure and she could just about make her way around German, but that was about it.

"They know what you meant," Zephon replied. "They're long-winded and they don't have much of a sense of urgency – eternity'll do that to you – but they aren't stupid. They picked you. They can pick others."

"They didn't exactly pick me though did they?" she asked, a little less play in her cynicism now. "I mean, they *did*, but like your boss said – how many people who fit the bill died at the right time? I'm guessing they had a pretty shallow pool to draw from."

Zephon paused, as if readying to address this, but was interrupted as Zotiel stopped in his tracks, forcing them to do likewise. He glanced back and forth and down at the moleskin, before beckoning Zephon forward to consult.

Deborah watched as they conferred, looking periodically from the moleskin to the thoroughfare ahead. Deborah stood a moment as their hushed discussion bounced back and forth, watching the milling souls pass this way and that. As Zotiel flipped a page of the notes and directed Zephon's attention to something ahead, her curiosity rose. She stepped forward to his back and glanced over his shoulder at the moleskin. She frowned, confused. The page was white.

"What are you looking at? It's blank…" She trailed off in amazement. The page on the right was blank. The page on the left was *partially* blank, but less so with each passing moment. A scrawl of cursive was filling in lines of script as she watched, handwritten by an invisible pen in a unseen hand.

> '...walked across the street, towards the diner. He looked around, feeling someone was watching him...'

Zephon caught her eye as she looked up and nodded across the street. A large man in a gloomy trench-coat and battered trilby had slowed his pace and was glancing around distractedly, his eyes narrowed a little. She glanced back down at the moleskin, which Zotiel held out now for her to view. The script continued writing itself silently.

> '...but seeing no one of interest, he scowled a little and continued, passing through the entrance...'

She glanced back up in time to watch the back of the trench-coat disappear through a swinging plywood door erected beneath a stone arch across the street. Above it, a poorly hand-painted sign read 'SALLY'S DINER'. She looked back up at Zotiel with fascinated inquiry.

"I told you, m'dear – we have our ways of finding people."

"That's a hell of a thing," she said, staring at the little book. It seemed so innocuous. "It writes the future?" Zotiel smiled.

"It writes the *present*. Nothing writes the *future*. Not for you crazy kids. Nothing but yourselves."

"Free will…" she said, nodding slowly. He nodded back.

"Mostly we can't use scrolls for any of our less *official* business, but we have a few like this one. Unconnected to the All-Mind. A gift from the Scribes. Useful tools around here, for sure."

"The Scribes?"

"Raziel was one, back in the day. These were made by Nuckey though. He was one of you actually, a long time ago. Weird guy, but he knows his way around a pen. And he knows Raz from way back. They've been through some shit together over the years. We can trust these."

Deborah considered pressing further, but thought better of it. Most of the time when she did seek further answers, the questions just kept piling up, and history lessons were not a priority right now. She needed to focus. She chose instead to nod and move on.

"So that's our guy?"

"Seems to be. Name's Raymond," Zotiel replied. He closed the moleskin – the 'scroll' as he had called it – and tucked it into the pocket of his jeans.

"Does he know who we are?"

"Nope."

"Best go introduce ourselves," Zephon added. He stepped towards Sally's with Zotiel in tow.

"Let's," replied Deborah, to no one in particular. She followed a few steps behind.

Sally's Diner was a bizarre sight indeed. An attempted recreation of a nineteen-fifties American grill, cobbled together from bric-a-brac and discarded materials. As if a skip had been emptied by talented children playing at restaurant. An L-shaped bar, pieced together from irregular sections of timber and plywood, was lined with stools of varying heights, fashioned from upturned cable spools and lengths of metal bars. A couple of booths around each side were crafted from some kind of boardwalk stall timbers, with occasional gaps, filled with seats that clearly belonged in cars or trucks. There was an area at the back where a kitchen would be in a real diner, but behind the open window there appeared instead to be some kind of chemical operations going on. Stills and pipes the predominant feature. It had the look of a meth-lab, or some kind of pharmaceutical processing plant. The acrid smell that filled the whole establishment emanated from back there.

Various patrons sat or perched around the place. There were a few glasses, some empty, some full, but no sign of food. That did not surprise Deborah in the slightest. Since her first timid steps in The Purgs, she had felt no desire to eat. Now, after however long she had been here – a fortnight or so she estimated – the oddness of her lack of appetite had abated.

Turning to Zephon she asked, "Why a diner? No one needs food here, do they?"

"Nah," he replied. "It's not to sate hunger. Not the hunger for food anyway. They make the Word back there." He nodded to the back.

"Synthetic stuff. Shit, but it keeps people fixed for a while."

"But a diner?"

"Sates a different appetite I guess. The appetite for normal."

Deborah nodded, understanding, if only academically. She could imagine the need people would have for something – anything – that approximated their prior reality. The satisfaction they would get from experiencing some facsimile of real life. She had, after all, sought the same thing her whole earthly life.

She walked ahead of her companions and headed towards the counter, leaving them to wait by the entrance. This she would do on her own. The trench-coated man sat on a stool with his back to her, conversing with a woman behind the counter.

"...Would have been around eighty-two or eighty-three. Probably female. Definitely young," he was telling her, with a gruff voice. A dull, all-American drawl. The voice of a cop if Deborah had ever heard one. She slid on to a stool beside his, resting her elbows on the uneven counter.

"Nope," replied the woman behind the counter. The eponymous Sally, Deborah assumed. She spoke with the same sad, lost air so common to her ear now. "I doubt I'd remember anyway. Now, you want a hit or not?"

The man, with a look of resigned deflation, reached into the breast pocket of a tattered waistcoat beneath his trench-coat and pulled out a stack of crumpled papers in an old fashioned money-clip. He removed one and dropped it on the counter. "Yeah, gimme one. And a bourbon if you got any."

Probably-Sally picked up the scrap, examined it scrupulously then looked back up to him.

"We got some," she told him, stepping away to disappear into the back.

The man fished in his trench pocket and produced a cigarette box, unbranded just like Zephon's, and a brass lighter. He lit up.

"Looking for someone?" Deborah turned her head towards him as she spoke.

"Yeah Blondie, I'm looking for someone," he sighed, exhaling smoke. He didn't turn to meet her gaze.

He was older than Deborah had expected. She didn't really know what she had expected, but he was older than it. In his fifties at least, and while his frame was powerful, he did not appear to be in great shape. Beneath the trench-coat he wore a beaten three-piece, complete with black suspender braces which bulged a little round his broad chest and broader gut. An old fashioned shoulder holster was strapped around his waistcoat, and she recognised with ease the source of the bump in his coat. A revolver stock. His build did little to hide it. A bruiser's build. Tough, but portly. His face was thick and his features petrous, but, behind the obvious despondency, his eyes held a glint Deborah recognised. An unerring steeliness. Drive.

"What you going to do when you find them?" she asked, pulling out a cigarette of her own. She had a lighter – Augustine had furnished her with one – but she left it in her pocket. Instead she turned to him.

"Arrest them? You must have a hell of a jurisdiction…"

He turned. Seeing her cigarette, he retrieved his lighter once more and offered the flame.

"It's not like that, kid. I just want to talk to them."

"Oh yeah? Why?" She drew in a drag – the first was the best, of course – and adopted her most approachable demeanor. Not sultry, not exactly sexy, but if coquettishness was required it wouldn't be too far out of reach. He paused as he returned the lighter to his pocket.

"You ever hear of the Rag Man killer?" he inquired with the light, offhand tone common to detectives. Standard issue. It came with the badge and the gun.

"No," she replied, honestly. He nodded, glum and unsurprised.

"Didn't think so. Depends when you snuffed it I suppose. And where. He was hardly Charlie Manson, but he was a big deal in the Frisco papers for a while. That's what *they* called him. The Rag Man."

He took a few quiet drags, looking around for an ashtray. Not finding one, he flicked ash on the counter. He eyed her up and down. Most likely sizing up whether she was worth making the effort to converse with. His conclusion was self-evident, as he continued.

"He killed a couple dozen folks up and down the Bay. In Frisco itself, San Jose, Palo Alto, up through San Mateo. Probably further. Street girls mostly. Couple of street boys here and there too. Used to leave them in sewer outlets and drainage ditches, their… *parts* all cut up. Scraps of their underwear shoved in their throats – so far down we were fishing threads outta their lungs sometimes. Nasty stuff. Saved bits of their clothes…"

"No, I never heard." She was attentive, but kept her responses to a minimum. Keeping him talking. Letting him tell his story his way.

"This was the late seventies, into the eighties. I worked the case for years. Chased that fucking guy all over the Bay. All over Oakland."

Deborah watched Eponymous Sally return from the back, carrying a little vial of snot-coloured sludge in one hand and a grimy glass and an unlabeled bottle in the other. Placing them down, she swept ash off the counter as she poured a decent measure into the glass. With an admonishing pout at Raymond she placed a tin coffee mug from beneath the bar as an ashtray.

Raymond nodded his thanks and picked up the vial, downing it neatly. Turning to the bourbon, he swirled it around in the glass and staring vacantly into its amber ripples. When Sally turned and looked to Deborah, poised to ask her for her pleasure, Deborah shook her head. She shrugged and pottered away once more.

"How'd you know it was a man?" Deborah asked.

"How's that?" Raymond asked distractedly as he surveyed the liquor.

"Your Rag Man. How'd you know it wasn't a Rag Woman?" She watched as he turned to face her.

"Because I found him." The glint she had observed in his eye glimmered a little. He gulped half the whisky in a swig.

"It cost me four and a half years, a marriage, a couple shots at promotion and Christ knows how many chewing outs from the chief, but I found him. I *had* him. Chased him all across this old waste ground near Fort Baker. To an old church up there. That's where he was living, you see. Had him bang to rights. Gun trained, cuffs ready." His tone was turning more and more wistful as he spoke, and here it drifted away into nothing.

"And?" she asked, gentle but coaxing. He downed the rest of the bourbon.

"Fucked it up. Too happy I had him. Didn't see what he had behind his back. Smashed my head in good with a brick. Grinned and giggled like a fucking harlequin the whole time." He sighed, shaking his head. "Now here I am."

Deborah sat for a moment, letting him have his silence. After what she judged an appropriate time, she spoke again, softly still.

"So you're still looking for him now? Here?"

"Ha," he grunted with a grimace.

"This place is hardly what I'd call Heaven – who fucking knows what's going on around here? – but I do know… it isn't Hell. After what I saw of his work, or his pleasure, or whatever it was for him, I know for sure this isn't where he went. He'd have had a straight shot, all south. Or will, anyway. Who knows if he's still living or not."

"So who are you looking for here?" she asked with curiosity. Part real, part pantomime, for his benefit.

"Like I said, he killed a lot of folks. Probably a lot more than I knew about. Probably a lot more after I fu… After I blew my chance." He tinkered with the empty glass, his gaze falling anywhere but back at her.

"Spent a long time looking for them now. They just keep on adding up."

"Why though? Why look for them?" He met her gaze, his eyes deep, dark wells in his granite face. His doleful expression sombre and genuine, as if the answer was obvious.

"To apologise. I owe them that."

She stared back at him, humbled by his answer. That was not what she had expected. Everything about his demeanour had led her to imagine him as a man of pure business – of vengeance and of action. A man who lived in the shadows of emotional reticence and moral ambiguity. This sense of simple, *moral* justice was not a trait his look betrayed. Zephon was right. The Archangels may have their flaws, but they were not stupid. They had an eye for the traits that mattered.

"You want to help them."

"I *failed* to help them," he replied grimly. "I just want them to *know*."

"So they can hate you?"

"Maybe Blondie, maybe," he conceded.

She paused, tapping ash into the tin mug.

"You were a victim too."

"They were victims of him. I was a victim of myself. I deserved what I got. They didn't."

Deborah thought about this as she stubbed her cigarette, dropping the butt into the cup with a *fizz* as the ember hit the residue within. She turned to catch the attention of Zotiel and Zephon at the door and cocked her head, indicating they join her.

"You want to help them? Really help them? Help everyone here?"

Raymond deposited the remains of his cigarette into the mug, and reached into his pocket to retrieve another.

"Hmm?" he asked with a humourless smile. "This place is *all* fucked up. I doubt anyone's helping this lot. What you got?"

Deborah slid one of the cards with 'SHEPHERDS' written on it and the little hand-drawn map on the back that Augustine had given her.

"Come and see us. There's something we're going to do. To help a lot of people. Something you'd be good at, I think. I have a hunch it's something you'll want to be a part of, Raymond."

At the mention of his name he animated, jolting his head around with a taken-aback grimace. Seeing Zotiel and Zephon now flanking her, his expression morphed into uneasy curiosity.

"Who are you Blondie? How do you know me?" His eyes were narrow. She smiled, inscrutably, but with as much warmth as she deemed appropriate.

"I don't. Not yet. But this thing we're going to do together? I expect we'll come to know each other pretty well by the end of it." She was carefully, scrupulously enigmatic. Keeping some mystery. She knew what the strongest play was here. Want to rope in a detective? Be a riddle he wants to solve.

"And what *is* this thing you think we're going to do?" he asked skeptically.

"Fix reality."

"Ha!" He laughed, but as his eyes flicked furtively across Zephon's then Zotiel's faces, seeing both remain stoic and solemn, his smile faded to stoney confusion once more. He frowned.

"How the hell are you gonna do that kid? You look like a damn candy striper."

Deborah stood.

"And you look like Al Capone. But we're not all just what we look like." She turned and headed for the exit flanked by the boys.

"Come and find us Raymond," she called back. "You're a man who believes in justice."

"So?" he asked loudly across the room.

"So we're going to deliver some."

Chapter Eight

POULTICE

Lena watched numbly from the bench as another rectangular nothing folded outwards from itself, depositing yet another timid soul into the open space across the way. The same lost look. The same childlike vulnerability. The same fear. Sitting on the bench, surrounded by the insane mishmash of steel and timber and scaffold and cages, the network of hellish construction – that was all she did now.

The first few years she had tried to help them. She tried to explain where they were – as much as she knew anyway – and to offer some kind of comfort. The futility of that, the insignificance of her help in the face of the crushing, unrelenting wave of their arrival was not what had stopped her. Lena had experience of that.

Most of her career had been spent in the accident and emergency wards of the Royal London Hospital. The 'pointy end' of the nursing profession, Dawn had always called it.

"You should think about a move to something less stressful auntie Leenie," she would tell her most every Christmas at Harold's, as they stuffed the bird and glazed the little strips of carrot and parsnip. "Lord knows you've paid your dues."

Lena would smile and reply that yes, maybe she'd think about it. It was a lie, but it was a white one. Lena knew she could do the job Dawn did. Dawn was a district health visitor. Technically it fell under midwifery, but whatever they called it, it took a full nursing qualification, and Dawn loved it. The bond with the children in her charge and their families, even the problem ones – it obviously brought her tremendous joy, and Lena had never wanted to diminish that. But the 'pointy end' was where she belonged. It took a certain type of person, she knew, a rarified breed even within the nursing community, to survive shift work in an emergency ward, and an even more rarified breed to thrive there. To find the little pockets of happiness in it.

Lena had always known she couldn't – wouldn't – transfer. Up sticks and leave it to the younger girls? No. She had liked to be where she could be the most help, even if at times it could feel futile. What she had never been able to adequately convey to Dawn was that while shifts might come and go where you felt you were just pushing against the tide, the people who you shielded against it – even with your rickety little umbrella –

saving them from a small amount of their pain was noble. Even if it only helped for a moment. It *mattered*. Regardless of the final outcome. And once in a while? Once in a while you could pull one back. Back from the brink. And nothing she could find in the less 'pointy' end felt quite like that.

It wasn't the endlessness of their arrival that had stopped her from approaching the lost souls. It was her inability. In her life she had had the bedside manner, and that was half the job on a good day and nine-tenths on a bad, but she also had the abilities. The tools to back it up. Here? Without a hospital and the doctors and the equipment and the girls? Here she was just a civilian. The terror in the neophytes' longing pleads for help – help she couldn't provide – every one was a sharp little cut. Each a little deeper than the last, building and building until the centre could no longer hold. Until you shattered completely, she had realised. Until their anguish, compounding, adding to yours, little by little, crushed your spirit completely. Until you were nothing but *their* sorrow, crystallised. So she sat and watched.

No one ever seemed to sit at her side. There was room for two on the bench, but somehow she had claimed it all to herself. Just her and the unending hunger. Back in her living days, on mornings after a night shift, when the chaos of the ward had buzzed in her head so loud that she had known that it would not yet allow her exhaustion to translate into sleep, she had often walked round to the little patch of green down Castlemain street. Vallance Gardens, it was called. Not much of a garden really - just a patch of grass with a couple of trees. Only a minute or so from the main entrance to the hospital, but somehow a million miles away. She would sit on one of the benches to gather herself. People had often come and sat at her side then. Not *with* her, but beside her. While she wouldn't often engage them unless they did so first, and they rarely did, the simple companionship of strangers had soothed the clang and clatter of the ward.

The clang and clatter of The Purgs, was a different chaos entirely. There was no Vallance Gardens to retreat to here and no end to the eternal night shift, but still she ached for the hum of another heartbeat at her side. An old gent on a constitutional, or a young mother watching her child mill around the grassy space. One of the old dears that would scatter crusts for the pigeons. Someone.

How many years had it been now since she emerged, frightful and pained, from her own nothingness across the way? Ten? Twenty? A thousand? She could never tell time anymore. It was funny, back when she was alive she had run her whole life by the ticking of the clock. A nurse always does, she supposed. Now, with no sense of it, time seemed to have taken its leave of her. No more need for you Leenie. You just hang around this bench. See you in a while. Maybe.

She watched as this newest soul stared around fearfully, and counted the beats as his fright turned to terror, terror to anguish, anguish to despair. After seeing it so often, the metamorphosis was as predictable as it was miserable. Another new inhabitant of this endless night. Another meek voice in the dark.

As he stared around, in hope of an answer to his awful predicament, his eyes flicked down to lock with hers. Their hopeful plead cut her anew, another fresh little slice in her soul. She lowered her head, averting her eyes. The Purgs were a tube train. No eye contact. Every time she did this she hated herself a little more, but it was the only way. She would drown in their sadness if she allowed it to flow into hers. There was little air left in this vessel as it was.

She maintained her self loathing stare at the ground for as long as she judged it would take for the poor kid to accept that she was no use to him, and lifted her head once more. Sure enough, he had turned and wandered a little down the way, off on the first steps of his own damnation. Someone else had arrived though. Someone at her side. Someone had sat on the bench. A heartbeat.

∽⌇∾

"Hello," the girl said.

"I…" Lena's voice cracked a little. How long had it been since she used it? It was rusty, in need of some practice. "Hello," she replied, gathering herself as best she could.

The girl was young, in her twenties Lena judged, a waify, white girl with blonde hair and a strange look about her. Innocuous, but deliberately so.

"Are you Caroline?" she asked with naive curiosity. Lena was stunned. Had anyone ever known her name here? Had anyone ever asked it?

"I..." She didn't know how to respond. Who was this little white girl?

"It's okay if you don't want to tell me." The girl was coaxing, Lena could tell, but not being pushy about it. Not making a show of it.

"I'm... It's Lena. Yes, I mean, I'm Caroline, but people call me Lena. *Called* me Lena."

The girl extended a milky white hand to her, and Lena looked down at it. It had been a very long time since she had had any course to recall the little courtesies of polite interaction. The girl's hand was smooth, though Lena's nurse's eye immediately noted the old scars on the inside of her fingers. Burns, not well treated. She took the girl's hand in hers and shook a limp greeting.

"I'm Deborah," the girl told her.

"Nice... Nice to meet you Deborah." The girl smiled and glanced forward.

"What are you watching Lena?" she asked. Innocently, but there was something behind it. Lena couldn't quite put her finger on what it was about this girl, but there was something. Something besides her forwardness and apparent credulity. Not exactly sinister, but... knowing, maybe? More informed than she let on?

"Just... Nothing." Lena sighed. What was the point? Soon enough a new poor soul would appear and tell the story for her, and besides, she didn't really have the words.

"Just watching them come and go?" the girl asked, helping her out.

"Something like that."

The girl, Deborah, nodded at this and glanced around the open area they sat in.

"You sit here a lot?" Still innocent, still guileless. Still harbouring some undercurrent Lena couldn't place. It hardly mattered though. Simply having someone – any heartbeat – at her side was enough to make this moment a little more liveable than the last.

"Quite a lot, yes." An understatement of course, Lena thought grimly, but if she told the truth – that she had sat here most of the past twenty-odd years as the cuts got deeper and deeper and deeper – she was certain she'd scare this little girl away. Or... maybe not? her unconscious replied. Maybe she'd understand completely. Who could tell with this one? What *was* it about this girl?

"Why here? Here specifically I mean?"

Lena stared out at the spot where the nothing would open.

"This is where I arrived." The girl Deborah nodded thoughtfully, but remained silent. Lena wondered if this silence was left for her to fill, or just in the absence of anything useful to say, but she filled it anyway.

"I think it has some kind of connection. To where I... Well, you know."

"To where you died?"

Lena's turn to nod now.

"How did you? If you don't mind me asking?" The girl's precociousness was still evident, but the innocence was beginning to slip. Lena was starting to figure out what was so unusual about this Deborah. She didn't seem lost. She seemed like she had purpose. It was an odd thing to see in this place, and especially odd in a young, white girl. They often seemed the most susceptible to the miserable malaise of The Purgs. The most easily broken by it.

"Nothing exciting really," Lena lamented. "I was late, it was icy, and in a fight between a Volkswagen Golf and an eighteen wheeler, the Golf will lose every time. Right outside the hospital where I worked."

"The Royal," Deborah confirmed. Lena furrowed her brow in curiosity as she turned to look into the girl's eyes. She did not turn to meet her. She just sat gazing out at the space ahead, as Lena had for so many years now.

"Yes, The Royal, how…?"

"I know a little bit about you Lena."

"How? *Why*?"

"How is pretty immaterial, though you'll find out eventually I expect. But *why*? That's the more interesting question."

Lena sat expectantly, waiting for her to elaborate, but instead the girl switched gears, seeming for the moment more content to discuss the past than the future.

"So the souls who arrive here – they come from your hospital?"

Lena thought for a moment about forcing the discussion back to her question, but instead decided simply to let the conversation go where it would go. There would be time, she hoped, to get back to that, but for the moment why not enjoy some kind of back-and-forth? It had been so long.

"I think so, mostly. I don't talk to them really any more, but I think so."

As she spoke, a new rip sliced the air thirty yards or so ahead of them, birthing a new lost soul into their sight. A young woman, dressed in motorcycle leathers. She still clung to a helmet and her tousled, brunette hair was plastered awkwardly across her brow and face. Matted, as if glued by some invisible, caked blood. Her eyes were wide with confusion and fear. Lena fixed her Novocain stare on the middle distance between them and her.

"Seems young," Deborah commented. "She didn't go from old age. You were on a trauma ward?"

"Accident and Emergency," Lena replied dolefully. "All ages. All sizes, all shapes. All broken up for the most part."

"Tough work."

"It was, but it was what I did." Lena could feel familiar disgust rising in her throat at the sound of her own voice. The miserable meekness of it. Back in the day she would have had harsh words for any colleague or intern, or any patient's family member who spoke in such disconsolate tones around her wards. But that was then. That was when she had a purpose and a place.

"You never fancied an easier path?" Deborah enquired. Lena felt a pang of painful nostalgia stab at her chest. Her eyes almost welled up. Deborah cocked her head in sympathetic curiosity.

"You sound like my niece. She used to ask the same thing. Used to try to get me to take it easy."

"She didn't like that you were a nurse?"

"She *was* a nurse, a community nurse. She didn't like that I was stressed is all."

"But you weren't stressed." Deborah was matter-of-fact. Lena smiled a little. This little white girl had some insight, that was for sure.

"No. I mean, yes, of course, everyone on the wards is, but I liked it."

"You liked to help. Regardless of the stress."

"It was my job," she replied firmly.

"You could have taken a different job though. Lots of jobs help people. It was more than that. It was your calling." Deborah was taking a shot, Lena could tell. Building to something, though she couldn't tell what.

"Yes. Yes I suppose that's a good way to put it." Lena smiled a little again. A thin spectre of a smile at best, but it was something. She couldn't remember when she had smiled last. Her facial muscles felt foreign in the configuration.

Deborah cast a long, slow glance around, surveying the monstrosities of construction all around. The hideous chaos of it seemed not to bother her, Lena noted. She was not new to this place. Or at least, didn't act like she was. She appeared unfazed by it all.

"How long have you been here?" she asked.

"Not long," Deborah replied, with an airiness clearly designed to steer the conversation away from her and back to Lena.

"It must be hard," Deborah said. "Having worked on the ward, helping people. To see them all coming here now?"

"I…" Lena didn't really know how to reply to this. Of course it was hard. It was a nightmare! All these people, all these people in the *worst* need. In the *hardest* times, and she, she who was supposed to help, who was trained to help, who had a *calling* to help, unable to do a damn thing!? What the fuck did she think!?

She wanted to raise her voice, to show her anger, her pain, but she couldn't. She worried that if she did, if she opened that particular floodgate, it wouldn't be a shout. It would be a shriek. All the awful years of helplessness and horror and pain and fear and useless self-loathing would burst out of her. She would be unable to stop. Instead she said nothing. But her eyes had flashed. Just for a second, but the smart little girl had noticed. A barely perceptible smile had drawn across her face.

"I know it must have been," she said, but her understanding sounded hollow to Lena now, without context for her smile. Had it been a smirk? Was this just some new cruelty to add to this place?

"Why are you asking me that? To hurt me? Who are you?" In her attempts to keep her emotions from exploding, her voice sounded small, childlike.

"I told you Lena. My name is Deborah. And I'm not trying to be cruel."

"So what do you want from me?" Lena struggled not to sound defeated, to retain her composure, though confusion scuppered her attempts.

"I want you to help me. *Us*, I should say. And by helping us you can help all of them." Deborah gestured out towards the empty space ahead.

Lena was having trouble. Every time she thought she had found a handle on this conversation, it turned out to be nothing but smoke.

"What? How?"

"There's a group of us, we're going to be doing something. It will involve a lot of travel, a lot of danger, and I suspect some broken bones along the way. We need someone who knows how to help us – keep us alive. Keep us moving. Someone who knows about medicine. Someone who knows about," Deborah paused for a moment. Lena wondered if it was simply to find the word, or maybe, she thought cynically, for effect. For punctuation. "*Trauma.*"

"You need a field nurse?" she asked, frowning. "For what? What are you doing?"

"Fixing reality." She replied with a comically matter-of-fact tone.

Lena slumped. This girl was obviously crazy. A different crazy from the rest, sure, a subtler crazy, but crazy nonetheless. Disappointment bled through her. She felt every old cut return.

"Reality is on the other side of those doors, honey. This place is not reality, and it's not fixable."

"You're wrong," the girl replied, earnest but still with the knowing glint in her eye. That glint. That glint was all that kept Lena talking. There *was* something about her. Something in that glint.

"And even if you're not – you want to try anyway Lena. You were never meant to sit by. You were never meant to watch people suffer."

Lena stared out vacantly, and as she did, another slice peeled the air across from their bench. A little hand folded out from the empty air clasping at the thick wedge of nothing as it swung open into the makeshift square. Behind it, a little boy stepped gingerly out of the air wearing a green hospital gown with red rocket ships patterned on it. His saucer eyes were pools of desperate timidity. Seeing his new surroundings he stared a moment, panicked, then bolted away across the thoroughfare and out of sight, his gait a limping, fearful zigzag.

The kids. Seeing the kids arrive, those were the deepest cuts. The cuts that never scabbed. Warm tears filled Lena's eyes. She felt one teeter on the rim then roll down her cheek. Deborah watched the boy with a sad horror also, and turned to her.

"Not the first kid you've seen arrive I suppose?" Lena sniffed and wiped the miserable tear from her cheek, shaking her head.

"What if I told you we had a shot at making it the last?"

Lena was not stupid. She knew manipulation when she heard it, and this was textbook. But the cuts ran so very deep now. So very deep, and there was no end she could fathom. Doing nothing was killing her slowly – doing nothing when there was nothing she could do. To do nothing when there was a chance that she could? If there was a chance this little white girl was for real? That would kill her a lot faster.

"What would I need to do?"

Deborah fished something from her pocket and pushed it into Lena's accepting hands, clenching them with her own.

"Just come and see us. Come and talk to us."

Lena stared into her eyes, trying to discern if it was madness or purpose that lay within them. She couldn't tell. Pulling her hands free of Deborah's, she examined the contents. A white business card, with 'SHEPHERDS' written on it, and on the back, a hand-drawn map.

"I… I don't know where this is," she told her meekly. This was all getting too much.

"Just look for it," Deborah replied, smiling genuinely. "Keep the card on you. It will guide the way."

Lena looked down at the card with undisguised skepticism. It seemed like a regular business card to her.

"What?" she stammered. "How?"

The girl, Deborah, stood and turned back to her.

"What am I, a magician?" She smiled again, "I don't know *how* it works, I just know that it *does*."

She turned away from Lena and walked around the bench behind her. Lena stared at the card in her hand a little longer, questions pulsing through her mind, all half-formed and wanting. She turned, leaning back, and saw, for the first time, Deborah standing. Tall and striking, flanked by two tall, male companions, silent, in jeans and white shirts. She stood resolute. Lena saw it now. The glint in her eye was not madness. It *was* purpose.

She looked back down at the card, up to the nexus point where the air birthed the new souls, then back to the card. Okay, she thought. Okay little white girl. She began to feel something within. A feeling she had not felt in a very long time – long enough that it took some time to identify. Hope, maybe. After having her own soul cut up all these years, maybe dealing with someone else's cuts would numb the pain.

"You got something in those baby blues, I'll give you that," she sighed. Deborah stared back at her, deliberate and steadfast, though Lena could detect just a hint of a satisfaction in there too. At the edges. Then she turned, leading her companions away from the bench and towards the alley behind.

"Where are you going?" Lena called after her. Deborah turned, still pacing backwards between her companions, and drew a canny grin.

"To find a magician."

Chapter Nine

GAMBIT

"You think she'll come then m'love?"

Zotiel walked at Deborah's back, behind her left shoulder. Zephon at her right. He had waited a good long time before speaking, ensuring they were far from the nurse's earshot.

"She will," Deborah replied. "She can't pass up the opportunity. She's given up on helping those people, but she wants to help *someone*."

"That's good then. Your band of heroes is filling out," he replied tepidly. Deborah slowed, allowing her chaperones to fall in line with her stride. The hint of pugnacity in Zotiel's voice had not escaped her notice. She was going to have to address the subject sooner or later, so, with a sigh, she elected for sooner.

"It's not like I don't trust you guys." They slowed to a saunter then stopped as the boys came around to the drift of the conversation.

"You think I prefer going into this thing blind? Giving up the only two people I know who both *do* know the terrain and *don't* make me want to punch their pompous teeth down their necks just to shut them the fuck up?"

Zephon grinned a little, boyish once more. Not terribly often did his apparent age diverge far from Zotiel's, but now he looked a clear ten years his junior.

"This is the only way this thing can work. You can't kill a leader with soldiers. Not secretly anyway, and if you had the numbers for a war you wouldn't need me." They looked defensive, poised to interject, but she continued.

"The one to kill a leader is the bellhop. The shoeshiner. The old woman who winds his clocks or the old man who delivers his morning paper. That's the ideal – close but invisible. If you can't swing that, though? If you can't have both close *and* unseen? Then unseen is the better choice. You go with a stranger. Have the blade come from somewhere unexpected."

"No one is unseen by The Office," Zephon objected sullenly.

"Maybe so, but we know for sure it's suspicious of you. You only need to look at those awful fucking scars on your backs. And besides, the more people who know the plan, the less secret it'll stay. That goes double when the people involved have... allegiances. Honest or otherwise.

"That's not gut feeling. It's fact. Von Stauffenberg *failed* to kill Hitler. Their plan was close, but not unseen. The blade was suspicious and the allegiances were muddled. Kennedy? Lincoln? Ghandi? All killed by lone outsiders. A conspiracy of one. No leaks. Invisible to their targets.

"You two are a part of the Office regime. I know you can hide it - like Cassiel talked about, shield your thoughts from the All-Mind – but that's a dangerous thing to rely on. Especially on their turf. He said as much himself: *'being far from Heaven makes it easier.'* Secrets are easy to keep in the shadows. In the home of your enemy? It's a whole different game. You want to watch this thing fail? Or worse, you want it to *almost* succeed? You want to be the Black Hand? The powder keg that *starts* a war?"

She could see the drawn look in her companions' eyes and hated it, but the wound was exposed now. Better to rip the bandage off clean and fast than peel away gently and drag this out for longer.

"The gunpowder plot failed because of the warning letter sent to Monteagle. A letter designed to save him alone. I believe you two can be trusted, but the All-Mind... You are connected to it right?" Zephon hesitated, then nodded in wilting resignation.

"So you're not completely in charge of your... mail. You could send the letter – accidentally. All it would take is your desire to help someone, *anyone,* within the regime." She turned to Zephon.

"All your kind still serve The Office. That's what you told me, right? I'm sure there are... brothers of yours, deep within it? Ones you would save if you could? What if shit goes bad and it comes down to them or us? Can you be certain – one hundred percent, cast-iron fucking *certain* – that under that kind of stress your shield would hold?"

Zephon opened his mouth, then closed it again and lowered his head. He would not meet her gaze.

"That's what I thought," she sighed. Her regret was deepened by their refusal to lie. That they would not deny their fallibility was the deepest cut of all. She nodded sadly. "We can't risk it."

The boys looked glum. Either she had convinced them, or they accepted that she would not be swayed; either way they argued no further.

"I'll be grateful to you two forever. And I'll do this thing – this crazy fucking thing – as much *for you* as for anyone."

Zephon stood a little taller at this, adopting a quiet pride in his stance. Deborah reached a hand out and very gently touched the ripple of white material at the top of his shoulder. Feeling the mound, the twist in the flesh where his scar began. He held his posture, steady and defiant.

"But I can't do it *with you*." She kept her face sombre. There could be no argument. She couldn't let them know it was a lie. A lie in part at least. She'd like to be doing this for them. For everyone. For the greater good. On some level, maybe she was.

"Who's next on the list?" she asked.

Zotiel smiled with resignation. He pulled a moleskin from his hip pocket and consulted it dutifully.

"Just one more for us. Guy called Whitman Czapski. Bit of a walk yet m'love."

A bit of a walk had been a decided understatement. From Shepherds to Sally's Diner had been a bit of a walk. From there to the odd little square where she had sat with Lena, that had taken a couple of hours. The march to what Zotiel and Zephon referred to as the Quarters, though? That must have been ten hours at least. Ten hours of trudging the endless haphazard constructs and ruins, this way and that, past what must have been tens of thousands of lost souls.

The monotony had remained unbroken, save once. As they passed through a wider, more populated thoroughfare, Zotiel had stopped dead in his tracks and engaged Zephon in a hushed tête-à-tête. Zephon had glanced ahead and then back to Deborah, and told her, with an imperative hiss, to hang her head and follow them.

"Look meek," he had whispered as they walked. Deborah had not immediately understood the reason – though her companions' urgency was enough to solicit her compliance – but as they had passed through the crowd, she realised the source of their consternation. Approaching from the opposite direction, their paths bisecting, were three other figures. A mirror of their own triangular formation. Two stood tall, either side, dressed in simple jeans and shirts like her fellow conspirators. Following behind was a downtrodden, hopeful looking man in a tattered shopkeeper's apron. Old-fashioned, like one would see in old black and white stills of war-rationing times.

As they had approached, Zotiel had nodded to the two tall men in acknowledgement. As they returned the greeting, Deborah had noticed the familiar ridges in their shirts. After seeing the scars on Zephon's back, she found it impossible not to notice them.

"Purah. Dagiel," Zotiel had greeted them. Not warm exactly, but familiar.

"Greetings Zotiel," one had answered. Deborah thought it was the one Zotiel had addressed as Purah.

"Who you got?" Maybe-Purah had asked nonchalantly.

"Just some girl. Not many details. You know how it is. Headed for the checkpoints. You?"

"Yeah, some guy. I forget."

"Never ends does it?" Zotiel had smiled dully, but kept the small talk vague. Shutting it down as neatly as he could.

"True that, Brother. True that."

The mirror trio had passed without incident, but not before Deborah had noted the sighs of relief from her companions. All done in a matter of seconds, but it had served as a stark reminder of how careful the revolution had to be. Of how careful *she* had to be. Living in and around Shepherds this past fortnight had been a dangerous seduction. The false sense of safety it whispered was sweet poison. Within that hive of clandestine affairs, her presence was disguised. Out here she was exposed. Better get used to that, she had thought with grim portent. That was but a taste of what would come.

Some six or so hours later, the boys led her to a wide open space. It was flanked at their rear by the ubiquitous spires of steel and timber, but, in front, a high, naval-looking structure stood. Stretching high into the blackness above, a tower, built in steps like an Aztec pyramid, fashioned from steel tankers. Ships on top of ships on top of ships – some upturned, some right-side-up, some on their sides, but all rotting and rusting and dead. Little alteration had been made to the vessels themselves, save for their bizarre placement, and only very modest additional construction to the whole. At first it seemed the ships had been piled and discarded without rhyme or reason, but, on closer inspection, there was a kind of system to it. Interconnecting routes through the open port doors and round the metal platforms and gratings had been erected. Even from the outside she could see – the maze of doors and platforms was a complicated and chaotic mess, but there was some byzantine order.

"This is it," Zotiel stated, looking up at the tower. "The Quarters."

Deborah stared up at its demented facade.

"The Quarters. As in living quarters?"

"As in gambling quarters," Zephon corrected.

Gambling for what? Deborah almost asked, then thought better of it. Who cared? Gambling always existed, everywhere you went, and generally was most prevalent in places where the people had nothing. The answer to that most obvious question was, itself, obvious: For whatever they can.

"Our 'magician', he's in here then?" she asked instead. Pulling the moleskin from his pocket once more, Zotiel consulted it.

"He hasn't left here for a very long time."

Deborah nodded. They headed for the closest of the numerous ground-floor port-doors ahead.

※

Inside, the Quarters was as much of a maze as Deborah had expected, though the variance in decor surprised her. The first few floors were nothing but rusted steel and flaking ancient paint, grated passages and narrow, steep stairwells. As they made their winding way through and up the levels though, the distinctions between the different ships became apparent. From the military, riveted form of the lower areas, they passed through several more civilian looking, ferry-like sections. Industrial still, utilitarian, but with some of the trappings of comfort one would expect from a well used leisure vessel. Through and through, up and up they wound, passing little huddles of figures engaged in muted conversations or some kind of bartering, and, more and more as they ascended through the levels of the tower, around little table games.

Cards mostly, dice, and some others Deborah didn't recognise. Further up the tower, passing through the upside-down world of what was once a container ship, upturned and listing to one side, weaving this way and that around light fixtures and ventilation housings on the once-ceiling and current floor, she had begun to notice the separation of game types into areas. Cards over there, mah-jong tile games here, some kind of board game with coloured stones on a square board that she did not recognise, seemingly played exclusively by men in very old fashioned garb, over yonder.

As they traversed the strange, nautical-themed scrapyard, she began to wonder if this was all heading to some great casino ship. She had images, formed by experience in her own world, of the grand gambling hall of a cruise liner. A chandelier-riddled, red carpeted, gold trimmed space, filled with felt tables of all shapes and sizes. People of all colours and creeds sipping champagne and nattering with jovial unconcern for the world outside. Nonsense in The Purgs of course, she knew that, but she at least expected whatever the miserable, hollow facsimile of that would be.

Instead, Zotiel and Zephon led her through a few tight passages and into a large room, more dimly lit than the others. A galley of some sort. Military. Soviet, if Deborah had to guess, though no text or markings remained. Long rows of fixed metal tables ran like rails along its middle, flanked by little round stools riveted to the floor, like pallbearers carrying the tables to their final rest. The room was far from fully occupied, but a few dozen pairs of figures were dotted sporadically along the lengths. Always in pairs, always facing each other. Between each couple sat a wooden chess board in some state of disrepair, and each figure hunched over it in contemplation.

Deborah turned to Zotiel, and whispered.

"So which one is it?" She took pains not to disturb the echoey quiet of the mess hall. The stillness of deep concentration. Library quiet.

"I don't know," Zotiel replied pragmatically.

"What? What about your little book there? The…" she lent towards haughtiness in her whispery strain to recall the word. "The *Scroll*. What does it say?"

Zotiel looked up at her with amused insouciance.

"It says he's playing chess."

She looked around at all the pairs of players here, every one a furrowed, lowered brow.

"Awesome," she sighed. "That'll help."

⁂

"Could be him?" As they paced the length of the hall Zotiel nodded to a thoughtful looking young man ahead.

Deborah glanced over at him, surveying the board. His game was still opening up, eight or maybe ten moves in, but his bishop was off already. Maybe trying to lure his opponent – but if that was the intent, it was coffeehouse. She was no master, but even she wouldn't fall for that one.

"Nah. This guy is meant to be good."

Zephon smirked at her brash assessment. He stepped ahead of Zotiel and her, surveying the far tables.

"This game is a staple?" Zotiel asked in a murmur.

"Hmm?"

"Of your kind. Humans. It has lasted a long time in your world."

"I suppose," Deborah replied distractedly, dividing her attention between the games around her. "It's war. Distilled into a simple form. War is what we do."

"It's what you do, but this is not how you like to do it," Zotiel replied, reading the moleskin. He held it out for Deborah to see. Whitman Czapski had just sacrificed a pawn. Deborah frowned as she read over the previous lines. She couldn't figure out his strategy.

"How do you mean?" she asked.

"It's an even playing field. Both sides have an equal chance. That's not how war is waged on Earth."

"That's true," she replied. "But it's how we like to think of it."

"The victors, you mean. That's how the victors like to think of it? In hindsight?" Deborah lifted her gaze from the boards and looked at him for a moment.

"No, the victors like to think they were the underdog. That's why our history books are filled with against-the-odds triumphs. They get to write it how they want. Every war is recorded in history as the hard-done rebels overthrowing the oppressive. I meant people in general. The non-combatants. *They* like to think of war as even-sided."

"Your sense of fair-play?"

"Something like that."

"It is apocryphal though?"

"Of course. Victory almost always goes to the greater force."

"I hope you are wrong."

Deborah smiled wryly.

"I said *almost*. We're not going to war."

"What about the defeated?" Zotiel asked with a cocked eyebrow.

"What about them?"

"How do they think of war?"

"They don't matter. They don't get to think at all."

Zotiel gave her an admonishing smirk.

"You really do still think like the living."

"How do you mean?"

"Of course they do," he replied.

Deborah stopped, considering this as she looked around at the silent souls engaged in their games. Zephon walked back towards them.

"Could be that guy over there. The old guy? He just lost a pawn." He pointed at a bald man at the end of the table, engaged in a battle with a younger, equally bald opponent. Deborah grimaced.

"I fucking hope not," she hissed. Zephon frowned.

"Why?"

"See that tattoo? On his arm? 1488 isn't a year. He's not our guy. The Arch's might be willing to overlook killing for hire, but I hope they'd have a problem with killing for colour. If *they* don't, *I* do. You can be damn sure that Lena woman will."

Zephon looked round at the skinhead with a confused scowl.

"The scar-ink means he kills?"

"That *scar-ink* means he *hates*. The other one – at his eye? *That* means he kills."

"For skin? That kind of colour?"

Deborah nodded, and Zephon frowned again.

"You people have very odd notions of what divides you."

"Whatever we can find."

Zephon quietened, and Zotiel tapped her on the shoulder, extending the moleskin once more. Deborah read the new entries, a smirk drawing across her face.

"We won't need to search after all," she whispered.

"How so?" Zotiel asked, rereading the text but seeing little to support her assertion.

"Just wait a moment," she told him, seeing the little notations write themselves, faster now. The endgame. She held up a finger in the air in anticipatory suspense, then watched the word appear.

'Checkmate.'

She glanced around the room and spotted one player stand, shake hands with his opponent and leave. Deborah smiled auspiciously and gestured to an empty area at the closest table. The boys dutifully took their leave, seating themselves, and she paced across the rusted mess hall to meet the victor.

※

Whitman Czapski was small in stature – Deborah could tell that much while he sat. He wore a pair of steel-rimmed spectacles, slung low on the tip of his nose, and his head was bald in the centre. A thatch of once black, now predominantly grey hair circled it, and covered his face in a scraggly beard. He wore a black, woolen suit jacket that didn't quite match his navy trousers, and, underneath, a white shirt, unbuttoned casually at the neck. A bowtie hung around his collar, real – no clip-ons here – but loose, untied.

"Mr Czapski?" Deborah asked quietly, still reticent to break the solemnity of the hall. He paused a second from his business resetting the board. Remaining still, he flicked his eyes up towards her.

"Well, that's curious."

He spoke softly, English with a Germanic slant. He seemed to regard her in that position a long time, then flicked his eyes back to the board, resuming his careful arrangement of the pieces.

"And who might you be schönes mädchen?"

Deborah didn't have much German to her vocabulary, but she recognised 'schönes mädchen'. It meant pretty girl. There or thereabouts anyway, though whether it was derogatory or not she wasn't sure. The difference between 'pretty girl' and 'slutty harlot' was often more in the cadence than the parlance. His tone felt enigmatic by design.

"I like the way you play," she told him.

"Pfft," he wafted a hand dismissively. "You were all the way over there."

"I knew it was over when he fell for your little ruse with the pawn – king's bishop six to king five – but you knew before that didn't you?" His eyes flicked back up to her. "When?"

He furrowed his brow in puzzled interest. After a long, pensive pause, he extended a hand to the chair opposite. Beckoning her to sit.

"How…" he began, but Deborah cut him off neatly as she sat down opposite.

"I'm just curious. When did you know he was done?" Enquiring eyes stared back at her uneasily.

"Queen's bishop to rook," he replied. A little shrug of modesty accompanied this, but his suspicious intrigue never wavered. Deborah nodded. That was nine clear moves earlier than her. Whitman Czapski was decidedly out of her league. She could play a decent game, but this guy was a master.

"Well, you certainly crushed him."

Picking a pawn of each colour from the newly reset board, he lowered his hands below the table. Deborah's hand twitched for a half second then stilled. Her natural instinct to reach for a weapon, or to attack, suppressed. Fight or flight was an inbuilt trait, professionally honed to a razor-sharp edge. At this point in her career, keeping her instincts in check required as much skill as applying them. More perhaps. She watched his eyes. He had seen the flinch, clearly, but he seemed simply to note it in silence and move on.

He raised both fists in front of her, and she pointed to his left. He opened it to reveal the white piece, smiled a polite nod of contrition and replaced the pieces on the board. She moved her queen's pawn forward two spaces.

"The Queen's Gambit," he remarked, staring at her. "Very appropriate for such a mysterious young woman." He made his move.

"You *are* Mr Czapski then?"

"I am. Though I have not been so formally addressed in some time. Whitman is my name." He moved in turn.

"You're German?"

"I was German," he corrected. "Now," he gestured around him, "I am of this place."

Deborah nodded and moved a bishop out into the field, watching as he noted it without concern.

"Whitman is an unusual name for a German isn't it?"

"Yes, mein girl, this is true. My mother was an avid reader of poetry. She loved it. Read every collection she could lay her hands on. I was named for one of her favourites." He shifted a pawn, freeing his king's rook. Deborah stared at the board for a second, considering his attack.

"Who?" she asked.

Whitman looked a little sad.

"A man named Walt Whitman, Schönes Mädchen. Before my time. Before yours also, I imagine."

"How could you know that?" she asked. He raised an eyebrow.

"You do not have the look of a long-time resident, my dear."

Deborah nodded at this. Surveying the board, she could not see the play he had in mind, it was too far ahead, so she elected to mirror and bide her time.

"Did she teach you? Your mother? I'm told there's a correlation between poetry lovers and chess players."

"Hmm, perhaps," he conceded thoughtfully. "The quiet rhythm, the pace, the beauty." He moved again. "But no. My father was my mentor."

"Mine too," she replied, shifting a pawn further forward to deny him the space. Whitman picked it off with his knight and raised an eyebrow.

"He could have taught you better my dear," he told her with a hint of puckish charm.

"He might have," she replied. "His death cut my lessons short." She moved once more. Whitman's impishness faded from his face.

"My apologies my dear, that was crass. To lose one's father is a terrible thing. A burden in life, often carried far beyond." He shook his head, and paused a while before he spoke again.

"My father was a horologist. A quiet, very intelligent man. He loved to play. I think as a watchmaker he appreciated the mechanised beauty of it. The paradox. The confining rules of the game and the artistry in their application. Fluidity within rigidity."

Whitman made another move, and Deborah could already feel the game slipping from her. She could see him coming, but not the extent of the play. The feel of the ambush but not the direction.

"He died?" she asked gently, carefully.

"We all did."

"All? All together?" She castled her king.

He nodded.

"All together. In a place called Dachau."

She paused and looked up at him, but his eyes remained fixed on the board. He could feel her look though, clearly, as he added, "You have heard of this place?"

"Everyone has heard of that place." She spoke softly, Whitman's shoulders slumping as she did. He sighed as he made his next move.

"Well, isn't that the way of the world mien dear," he remarked sadly. "Everyone remembers the horror. The injustice and the death. The bad things done by bad people. Few remember Leaves of Grass though."

She stared at the board.

"Leaves of Grass?"

He smiled a sad, small smile.

"Walt Whitman."

Deborah pondered this, but had no good answer. No pearls of wisdom. Her life had been devoid of poetry as far as she could recall, but rife with bad things done by bad people. She was a bad person herself.

"It's easy to remember the bad stuff. It's more common," she told him as she took a pawn.

"Indeed mein girl. Indeed. Most particularly in this place."

"Your father… he was a skilled tradesman… They didn't give him a chance to use that skill? To save himself? To save you all?" Whitman sighed.

"No. Perhaps they might have. Some were spared for such reasons – at least for a time – but the literature in his collection, when discovered, put any chance of such mercy to bed."

"How so? He was devout?"

"He was, in his way, but his faith in the Talmud was not his undoing. His interest in mysticism was. My father had a keen interest in the occult. Of all religions, but particularly of the Kabbalah."

Deborah peered at him. Whitman, seeing her lack of comprehension, smiled.

"Jewish mysticism. He was no practitioner. His was an academic interest at most. But the presence of such texts in his library… well… it did us no favours. No amount of poetry and other innocuous texts were ever going to hide such literature from the prying eyes of the Schutzstaffel."

He pondered his next move closely, though Deborah suspected his delay was related more to his story than his ability.

"A shame. The irony is, I believe both my mother *and* father put more stock in the beauty of the verse than the texts that were their undoing."

Deborah cocked her head, understanding.

"As do you?" she added.

"Indeed. After so much time here? At times my love of verse has been all that has held me steady."

"This place is certainly not on the side of poetry."

"It is not on the side of *us*," he replied firmly. "It is wrong. It is not..." He moved his queen, freeing her from her shackles and opening up his game. "It is not as it is supposed to be."

That's interesting, thought Deborah as she returned a move. He's half way there already. She wondered if his assertion was based simply on faith. Or knowledge perhaps? Though how could it be? She watched him as he took her bishop with the freed rook, further asserting his dominance on the board.

"You're right you know. More so than you may realise. This place, it's *not* as it should be."

He shrugged, adopting a more pragmatic tone.

"It is as it is. However it became this way, this is how it is now. We can play at least." He pulled a sorrowful smile. "That is something."

Deborah watched the board, seeing no obvious route to take the game. She was floundering, and could tell he knew it.

"If there *was* something more, something that could be done… something that might fix this place… would you do it?"

Whitman paused and shuffled back in his chair a little, looking up above and behind her. As she turned, she saw Zephon had made his way from the end of the table and now stood at her side. He leaned down, his mouth an inch from her ear, and whispered.

"*Queen to king's bishop four.*"

Deborah stared at the board and, seeing the play, she made the move. With an insular smirk she realised what was happening. The boys were reading Whitman's scroll. Keeping her in the game.

Whitman clearly noted that she had received help, but did not seem to mind. Deborah suspected, given his mastery of the game, that he likely welcomed a challenge, whatever the source. She was happy to provide it.

Zephon stepped back to Zotiel, who had followed behind him, and stood now a few paces back. Moleskin in hand.

"Something more than just accepting things the way they are. Just playing this same game, over and over," Deborah added.

He scoured the board, more thoughtful than before. When he made his next move, he did so a tad more hesitantly.

"If there was something more to do…" He pondered quietly. "To change it you mean? For us? To… alter our collective fate?" he asked.

She nodded. "Something to change this place, yes. To change *all* places."

Zephon leaned in and whispered another move to her. As she made it, Whitman analysed the board carefully.

"Your friend... I'm sorry to say, is better than you." He wagged a finger back and forth playfully at her.

"We're a team," she replied with a smile. "So... would you?"

"Nein. No. I do not think so," he said as he made another, more cautious move. He looked up at her, fixing on her eyes as she frowned.

"I don't know who you are Schönes Mädchen, but I do know *what* your friends are. I have been here longer that the duration of your life on earth. Longer than the duration of my own by now, I imagine. It is an awful place. It is not right, not as it was intended. That much I can see, I can feel. But it *is* how it is. To refuse to accept it? To try and change it? Down that path lies madness."

Deborah grimaced. She had not expected this. After seeing Whitman's comprehension of his situation – far more lucid and pragmatic than her previous recruits – she had expected him to jump at the chance to be a part of its improvement.

"You don't believe in changing things?"

He cocked a cynical eyebrow at her.

"My dear, change comes in many forms. In my life I saw much change. Sometimes for good, often for bad. The change you offer – it is of a... violent nature?"

"Violence comes in many forms. It's usually the catalyst for change."

He nodded, his suspicions confirmed.

"A putsch."

"I suppose," Deborah conceded.

"The last time I witnessed a putsch, it led not to the promised salvation of my country – of my motherland – but to its descent into hell."

"We're not the Nazis." She made another move, at Zephon's advice. Taking Whitman's rook and, she saw now, hamstringing his strategy.

"No one ever *seems* like the Nazis. Not at first," he told her disparagingly.

On the board he switched tactics, focussing his attack across her other flank and putting his queen's knight on the offensive. Plan B maybe, or perhaps simply the next step in a devious Plan A. Zephon, after some hushed consultation with his partner in crime, leaned in and advised a defensive move. Deborah dutifully adopted it.

"Your analogy is flawed," she told Whitman stoically.

"How so?"

"Because it's the current regime that are the Nazis. Look around you. You more than anyone must see that."

He peered up at her once more, sharpness in his eyes now.

"You think this is like the camps? Maybe it is, maybe it isn't, but what would you know little girl?" His knight marched on, taking her sacrificial pawn.

"I wouldn't, not really. Just what I've read in history books. But I do know one thing that perhaps you don't. At least, that you don't know first hand."

"And what is that Schönes Mädchen?"

She didn't need Zephon to show her the move here. She pulled her bishop back, slaying his now open knight.

"The Nazis lost. In the end."

He watched the board, seeing the trap he had fallen into and surveying the new situation. The game had evened up considerably.

"I had heard. Not by way of assassination though. War is not what you have planned, that much is obvious." He played his final gambit, ostentatiously shifting his queen into position. It left it open, she could see that. The game was set for her victory or defeat.

"War can't work in this case. Not every wrong can be righted by an army. Sometimes a roll of the dice is all you can do. Take a shot and hope your opponent misses the signs."

Zephon leaned into her ear and pointed out what she already knew.

"*Bishop to Queen, checkmate.*"

She looked down at the board a while, allowing Whitman to ponder what she had said, then shifted her rook uselessly forward. He took the bishop with his queen.

"Checkmate," he said, with an accusatory look.

He sat back in his chair, surveying her with surly caution. His demeanor fell short of hostile, but not too far short.

"You think you can throw a game and your point will be made? I'll join up for some hoffnungslosen plot, just because you ignore your friend there?"

"No," she replied honestly. "My German is weak, what is hoffnungslosen?"

He narrowed his eyes a little.

"Without hope. *Hopeless.*"

Deborah shrugged a little and adopted a more directly conspiratorial tone.

"No. I doubt you are that easily manipulated. Even if you were, I'm not looking to manipulate you. I'm not looking to manipulate anyone. Not for this. This thing we are going to do, it's going to take a while. It's going to be hard. It's going to seem," she paused. "*Hoffnungslosen* at times, though I'm not sure that's quite the right word. The whole basis of the desire for change *is* hope. I think you know that well enough. Hope is *all* we have. People who feel manipulated won't do me any good. I need people who *want* to do it. For their own benefit if that's all they can muster, but for everyone's benefit ideally. They need to want to be there. They need to have *chosen* to be there."

"Free will," he stated, nodding in thought. The rancour had slipped, replaced with curiosity, but his reticence remained palpable.

"Then why me? Why come to me?"

"You're smart, you can think ahead, and you have first hand knowledge of fascism. On Earth as well as here."

"They are hardly the same thing."

"It's a start," she replied flatly. "Plus," she measured her tone carefully. "You've spent seventy years here looking for a challenge." She watched as he cocked his head to one side, in contrition. "I'm offering you one."

He toyed with his beard aimlessly as he sized her up. Deborah remained unflinchingly still, staring back at him. She pulled out one of the Shepherds cards and placed it deliberately at the centre of the chessboard. A flat rectangle of snow in the midst of the battle's aftermath. The remaining veterans on the battlefield seemed to eye the card with the same suspicious scrutiny as her victorious opponent.

"Come and meet with us. That's all I'm asking for now." She looked into Whitman's eyes deeply and honestly. "Nothing is *hoffnungslosen* by its own force. Hope can't be *taken* from you. You have to give it up willingly."

She stood, and, looking down at him, she dropped her final word with a beseeching whisper.

"*Don't.*"

Whitman rubbed his forehead with his thumb and forefinger as he stared down at the card, but said nothing. Deborah walked away from the table, Zotiel and Zephon by her side.

Fracture seven
LAMENTATIONS

Deborah burst through the door and stormed forward, oblivious to the room's two other occupants. Her eyes were fixed on Mr Rust.

He stood at the far side of the room, a document in one hand, a coffee mug in the other. She had managed to keep her rage in check as she was frisked and scrutinised at the underground entrance by the unremarkable, besuited guard, but she could hold it close no longer.

Rust barely had time to register her approach as she strode across to him. Slapping the mug from his hand, sending it to shatter on the wooden boards, she grabbed his throat.

"What the fuck was that?!" she bellowed.

Fury burned from her face and up through her arm, sending tendrils of strength she didn't know she had through her fingers as they clamped round his trachea. He appeared to have genuine panic in his eyes, at least for a second or so, before she felt herself pulled from him.

It took considerably more force than one might have expected for the two men, whose affairs she had interrupted, to remove her, but they managed. Ripping her slight frame from his, they threw her back across the room where she landed, ass first on the floor. She sprung back up, ready and willing for a second go at him, but, as she took her first step, she heard a click. A sound she had not heard before, but would hear many times in her future. One of the men aimed a gun at her head.

She stopped, but rage continued to smoulder behind shaking features. Rust looked at her. His cold composure was returning, though it was hindered a little by his rubbing at his newly bruised throat.

"Well, I'd call it a job well done Princess," he replied.

"Don't get *fucking* funny with me you spooky cunt!" she roared. "You never said we'd be killing anyone!"

Two guns trained on her now, but she barely gave them a thought. They were enough to hold her back, but they weren't going to quell her wrath.

"No," Rust replied, measured as always. "I didn't. But hey," he shrugged, "there you go. You did anyway. Remarkably well, I might add. Most operatives in that situation would have gone for the target's gun. At worst they might have hit him with something blunt, taken him down cleanly." He wagged a finger at her playfully. Toying.

"Not you though Deborah. You're nothing if not exciting. You went *bloody*." Directing his voice at his two associates he added, "Not squeamish this one. And not short of rage to channel."

"Got that right Sir," replied one. He spoke stoically, though breathing a tad heavily after his scuffle. His gun barrel didn't drift an inch.

"We would never have agreed to…" Deborah began, but was cut off.

"Just drop the *'we'* would you please Deborah?" Rust said curtly. "*You* are the one who did the heavy lifting. *You* are the one who called all the shots in there, and *you* were the one who eliminated the target. There is a reason I requested that only *you* come and meet me here. Your friend Mr Greene? He is of no interest to me. Not after his rather hesitant and decidedly *lacklustre* performance. If it were not for you, he would likely be lying on a slab right now, with a revolver slug in his thick head."

The callous way the man talked about a murder, a murder she was now complicit in, sickened Deborah.

"He's a good person! He doesn't kill people!" she screamed. "I thought I was too!"

Mr Rust smiled, but not his crocodile grin. This time, against everything she had come to know of the man, it seemed an honest smile. Almost compassionate.

"Deborah, *no one* is a good person. No one. And I can guarantee you – killing someone? That alone does not change one's standing in that regard."

"The hell it doesn't!" she shouted back, though with a little less fervour behind her anger. Partly owing to the unexpected earnestness of his new demeanor, but mostly because she so desperately wanted his words to be true.

"What do you know of the man you killed?"

"Nothing!" she replied, anger ebbing to quizzical haughtiness.

"Would it help you to know some of his many – and there are *many*, Deborah – some of his *many* crimes?"

Deborah thought about this genuinely for a moment.

"No," she replied flatly. Rust smiled.

"Good answer," he remarked with conciliatory acumen. "And why?"

She stood now, the fire of her anger dulling to an ember. Not gone entirely, but subdued to the point where she could think and speak with some measure of objectivity.

"Because it won't change anything. He's dead, I'm not. My fight isn't with him, it's with you."

Rust smiled again, and signaled the two men at either side of her with a flick of his wrist. Deborah never dropped her stare from him, but she felt the shift of the air by her sides as the guns were lowered.

"Taking a risk, aren't you?" she told him coldly. "How do you know I won't rip your fucking throat out this time."

"You won't."

"And why?" she asked, mirroring his tone caustically.

"Because your fight *isn't* with me, and you know it." He cocked an eyebrow at her.

"You're not here looking for a fight, Deborah. You're here looking for a purpose. You know *exactly* why I asked you here. You knew before I contacted you."

"I came here because I wanted answers," she spat.

"No you didn't," he replied impassively. "I'm *offering* you answers. You're too smart to need them."

"I came because I wanted to make sure you won't follow through on your threats. To have us arrested. To hurt me and my... To hurt me and Mark." She sounded half-hearted, even to her own ear..

"Why would I? I got what I wanted. You knew that too."

She was floundering. The truth was rearing its ugly head, the truth she didn't want to admit. Rust already knew it.

"I came..."

"You came because you know what I know. That you didn't do such a good job in that office because you were *forced* to."

"I..." She didn't want him to continue, but she couldn't find the words to make him stop.

"You did a good job because in that moment, in that office, you found something in yourself. You found your talent. And you *liked* it."

Deborah simmered. She wanted to refute him, to yell and to scream. To admonish his idiotic, sick, mean, cruel lies. To call him a twisted fuck, preying on a poor, down-on-her-luck, homeless runaway. To twist his fingers from his hands and gouge his eyeballs from his head. She wanted to kill him. But she didn't. She couldn't. Because he was right.

Mr Rust seemed to see every individual one of these thoughts pass through her head, and his quiet colleagues certainly saw the latter ones. Their guns began to raise once more, to defend their boss from the rekindling fire behind her eyes, but with a glance from Rust they paused and hesitantly re-lowered the weapons. He maintained his sympathetic demeanor as he continued.

"When I was young I loved the piano," he said.

"I... What?" she asked, confounded by this spontaneous, left-field comment.

"When I was young I loved the piano," he repeated simply.

"I practiced for years. My mother and father were strict. Uncompromising people. Successful too. They thought they saw potential in my childhood interest, and they encouraged it. In their way, at least. Some people would call it forceful – and it was – but that was encouragement in their eyes. They were convinced I could reach some heights in the field, and would tell me so whenever they felt my drive slip, even a little. At times I hated them for it, but mostly I felt pride. Pride in their belief in me. I loved my parents."

"So?" she asked, vexed both by this odd change in direction and at the mollifying effect it was having on her.

"I spent countless hours studying the notation, the theory. I learned all there is to know about the great pianists of history, listened over and over to the works of Beethoven and Mozart and Haydn. I laboured day and night to memorise them. I had a dream of being a concert pianist – my parent's dream imposed upon me, I suppose – but I pursued it relentlessly. It was all I wanted in my life. All that mattered to me. I was raised for it. Hot-housed to believe it."

Rust's story was clearly a nostalgic trip for him, but at no point did his eyes glass or mist. He told his story with a steady beat; his stare remained piercing, unblinking.

"When I was seventeen, I had an audition set up for an advanced programme at the Curtis Institute in Philadelphia. A conservatory. A magnificent school, one of the best. I had travelled a long way to get there. On my own – I wanted to do it for myself. I convinced my parents so."

"What the hell does this have to do with…" Deborah began to ask, but drifted off as he tilted his head. His unflinching stare was stoney as he lifted a solitary finger, silencing her.

"The night before my audition I was ready. Feeling great. Practically mapping out my rise to super-star status in my mind. I was not nervous, but I didn't want to let myself get restless in that hotel room. I headed out, to a club I had heard of. A jazz club.

"As I sat having a drink – soda, I didn't want to be hung-over for my big day – the hostess announced that a pianist was coming on to do a set. Unusual in a jazz club for a solo pianist to do a full set. I though it was fate. It was in a sense."

Rust's stoic timbre never faltered. No hint of sadness peppered his words, though Deborah wondered if she would be able to identify it if it did. He was enigmatic at the best of times. He did appear, to her fairly astute ear, to be recalling a true story. Her short life thus far had given her a keen nose for bullshit. She smelled none.

"So this little black kid comes on. I mean a *kid*, in the most literal sense. Little nigger couldn't have been older than twelve. His suit jacket was three sizes too big. His shoes were more glue than leather, and he needed a meal and a fucking haircut. Walking up to the baby-grand, he didn't look tall enough to hit the fucking pedals. I thought it was a joke. He sits down and… well." He paused.

"I had never heard anything like it. The kid was a genius. He played like I've never heard a piano played, before or since. Like he was a *part* of that baby-grand. Before he sat down he looked like a frightened kid, but as he played he transformed. His face was *alive*.

"He was pulling in harmonies and themes, three and four and five at a time, playing on them, seeming to discard them, then working them back into each other like musical chaos theory. Like auditory mathematics. Like the melodies were *fucking* right in front of me. It was magnificent. Spectacular. Some was prepared, but parts of it were improvised right there in the moment. Most of the audience might not have realised that, but *I* did. My own abilities were the cruelest curse. I could appreciate the genius. I could *see* it.

"I saw then, right there in that club, something that changed my perspective forever. I saw what *true* talent was. *Natural* talent."

Deborah shot a *'so what'* look at Rust.

"I went back to the hotel, and lay awake all night thinking about that nigger kid. In the morning I got up, I checked out and I went to the train station and I bought a ticket home."

"You never bothered to even try?" she asked coldly. "Pretty defeatist."

"What was the point? If I could practice for a decade or more – longer, probably, than that kid had been alive – and still couldn't play like he could? Feel the way he felt when I did? Then what did it matter? No amount of practice or theory can compete with natural talent.

"It took days to get home by train. I had plenty of time to think. Through my realisation, through my failure, I had a long time to consider the difference between his natural talent and my mere assimilation of practice and knowledge. To think about how I had been encouraged to believe in a lie. And to consider where *my* natural talent might lie."

Deborah resigned herself to his musings. Giving up on trying to halt his story, she resolved simply to hurry him along to its conclusion.

"So what did you do instead?" she asked with weary disinterest.

"I arrived home, late in the night, and choked my mother and father to death as they slept."

Deborah looked at him dead-eyed, but inside she felt a cold fascination creep through her. His impassivity was chilling.

"*I* had mistaken my talent for drive, the drive to play the ivories. *You* have mistaken yours for rage. Believe me Deborah; neither of us would be happy with those false realities. No matter what we did to convince ourselves otherwise."

He watched her with an equivocating eye. She stood a moment in silence, staring back.

"All that story proves is that you're a murderer, the same as me," she told him, uneasy confusion in her words.

"Murder is a civilian word," Rust responded. "One for all those people out there. All those... Mark Greenes."

Deborah's eyes narrowed. How dare he invoke Mark's name like that? She wanted to grab at his throat again, but sucked breath through her clenched teeth and restrained herself. If she didn't, she knew his accomplices surely would.

"Do you deny that when you killed that man you felt good? That it felt right?"

"Yes!"

"You're lying."

Deborah scowled at him, but his gaze went right through her. The time for flat denial had passed.

"...yes." She wilted. Rust nodded, satisfied.

"You're young. You've not had much luck in your life. I think you *have* had drive, in your way – the drive for some kind of future with your young... consort. But you know. In your heart you know. That is not your path."

"How the fuck would you know?" she asked with malice.

"Because you're here," he told her softly. An odd empathy cut his acid tone now.

"Because you know that you mistook your talent for other things. A dream of a future. Passion. Love maybe. But when I asked you to kill? You killed. I suspect that that was the first time you felt *right*."

Deborah's anger had melted fully now, replaced by a sickly vulnerability. She felt like she was being inspected, naked.

"I do love him," she told Rust honestly.

She couldn't recall ever saying the word love out loud to anyone, including Mark himself, but it had the ring of truth. She did love him.

"It doesn't matter," Rust replied, empathic still. "He *saw* your talent. I was watching, remember? I know that look in his eyes. He won't understand, no matter what you say or do. Not really. You know there is no life there for you."

Deborah felt the miserable truth he spoke waft through her. She remembered Mark's horrified stare at her blood-splattered kill-face. She couldn't forget it if she tried. Standing above a fresh corpse, in a room filled with blood, surrounded by the stench of piss and shit and acrid adrenaline; it was that look in his eyes that had horrified her the most. The crown of sorrow she wore was forged in the fire of that look.

"We can offer you a life. One where your talents will be useful. Where you can do what you know you were born to do. What you are good at. One where those talents will ensure you never know the hunger and cold of street-life again. Your fantasy? It can offer you nothing but unfulfilling want."

She tried to picture the future she had planned with Mark. A little studio flat. Mark coming home after a hard day's graft at some menial job, her acting the kept housewife. A meal prepared. Carpets and sofas. Curtains. It seemed more distant than ever. Vague and shadowy. Nothing but fleeting, sepia-toned images in dust. Then she recalled the feeling of power. The rush. The burst of her... talent. Manifest in the wrathful plunge of a fountain pen into the neck of a stranger. Her face flushed, prickly and warm.

"Who is we?" she asked.

"I work for a group called The Orchard."

"The Orchard? I've never heard of them," she stated incredulously.

Rust smiled.

"Of course not."

Deborah paused.

"What would I have to do?"

"Nothing you weren't born to do," he replied emphatically.

"I mean now. Right now, what would I have to do?"

Rust looked pleased.

"Well, you're done in Scotland. In the UK too. Can't have you operating in a country where your fingerprints are on file, and where there are missing persons reports with your grade-school photos lying around. We'll set you up in an apartment. Somewhere in Europe. Paris maybe? Or the States? You'll be assigned a handler. Someone who'll be your contact."

He spoke up a little, turning his head to his colleagues who, during Rust's lengthy monologue, had resumed their business around the files in the boiler room basement desks.

"We have anyone in mind?"

"Got that young kid looking for a new operative. That shit in Uruguay freed him up," one of them replied. A raised brow indicated that 'that shit in Uruguay' had, indeed, been some shit. Deborah thought this was the one who had spoken before, with his gun trained on her, though it was hard to tell. The pair were virtually interchangeable in their scrupulous ubiquity.

"Ah yes," Rust replied, nodding thoughtfully.

"Seems like dangerous work," Deborah remarked cynically.

"So is living on the streets." He spoke with faraway detachment, then, seeming to reconsider his tone, looked up at her closely. "But yes, it is. Does that bother you?"

"No," she replied after a thought. It didn't really. Her past six months had been among her happiest, and those had been fraught with danger.

"You aren't my contact then?" she asked him.

"Whether you accept or not, you'll never see me again."

"And we were just getting to know each other too," she breezed with acerbic sarcasm, masking her flooding emotions.

This thing was really happening. She had known in her heart that this was how it would go. She suspected that she wanted it, but it didn't make it easier to let the last six months go. She felt, all of a sudden, very young. As young as she really was.

"You off to wait around for another poor sap to try and take the wrong briefcase?"

He eyed her with a contemptuous, if marginally amused look.

"Something like that."

"Hell of a job you have," she told him coldly.

"It has its perks. I meet some... interesting people," he replied coyly. She saw one of the quiet, interchangeable suits grin a little to himself.

"You won't ever have any direct dealings with The Orchard, except via your contact. You are free to pass or accept whatever contracts come your way, but I advise you to rely on the judgement of your handler. You have your skills; he will have his."

Deborah spent a moment or two thinking about the enormity of what was happening here. Life changes fast. The little conversations that reshape our worlds, they come on like a freight train – unstoppable and destructive – but as they happen, they flit by in an instant. Leaving only the scattered remains of the life they smashed apart in their wake.

"I want to say goodbye," she told him with flat certitude. "To Mr Gree... To Mark." He surveyed her keenly.

"That's not a good idea."

"Fuck you," she replied, as cold as ice. "I'm not just going to disappear on him. I owe him some kind of explanation."

Mr Rust cocked his eyebrow once more and shook his head a little. In frustration, or in remorse perhaps?

"And tell him what, exactly?"

"I'll lie. I'm not going to give away any of your dirty little secrets. It's not like I know anything anyway. But I'm not just vanishing. Not from him."

"Our secrets are dirty, Deborah, but far from little." He wilted a little.

"Fine. It's up to you. You're free to do what you want. I didn't force you to come here, all I did was ask. And I'm not forcing you to stay, or to accept. I'm certainly not forcing you to leave your current life. That choice has to come freely, and must be made by you alone."

Deborah nodded.

"When you're finished with your…" Rust paused a moment, "with whatever it is you want to tell him, call this number. They'll ask you for a shibboleth. Just tell them this."

He leaned and wrote something on the back of a business card. Deborah hid her frown. She didn't know what shibboleth meant, but she was damned if she was going to let him know that. She wouldn't allow herself to loose any more ground in this encounter.

"It won't be me you speak to, but whoever it is, you can trust them." He handed her the card, which she took and examined.

+240 7321

"Don't leave that anywhere," he told her with gravity.

"Good tip," she replied.

She pushed the card into her hip pocket, then turned and walked out of the boiler room, leaving him to his clandestine paperwork.

Mr Rust was true to his word. She never did see him again. Not in this life.

Leaving the underground basement office, through the corridor and past the guard who has frisked her without obstruction, her intention had been to make her way straight home. Back to the floor above the Gomorrah, to see Mark and make her attempts at a goodbye. As she climbed the stairs that lead up to the nondescript service door and out into the subway station, however, her stride became a slow step, then a saunter. What *would* she tell him?

Down in the boiler room basement, it had seemed simple. She had told Mr Rust she would lie. Easy to say. Easy to tell someone you'd lie to the only person who truly trusted you. Harder to do it in reality though, and exiting the station into the bright daylight, reality took a much firmer hold than it could while she skulked in Rust's shadowy world.

Even if she did lie – and she knew she would have to – what could she say? She and Mark did not live in the nine-to-five world of this sunlit street. They didn't live in the world of Starbucks coffee and Subway sandwiches. Of office workers out to lunch and mothers pushing prams along the pavement, twisting in and out of the passing people and the set-outside tables and chairs of the little cafes. Their drum didn't beat to the rhythm of everyone else. Legitimate excuses would be hard to come by.

She couldn't tell him she had a job, that she had to move to another city to follow a career. She was fifteen, and besides, nothing tied him here. He would tell her he'd come too. She couldn't tell him she had met someone else. Who could she have met? Besides, if the intent was to spare his feelings, that would be a sick move. She couldn't, she *wouldn't* tell him she just didn't love him. It wasn't true, and the pain she felt now thinking about it, that would be magnified a hundredfold if she shared it. That kind of hurt fed on itself. It multiplied like cancer.

No. In truth, she had no idea what she would say. She couldn't go to him like this. She had to think. She fished around in her pocket and pulled out what money she had. A twenty pound note and a few loose coins. The twenty she had taken from their stash before she left this morning, not knowing what was in store, or how long she'd be gone. Not much, but enough to carry some guilt along with it. She didn't like to lift cash without telling him. That was *their* money, hard-won together. She grimaced. This morning, taking a twenty pound note she had earned alongside Mark was enough to make her feel guilty. What would she feel like by tomorrow?

She crushed the note in her fist and looked around the street. Spending it alone seemed wrong, but she would anyway. She had to start thinking solo again. She had to stop thinking of things, the money included, as shared property. And she had to re-evaluate her standing in this world. What she considered her place in it. She turned from the station entrance and headed into the Starbucks.

It was called a vanilla latte, and it tasted like candy-floss and watery dirt. The number of questions she had had to answer of the flapping, air-headed Bimbette behind the counter – size, strength, whether she was staying or going, the inclusion, or not, of syrup and sprinkles, whatever the fuck they did – she had expected something magnificent at the end of it all. Not this disappointing piss.

It had been a long time since Deborah had sat in one of these places. Back in Edinburgh, with Trisha, in her earlier tenure in that city. Before her relationship with her aunt had descended entirely into bitter feuding and seething resentment, and, crucially, before she had cared to try coffee. She didn't see what all the fuss was about. Must have something though, she thought cautiously, the price all these people were paying for these various cocktails and concoctions. There had to be something she was missing.

Six or so months on the streets had, she realised, dulled all sense she had once had of the practicalities of easy living. If Rust was telling the truth, and she suspected he was for the most part, she would have to readjust to this side of life. Heating tinned food in its can over a camping stove would be a thing of the past.

She would need to relearn the real world. The trappings of it anyway.

She sat in a quieter upstairs area of the shop. The unseasonable sunshine outside had drawn the majority of the patrons to the lower level, where the big glass windows shone bright, or outside to the benches that lined the bustling street. Up here, there were no windows, just the tables and chairs and sofas all sitting empty around her. That suited her fine. The thoughts that played on her mind now, they were more suited to the gloom. They scurried around too frantically when the sunshine hit them. Scuttled away from the front of her mind like bugs. What the fuck was she going to do about Mark?

Deborah knew that she was going to accept Mr Rust's offer. Like he had said, she had known since before she walked in his door. Not just because she had been good at killing. Not just because she had, in a perverse way, enjoyed it. No. Not *enjoyed*, she thought with a frown. That was the wrong word. A junkie doesn't *enjoy* a hit of smack, and a lover doesn't *enjoy* a kiss from their beau. They *need* it. It releases them, it… *fulfils* them. Try as she might, Deborah could not deny, not to herself, the rapturous rush she had felt in the midst of that frantic horror three nights before. That wasn't a feeling of enjoyment. It was a feeling of… something else. Something more. Something primal, something… carnal. The intimate details of that moment were jumbled and messy in her mind, but the afterglow she could recall clearly. The sweep of the adrenaline euphoria leaving her, and the moist patch at her crotch that had remained. What that meant? What that said about her? She was not sure. Nothing good.

Mr Rust would no doubt tell her it was normal. Nothing to fear, no explanation required. He was, after all, a killer himself. Anyone else though? Anyone else would likely say she was insane. Deranged and sick. Deborah suspected that she would have said so herself, had the story been relayed to her by someone else, mere days ago. She had thought of herself as a good person. She supposed everyone did though. No one strives to be bad – that happens in the background. Everyone casts themselves as the good guy in their own story. Most people never get a true test of it like she had though. Most people never have reason to push their moral boundaries that far. To see if they snap or not. To discover the yield point.

She was going to accept the offer because it would give her the chance to feel alive, but with limits. Deborah knew two things unequivocally. She knew that she never wanted to kill an innocent person. That much remained of her. She knew that. But she also knew, without a shadow of a doubt, that she was going to kill again. That she had to. She needed a way to meet both those desires. The Orchard seemed ready and willing to provide.

The Orchard she thought with a full roll of her eyes to the empty room. What a stupid fucking name. What the hell did it mean? What did they think they were doing? Clipping leaves? Scrumping apples? She stared down at the card Rust had given her. Two trees: one alive, one dead. She had no idea what significance, if any, the imagery carried, but the sight of the smaller tree, the dead-looking one, unsettled her. No real reason for that, she told herself, her pragmatic side scolding her a little, but it did anyway. It seemed to loom from the card at her knowingly. Seeing her. Seeing what she was. She shook her head and pocketed the card once more, refusing to be drawn in by its voodoo. Real or imagined, she had her own problems.

She *was* going to accept the offer. So all that was left was the sad goodbyes to her former life. She sipped the candy-floss piss and thought about Mark.

The unseasonal sunshine had given way to a brilliant orange evening that, in turn, had succumbed to darkness. Deborah had spent some of that time, and most of her money, in the coffee shop and some more sat on a bench in the botanical gardens watching the light fade. The rest she spent in a sombre, lonesome walk through the city. The city she would soon depart. All of the time she had pondered what to tell her dearest – her *only* – friend. After all the long hours, she had come up with nothing.

She had barely been aware of the direction her aimless wandering took her at first, but had become conscious after a time that her homing instinct had swung into gear. Her autopilot footfalls driving her loosely in the direction of the Gomorrah. Standing, watching the comings and goings of the try-hard casuals that made up its fashionably shabby clientele from across the street, her eye drifted up to the top floor of the building. A keen eye, and foreknowledge was required, but she could see, just barely, a hint of orange glow behind the corner of one of the steel sheets. Mark was still awake.

Of course, she thought. The music was still blaring from below. Besides, save for that one fretful night in the holding cells that had been forced upon them, he had not slept without her warmth by his for a long time. Since they day met.

Deborah felt a warm tear run down her cheek. His first gestures of kindness, lifting his own mattress from his bed and separating out the sheets – unevenly, giving her more than he retained – that remained her benchmark of happiness. A highpoint of childlike joy, set against the torrent of shit that had preceded it. Higher even, she realised with a moment of surprised clarity, than any she could recall, even back with her father. Maybe because those older memories were losing their place in her mind, filing away in little compartments at the back. Forming abridged versions in her mental archives, making room for new thoughts and memories. Maybe not though. Maybe she really was about to walk away from the happiest time in her life.

A second tear came. Rather than wipe at her face, she felt them run. It felt good in a way, cathartic. Weeping meant she was not a monster. Not entirely. It meant what she had had, for a while there at least, had been real. It *had* been meaningful. It *had* been beautiful.

It was exactly as hard as she had imagined it would be, standing in the dark street looking up at the broke-down palace. The draw of the place? The desire to pull Mr Rust's card from her pocket, rip it into pieces and scatter it on the ground, to run to Mark and forget The Orchard and the killing and the Artist-Formally-Known-As-Mr-Briefcase? To forget the mess and just lie down beside him and feel his body next to hers? It was forceful. Unrelenting. Like gravity itself. She toyed at the paper corners of the card with her fingers, folding and pressing it against the edge of her pocket and into her thigh. It would take no effort at all. It would be so simple. So easy.

But it was a mirage. That which drew her in? It was a phantom. Nothing more. Just the ghost of a previous life, haunting her. Toying with her. Those days, her halcyon days, they were over. They were over the moment Mark saw the fire in her eyes, and she had known it the moment they met his. There was no going back. She realised now with crystal clarity that which had eluded her all day. That which Rust, in his taciturn way, had tried to tell her. There was nothing to say.

She allowed herself a moment more to look up at what had once been her home. Just a moment, allowing a few more tears to flow freely. Then she wiped her face, turned and walked away.

2. 4. 0. 7. 3. 2. 1.

...
Ring.
Ring. Ring.
"Good evening, Grove cars?"

Deborah paused for a second, unnerved. Had she dialled wrong? She stared at the number on the card. Nope, she didn't think so.

"I... Sorry... who am I calling?" she stammered.

"This is Grove Cars, do you have an account?"

What the fuck? Grove cars? That's what the woman's voice had said. Deborah fretted for a moment, her brow furrowing, and then it clicked. Grove Cars. Grove. Orchard.

"Yes, I... Yes. I have an account," she stuttered.

"Excellent ma'am. Can I have your account safe-word please?"

Safe-Word? Deborah thought puzzled. What fucking safe word? She raced back over her encounter with Mr Rust, and then, with a flash, remembered. That word she hadn't known. A 'shibboleth.' In first her desire to keep the upper hand in her dealings, and then in her eagerness to get out of that boiler room, she had never looked at what Rust had written down on the back of the card. In all her troubled musings, all day long, she had looked at the card a dozen times, but had never flipped it over. She had been too hypnotised by the eerie logo on the front.

She spun it in her hand and let out a grunt of emotion as she read the words scrawled on the back. She didn't know whether to laugh or cry.

"Ma'am? I need your safe-word before I can connect your call."

"Yes," she replied, swallowing painfully over the lump in her throat. "Yes, my safe-word. It's..." she smiled a little to herself.

"'Right Briefcase."

"Connecting you now."

She stood for a moment in the phone booth, looking out through the dark, over the edge of the road bridge and past, to the canal below. After a couple of soft clicks, a man's voice came on the line. He sounded young, and had an American accent with a slight southern drawl.

"Deborah?"

"Yes," she replied, staring through the grimy glass and out over the rippling dark of the water. The dancing reflections of the city lights on its surface were hypnotic and beautiful. Most people, presented with this scene, would be captivated by those pretty reflections. Deborah thought of the inky black, unknown depths they disguised.

"My name's Eli, nice to hear from you."

Chapter Ten

AT SIXES...

After five days - or was it six? - they had all arrived.
Raymond had been first. His cop's inquisitiveness had driven him to Shepherds the very night Deborah and her chaperones had returned.

Deborah had been reticent to divulge any more specifics to him prior to the arrival of the others, but he had been happy enough to wait it out. Despite being human, he seemed to fit perfectly into the milieu of the establishment, and had been more than happy to partake of the beer and whiskey that the Angels drank. Particularly so after he had established, with intrigued pleasure, that Augustine the bartender was not interested in any of his folded barter papers. On-the-house wasn't a concept he was familiar with in The Purgs, but he was most pleased to make its acquaintance.

Deborah wasn't sure whether he ever returned to the upper floor room he had been given the use of, below hers. She never heard any movement down there, and every time she had ventured down to the bar, to play chess with Augustine, she had found him, drinking or in quiet conversation with the Angelic patrons. He never seemed drunk. One of the habits ingrained by life as a detective, she imagined. Having to look like you were being social, all the while working an angle, would certainly teach you to nurse a drink. To keep your head. While other men were losing theirs.

Deborah had expected Lena to arrive before Whitman. To be honest, she had wondered if Whitman would come at all. Of the three recruits she had been tasked to assemble personally, he had seemed by far the most reserved. The least receptive to her deliberately mysterious offer. Sure enough though, two nights after Raymond's arrival, she had descended for her nightly games and had found him sat in her usual spot at the end of the bar, engaged in an epic battle with Auggie. Auggie, who had looked distinctly more engaged in this match than in any he had fought with her.

In the time they waited for the last of their troupe to arrive, Whitman and Augustine played often, and formed a loose friendship in their small-talk over the board. Deborah had once or twice sat and followed the battles in their campaign. There was much she could learn from these two masters, but her interest in the game was waning. Waxing instead was her focus on the task that lay ahead.

She had numerous discussions with Raziel on the subject, down in the naval-looking office below the bar. The Officers' Quarters she had taken to calling it, and no one had objected or offered alternative nomenclature. These conversations she entered into with Raziel alone, keeping discussion of the job from her potential team members until they could be addressed en masse.

They were simple talks, of the most practical aspects of the task, though they would often veer off on wildly tangential tracts. That still irritated her, but it was just Raziel's way, she had learned. There was no getting around it with him. In a choice between too much information and no information at all, generally the former was better. In the cases where she felt the latter was most appropriate she would simply say so, and now, with some trust on her side, he appeared more obliging to her forced conversational hiatuses. He was, she began to realise, fascinated with her.

They discussed the structure of The Purgs, the Hierarchy of The Office, the checkpoints and judgments that the souls leaving The Purgs had to face. The nature of God and the old ways versus the new. She knew she gleaned little substantive information, but it was a start. Where he was vague she could always consult with Zotiel and Zephon when they returned.

The Boys, as she had affectionately begun to refer to them, had returned with her to the bar after their dalliance in The Quarters, but had been almost immediately dispatched once more. Off on their 'official' business. Deborah had not pried on this subject, but she had some idea what it would be. She recalled their brief encounter with the other two Angels, Purah, the forgetful one, and Dagiel. *'It never ends'* Zotiel had joked. Alongside their clandestine business with the Resistance, they had significant 'real' business, *Office* business, to take care of. Keeping up their duties. Keeping the suspicion off.

Raziel had spoken in sad tones as he had relayed this. Wistful, like when he had discussed the old days. Among all the hifalutin nonsense and the grandeur and archaism of the Archangels' language, among the awesome enormity of the task that was to be her charge, every now and then something would happen to reaffirm the little parts. The private, small reasons to do this thing. Seeing an Archangel sound so meek certainly fell in that camp. Like feeling the twisted flesh of Zephon's scars, it humanised these ethereal beings. Made them nothing more than people. People in pain. She wanted that to be the reason she was doing this. She desperately wanted that to be it.

After several more days of waiting, Cassiel had emerged from the archives and had informed Deborah that they were ready. That a 'Guide' had been selected. One who could walk the Great City without suspicion, whose purity was pristine, but who's goodness extended further. Extended far enough to believe in the righteousness of the Old God. To believe the goals of the Revolution were just. He also told her that her 'Rogue' was here. Had been found. That was the word he used. *Found.* As if this member of her merry band, as if his involvement had been predetermined. They had to *select* her guide. All they had to do was *find* her rogue. Deborah had noted this, noted it keenly, but had pressed no further. She had found that doing so with the Archangels was generally less than fruitful. When they wished to impart something, they did. When they did not, coaxing was useless, and forcing was painfully laborious. Best simply to wait and see for herself.

That evening, just as Deborah had begun to re-evaluate and accept that two out of three was not a bad return, Lena had stumbled into Shepherds. She had looked terrible. As drained and hollow as any soul she had seen in The Purgs. Far more so than when Deborah had sat with her, so many miles above.

Deborah had immediately thought that a mistake had been made. There was no way this poor woman could make the journey. It was a fucking miracle she had made it to the bar at all. That she hadn't just keeled over on the way and given up.

Augustine had looked with horror at her, and had dispensed with all his usual formalities and peculiarities as he shot round the bar and across the room to her near collapsing figure. He had produced a vial of The Word, and held it out to her. Deborah had been flabbergasted by her reaction. She had looked at it without comprehension. She didn't know what it was.

Deborah could hardly wrap her mind around it. She had talked to this woman, had a long conversation with her. She was sad for sure, depressed and broken, though those words had little meaning in The Purgs, where everyone suited them to some degree. To say someone was depressed here was akin to saying they were in possession of a head. Even by the standards of this place she had seemed longing, but seeing this scene, Deborah could hardly believe she had managed as well as she had. It took Deborah two days in The Purgs to feel the hunger so debilitating that she could barely stand. *Less* than two days. Lena had been here for more than two decades.

After her trek, she had barely had the strength to lift the tiny vial to her mouth. Augustine had done it for her. As the airy liquid had slipped over her lips and down her throat, Lena's eyes had widened. She had slipped from his grasp down onto her rear in a pile on the floor, her shaking legs unable to withstand the force of the shudder that ran through her. After a moment she had stood back up, with wonder in her eyes. Wonder and glassy tears.

"Am I alive again?" she had asked Augustine. A genuine question. She looked into his eyes as though he himself was her saviour.

"I'm afraid not my dear," he had replied, adding a comforting salve to his tone. "I can't grant you life. I got whiskey though?"

They had both smiled, as she had nodded and allowed him to help her across the room to the bar.

Respect swelled within Deborah. Lena had endured a hardship she could barely fathom, but she had still dragged herself through. Nothing to drive her but the promise of hope. Of a *chance* to help. She was perfect.

⁂

Introductions, formal ones, had been perfunctory in some cases. Raymond and Whitman had certainly already engaged in some back and forth over the days in the bar above. Lena, after her swift recovery from the hunger by way of the vial – the Miracle Juice, as she referred to it, much to the amusement of the Archangels – had been unflinchingly warm in greeting both of them, and the cynical way she had eyed Deborah on the park bench a week ago was replaced now with only mildly hesitant familiarity. Her gratitude stemming from her introduction to The Word had negated any reproach over the gruelling walk she had endured.

The three sat in the archival room, side by side on wooden stools. Apprehensive, but enquiring. Like the waiting room outside an interview, or an audition. Behind them, the formidable, grim figures of Raguel and Yahoel stood. They watched in sombre silence, like ancient statues at some pagan alter. Deborah sat facing the group, with Cassiel at her side, sat in his own chair. Waiting also.

"Do we need to wait for the others?" Deborah asked him.

"No," he replied. "Your guide and your... rogue, they know of our endeavour. They will join us shortly, I am sure."

"Okay," she nodded.

She turned to the trio. Lena's enquiring face, Raymond's stoic grimace, Whitman with his testy, yet curious eyes set on her as he toyed with his beard. She pulled in a breath.

"I'm going to tell you a story..." she began.

Her three recruits sat in silence, like pupils in a class after a lengthy lesson, staring back at their tutor through the musty classroom. The air was thick with disbelieving suspense.

"Well," Raymond was the first to break the silence. "That's probably the most insane thing I've ever heard."

"Yup," Deborah conceded.

Her voice was thin after so much talking. At various points during her long relay of their situation and the desires of the Revolution, Cassiel had made to interject, to relieve some of the conversational burden, but she had gently hushed him. She had to be the one to take on the role. As leader, the tale had to be spun by her and her alone. Her long discussions with Raziel had been in preparation for this. She was human, and she knew the ways of humans. The story was too big, too grand to convince, coming from the Angels. It had taken a long time for her to accept it from them. She needed these three to hear it from a more familiar mouth.

"It's blasphemy," Lena added, with narrow-eyed incredulity.

"It's not," Deborah stated flatly.

"*Killing* God?! How can you say it's not..." Lena began, but Deborah interjected.

"Killing *a* God. To reinstate *the* God. That is *not* blasphemy. The current state of things? *That* is blasphemy."

Lena opened her mouth, then closed it again, in thought.

"I thought you were an atheist?" she asked with a cocked eyebrow.

"I believe only in what I can see and feel and prove, not in what I need to rely on faith for. I'm *here*. I don't *need* faith. I *know*."

"So what does that make you?" Lena pressed.

"It doesn't matter," Deborah replied. "Philosophical terms have no meaning any more. This isn't Schrodinger's Cat. I've *seen* in the box. The cat is alive. And it's not a good cat. It *should* be dead."

"And we're the ones to fix that?" Raymond asked.

"Yes," she replied firmly.

"An old detective, a nurse and a…," he looked at Whitman, who had sat in silent thought until now. "Excuse me buddy, but a concentration camp victim? And whoever else your big pals bring in here, we're going to change the course of reality?"

"Yes," she replied again, just as firm. They had to see her resolve. If she willed it hard enough, it would be contagious. It had to be, she was counting on it.

"What makes you think we can do that?" Raymond asked with a dubious tone.

"Because little groups of hopeful people are what *always* changes the world," said a voice.

All heads turned to the speaker, who sat stroking his beard. He turned to Deborah with a funereal glance.

"More often than not they fail though. Most often."

Deborah felt relief swell inside her. Whitman. Who would have thought?

"That's true," she replied, "but they try anyway."

"Because they know in their hearts, that to not try? To not act? Would be the worst betrayal of all." He nodded with conciliatory gravity as he spoke.

She allowed only the tiniest hint of her smile to crack across her face. Just the slightest bit of it. Just for him. Who would have thought? Whitman Czapski.

"Yes."

Both Raymond and Lena were looking at him in suspense.

"Just think of the challenge," Deborah told him with conspiratorial playfulness. He smiled a little, seeing the mock manipulation and not caring.

"Okay Schönes Mädchen. I'm in."

Raymond let out a skeptical grunt.

"For the challenge?" he asked Whitman cynically.

Whitman turned to him and replied with quiet resolve.

"For the good. I stood by as a fascist government ravaged my country and my people and finally my family and me." He turned back to Deborah. "I won't stand by and watch it again."

Deborah fired a thank-you from her eyes, and watched as he nodded back. He then stood. Deborah wondered for a moment why, and eyed him with curiosity as he flipped and tied his bow tie at his neck. After a moment, once he had finished and was happy with it, she watched, humbled, as he lifted the stool on which he had sat, walked the few feet towards her and placed it gently at her side. He sat, now looking back at the two remaining recruits. On her side, and at it.

Deborah loved this gesture. The quiet, dignified courtliness of it. She wanted to kiss him on his bald head.

Lena and Raymond, virtual strangers to each other, shared a pensive glance. Turning back to Whitman, Lena spoke softly.

"You don't think it's futile? All that she told us… You don't think it's hopeless?"

Whitman glanced at Deborah and then back to her.

"Hope does not reside in the task. It resides in the man. It can't be *taken*. I won't give it up."

Deborah smirked and said nothing. Odd to hear oneself paraphrased, she thought. Raymond remained silent for a while longer, then, with resignation, he grunted.

"Fuck it."

He stood, and picked up his trench-coat. Deborah watched him with dismay. He hooked the coat over the crook of his arm and looked across the room at the exit. For a moment he stood in consideration. Then he turned, picked up his stool with one of his broad shovel-hands and set it next to Whitman's.

"The sins I got following me around? I'm not going anywhere quickly, and likely not anywhere good." He squatted down on the stool, and pulled his cigarette packet from the trench. He slid one out as he watched Deborah's smile broaden and lit it, snapping the metal lighter shut with a resonating clink.

"What've I got to lose?"

"Your *soul*," Lena told him, desperately. Her place opposite them now a lone vigil. Her face caked in the anxiety that instilled.

"Not much of that left now," he remarked, taking a long drag on the cigarette and billowing thick smoke into the air. "Maybe I can use what's left for something more than regret."

Lena looked small. Small and fearful across from them. But she didn't move.

"It's your choice Caroline," Deborah told her. "Free will. We won't force you. All we can say is that we want you. We *need* you."

She sat timidly, a rabbit in headlights.

"I'm afraid."

"We all are," Deborah replied.

"I don't want to stay here."

"You don't have to."

Lena hung her head a moment, and when she looked back up, tears hung in her eyes.

"I don't know how I would help."

"None of us know that. All we know is that we can try."

She nodded, passively, and looked around the room at nothing in particular. Then she stood. Whitman stood at the same time, and stepped towards her. He leaned in toward the stool and turned his head to meet her eye with a questioning glance. Lena stood a second more, staring back at his gentlemanly gesture, then nodded again. Whitman smiled and lifted her stool, walking it across to place it by Raymond's.

Raymond, witnessing this unpretentious, comforting gesture, shuffled over to the stool next to Deborah, allowing Whitman to take his place. Whitman nodded his thanks and sat, and Lena sat beside him. She held his hand as she did, and kept it in hers afterwards.

Shortly after Deborah's solo had become a quartet, the door opened, and Raziel emerged from behind it. In seeing him arrive, walking tall, his black void eyes scanning the room and assessing the mood therein, Deborah thought for a moment how fortunate she had been.

Whitman, Raymond, even Lena whose resolve had wavered the most; all had accepted quickly and without question some of the more outlandish aspects of their business. Things she herself now took for granted, but which had once thrown her for a loop. The Angels, the Archangels with their obsidian eyes and dizzying quality, the archaism of their manners: all had been glossed over without much fuss. Deborah wondered if this difference was entirely due to the speed with which she had been introduced to it all, mere days after her own death, in comparison to their various periods of years, or decades, her recruits had spent in The Purgs. Or perhaps, she mused, she was simply different by nature.

Raziel acknowledged her presence, but made his way to Cassiel first, whispering in his ear. Cassiel nodded in confirmation and turned to Deborah and her troupe, who, having pulled their stools into a loose square, sat in muted conversation.

"Your guide is ready," he told them.

"Where is he?" Deborah asked.

"She," Cassiel replied. "She will be here momentarily, though the meeting must be brief. Leaving the Great City in the manner she has is *extremely* dangerous. Impossible for anyone of even mild impurity, and her return must be swift. She cannot be tainted by this place."

"She's coming from The City?" Deborah replied, confused.

"Yes. By way of a most ancient passage. One not employed for eons."

"That's not how we'll be sneaking in?"

Cassiel grinned a sickeningly grim smile.

"To even attempt so, my dear child, would burn your stained soul from your body and send it shrieking through eternity."

"Okay," Deborah adopted a casual sarcasm, the antidote to his grave theatrics. "Good tip. Let's not try that then."

"Indeed," Cassiel remarked. He seemed then to sense something about to happen and braced himself.

"Deborah." He addressed her alone, with sincerity. "You must trust us. She *is* the way. She will help you."

"O…kay…" she replied uneasily. What the hell did that mean? What was wrong with this guide?

She barely had a chance to think further, before a familiar static feeling rose in the air around her. Raymond and Whitman looked up and around. Lena, all too familiar with the feeling, simply bowed her head. That static, to her, brought nothing but painful memories.

In front of her, in an empty space next to their group, a slice of pure white light cut the air. It peeled not in a line, as she had seen elsewhere, but in a perfect circle in the air. Perhaps eight feet in diameter, sitting a few inches above the ground. As this round version of a nothing-door peeled open in a circular sweep, radiant white burst into the room. It was blinding. Deborah, along with her troupe, turned her head violently and shielded her eyes. Even through her lids the light was intense. Burning. It rose in a flash, then dissipated, leaving the room a blurry blob as her irises strained to readjust to the gloom of the archives.

As the haze focussed, her lenses recovering from their flash-frying, she made out two silhouettes. One large, one small. The larger had something massive spanning across its back. Their blurry edges were closing, sharpening around them as they stood, her returning vision creating a focus pull around them.

Finally the colour ran back in to the world and she saw Raphael, standing tall, in a robe and resplendent silver regalia. He was transformed. Barely reconcilable with the boyish looking, cropped blonde in the linen suit she had sat with in this very room only weeks ago. His wings were out. Great, swan wings, folded, but Deborah could tell from their height that their span would be enormous. Fifteen or sixteen feet at least and beautiful, pearl white. The sight of him was awesome and terrifying.

At his front stood a young girl. A slender slip of girl, with long fiery-red hair and piercing green eyes. She wore a simple, green dress with a stitched band around the waist, of a darker material. It matched a small slung bag, more purse than bag really, on a delicate strap over her shoulder. Around her neck she wore a wide green ribbon, on which hung a golden clasped pendant. It did not hang low; the ribbon was tight. She stood watching the group in silence. She did not seem fazed by the sight she saw, or by the manner of her arrival for that matter. She was unconcerned by the presence of the Archangels, even her chaperone in all his glorious finery. She did, however, seem sad. Melancholic. Not sad in the fashion of the Purgs. Not the hollow and fearful pathos of those lost souls that filled every crack and crevice of this place. Her sadness was different. Somehow… peaceful. A serene heartache.

Cassiel, who, along with his brethren, had not flinched at the light from the door – indeed, had seemed to bathe in its emanation and afterglow – looked tensely at Raphael's towering figure.

"You encountered no trouble?"

"None, Brother," Raphael replied. "Luck was on our side."

"Let us hope the same for your return. These channels grow less safe year by year." His hurried whisper was fretful.

"Indeed" Raphael replied gravely, and then turned his attention to Deborah.

"May I present your guide ma'am. Miss Arianna Selena Durante," he told her, and added, "L'oiseau Chanteur de la Nuit."

At this the young girl turned her head and looked up at Raphael with a sad admonition in her eyes. He looked back down at her, without any defensiveness. Just a look, nothing more. The girl, Arianna, turned back to the group and smiled shyly.

Deborah couldn't quite decide how old she was. If she were to close her eyes Deborah would have guessed around eighteen. But with them open she couldn't be so sure. There was incredible depth to them. Deborah had to remind herself often that the age people appeared to be had little relevance here. That was simply the age they had died. The time passed since their birth? That was something else entirely.

"It's a pleasure to meet you Miss Durante, my name is Deborah."

Arianna smiled and nodded a greeting.

"You know why you are here? What we are doing?" Deborah asked her. Keeping business at the forefront for now. She wasn't sure quite how long Cassiel would consider 'brief'. She wanted to ensure the most important questions were dealt with as a priority. The girl nodded again, with a solemn conviction unnerving on a face so young.

Whitman piped up from Deborah's side now. Wishing to cut some tension, she assumed.

"L'oiseau Chanteur…" he asked curiously. "Are you a singer?"

Arianna hesitated a little.

"She was," Raphael replied for her. The girl still hadn't spoken a word. It was becoming conspicuous. Deborah and the others had begun to cast occasional, uneasy glances at each other.

"With your permission?" Raphael addressed Arianna now. She looked up at him and nodded. He turned to the group.

"Arianna Durante was a singer. A rather famous one in her day, something of a prodigy. I imagine you could still find some record of her in a library somewhere, even in your time." He spoke to Deborah directly.

"What was your time?" Deborah asked Arianna.

"She was born in 1831, in a town called Landerneau." Arianna nodded along.

"Her voice was incredible. A beauty like no other. Haunting. She travelled from Landerneau to Paris when she was fifteen, with her beau, an older man named Achille who would be her manager. To pursue a life on the stage."

Arianna listened to Raphael speak, unfazed, if a little embarrassed at his more fawning accolades. At mention of her 'beau' though, she seemed to wilt a little.

"She was successful. Wildly so. Her voice was the talk of the city. The name 'L'oiseau Chanteur de la Nuit' was applied by the newspapers of the day, and it was aptly adopted. The Songbird of the Night. Her star rose very quickly. Her admirers were plentiful. Potential suitors abundant. Achille was displeased, despite her devotion. Despite her love for him."

Arianna's head bowed. Deborah baulked a little at this unsettling scene. It seemed cruel. Why tell this part of the story? But Raphael did, and Deborah assumed he must have her blessing. Certainly she never attempted to interject or to impede him.

"Upon finishing a performance, at the height of her fame – a most successful one at L'Salle de la rue Le Peletier – and after multiple curtain calls, she retired from the stage. Rather than return directly to her dressing room as she normally would, she went instead to her manager's office. To find her love. She did not find him there. She did, however, find his ledger."

Raphael appeared to check his footing here, glancing down at Arianna. She nodded, beckoning he continue, though she bowed her head thereafter.

"Her discovery that he had been stealing her performance money rather than, as he had assured, storing it safely... was the first tragedy of that evening. His reaction when she confronted him was the second."

Deborah waited for him to continue, but he didn't. Instead, Arianna looked back up at Deborah and the group, and lifted her hands to untie the ribbon around her neck. As she slipped it off, Deborah grimaced. A vicious scar ran the width of her throat. Deep enough that, looking face to face at her, one could barely see where it ended at the sides of her neck. It might as well have been a decapitation. Her deep green eyes remained steady and mournful.

"Oh my lord," groaned Lena, standing instinctually to go to the girl. The innate nursing tendency had clearly returned in full along with her strength. She stopped herself, however, as Arianna replaced the ribbon carefully, tying it back up neatly behind the coppery waterfall of her hair.

"A messy cut," Raymond said gruffly. "He was an aggressive guy?"

Arianna nodded dolefully.

"Why is she mute?" asked Whitman. Deborah shot him a look of disbelief.

"Are you serious?"

"I mean why is she *still* mute?" he corrected. He spoke softly. Not without compassion, though not necessarily with it either.

"I myself was gassed. No physical marks there I grant you, but you?" He looked to Deborah. "You died with a bullet in you did you not? And Raymond mein freund, your face… I'm sure it, was not quite as it is now after your dalliance with your killer. Your… Rag Man." He turned to Lena. "Ms Caroline, you have not told us of your demise, but a woman of your age, I cannot imagine it was anything natural?"

"A car crash," Lena confirmed, a little sad, but with a questioning tone rising. She, along with the rest of the group, was beginning to see where Whitman was going with this. He nodded with solicitude.

"I'm sorry. I imagine that at the moment of your passing you did not look so very lovely, my dear. So my question is," he turned to Arianna. "Why are you mute? It does not seem fair that you retain the mark of your death-stroke, where the rest of us do not."

The group stood in querying silence. Lena, seeming to recall something, stooped and raised the leg of her trousers.

"I still have this," she said, pointing to a lighter patch of scar tissue on her shin.

"You were young when you received this injury?" Cassiel asked her.

"I was nine. I pierced it on a fence."

Cassiel nodded.

"I still have these," Deborah added, holding up her fingers. The burns were as present as they had ever been. "And yes, I was young."

Cassiel nodded again.

"Those are a part of you. The you that you are in your own mind. Part of what made you as you are now. Your soul carries such things. It is unusual to carry the *fatal* injury on beyond death. Such things are not ingrained. The soul has no time to live with them, and no wish to recall them."

Deborah frowned.

"So why…"

"It is unusual, but not unheard of. To carry the killing blow? The soul must *wish* to. Their sorrow must carry it for them. Envelop it. The wound itself must be such a great part of themselves, that it *cannot* be let go." He turned with solemnity to Arianna.

"You carry your burden of your own will, child?"

She nodded, and, delicately unclasping her purse, she reached into it. Cassiel looked back with understanding. Deborah could not grasp this.

"Why?" she asked, unnerved.

Arianna produced a little leather-bound notepad and a pen. For a moment Deborah thought it was a Scroll, but no. This was a notebook like any other. Good for writing and nothing more. Arianna scribbled, and held the pad up for them to see. What it said hit Deborah right in her chest.

'I Love Him'.

Well, she thought with fascination. What was there to say to that? Cassiel smiled. Lena, with her wide eyes doleful, was the one to ask what Deborah had wondered, but had chosen not to vocalise.

"Where is he now?"

Arianna looked mournful and scribbled another note, ripping it off and handing it to Lena.

'Below,'

it read.

Lena stepped forward to Arianna, ignoring the imposing figure of Raphael in his finery. She took her hand in her own and embraced her tenderly.

It was a moment no one in the room would voluntarily disturb. Whoever knocked on the door, from the Officers' Quarters, did not know this. All eyes turned as Raziel stood and paced towards it.

"Our group numbers five now," he said as he walked. Arriving at the door, he added, "Now comes our sixth."

He opened the door, and through it came Zotiel and then Zephon. Both nodded familiar greetings to Deborah and the room. Behind them followed a young man. A boy really. His dark, curly hair was matted and his frame was lean. His features gawkish.

Deborah's eyes widened and a bowling ball fell through her stomach. Her face turned white as the blood raced from it, repelled by the swell of her thoughts. *No*, her mind groaned at her. *No no no. Not him. Please.*

A rogue, she had asked for. *'Someone with a good slight-of-hand. Someone proficient at con-art.'* Her own words thundered through her head, fragments of conversations flitting like a zoetrope behind her eyes. In front of them stood her past.

Chapter Eleven
...AND SEVENS

He was so young. So very young in front of her. Memory is an odd thing; Deborah knew that. Those people we remember from our past, the childhood friends, the school classmates, the neighbour kids from across the halls of our youth – we think we remember them as they were, but we don't really. When we think back, we don't remember them as young as they truly were, because we don't remember ourselves as young as we truly were. Rather, we project our current selves back into those memories, like ghostly visitors.

Deborah had read once that every time we remember something, we recreate it anew. This was no doubt true, she had thought, and every time we do, we change little aspects. Little aspects about ourselves and, by projection, little aspects about the other players. When we look at a photograph of a childhood day captured in perfect clarity, even one we think we remember vividly, there is only ever one response.

'*My my,*' we say, '*don't we look young!*'

Deborah had no photographs of her past. But here one stood. Live, in living colour. Right in front of her horrified face.

And my my. Didn't he look young.

⁂

"Mark?!" She spat the name out over the rising lump in her throat.

"Hi Deb," he replied with his boyish smile. Fifteen years disappeared. She was right back in an alley in Glasgow. Two Mars bars and a Twix.

"How…? How are you here?!" she stammered.

"They brought me," he replied, directing a thumb towards Zephon and Zotiel, though never averting his gaze from her.

Raziel, seeing the familiarity and the calm way Mark spoke, stared inquisitively. His black eyes narrowed a fraction.

"You knew who you would meet here?"

"You said the assassin was someone from my past. From my *life*, you said. Look at me." He glanced at Raziel with admonishing cynicism.

"I don't know if it escaped your all-seeing eyes or whatever, but I never *had* much of a past. How many people – people that might have become *assassins* – did you think I would know? Did you think I went to some junior hitman-camp on my summer holidays or what?"

Raziel glowered. Whether anyone else noticed Zephon and Zotiel's stifled chuckles was debatable, but their lowered heads didn't quite manage to disguise it from Deborah. She watched this little exchange in a fuzzy haze, but their reactions snapped her back.

"I mean *how* are you here, Mark? *How* are you here?!"

He looked at her earnestly. "Isn't it obvious? How are you?"

Deborah closed her eyes to prevent any tears from forming. She wasn't successful, but she did at least prevent them from escaping the confines of her eyelids.

"I died," she said, the truth looming large over her.

"Bingo," he replied.

She baulked.

"But you're... you're exactly as I remember you Mark. *Exactly*. How..." She paused. She knew she was going to have to ask. She didn't want the answer, but she needed it. She braced herself.

"How old were you when..."

Mark tried a small smile. Trying to comfort her. That only made it worse.

"It was the next winter," he said, free of malice. "After you... after you were gone. Just a cold snap. Nothing earth shattering. Nothing violent. I went to sleep, I didn't wake up." He paused a moment. "Well, not *there* anyway. You look... older."

"You look *so young*, Mark." Deborah's fortifications against her tears were faltering. One hard blink and they would crumble. She knew it.

"Well," he shrugged, "I was, I guess. We both were."

Deborah was aware of the group around her, of their presence, but she couldn't bring herself to look at them. She had begun this day, her first day as their leader, with every intention of being the rock they would need. The staunch captain. The cast iron tip of their spear. It had taken about seven hours for those intentions to fall apart. She almost cared.

"Wait." A frown crossed her face as recollection dawned, morphed into a gargoyle scowl by her thickening throat and reddening eyes. "Wait, the *next* winter?"

Mark nodded, curious.

"How the fuck did that happen Mark?!" She stepped forward and grabbed a hold of his shoulder, shaking him. She was a clear three inches taller than he was now, and it felt very strange as a thirty year old woman to be violently manhandling a teenage boy. But she wasn't a thirty year old woman. She was a fifteen year old girl. She was a thirty year old, cold-blooded killer. She was a fifteen year old, lost little girl. Her present and her past had collided. They both lived now, struggling for control of the same body.

"You had the apartment! You had the…," memory flooded back. "The broke-down palace!"

Mark smiled reflectively.

"I didn't stay there," he replied softly. "That was where *we* stayed. I… I didn't stay there any more."

Deborah was shattering as he spoke. Her glass body cracking under the strain of this. The memory and the guilt and the shame. Killer or not, it turned out, to her mournful surprise, that fifteen year old lost girl had been waiting and watching from within her all along. What terrible things she must have seen. What must she have thought?

"You had money! You had all the *fucking money*, Mark! Why were you sleeping outside you *stupid fucking idiot*?!" She was screaming now. Shrieking in his face hysterically.

"That was *our* money," he said flatly. As if this was totally obvious. As if she should know better. As her face contorted with her grief, he added, "What if you came back?"

The final crack. Deborah shattered. Her dam broke and the tears burst through. She dropped to her haunches and buried her face in her hands.

"Deb, I…" She felt his hand touch the top of her head gently. She threw her hand out wildly, shoving his away.

"No," she moaned through the guttural cracking voice of her tears. Violent tears. Like knives in her eyes. Knives in her throat.

"Deborah, it's *okay*. It's… You shouldn't…" He tried again, but this time she smacked his hand away with more purpose and stood. Her face was blotchy and swollen, her throat painfully stretched.

"No," she said again, trying to compose herself.

"No what?" Mark asked genuinely.

"I thought I hurt you. I *knew* I hurt you, badly, and I knew you would hate me. I saw the look in your eyes when we… when I…"

She forced the words. Deborah never had trouble finding words for anyone else, but this was different.

"When I killed him. I saw. I knew we were finished, so I left. I knew that it would hurt you."

She sniffed like a child, and hated herself for it. What right did she have to cry? She stepped back from him and summoned as much composure as she could muster.

"But I never knew that I killed you."

Mark furrowed his brow in genuine, sorrowful confusion.

"You didn't kill me Deb."

"Yes I did," she replied in a miserable whisper. "Yes I did." She turned to Raziel, who stood in silence watching her.

"Well, your little number theory is out the fucking window, isn't it?" She threw her words at him like weapons. "Turns out my count was off all along. Right from the fucking start. I'm not at thirty-nine. I'm at forty already."

Raziel remained, for the first time since she had met him, appropriately silent. She turned back to Mark, and placed a hand gently on his cheek. His young cheek. Just like her young self had so often.

"I killed you." She smiled at him with painful, fatal beauty. "I killed you my love. I *will not* do it again."

Mark's brow lowered as she turned back to Raziel.

"No," she stated with finality. "He will *not* come with us. No *fucking* way."

She turned, all thought of her task gone, and stormed out of the room. The group looked back and forth at each other in uneasy disorder.

When Mark, accompanied by Raziel, followed her into the Officers' Quarters, Deborah was lying on one of the green couches. Her head pointed towards the wood panelled ceiling, one arm resting askew across her face.

Raziel, seeming to have discovered in the past few minutes some understanding of human social norms – or maybe he had had the knowledge all along and had simply not cared to employ it – remained at the entrance, silently. Mark approached the empty couch and sat opposite her. He sat there for several minutes before he spoke, and when he did, his tone was light.

"You remember when I got that CD player?" he asked her. Deborah remained motionless on the couch, her face still buried in the crook of her elbow.

"Deb?" he coaxed.

"For my birthday," she said, muffled, from beneath her arm.

"Yeah. I was all excited cause I managed to get it without cutting into our stash? Got it wrapped and everything? It looked like shit, the wrapping, but I did get it wrapped at least."

"Yes." She sniffed hard, still hiding her eyes and face from him.

"And I was so excited that I forgot to get any CDs to go with it?"

Deborah grunted in a painful half-laugh. It cut through her bruised throat.

"Yeah."

"So we went down to the Tower Records, and I hung about for like an hour, trying to get a moment to pocket that goddamn copy of Nevermind."

"That big, ginger clerk," she told him.

"Right! That dude. He was all over me. What a chump. You think he was making anything more than minimum wage?" Mark spoke in an amused recitative. "Why the hell did he care so much?"

"I think he fancied you," she replied from under her arm.

"Well, I was *terribly* fetching in my delightful ensemble that day. Homeless chic don'tcha know."

She laughed again, and pulled her arm down from her face. Tilting over on the green leather, she rested her puffy, warm face on her arm. All the body language of adulthood had slipped from her.

"I eventually got the security thing off and pocketed it, and I was almost out the store when he grabbed me, face on him like I pissed in his chips."

"I remember," she smiled sadly.

"He was about to get the manager when you came in and grabbed his arm, stuck his hand on your…" he trailed off, and Deborah smiled again. He was still shy about these things.

"On my tit, Mark. You *can* say it you know."

He looked somewhat bashful, but continued.

"You stuck his hand there… and he goes all shocked. Looked like that kid in Home Alone when he puts the aftershave on? You start shouting about how this pervert is trying to grab you to the whole shop?"

Deborah did remember. In spite of everything, she began to giggle. Girlishly, like she hadn't in more than a decade. Mark began to laugh.

"He starts shaking his head like a little kid caught stealing sweets, with his mouth hanging open? He stepped back so quick he fell through the whole CD rack?"

"He looked like a fucking turtle rolling around on his back going 'no I wasn't, I wasn't!'" Deborah squeezed the words between her giggles. They were both laughing like children. For the briefest of moments it was beautiful. Then, as the laughter faded, Mark looked at her with a soft, serious gaze.

"I'm coming with you." He was quiet, but spoke with clarity. "You left me behind once. You're not doing it again."

Deborah sat up now.

"Why aren't you mad at me Mark? Why don't you hate me?"

He shrugged a little.

"I was, for a while. I was mad. I was angry at you. I don't know if I ever *hated* you. I told myself I did for a while, but I don't think it was true. I never thought you were evil or anything. And it's been a long time. Being here? If it gives you anything, it gives you perspective."

She felt dejected, horribly so. His lack of anger was as humbling as it was cutting. She wished he did hate her.

"You're not coming," she told him.

"I know the plan. This big weirdo told me." He cocked a thumb back at Raziel, who either hadn't heard or elected to feign so.

"You might need me. What if you need a briefcase nicked? You *know* I'm your man."

Deborah smiled at this, but shook her head.

"You're too young Mark."

"I'm older than you are Deb. I was born in eighty-one. You were born in eighty-three. Whatever I look like, I'm still older than you. And I'm definitely older than the wee redhead in there."

While Deborah knew this was true, it didn't matter. She couldn't bring him along. She wouldn't subject him to it.

"This thing we're planning? It's going to be difficult. It's going to be virtually impossible, I think. We're pretty much guaranteed to fail. And the consequence of that? I can't do it Mark. I won't do that to you."

"The consequence?" Mark's voice began to rise a little.

"There's no precedent for this, as far as these guys know." She nodded towards Raziel at the door. "No one knows exactly where we'll end up when we… *if* we fail. But *down* seems the only feasible scenario."

"So?" Mark asked with a little haughtiness.

"What do you mean so?" she asked tempestuously. "You think that's something to joke around about? To take lightly? Have you looked around *this* place? This will be a walk in the park compared to what's down there."

Mark narrowed his eyes.

"Yeah, I *have* looked around this place Deb, I've had fourteen years to. Have *you*?"

"What do you mean?"

Pique rose in Mark's voice.

"I mean have you looked at the people here? *Talked* to any of them?"

"I…" She wanted to tell him yes, those people in the room – Whitman, Lena, Raymond – but really she hadn't. Not to any of the random souls that milled around in their quiet misery. Not at any length anyway. She didn't know what he meant exactly.

"Well I have," Mark shot at her, pained. "Folks are not here waiting to get *above*. They're here hoping not to go *below*. But that *is* where most of us are going. Eventually. Its just a matter of time."

"I don't…" she began, but he cut her off.

"The *'sins'* that stop you going up? Some of them are tiny! Insignificant shit!" His pique was building to anger.

"Had an affair and killed your mistress? *Fuck off.* Stole sweets as a kid? *Fuck off!* It's all the same to the bigwigs. Nicked a loaf of bread for a hungry kid, talked in church, coveted your neighbours wife? All mortal infractions. Unless, of course, you were a fucking hypocritical religious zealot. Then you get a free pass. It's all back to front and fucked up. I doubt I need to tell you where I'm going. Plenty of sin to draw from in my well."

Deborah watched his temper build. It seemed odd to her. Through all her time with Mark back in the day, she realised, she had never heard him raise his voice in anger. It seemed wrong.

"Whether *you* think I should be or not, whether you think I'm a bad person, doesn't matter. I'm damned. The only reason I'm still here now is the fucking backlog. I know it, they know it," he nodded towards Raziel, "and I can fucking guarantee that your little group know it too. Why do you think they're all willing to risk it with you? It's not because they want to help fix the world. Not completely anyway. It's because it *isn't* really a risk. They don't stand to lose anything that won't be taken from them, in time, anyway!"

Deborah stared at him. It was hard to reconcile the dissonance of this angry, astute outburst with the sweet, funny, earnest boy she once knew. They sat in silence for a long moment.

"When did you get smart?" she asked eventually.

"I'm *not* smart," he replied, his tone cooling as his anger ebbed. "I've just been here a while."

Deborah gave an admonishing look, but feeling the insult in her words, she corrected herself.

"You *are* smart. You were before, I didn't mean that. It came out wrong. I just meant… I don't know what I meant. You *were* smart, Mark. You always were. You just weren't…"

"Jaded?" he asked knowingly.

"I suppose," she conceded.

"I'm not. Not now anyway. Now I have a chance to actually do something. Don't take that away. It's been a long fourteen years."

She sat in contemplation, in the glow of his resolve.

"Mark," she began with a sigh, "I *know* you're not a bad person. I *always* knew. But *I* am." She began to try and regain her composure, straightening out her shirt and smoothing her hair back across her head.

"Even if we somehow succeed, if we manage to beat the worst odds I've *ever* known? Return things to the way *they* say they were? How they are supposed to be?" She drew a low breath. "I'm *still* headed down."

Mark was clearly disconcerted. He looked ready to offer a response, but failed to find a fitting one.

"I don't do what I do for the money. And I don't do it out of circumstance. I do it because… I choose to. Because I *need* to. Whatever happens to the world – wherever the standard of good and evil are set – it doesn't matter for me. I'm too far in one direction. The fulcrum's never going to slide far enough to save me."

"I don't believe that."

"It's true, Mark. You know it, deep down. I still remember how you looked when you saw me. When I killed my first."

Her glance at his face confirmed it. He did recoil. Just a little, but it was there in his face, when she spoke of that fateful night in the offices of Swinton Legal.

"Hitman is a very apt word, Mark. A *hit*. The same word we use for a kill, a junkie uses for a shot. We're…" she thought for a second, then admitted the truth that she had feared for years, though never truly accepted. "We're *addicted*. Just like they are."

Deborah had never discussed the intimate side of her profession, her *talent*, with anyone. Not ever. Saying it now, to him? It was both a tremendous relief and a hideous betrayal. Unburdening herself to the only person she didn't want to burden with anything more.

"You do it for fun?" Mark asked with an oddly unprejudiced cadence. No judgement in his inquiry.

"No," she replied thoughtfully. "I do it for a living. But I can't deny the feeling I get when I do. I could have stopped Mark, but I never would have. I needed it. I… I still need it."

Mark said nothing to this, but nodded slowly, pensively.

"You wouldn't understand," Deborah sighed sadly. "And I sure as fuck wouldn't want you to."

Mark looked back at her with steel behind his eyes.

"I don't need to," he replied. "You are who you are now. But that's not *all* of what you are. You're not *just* some ice-in-her-veins assassin, whatever anyone else thinks. Whatever *you* think. You might be that, but you're other things too. You're the girl with two Mars bars and a Twix that she shared, without knowing where her next food was coming from. You're the girl who knows that Americans put the month before the day. You're the girl who scared a big, ginger shop clerk into rolling about like a turtle just to help out her friend."

Deborah smiled another pained smile.

"You were a lot more than my friend Mark."

He smiled back, hazy nostalgia in his complexion.

"Yes. Back then. But I'm a friend now. I don't understand why you do what you do, but that hardly matters now. Not here. You can think what you like about yourself. That's your prerogative. But you don't get to decide what I think of you. I was your friend then. I'm your friend still."

He stood from the couch.

"I'm coming with you."

He extended his arm out towards her. She stared at his hand and then at the resolve in his eyes.

"What are you going to do? Fix me? Save my soul?"

"Yeah," he replied. "I'm quite the carpenter, and a hell of a cobbler."

Deborah smiled a warm smile. Just to herself. Just for her. She had missed Mark. Whether she had known it or not, his absence had left a hole in her. A cigarette burn in her heart. She reached out for his hand.

"Okay, Dickhead," she sighed, smiling.

She took his hand and let him pull her up. The pair walked back towards Raziel, who silently opened the door for them.

⁂

When they returned to the archives, a muttering hush had descended. Whitman and Lena sat at an angle to each other, talking quietly. Raymond and Zotiel stood in conversation, or whatever passed for it, with Arianna Durante, who remained standing by her gilded chaperone. Cassiel, Raguel and Yahoel stood near the back of the room, a trio of furrowed faces. Zephon, curiously, stood alone. Unerring and unflustered, in a watchful vigil at the door. As Raziel led Deborah back through the door with Mark behind, he smiled. He seemed the only one to be sure she would return.

"All straightened out?" he asked, free of condescension. Deborah gave a brief nod, but did not slow her pace as she stepped to the centre of the room. The *clickety-clack* of her boots on the wooden floor drew the attention of all its occupants. When she stopped, turned and drew in a breath, all eyes were on her.

"I'm sorry," she said simply.

Her audience remained silent, though Whitman offered a conciliatory nod.

"That wasn't the best way to earn your confidence. It was... unprofessional. It won't happen again."

"We all have a past, Schönes Mädchen," Whitman said, acceptingly. A couple more nods from the room. Deborah smiled at him in thanks.

"Yes we do. And we all have burdens. And mine won't be yours again. Thanks. All of you."

Deborah had not been sure how she was going to fix this thing, to correct the damage her outburst may have done, but that seemed to be that. Easier than she thought. The air of tension lightened fast, as if the room itself exhaled after a long held breath.

Cassiel broke from his trio and paced the room to her spot at the centre. Seeing he meant to speak, Deborah stepped out into the audience, taking her place among her newfound acquaintances and re-found friend. Cassiel took the stage and looked over the row in front of him.

"A Warrior, a Guide, a Healer, a Mage, an Assassin and a Rogue." He spoke in a commanding voice. Giving a sermon. "We are complete."

The members of the group looked back and forth at each other. Despite the gravity, despite the terror and despite the impossible task which loomed large in their minds, it was difficult not to feel, in a sense, enlivened. Their merry band was assembled. Their grand adventure was on the cusp of its beginning.

"No," said a deep voice at their back.

Deborah and her troupe spun around. Raguel stood, tall and impassive as always, but he had jettisoned his usual silence.

"They are six." He shook his head. "They need another."

Had Raziel, or even Cassiel, suggested further delay, further addition to their group, Deborah might have shot back with some sarcastic or withering remark. She might have groaned. She might have wilted and sighed. But it came from Raguel. Raguel, who had always remained tight-lipped, except once. To help her. Raguel whose voice was like thunder and whose hands were burned ashen black. Raguel, who she trusted still, to lend voice to thought only when the thought was of import.

"Why?" she asked.

"Six is a *bad* number," he replied.

Oh fuck, really? You with this numerology shit too? she thought, but did not say. To Raziel or Cassiel, she might have, but not to him.

"He is correct." Cassiel spoke up now.

Deborah felt herself ready to deflate, but caught herself. After her outburst in front of the group she was to lead, she would not show them any more reason to doubt her today.

"So we need someone else?" she asked. "We're not going to lose anyone. There's no one here who's expendable."

"That is true. We are, as you say, going to need someone else," Cassiel replied. "Seven is a *good* number."

Deborah rolled her eyes. No one else saw, and Cassiel elected to continue, rather than address this doubtful gesture.

"There *is* a gap in the expertise of your group, child." He was ponderous, his cadence measured. "Heaven is a system. The City an intricate facsimile of myriad aspects of your world, rolled into the less confining parameters of ours. As above, so below. As below, so above." Cassiel seemed to be getting to a point here, though it eluded Deborah.

"There are many facets to your task that may require the knowledge of the systems. Of the paths of the energy of The City. You may have need of a… Paraclete."

"A Paraclete?" Deborah asked.

"An Enabler," Whitman added with a nod.

"What… does that mean exactly?" She asked hesitantly.

Raymond spoke up.

"I think he means a whiz-kid. Electronics and that kind of shit? Computers and microchips and what have you?" He spoke to Deborah, but eyed Cassiel as he did. For validation as much as anything. Raymond clearly had little understanding of the concepts of which he spoke, beyond knowledge of their existence. Cassiel meditated on this for a moment, then nodded.

"In Earth-parlance, yes. Someone who can understand, or at the least fathom, the intricacies of the energies of The City. But more than that. Someone who can comprehend such factors as they relate to *you*. The dangers they may pose to you."

Deborah began to realise what they meant. The answer to the question dawned.

"You mean a *handler*. That's what we called it in…" She almost spoke the name of The Orchard and then stopped herself, though she wasn't sure why exactly. It would have been unthinkable to do so in life. Probably quite immaterial in death, but instinct had a long wake. "…in the company I worked for. A handler. I had Eli."

"So we need to find one here?" Lena asked.

"That won't be as easy as these guys might think," Deborah replied, turning to Cassiel. "For starters, handlers aren't as expendable as us. As *me* I mean — as field operatives. They don't get involved hands-on, not in person anyway. They don't get killed in action. It took you guys long enough to wait for me to die. That's what you told me, wasn't it? You could be waiting a hell of a lot longer for a handler to die in a fit state to help us. They don't die, they retire. Unless you want us dragging around some geriatric who remembers how to crack the Enigma machine. Or want to sit tight, hoping a young one gets hit by a bus."

Cassiel nodded, understanding her point.

"Plus," she continued, "a handler's relationship with his operative is… I don't know how to describe it. Close. Intimate, I suppose."

Mark's face twitched a little. He took a keen interest in this comment, she saw. Oh Mark.

"And they are… an eclectic bunch. Oddballs for the most part. Finding one who would be happy to join your — *our* — cause is one thing, but finding one who could easily fit with me? With our group? That's another." She sighed.

"It's not like I'll find another Eli. And he was my handler for my entire career."

"I understand child, but the requirement remains. You should bring someone," Cassiel told her.

"And I understand," Deborah replied, "I just don't know *how* we're going to. Good handlers are rare enough. Finding one that works well with an operative is like catching lightning in a bottle."

She was having trouble conveying exactly how fruitless their search would likely be, and she knew it. It was not an easy thing to describe. A good handler had to be like an extension of yourself, and you an extension of them. It was an inherently intertwining relationship. A symbiosis.

The whole group was silent, each feeling the strain of the gloom, but none wishing to break it without anything to add. Deborah leaned on the table around which they now stood, head lowered in frustrated thought. As she did so, she felt a gentle tug at her arm. Turning, she saw the willowy figure of Arianna Durante, her big, green, soulful eyes looking up at hers. Obliging eagerness to please shone in them, but behind it, an iron will. She had her arm outstretched and in it was a sheet of her notebook.

Deborah took the paper and read the script, then lifted her head back to meet Arianna, with a look of confounded curiosity.

"What does this mean?" she asked Cassiel.

She held out the piece of paper to him, never breaking from the obliging gaze of her newest friend, L'oiseau Chanteur de la Nuit.

Cassiel looked down at the paper, then back up at the group. First confusion, then, as comprehension dawned, a sunken, sallow look drew upon him. Deborah had not seen such a disposition in any of the Archangels. Never before had one of their kind looked more like a man to her.

"Brother?" Raziel asked him, reading his concern and extending his hand to take the note. Cassiel handed it to him and turned to Arianna.

"How do you know of this?"

She, of course, did not reply, nor did she reach for her pen. She offered him nothing more than a coy shrug. Her piercing eyes remained steady.

Raziel read the note, and Deborah watched for his reaction. It was as grave as Cassiel's for sure, but there was something there. Something else. She thought it might be mettle.

All this consternation, all this disquietude over so small a phrase. All the note read, in Arianna Selena Durante's neat little handwriting, was six words.

'He does not have to die'.

"It is folly."

"It could work, Cassiel. It has in the past."

"Occasionally maybe, but how long ago? And for what nefarious purpose?"

"*Our* purpose is nefarious, Brother. And yes, a long time ago, but the ways still lie open."

"How could you possibly know that?"

"Who would seal them? It is the dominion of no one."

"We don't know that either, Brother."

"Cassiel, it is the dominion of no one. No one but the lost. It is dangerous, granted, but it *could* work."

"And if it doesn't?"

"Then it doesn't."

...

"You are changing, Brother. Your discussions with her. You are becoming like her. Rash. Reckless."

"Perhaps. How long have I watched her? Besides, are those such terrible qualities? They are why we chose her."

"They are *human* qualities. Admirable in *them* perhaps. Not in us."

"Nonsense, Brother. They are qualities we *lack*. Why else would we come to her? Why else would we ask that she see victory where we see only defeat?"

...

"You would have the entire Revolution jeopardised for the sake of one recruit?"

"I would have it tempered. They will have to endure hardship, we are *asking* them to do so. The Void is dangerous, but they can succeed. And doing so? Venturing there, for the completion of their assembly? That would strengthen them. Steel them for the journey ahead."

"You speak of it like it is a gauntlet to be run. A test."

"It would be."

"The Void is no test, Raziel. It would be their undoing."

"If The Void were to be their demise then they are not a fitting blade anyway, Brother. It *is* a test. In comparison to what will come? A most fitting test."

"That is foolish talk."

...

"It is their choice to make Cassiel. Her choice. At some point we must relinquish our reins. Stand aside and play the watchmen."

"Can you even be sure this man, this Paraclete – that he will come willingly?"

"She thinks he will."

"She *thinks*?"

"Free will, Brother. She knows him better than any. If she thinks he will come then I bow to her judgement."

"Hmm."

"She must be allowed to lead her troops, Brother. A puppet leader is of no use to us. If she is to be our saviour, she cannot also be our marionette."

…

"You believe Lord Gabriel would approve of this?"

"Lord Gabriel is not here."

"*Brother!*"

"He is *not* here, Cassiel. *We* must make the decision. But I believe that His Lordship would agree that his Hand must do as she sees fit. That for us to overrule her, after so much effort was made to find her, would be misguided."

"Perhaps."

…

"They will need to be escorted. The Void must be passed with great speed if it is to be passed at all."

"My footmen will take them."

"They volunteer? Or you volunteer them?"

"They will go willingly. They are loyal to the Revolution. And they are fond of her."

"As are you, Brother."

"I know what she is…"

"Do you?"

"Yes."

"And still you allow your misplaced affection to rule your judgement…"

"I allow my reverence to strengthen it. Fearful though it may be."

…

"And what of her questions?"

"Questions?"

"She is not stupid, Raziel. None of them are. If she is to recruit her Paraclete in this manner? She will put it together."

"There is nothing to put together, Brother."

"You know that is foolish. She is what she is. She will wonder. *They* will wonder, and they will ask."

"She has her own reasons, Cassiel. She would help regardless."

"I doubt that."

"You have not watched her as I have. She would. I am sure of it."

"And if you are mistaken?"

"It does not matter. It will not come to that. She will not know."

"You are naive."

"You are over cautious."

…

"If they should fall, Raziel… if they fall it will be a deep wound to us."

"*If* they fall, Cassiel, it will be a *fatal* wound to us."

…

"Very well. Bring her in."

Fracture Eight
PROVERBS

Deborah stood in her apartment by the windows, looking out over the dark city, past the Space Needle to the black water beyond. The dial tone buzzed softly in her ear.

"Deborah?"

"Hey Gorgeous. How you keeping?"

"Been worse darlin', been worse. Not much though. Where are you?"

"Back in the apartment."

"You're back in Seattle already? I thought you were gettin' the luxury treatment in Barbados or some such place?"

Deborah smiled. For a man in his position, Eli had little grasp of geography outside of what he learned for each job.

"Taipei. And I was. For a month now. See? I do take your advice from time to time. You didn't miss my sultry tones?"

"Yeah. One holiday in six years. You're quite the layabout. Nah, I've been busy y'know? Had to move around a bit."

"Trouble?"

"Yeah, girl trouble."

"Yeah I heard about that Gorgeous. Her name was Katrina right?" Deborah shifted, peeling her damp, bare feet from the floorboards, and paced across to the big sofa. She lay across it, pulling her bathrobe up around her, slid a pack of Virginia Slims from the coffee table and lit one.

"Yeah. Damn bitch flooded my place, would you believe it? Women, eh?" Deborah smiled at this. Eli was pretty much the only person who could make her do that. Then again, he was also pretty much the only person she knew.

"You wanna watch that darlin'. You're not meant to know where I hang my hat, remember?"

"With your accent? That's always been a dumb rule. I can practically hear the Po-Boy digesting."

He laughed at the other end.

"Had to call into the home office. Get them to send round Customer Support to clear out all our shit. Quite an operation in the flood."

"No trouble I hope, Sweetie? I hate to think of you struggling," she toyed.

"Nah, got a new office all set up now. Just final touches to go. So what you up to?"

She picked up the glass of red and sipped a little.

"Nothing. Just lounging about. Wanted to check in. Catch up. What's the crack?"

"Never gonna drop that Scottish shit are you? Don't they look at you funny around Seattle, talking like a leprechaun?"

She laughed, tapped in the ashtray and placed it in her lap, crooking the cellphone in her neck.

"Leprechauns are Irish. You mean a kelpie or a brownie or something."

"A what?"

"Never mind," she sighed exaggeratedly. "That Scottish shit is why I chose here, Gorgeous. I *like* the rain. Reminds me of my misspent youth."

"As opposed to your misspent present," Eli replied. *"Well, I'm a bit out of the loop, so not too much company gossip. You hear about Rust?"*

"No, what about him?"

"Moving up I hear. Quite the climber. Head of operations for all of Europe now. Could be a candidate for the big chair soon enough."

Deborah had never seen or spoken to Rust since her final meeting with him below the subway station in Glasgow. Eli, who kept abreast of the comings and goings of The Orchard by whatever means he had, had kept her informed of his rising star within it.

"Well, if he does, you'll never hear about that promotion. He'll just drop off the edge of the world."

"True that. He should thank you."

"Me?" She stubbed her cigarette in the ashtray and reached for another.

"That business you took care of in France? That was his fuck up."

She sipped more wine and lit her second. In France? she thought. Lucille? How was Rust involved with Lucille?

"He knew about Lucy?"

"He hired her. He brought her in. He was supposed to have kept an eye on her. If you hadn't have done such a good job he'd have got plugged along with her."

"She was a good operative Eli."

"Sure, but she was a sadistic fuck."

"In the end, yeah," she conceded, with a slight melancholy.

Deborah's last contract, her sixteenth, had been atypical. It was very unusual for a contract to be raised without an outside customer. Eli had been reticent to accept, knowing that the client was The Orchard themselves; he was uneasy not knowing the target. Deborah had known though. As soon as he had spoken of the hit. An *internal* contract. She knew, of course, that it would be another operative. She had considered it might be Lucille long before he had reluctantly accepted on her behalf and confirmed it.

Deborah had always suspected that Lucille's illustrious career would end this way. She had met her four, maybe five times, and had felt something of a kinship mingled in with her admiration for her. The simpatico they shared was not purely based on their shared profession. She saw the same thing in Lucille's eyes that she struggled with herself. The same want. The same hunger.

Lucille had finally snapped. She couldn't fill the vacuum inside her solely with the drip feed of her professional endeavours any longer. She had slipped into personal kills. Kills just for her. Who knew when? For all Deborah knew, she had been engaged in her own secret satisfactions back when they had shared a meal in Moscow. Or before even, when they had worked together on that Budapest nonsense with those cocaine-headed banking clowns. It could have been going on for years. However long, it had finally come to a head when she could no longer cover her tracks. When the trail of extra-curricular corpses became too long to ignore, and The Orchard had finally dealt with the problem the only way they knew. Well. Deborah had, really.

"You liked her?" Eli asked curiously.

"I didn't know her very well. She had her demons. We all do."

"I suppose," he conceded. *"You didn't have to take the contract. It's not like you to want to take a holiday. You wanted to, what? To cleanse yourself? After her?"*

Deborah took a long drag on Virginia number two and closed her eyes, feeling the burn as she exhaled.

"Something like that."

"Well, probably did you some good anyway. You should have invited me. I'm good with the suntan lotion."

Deborah smiled.

"I'm sure. How would I know? For all I know you could have been on the next sun-lounger over."

"Were you in a bikini?"

She paused for a moment with a squint as she quaffed some more red.

"Yes."

"Was there a man in the next lounger?"

"Probably."

"Did he ask you to marry him and run away to start a new life together?"

She broke out in a broad smile and laughed.

"No."

"Can't have been me then."

"Ah," she sighed with dramatised dreaminess. "Such a hopeless romantic."

"Damn straight. One of these days we are going to meet though."

"My stars, such tempestuousness Sweetie," she declared, theatrically beguiled. "What would The Orchard say."

"Eh," he dismissed. *"I work for you, not for them."*

"Don't kid yourself Gorgeous, we all work for them. Besides, I'm sure there'd be a string of young lassies all over Louisiana broken hearted if we did. A romantic soul like you?"

She could hear Eli's grin through the static line.

"I do fine. But you're the only girl for me Darlin'."

"Yeah yeah… big talk."

"Anyways. I'm glad you're feeling better. I haven't had much of a chance to check the wires for anything new, but are you ready if I do? Or you taking a bit longer?"

She stubbed her second cigarette, considered a third, then decided against it. She slid the glass ashtray back onto the coffee table.

"No, I'm ready," she told him. "Don't want you to start thinking you need to find a new beau."

"What I just tell you?"

She grinned again.

"I'm the only girl for you."

"Damn straight. Where you go, I go."

"Your cameras at least," she replied, toying playfully with him.

"Say the word and I'm on a plane. You want to test me? Wherever you go, I go. That's a pact for life darlin'."

"Well, let's see about our next contract and take it from there shall we?"

He mock-sighed.

"All business. Okay. I'll be fully up and running in a day or two. A week at the most. Then I'll see what's in the wires."

"Okay Gorgeous. Don't work too hard."

"Take'er easy... And Deborah?"

Deborah pulled the phone back to her ear.

"Yeah?"

"You did the right thing. She was crazy."

She paused a moment.

"Yeah. I know. Talk to you soon." She hung up and lay back into the sofa.

Lucy *had* been crazy. The look on her face as Deborah had slit open her throat, drained the last of her life from her? It had been haunting. It *was* haunting. The look of rage, and of gratitude. She had fought for her life, fought bitterly, but in the end, she had relished in her own death. Deborah could not tell then, or now, if that pleasure she took was in the ending of her tormented needs, or simply in the death itself. Her own grizzly passing the final, blissful smack-hit in a life of chasing her addiction. Chasing it down that dark and lonely path.

Deborah knew that path. She may not have walked it, but she lived at its entrance. At its first marker. From time to time, she could not help but glance down its deceptive, tempting trail. Just for a moment. Every now and then. What easy prey? What ecstasy lay there?

All that ever stopped her was the knowledge. The knowledge that those who did venture down that path? They never came back. She had known, the moment she suspected the contract was Lucy, that she would accept it. Not because she hated her. Not because she didn't understand her. Because she did. Because she wanted to be there, at the end of her path. To meet her there perhaps, to lift her burden from her, but that wasn't the only reason. It was not altruism that drove her. Deborah wanted to bear witness to the gruesomeness of that path's end. Shock therapy for herself. To reinforce her own aversion.

It had worked, in some sense. Seeing the finality. That moment, that rush moment of the kill, and that look in Lucy's eyes as inevitability dawned, clung to her still. Deborah could picture it so very clearly. Its ruthless beauty. Its bloody seduction. As she did, she slipped a hand beneath her bathrobe, closed her eyes and lay back.

Chapter Twelve

THE VOID

The tunnels had begun to widen considerably as the truck made its way along their vast lengths. Deborah rode up front, between Zephon, passenger-side, and Zotiel, at the wheel. Raymond, Whitman, Lena and Mark rode behind, strapped into seats side-on to the length of the empty container transport.

Progress had seemed sluggish at first. Zotiel had manoeuvred the vehicle carefully and painfully slowly through the tight network of sewer tunnels – or whatever they were. This crisscrossing system of brick-built, subterranean passages beneath The Purgs. After a time though, the arched stonework opened up and straightened, allowing for more speedy travel.

After the first few hours, the immediate questions had all been asked and answered. Of the truck (one of the old models used for transportation of souls, defunct and recovered by the resistance for times of need) of their current location (referred to by The Boys as 'the tunnels' with little additional detail offered) and, crucially, of their destination. Something they had called The Void. On the specifics of the place they had been vague, though Deborah suspected that this owed not to any desire to be deliberately effusive, but rather to their genuine unfamiliarity. It was obvious they were trepidatious about entering it. They feared it. From what she had gathered, it was a kind of no man's land. A DMZ, between what they called the celestial plains - encompassing The Purgs and Heaven (Hell too, Deborah assumed, though she would not ask) and the living world. Earth. How exactly they were connected at the Earth side she could not imagine, but how they were connected at this end was clear. The tunnels. The long and winding tunnels.

As he glanced around at the widening arch of their current passage, Zephon flicked his eyes down at the map in his hand, then back.

"We're going to be there soon," he muttered.

Zotiel gave a stilted nod. He shared Zephon's sunken, if determined, mood. He drove through the tunnel in silence.

Deborah glanced back over her shoulder at her band of heroes. They sat in muted agitation. Tremulous. Raymond and Mark on one side, Lena and Whitman facing them on the other. Arianna, of course, was absent. Her guidance would be of no value where they were going, and her return to Heaven by way of the passage of purity was required to be swift. As Cassiel had been quick to remind her, her every moment she spent in The Purgs increased both the potential of suspicion, and the terrible danger of her method of return. The group would not see her again. Not until their rendezvous in Paradise.

Deborah felt she should say something. Something to lift the mood perhaps, to try and buoy the group, if only for a moment. She was about to try, when she felt her body shift forward in the seat. They were slowing. She turned back to the windscreen and saw why. Through the glare of the truck's headlights she saw, a hundred yards ahead, and closing on them, a massive gate of solid iron. It barred the tunnel.

"Problem?" she whispered to Zotiel.

"Yeah. Big problem," he replied cynically, slowing to a halt in front of the forbidding barrier. He pulled the handbrake up with force but left the engine running. "We're here."

He and Zephon shared a glance, then both opened the doors of the cab and hopped down to the puddled stone floor of the tunnel. Zotiel leaned back in for a moment, touching his hand to a rolled slip of cloth by the edge of his cab door. Confirming its presence, or perhaps making to retrieve it, though if so, he thought better and left it where it lay. When Deborah made a move to follow him he held up a hand to stop her.

"You stay in there m'love. And strap in. Tell your merry men to do the same." He glanced at the gate suspiciously. "We might need to get going in a hurry."

She did as they bade and watched through the grubby windscreen as he and Zephon stepped to the door and examined it. They spoke back and forth as they paced its width, though she heard nothing of this exchange. Zephon found something of interest to one side, under a length of the huge chain links that bowed inward, flanking the door, and summoned his partner. After some close inspection and gesticulation back and forth, they appeared to reach a consensus. Producing something from his person, a key or some arcane mechanism she assumed, Zotiel interacted with whatever it was they had found, and stepped back. His compatriot pulled down on an ancient, black-metal handle on the side wall. It took all his force, clearly. Both his feet left the cold ground, his entire weight suspended. For a moment Deborah thought the lever would not budge, but sure enough, as he jolted his hanging body downwards, it freed from its rusted position and he crumpled to the floor, pulling the handle with him.

The great chain links shook off their bow, pulling taught then filing upwards into the gloom. The door gave an earth-trembling groan of sleepy displeasure, belching a great cloud of dust and stagnant filth into the air around the truck. It began to creak slowly downwards as the chains rose. Zotiel and Zephon, the latter having pulled himself up from his pile on the wet tunnel ground, made haste back into the cab at either side of her. Tension hung thick in the stale air as the trio sat staring ahead, the quartet at the rear craning their necks to do likewise. The door grumbled and strained as it was drawn down into a grime encrusted trench in the stone floor, and, as it did, they beheld what lay beyond.

First a crackling purple-grey sky, ripped here and there and everywhere with lightning scars. The rumble of the gate's descent was peppered by the smacking and groaning of thunderclaps and fizzing electrical buzzing.

As the gate lowered further, they saw distant peaks. Forbidding spires of rock, biting up at the frenetic sky like great fangs, and closer, crags and rock-crops and boulders littered a grey dust ground. No trees or vegetation grew. They saw no movement of any kind, save for the endless spasms of the pulsing, fractured sky. It was a dead land. Apocalyptic and lifeless. Nothing but rock and dust. The door disappeared with a resounding clang and an ominous thud. Seven pairs of eyes stared out across the hollow landscape.

"No wicked monsters..." Deborah breathed, breaking the silence.

"Not yet," Zotiel replied, scouring the horizon skeptically.

Whitman glanced at Lena, and she back at him. Raymond and Mark stared out across The Void with sullen concern.

Zotiel, releasing the handbrake, drove the truck slowly through the door to the dust beyond, stopping with the rear of the truck a few feet from the opening.

"Do we close it?" Zephon asked him.

"No," Deborah answered for him. "It's quiet here now. Who knows what hurry we might be in on the way back."

"You believe we're *coming* back?" Lena asked her, lending voice to the fear that clearly engulfed them all.

Deborah stared across the barren wasteland for a moment.

"Look at this place." She twisted around to look Lena in the eyes. "I'm not fucking dying *here*."

Her spirit was as infectious as she had hoped it would be. Zotiel grinned.

"Well. Let's get fucking going then." He revved the engine and the truck purred to life. They rumbled forward across the dead ground.

⁂

They sped across the landscape in a dusty streak, a great cloud billowing into the electro-static air in their wake. The excitement of their departure did not last for long, but as it ebbed, it left the mood of the truck somewhat less pessimistic. Despite some jostling back and forth, those in the rear of the cab were able to release their straps and stand on occasion. Raymond and Whitman took advantage of this, and were engaged in a hushed conversation by the truck's rear windows. Lena and Mark remained seated, quiet. Zotiel kept the vehicle on a steady route, making for the mountainous horizon.

As they rolled on, Raymond peeled away from his whispered conference and, carefully stepping to the front of the cab, leaned on the back of the passenger-side seat. He whispered in Deborah's ear.

"Whitman and I been talkin', Blondie."

Deborah didn't care much for the moniker, but it had stuck now. She wasn't going to force him to change it. Not yet anyway. Not when he had done so much for her already. She tilted her head, raising her ear to him.

"If this is possible," he said in a low, conspiratorial tone, casting a suspicious glance at Zotiel, "why did they wait for you to die?"

The question bothered Deborah. He had a point.

"I guess... maybe they figured I'd be less disposed to helping them if they just grabbed me and pulled me here?" she whispered back.

Raymond shrugged, but looked unconvinced.

"You think this guy – your friend – he will? Be disposed to help us?"

"I'm going to give him the choice."

Zotiel seemed almost to interject here, but before he could, all their eyes were pulled to the windscreen. They had just sped past a figure. Grey and translucent, but a figure nonetheless. A human figure.

"What the fuck was *that*?" Mark shuddered. He stood and approached the front of the truck.

"The Void Lost," replied Zephon.

"Oh, of course, how silly of me," he replied sarcastically. "What the hell are Void Lost?"

"The way we came, through the tunnels? That's one of a few ways here from The Purgs," Zotiel replied. "There are others. Sometimes folks find them. Get the notion to try and walk across. Walk back."

"I've been there fourteen years. I hadn't heard that."

"Well, they don't come back to tell their stories, kid."

"Does it ever work?" Deborah asked curiously.

"Not very often. Never the way they would want. Most lose what sense they had. They end up just wandering around here for eternity, I think. Nothing left of themselves. Just the hunger. The few who do make it all the way... It's not like simply *reaching* the living world makes them *part* of it. You can take the horse to water, an' all that. You ever seen an apparition? A spirit?"

"I'm in a truck full of them," she replied.

Zotiel smirked.

"I mean in your life."

"No."

"Well, they do get through, I'm told. Occasionally. But mostly there's no more mind left when they do. Just the most basic instincts. They might end up returning to where they lived or worked or grew up – someplace meaningful. Ingrained. They can't get their lives back though. It doesn't work that way. They just end up hanging around."

"Poltergeists?" Mark asked.

"Sure."

The truck trundled on, and past a few more of the figures.

"I always thought those kind of stories were made up."

"Mostly they are. I don't think it's very common for any to actually make it that far. You guys should sit. If they start taking notice of us we might need to turn sharpish. Don't want you smacking off the sides."

"They can hurt us? They look like ghosts."

"You're *all* ghosts."

Mark furrowed his brow, but, along with Raymond, returned to his seat obligingly. Out the window, another spectre whizzed by. Then another. Then another.

※

They journeyed on. The frequency with which they saw the shambling Lost increased steadily. After an hour or so, as they sped past another little group, Deborah noticed something else breaking the endless desolation of the land. At the centre of the spectral congregation sat a tall spike. It appeared to be wooden, though from what tree it was cut, in this place, she could not imagine. It stood about four feet from the dusty ground, and perched atop was the skull of a goat. A grim and menacing marker in a grim and menacing land.

"You see that Zote?" Zephon asked him cautiously.

"I saw," he told him, his gaze straight ahead.

"You know what that means?"

Zotiel glanced at him cautiously.

"Could be a lot of things."

Deborah watched him as he spoke. His face was not confused. It was fearful.

"Could be..." Zephon began, but Zotiel spoke over him quickly.

"Doesn't matter what it is, Zeph. We got our plan. In and out. Shouldn't matter. We're not bothering anyone."

"What *does* it mean?" asked Deborah, looking to each of them in turn.

"Not sure m'love. Pay it no mind. Should be nothing."

He knew more than he said, clearly, but with the group behind, she did not wish to press him. If he elected for secrecy, she trusted it was warranted. She quieted, for the moment, though remained ill at ease.

Their speed did not relent. The tense atmosphere in the truck did not diminish. Time marched on from hours into days. The only indicators of progress were the mountains; distant still, but looming closer and closer, higher and higher as they travelled.

Deborah and the rest of her group began to feel the effects of the slow march of time. Their hunger cried out. She badly wished they had some of the little yellow vials, of The Word. The 'miracle-juice' as Lena called it. She had implored Cassiel to provide some for their journey, once its duration had been made apparent to her, but he had shook his head in refusal. Not unsympathetic, but emphatic.

"There are things there," he had told her, "that would sense such a trickle of life. The hunger is better. It will be your burden, but will also be your cloak."

She had not fully understood then, but now it made sense. The more and more frequent Void Lost that they saw dragging their disorientated way around the electric wasteland – sometimes grouped, sometimes lone – would, on occasion, lift hollow, spectral eyes in the truck's direction, but seemed, for now, resigned only to watch. They made no move to approach or impede the speeding vehicle. The sense of the life they so craved was not palpable in her group, she realised.

Their own hunger masked their scent from the ever-hungry.

Still though. Their interest *was* growing, along with their prevalence. Where once they ignored completely, now they glanced. Stared with vacant eyes. She had seen more of the goat head markers too. Their sight did not instil comfort. The Boys might try to play it off as nothing, maintaining calm by keeping their significance from her and the group, but it had not escaped Deborah's notice that the markers all faced in the same direction. Someone, or *something*, put them there. Placed them with purpose. As a warning perhaps. Or as a stake of claim.

***

As they neared the great spires of filthy rock that engulfed the horizon, clawing nastily at the epileptic, bruised sky, the sporadically dotted Lost began to thicken to a horde. The truck was forced to a slower pace as Zotiel, silent and grim, edged it left and right to avoid the crops of them. Their prior disinterest had entirely faded. Everywhere now, spectral eyes followed their path. Deborah and her companions could feel their claustrophobic stares pressing in on them, choking their resolve.

"We're not going to make it to the mountains without them doing something, are we?" said a voice from behind.

Deborah swung around in her chair to see Lena, steadying herself on the seat-backs and staring out the windscreen at the silent masses.

"Without them trying to stop us?"

"They haven't yet…" Deborah replied warily. She had been thinking the same thing.

"What do they want?" Lena asked fearfully.

"What you have and they don't," Zephon replied. "Life. Purpose."

"We're not alive though." Zotiel's face tightened as he weaved among the Lost.

"You're more alive than these poor fuckers."

They passed another goat skull marker. The group followed it with reticent eyes.

"Who put those here?" whispered Lena.

"No one good," replied Zephon gravely. Zotiel stared straight ahead.

"Do you know?" Lena asked him.

"…No."

"Yes you do. You suspect, at least?"

"I…" Zephon might have answered her, Deborah was not sure, but a grating scrape that resonated through the inside of the truck clipped his words short. Whitman, Mark and Raymond in the back whipped their heads to one side. No one spoke.

A second scrape, this time from the opposite side of the vehicle, pulled their attention. Then another.

"They're getting a bit feisty now," Raymond growled. Another scrape and then another.

"They're trying to get in!" Lena moaned, her voice rising.

"Yup," Zotiel told her, lifting his own volume to meet hers.

"What do we do?"

"Strap in," he barked over his shoulder. "We're not playing nice anymore!"

He revved the engine and slammed his foot down to the metal. The engine roared over the buzzing static of the sky and the truck barrelled through the crowd, sending limp, grey rag-dolls flying. The host of watchful eyes blurred past the windshield, and as they did, Deborah saw their manner change. The curious malice in their collective stare dropped in an instant. Replaced with clawing outrage.

※

Their tearing streak through the crowd was sickening and exhilarating. The bounce and crunch over the spectral corpses as the wheels crushed their sallow numbers or battered them to one side or the other was a frenzy. Deborah watched with anxious respect as Zotiel gripped the wheel, gritting his teeth as he battled to hold it steady against the onslaught. His eyes flicked from left to right but never deviated long from his goal. A single peak rising above the others, dead ahead now, in the mountain line.

They made progress, despite the mass of impeding bodies thrown at their front, and Deborah began, as the spire that marked their destination filled the sky, to believe they would endure this last stretch without deeper horror. With a splintering crack, that hope disappeared.

The truck smashed through the black wood of the stake, and the goat skull burst against the windshield like a porcelain firework. Through the dust came flying the grey, half-translucent body of a woman.

She splayed across the windshield of the truck like a cat, filthy bare feet planted, toes hooked between the bonnet and the base of the windshield. Boney fingers gripped the outer rim. Nothing clothed her but caked dust and filth. No hair grew anywhere on her corpse body. It looked as dead as the earth in this hollow place, but her face was painted. A ghoulish smear of makeup, like a child had raided her mother's beauty box. Her eyes were live with malicious desire. Time seemed to stop as the group stared in horror back at her, and she tracked them with a predatory, animalistic glare. Then she scuttled upwards to the top of the cab, out of view.

"Shit!" shouted Mark. "It's on top of us!"

"Shake it off," Zephon told Zotiel, his attempts to keep cool admirable, but strained.

Zotiel had little hope of this, Deborah knew. As they scraped and bounced towards the mountain it was all he could do to keep some variance of a straight line at all. He had little, if any, control over the finer movements of the truck in this maddening crowd. Luck was all they could hope for.

A few hard bounces shook them as they pummelled through and the scuttle of her feet on the roof seemed to stop. Whitman, Raymond, Mark and Lena stared up tensely, each straining to discern any trace of the sound over the carnage outside.

"Is it gone?" asked Mark reluctantly, looking around at his companions.

"I…" Whitman began, but as he did a piercing shriek cut the air from above. A hideous harpy-cry. The sheet-metal roof punctured, birthing a grotesquely broken and twisted hand into their carriage.

"Jesus Christ!" Mark yelled.

Unbuckling his seatbelt frantically, he jumped to the other side of the vehicle, away from the newly punched hole above. The broken-fingered appendage jolted and spasmed as it was pulled, then ripped back through the metal hole and disappeared. It left behind a sickening ribbon of grey flesh, dripping with thick black ooze and hanging on the ragged edge. A single finger, broken and twisted, dropped into the seat he had occupied. No one but Lena noticed the sad reminder of its owner's past life, and its downfall; the little gold wedding band. It was bent outwards where it had caught on the edge of the punctured steel.

The truck continued to sway and swing over and between the angry horde, and at the hole in the roof an eye appeared, pressed against the roof, peering viciously this way and that. It locked when it spotted the quartet, huddled into one corner of the transport. It disappeared, but as quickly as it did, a second hand appeared, the unbroken one, and wrapped its grey fingers around the metal. Both the steel roof and its attacker screeched as the metal began to tear and bend open like a tin of sardines.

"I thought they were weak!" Lena shouted forward at their driver. "How is she doing this?!"

No one answered, but Deborah knew. It didn't matter the state of your body or sanity. Hunger has to be sated. Hunger won't be denied. Hunger finds a way.

"I can't get rid of it!" Zotiel hollered in dismay.

The roof peeled back further, revealing the pulse of the sky and heightening the din of the thunder and the chaos outside. Then, blocking the sky, the Lost woman appeared. Her sunken face and grey sallow skin, smeared in clownish makeup, shook and flapped with the vibration of the speeding truck, but her eyes were fixed upon her prey.

She glared in triumph as she scuttled across the ripped hole, then leaned her whole torso into the truck. The razor sharp edges scraped at her rancid flesh, shaving the skin from her shoulders and breasts, revealing black, viscous jelly-blood beneath. Her bared teeth clenched painfully, but she did not slow. She squeezed, forcing her body through, head first.

"Do something!" shrieked Lena, though to whom she wasn't sure. To anyone. It turned out it was Raymond who answered, though not with words.

A deafening crack rang out, magnified in the echoey chamber of the truck. Deborah watched as the body of the Lost woman ended her desperate squeeze in apparent success. Her limp, battered body slammed to the metal floor in the centre of the transport. It did not move. She lay in a malformed heap, the oozing, slashed flesh of what remained of her breasts mashed into the metal floor. Her legs were splayed wide and the thick crust of dust and foul smelling waste caked around her rear and legs and crotch filled the air with its stench. Her neck was twisted painfully around on itself, and through her bald, harlequin head a great hole had appeared. Right between her vacant eyes.

Raymond stood at the rear of the truck, an arm extended. The barrel of his revolver trained on the still body. He looked, for the first time, like a warrior. All the group stared at him in shocked wonder.

"Just testing something out," he growled.

"Nice shot, Dirty Harry," Mark told him breathlessly. "How did you know that would work?"

"I didn't," replied Raymond.

Deborah said nothing, but gave a little nod to Raymond, which he returned. She turned back to the carnage out front.

The single peak that had been their beacon was no longer visible, they were so close to it. The swarm of grey bodies was still thick, but in the distance she could see what Zotiel and Zephon had been looking for. At the base of the mountain, a half mile or so ahead, was a rough road winding up to its base. At its top she saw the dark, gaping mouth of a cave.

∽⌇∾

The cave entrance in the base of the mountain had marked the end of their encounter with The Lost. Some, of course, had trailed after them at its mouth and beyond, but without further figures in front, their numbers had been swiftly left behind. To wait, Deborah thought grimly. To wait for their return.

The winding rise the road took to the mouth of the tunnel had continued inside. Zotiel drove them in a great sweeping arc, curving back around upon itself. It was a spiral, circling up and up, within the mountain.

After a long period of silent driving, seeing no new sign of threat, they had considered it safe to stop a few minutes. Long enough, at least, to excise the foul body of the Lost woman from their transport. Raymond and Whitman had lifted her limp corpse with distaste, and, as Zephon swung open the rear doors of the truck, had heaved her out onto the stone road behind. Lena had winced at the hollow, wet crunch of her boney body as it hit the ground. Feeling some inescapable sorrow at the action she had hesitated a moment, but had then cast the finger, along with its damaged wedding band, out also. The sight of The Lost as a menacing horde was terrifying. The sight of this crumpled pile of limbs, lying, alone and battered and naked at the roadside, was just sad. As they continued their spiralling ascent the stink of her remained, clinging to the truck as a miserable reminder, but at least the horror of her was now a vivid memory and not a visual reality.

"What is this place?" Lena asked Deborah and her consorts at the front of the cab.

"It's a nexus," Zotiel replied for her. "One of a number I believe. Very old."

"A nexus between this world and ours?" Whitman asked. Zotiel nodded.

"How does it work?"

"I don't know," Zotiel replied. "It hasn't in a long time, as far as I know."

"Still a long way to go," Zephon told the driver. His head was bowed as he consulted a moleskin Scroll.

Zotiel nodded and drove on.

༺༻

After many more hours of their slow spiral up the inside of the mountain, some features began to break the endless wall of rock at their sides. Crusted lines in the dead stone. Faint, caked with powder ash and dust, but there all the same. Outlines. As they climbed, these markings became more frequent and better defined.

Mark stepped up behind the front seats and stared out at the illumination of the headlamps.

"Those are doors aren't they?"

"Yes," Zephon replied.

"To where?"

"Earth."

"I mean where on Earth?" he asked.

"Everywhere."

Deborah turned to Zephon.

"So how do we find *our* door?"

Zephon did not answer, but held out the moleskin, offering it to her. She took it and opened it at a blank page, slowly flipping forward until she found the spot where the neat cursive was scribbling itself.

> *'...across the market from him. He sat a moment longer at the square, watching couples pass by, then stood, leaving Jackson Square. He headed up Chartres Street to the coffee shop, watching the...'*

She closed the book.

"This is Eli?" she asked.

"Yup."

She stared down at the leather cover of the book. The concept of the Scrolls still boggled her mind.

"I don't understand. How is this going to tell us which door we need?"

She made a move to hand back the moleskin, but Zephon shook his head.

"Hold onto that. Keep reading. It's not gonna tell *us* which door. It's gonna tell *you*."

She furrowed her brow, but did as he bade. She sat back and opened the Scroll again.

༺༻

The spiral of doors was enormous. After hours of driving in an ever ascending loop, watching doors flit by the windows by the thousands, Deborah realised with wonder that as big as the mountain had seemed from the outside, it could not possibly be this vast. The space inside was not connected to the shell outside. Not at a one-to-one ratio anyway. She supposed that in a world of doors that opened from thin air and closed again without trace, in a world where doors were not connected entry to exit, this should not be such a difficult concept to accept. Somehow though, this was more disquieting to her senses. The rules of this world were still unclear in many ways, but this was the most perfect example of its baffling unfamiliarity that she had encountered thus far. Trying to conceptualise it was dizzying. Like vertigo.

She spent much of their long ascent watching the script write itself in Eli's Scroll. Doing so filled her with guilt, but she couldn't stop. It was voyeuristic and deeply wrong. It was a violation, but she had spent fifteen years being watched by him. It was an odd thrill to turn the tables now. Nothing quite as exciting here, of course. Eli had watched her as she engaged in assassinations all over the world. High stress missions, emotionally fraught, dangerous and tactical and deadly. She was watching him have a lonely coffee, a lonely walk home and a lonely afternoon in his lonely apartment. Still though, the unfettered access to his thoughts and actions was as compulsive as it was creepy.

Outside, the zoetrope of doors that flitted by the truck windows had slowly transformed. Where they had begun as nothing more than stone crevices following the formations of the rock wall, now they took much more familiar forms. Doors. Wooden castle doors, metal jailhouse doors, glass patio doors that seemed to open only to the rock face behind them. Shed doors and attic doors and shop doors and cottage doors, office doors and sliding elevator doors and submarine doors with great wheel locks on them. If a door existed, anywhere in the world, it seemed it had a brother or a sister or a cousin that lived here.

"I really don't know what I'm looking for here guys," she sighed. She was long past the point of disguising her deflation.

"I do," said a voice from the back. Lena's voice.

Deborah turned, surprised.

"Haven't you ever felt like someone was watching you? Even when you're alone?"

"Well... yes," she replied hesitantly. "But in my line of work someone usually *was*." She held the Scroll up.

Lena smiled.

"I mean when you're just going about your day."

"I… No. I suppose not. I…" She paused, uncertain exactly what they meant. "For me… I would have known if they were."

"I have," Mark told Lena.

"Most people do at some point, I think." Whitman added and glanced at Raymond who nodded.

Deborah thought about this curiously. So often in her life she had attributed positive qualities she possessed to her occupational prowess. It was disquieting to think that those same sharpened skills that had been her best asset, had actually blocked out something from her perception entirely. She prided herself on her sharp instincts. But those same practical instincts had apparently blinded her to the more impractical ones others possessed naturally. The human connection to the otherworldliness that existed all around them.

"So… what are you saying? That if I keep reading I'll just *know*?"

"No," Lena replied with a supportive smile. "I'm saying, if you keep reading, *he'll* just know."

༄

Lena was right on the money. As they sped around the never-ending spiral of doors, the textual descriptions of Eli's actions began more and more to betray a disquiet in him. Sudden glances around, pensive moments, furtive glances around rooms and out of the windows of his apartment. So much so, in fact, that he had left the apartment and was making his way back down the streets he had walked before. He was heading back to the coffee shop on Chartres Street as she read.

It had not escaped her notice that her own name had popped up in his Scroll several times. His vague anxiety had more than once turned his mind to her, and she had read with fascination the guilt he felt over her passing. The self-loathing in him. It was a grim spectacle to read one's own name in such a context. Grimmer still that on some level, some dark, primal level, she was glad. Glad that he felt guilt. That made her sick.

She had not quite been sure what sign she was waiting for, and had almost angered at her group's conviction that she would simply 'know', but as she discovered soon enough, their faith was well founded.

> *'...towards the entrance of Furey's and paused for a second. He stared down the side alley. He had passed it often, but had never noticed the oddly placed green, wooden door at the end of it, the one with the golden knob. He could not work out from which establishment it lead. Strange, he thought. The door seemed innocuous, but it made him anxious. Attempting to shake the feeling, he headed...'*

Deborah whipped her head up to the windshield. There it was, right in front of her. Illuminated by the headlights, between a rusting portcullis and a grubby fast-food door with 'Best in the West' written in poorly crafted, hand-cut lettering, was the door. An emerald green door, with a golden doorknob.

"Stop!" she cried in shocked triumph.

Her surprise imbued her voice with childlike eagerness. Despite the horrors their journey had presented, her fellow travellers could not help but smile. Zotiel pushed on the brakes and brought the truck to a halt next to the emerald door. The group piled out of the truck, and Deborah began to prepare.

Zephon took Mark aside.

"Are you sure about this? You don't have to," he told him.

"I want to," Mark replied with resolve.

"Okay. It's up to you, kid. But if you're going to insist on going in, there's something you should take."

He led Mark round the truck and out of view. Zotiel approached Deborah.

"They explained how this works?" he asked with inflection. Deborah nodded, shrugging.

"Sort of," she replied.

He extended his hand to her.

"You'll need these."

She peered into his white hand to see two little contact lenses in a little silver box.

"My vision's 20-20," she said, raising an eyebrow.

"Not like ours it's not," Zotiel smirked.

She took them from him.

"So, how you gonna ask him? You know it won't be simple…"

She shrugged again, but looked back at him with steady nerve.

"I'll improvise."

Chapter Thirteen

GHOSTS

Eli stepped into Furey's for the second time today. Not a record since he had begun frequenting the joint more often this past year, but still relatively unusual.

Unusual was an apt word today. He had been *feeling* unusual. All day long. Tense. Without any reason he could fathom. It was not a pleasant sensation. He wanted to be somewhere familiar, somewhere with people around. Where everybody knows your name, as the song went. There were no places where everyone knew Eli's name, but Furey's was the closest thing.

"Just couldn't stay away, Hon?"

Beth smiled at him from behind the counter, where she stood working the coffee machine. He forced a smile back, hiding his vague disquiet.

"This place just got something my apartment don't."

"Oh yeah? What's that?"

He smiled.

"You of course darlin'." He cocked an eyebrow flirtatiously.

"Ah!" Beth nodded, amused. "Of course. You want to keep your refill going?"

"That allowed?"

"Bill's gone for the afternoon."

Eli smiled and nodded to a booth by the window. His usual booth.

"Be over in a moment," she told him with another big smile. He slid himself into the booth and the previous occupant's detritus aside. Resting his head on his hands, he glanced suspiciously out the window at the street beyond.

Why did he feel like this? It was infuriating. All morning he had felt someone on him. Watching him. He glanced around the street, knowing he would see no one, knowing looking was a fool's errand, but he could not shake the feeling. It followed him everywhere he went, like a lingering smell.

Could it be The Orchard? In the year or so since his last fateful assignment had ended with a bullet in his operative – in his friend – he had not had much contact with them. Early on they had sought to connect him with some new kid, but he had flatly turned it down. He hadn't been sure he wanted to stay with the company at all at that point. He still didn't know. Twice since then he had made contact himself, just to check in and keep his options open, but had never allowed any of the back and forth correspondence to stray too close to the subject of a return to active assignment. Not yet.

Would he do it all again? Start over? New contracts, new operative? Deborah had been his charge for fifteen years. Since they were both basically kids. Thirty-eight contracts. Most operatives lasted six point three. He knew the numbers, and more than that, he knew how the numbers worked. Six point three. That was the average. That number took account of the great ones. The masters. The Brents, the Barbesis, the Zizzos. The Lucilles. The Deborahs. The ones with dozens and dozens of successful hits to their names. Take them out the equation? You were looking at an average more like two. Most handlers had a pretty quick turnover. It was why you didn't get involved. Why you weren't supposed to care on a personal level. You were supposed to be clinical. Stand-offish. Don't become friends. Certainly don't fall in love.

"Here you go, Gorgeous."

Eli was snapped out of his thoughts with a punch. He knew that voice. He whipped his head around. Beth stood by the booth, holding two jugs of filter coffee.

"What did you say?!" he stammered, rattled.

Beth frowned, a little warily.

"I… said here you go, Hon?"

He peered at her cautiously.

"Sorry, I…" he trailed off.

Beth was a good looking girl. Tan-skinned and sultry. Thicker around the hips and chest than some, but in a way that leaned sexy rather than matronly. Her wavy, brunette locks were usually pulled back, though today, Bill being away, were loosened. They fell across the shoulders of her white waitress' blouse fetchingly.

"Never mind. Sorry. You… sounded like someone is all."

"A girl, I hope?" she asked with playful inquisition. "Some dalliance for your past?"

He smiled.

"Something like that."

"And I thought I was the only girl for you."

She said it offhand, but Eli stared at her like she had just slapped him across the face. He felt like she had. Beth noticed, clearly.

"Maybe you want the decaf, Hon? Look like you could use some sleep tonight…"

He smiled, covering his unease as best he could.

"Yeah, maybe. Thanks."

She poured and left him to his thoughts, casting a bemused, if a little concerned, glance back over her shoulder at him as she left. He drank, deep in sullen thought.

◈

Decaf or not, his return walk to his apartment was no less anxious. The feeling of being watched was not dissipating, despite his more rational tendencies' attempts to overrule it.

Not The Orchard. This may be their style, but he was a veteran at this point. He would know; he would be able to tell. And why would they? He was one of them, still. Active or not, they knew he was not a threat. How could he threaten them? They had total deniability in everything. Any job went sour, it was never on them. Just on the operative and the handler. Like his last job. Ask them about it now – even him, one of their own – and it never happened. Job? What job? Deborah? Never heard of her.

It certainly wasn't the police. They weren't good enough for him not to see some sign. Local cops were, at least, unsophisticated enough not to even know how unsophisticated they were. They were about a subtle as a sledgehammer. He would know in a half second if they had his scent.

So who? Interpol wouldn't give a shit about him, neither would the Feds. The CIA? They likely knew about The Orchard – parts of it at least. Eli suspected that more than a few contracts originated at Langley – but one inactive handler going about his humdrum routine? What would they care?

No. This was something different. The metal taste of fear that rose, apparently baseless, in his throat, it stemmed from elsewhere.

Something else was bothering him too. Everywhere he looked, signs seemed to draw his attention. Advertisements. Billboards. Bus Ads. Flyers in shop windows. Eli was not one to pay them a second thought normally. Between his rarified profession and his self-imposed life of solitude he was hardly the demographic for anything they would have to offer, but now? They seemed to call out to him. They seemed, all of a sudden, *important*. Why, he did not know, but they were all the same.

As he walked, a Land Rover Discovery billboard, like a beacon, drew his eye. Something about it. Something... within it.

The car itself? No. Eli didn't care about cars. He could drive, but he rarely did, and his interest in vehicles began and ended with one question – will it get me from here to there? Could just be the smiling model? Beautiful girl, with the sultry, beckoning eyes that were the hallmark of car, perfume and lingerie ads – sex sells of course – but unremarkable within that confine. No. Not her. It was the tagline. That was what drew his eye. At the bottom of the ad, the text read *'ARE YOU REALLY HAPPY WITH WHAT YOU HAVE?'* Eli's eyes flicked up at it continually as he walked, unable to resist its question.

What the fuck was wrong with him? Why did he give a shit what some car ad said? He glanced back up and was about to mutter something to himself about how dumb he was being. To chide himself for his baseless paranoia. Right as he did, a bus honked its horn like a wall of noise, inches from his ear. He jumped back. In his hypnotic contemplation he had not looked as he stepped from the sidewalk to the street.

His heart pounded against his chest wall and his pores yawned cold sweat. He stood still, breathing deep, watching the bus rattle on down the road. Even despite his violent shudder at what so very nearly just happened, his focus was pulled to the ad that ran along its side. The vertical strip showed nothing but the image of a tall white building. Across the length of the bus though, in bold capital letters, it shouted, '*SHAKE. REDO. BE.*'

Not a great ad, he thought, forcing practicality in the face of his carelessness. I can't even tell what it's supposed to be selling. He stood a moment as his heartbeat returned to something closer to normal, looked both ways several times, then carefully crossed the road. He headed home.

༄

Over the course of the next few days Eli began to feel a sick, sinking dismay. His mental state was deteriorating. He could feel it. How truly horrible it was, he thought, to have the full faculties required to identify the spiraling decline of his mind, yet lack the wherewithal to halt or reverse it.

His routine remained the same as it had this past year: wake, emails, Furey's, walk, home, internet, out, bar, home, computer, sleep. To a casual observer he would seem to be habitual as ever. Business as usual. From his privileged viewpoint though? From the inside? He was in turmoil. The routine was becoming a laboured struggle against a tide of paranoia. His sleep was becoming a restless fight against his own dreams.

Eli didn't remember much of them upon waking – he never had – but now, many times each night, he would burst from his agitated, fidgety slumber in a sweat, with nothing but a feeling of displacement and the image of a curving road in his mind. A stone road. However long he managed to keep up the fight, however long he could stay asleep, he invariably felt less rested upon waking.

Nothing gave him release from the feeling of observation. At first, he had likened the sensation to that of an animal in a zoo. The watchful eyes of the patrons on him, powerless to hide. Forced to live his life in full view. But this analogy had fallen flat after some thought. He wasn't like an animal in a zoo. The animals could see their observers through the bars or the glass, and they, at least, lived their captive lives in the cradle of protective hands. This was different. This was like he was the ant on the sidewalk, under the scrutiny of the unseen bully as he readies his magnifying glass. The sense of an impending... an impending *something*, hung over his head.

Everywhere he turned, he saw the signs. Or perhaps they saw him. Every one innocuous, yet imbued with sinister meaning by his straining paranoia.

A lawn sign he walked by, stuck in a garden, spoke of its realtor, '*GETTING YOU PLACES! YOU'LL BE GLAD YOU DID!*'. A political affiliation sticker in the rear window of some out-of-towner's Chevrolet Blazer, for some candidate Eli had never heard of, declared '*ACCEPT THE CHANCE FOR CHANGE!*' A poster hung on a shop front window telling him he should '*VISIT BEAUTIFUL KISATCHIE NATIONAL FOREST*', declared that it was in his interest to '*SEE THE HIDDEN WORLD!*' It seemed that everywhere words existed for reading, they somehow were targeting him. All perfectly explainable individually of course. All perfectly normal. Unless, Eli understood with grim realisation, your mind was broken enough to view them all as a whole. As a pattern. If you were far enough gone for that? Then their rantings became impossible to ignore.

The worst was the pop-up. It seemed both the most meaningful and the most sinister. For three nights now, every time he ventured onto the internet in his apartment, the same obtrusive pop-up ad had jumped out. As if waiting, just for him.

His setup was secure. Eli knew what he was doing, his IP address was untraceable. Masked and re-masked, bounced back and forth, here and there and everywhere across the globe. His firewalls and filters were the best in the business. He should know, he helped write some of them. Something as rudimentary as a basic targeted advertisement should never be able to get through to his machine. None ever had before. Nevertheless, several times each night, the same ad. Over and over. A white building. *SHAKE. REDO. BE.*

Every time it appeared he had wanted to hit the 'X.' Dismiss it. Get rid of the irritation and the paranoia with it, but every time something had stopped him. Every time he had paused, a little hypnotised by its mysterious image, and instead hit the little button at the bottom. The one that read '*REMIND ME LATER.*'

He didn't really know why. He didn't want to be reminded later. He wanted it to be gone for good.

Didn't he?

∽∾

Six days had past since the sickly feeling began. Eli sat in his booth, drinking his coffee. Not decaf this time. He wasn't sleeping anymore, but that had little to do with his caffeine intake, he was pretty sure of that. He wasn't sure of much of anything anymore, but he was pretty sure of that.

It was dark outside. He had decided after last night's sorry, miserable activities, that heading to a bar or a jazz club of an evening was fruitless at this point. His mind was going. It was shattering inside him, and no amount of alcohol or music was going to lift his mood from that. Better he go where he could at least have some kind of human contact, however brief. Something to keep him sane. Beth. Sweet, happy Beth. The closest thing to a friend he had left, since his career took a plummet last year.

"You get lucky last night, Hon?"

"Hmm?" He glanced round at her.

She stood at the end of the table, two jugs of filter coffee in her hands as usual, though the look on her face, the look of concern, that was less usual. Well, he thought unhappily, it would have been unusual a week ago. Not so much recently. That look sat wrong on her pretty face. Her waitress attire was, as always, not particularly flattering on her hips and ample chest. Bill wasn't one for sexing the place up, and he must have been around today as her thick, wavy, brown hair was pulled back in a high ponytail, but she was a beauty nonetheless. Seeing her look at him like he was an injured patient in a hospital was dismaying.

"It's just... Those are the same clothes you had on yesterday..."

Eli looked down at himself, though he barely had to. He knew he looked a mess. Hell, he *felt* a mess. Why shouldn't he dress the part?

"Oh, yeah I... well I... haven't really been to sleep yet. So, y'know, this sorta *is* still yesterday. For me."

"Up all night huh?" Beth looked at him with an exaggerated sympathy. Trying to mask her actual sympathy, Eli thought sadly. "Those computers just won't play ball?"

Beth knew nothing about technology. It was part of what Eli liked about her. His whole life, it seemed to him, took place on screens, in a digital realm. That she would have trouble finding an 'on' switch, let alone an email, made her just about his favourite living person. She knew nothing of his actual line of work of course, but when she had asked what he did for a living he had told her data gathering and digital analysis. Both of which were, largely, true. The closer the lie is to the reality, the easier it is to maintain. A tenant of The Orchard if ever there was one.

"Yeah," he smiled as best he could in his foggy, insomniac state. "Kicking my ass."

She held up the blue banded jug – the decaf – with a hopeful look. When he shook his head, she grimaced a little. She glanced at the red-banded one. Eli turned from her disappointment to view the dark street outside.

"Well, you show them who's boss, Gorgeous," Deborah replied.

Eli's eyes bulged as he saw her. Her slim figure was wrapped in a waitress blouse. Cherry lips, blonde hair pulled up in a bun. Reflected perfectly in the dark window glass behind him. She poured from a red-banded jug.

He jerked around in his seat. Beth flinched at his sudden movement, spilling coffee over the edge of the cup.

"Jesus, Eli!" she scolded, a little flustered. "This is why we have the blue-band. You need to get some rest."

Eli sat a second, staring at her. At Beth, he told himself. It's Beth. It's *Beth*.

"Sorry. You're right. I didn't mean to... Sorry. Maybe I *will* go blue after this one." He forced a comforting smile, but it must have missed the mark. Beth sure didn't look comforted.

"Maybe you should go *home* after this one, Honey. Get some rest. Seriously." She frowned. "I'm worried about you."

Eli said nothing. He had barely heard her. His attention had been caught by something. Something that had hit him like a freight train. Here too? Not here too. Please. *Come on*, not here *too*.

"What *is* that?" he asked, staring at the little white name-tag pinned to her blouse. She cocked her eyebrow at him uncertainly.

"Um... well those are my tits Eli. Generally it's considered polite to be a little more discreet when you ogle..."

"That." He pointed at the name-tag.

"Oh." She shrugged. "Bill wants us wearing them now. He's going to be redoing the signage outside, that's the new logo. What'cha think?"

Her question was cordial, but Eli wasn't listening. Blood was thundering through his ears. Below Beth's name was the new Furey's logo. Below that, in little script it read '*COME ON IN, WHAT HAVE YOU GOT TO LOSE?*'

※

Ghosts, he thought miserably. I'm seeing ghosts. Eli didn't believe in ghosts. He wasn't the spiritual type – he never had been. But he couldn't deny what he was seeing. Reflected in shop windows, in the fleeting images of strangers in the wing-mirrors of parked cars, through the windshields of moving ones. They weren't spirits. Not the spirits of the dead come back to haunt him. Those were just stupid stories for stupid people. Spooky tales for children and comforting white lies for the spiritually needy and the emotionally weak. But he *was* seeing them. Ghosts. Ghosts of his past life.

As he trudged home in the dark, he pondered, bitterly and for the thousandth time, what it all meant. For the thousandth time, he came up with nothing. He preferred to walk in the dark now. The billboards and the advertisements, they were still out there, in the warm black of the Louisiana night – they were still watching him – but at least in the dark he could try to ignore them. The fairy-lights strung from the iron verandas above were bright, but decoratively so. They didn't cast too far. Not far enough to illuminate the seductive messages.

He knew Deborah's death had affected him. That much was obvious, and not just to him. Why else would The Orchard allow him such leeway to step back as he had done, and for so long? It wasn't just his long service being paid off. They wanted him back, and were willing to wait if it meant his return would be at full capacity. They weren't compassionate, but they were smart in their self-interest. He knew it had affected him, but he had not considered how much. How long its wake would be. A year of quiet gathering of himself, and right as he had begun to feel he was getting through, that he was turning a corner – now his mind began to break down in the mire of it. How miserable. How pathetic.

He was seeing her *everywhere*. Every back that was turned on the street was a slim blonde, until they turned around. Every reflection in every shop window was a tall girl with cherry red lips, until he turned to see the real person. Every greeting was a 'Hey Gorgeous' until it wasn't. Everything, everywhere reminded him of how flimsy and fake his new life was. His mind had revolted. It didn't like its new place in the world, clearly, and it was no longer putting up with it. It had had all it could stand, and it couldn't stand no more.

⁓

He sat staring at the pop-up window on the screen.

When he had given up on trying to rest and flipped open the laptop, hoping to alleviate his restlessness for a brief moment with what men do in its face, he had found himself unable. Every one of the pouty, shameless girls doing their pouty, shameless thing on the screen kept morphing into her. Brunette or redhead, black or white or Latin or Asian, they were all a slim, familiar blonde, with coquettish judgement in their eyes.

'*Tut-tut*' they told him, toying. '*And I thought I was the only girl for you.*' Wink.

Now, his world all broken around him, unable to take some brief, fleeting pleasure, even in that, the pop-up ad had appeared once again. SHAKE. REDO. BE.

His first instinct, as usual, had been to hit the little 'X' at the top. Finally. Dismiss it for good this time. Bite the bullet and stop this silly dance. But not this time. He still couldn't bring himself to pull that trigger. He dragged the mouse indicator over the 'X' then paused, as usual. This time though, at '*REMIND ME LATER*' he paused again. His finger hovered over the touchpad.

Maybe it was his exhaustion, his lack of sleep. Maybe it was his mind further spinning down into the depths of his own private madness. Maybe it was just plain old curiosity as to just what the *fuck* this ubiquitous goddamned ad was for? Whatever it was, he hesitated, staring at it. Staring at the picture of the white building. Staring at the words. Staring at the little box at the bottom left that asked '*WANT TO KNOW MORE?*'

Fine, he thought with resignation. Fine. You win. I do want to know more. What the fuck else am I going to do? Just sit and wait as my mind turns to mush? Wait for the point – the inevitable point – where I can no longer keep up the veneer of sanity, and the men in white coats come and drag me to the psych ward. Or worse, he thought grimly, The Orchard gets wind of it, and has to take care of me? Make sure their secrets are safe the only way they know how?

Who would be the one to do it? he wondered. Maybe it'd be that kid, the one they tried to pair me up with, he thought with funereal amusement. Wouldn't that be ironic? I'd meet him after all. Maybe I'd be his first assignment.

No, he thought, defeated horror gripping him. You win. I want to know more. I want to *Shake*. I want to *Redo*. I want to *Be*. With tension wringing his stomach, he clicked on the button.

What he saw was rather disappointing at first. Nothing changed but the picture. The image of the white building faded slowly, and in its place a picture of a door appeared. A green, wooden door. Eli frowned.

After all that? This is it? he thought with bitter deflation. I still don't know what the fuck this means. Anger began to rise. Partly at this dumb goddamn ad, too fucking clever for its own good – advertising a product that no one could possibly understand – but mostly at himself, for building it up. For allowing his mind to imbibe it with such power. To construct it into his own false salvation. For expecting answers from a source so fucking stupid. He was ready to lift the laptop and heave it from the bed in frustration, but as he grabbed its frame, he stopped.

Wait a minute, he thought, staring at the image. Wait a minute. I *know* that door.

∽⌇∽

Eli stood across the street from Furey's, glancing around. He had changed his clothes today. He wasn't sure why exactly, for what, but he had anyway. Still a pair of blue-jeans, but now his old Wu-Tang shirt. His lucky shirt, from a time when luck still mattered. It was clean, at least. In preparation, for what he did not know, he had pulled on his brown boots. His hikers.

The sunglasses were not in preparation for anything. They were just to disguise his bloodshot hysteria from the masses. Without them, his paranoid flickering eyes looked crazy now. Red and strained from lack of sleep.

There was the alleyway. The detritus of Furey's and the surrounding eateries piled in and around the metal cans that ran its length. Pick-up day must be coming soon.

He crossed the road, carefully, and stepped past the glass front of Furey's. Past his booth. Inside he could see Beth's comely curves working the barista machine with a smile as she exchanged pleasantries with a customer. Eli couldn't be sure why he felt such finality as he looked her way, but he did. As sure as night followed day, as sure as he stood here now, as sure as he was not, as the billboard had asked, *happy with what he had now*, he would not be seeing her again. What he *would* be seeing, that was another question entirely, but he would not see Beth again. A twang of regret ran through him.

He glanced around to see if anyone was watching him on the street. No one was, though that didn't mean much. It didn't make the feeling of observation any less. If anything it was more palpable here than ever. Like he was approaching the observation deck. He turned into the alley and walked its length, his eyes trained on the green, wooden door ahead.

Stepping to it, he wrapped his hand around the gold-leaf knob. Was it leaf? It had appeared so, from a distance. Now though, holding it in his hand, it felt like solid gold. Who would leave a solid gold doorknob out for the taking in a shitty garbage-dump alley? he thought. That's stupid. Of course it's just leaf. Nevertheless…

Shake.

Redo.

Be.

He turned the handle and the door opened inwards, revealing nothing but darkness within. With a last glance around at New Orleans, he took a long, slow breath. The city felt more and more like his past than ever.

He turned and stepped through, into his unknown future.

Chapter Fourteen

SPIRALS

The darkness was unbroken. Dense and thick. Eli's footing on whatever lay below felt solid, but he could not see any floor. He waited a moment, hoping his eyes would adjust, but all they did was strain against the black in vain. There was nothing for them to cling to.

He was afraid. What was this? Where was he? What had he done? He turned back to the door through which he had entered, but saw nothing. Felt nothing. Nothing but the empty dark. Nothing but the black abyss around him. Oh my God, he thought, instantly regretful. What had he *done*?

He stood motionless. Every sense clawed to find anything to latch on to. A sight, a smell, a taste in the air. Something to give away the nature of this void in which he found himself. After a moment or two, his straining ears identified the trace of a sound. A hum. Distant, but there all the same. It was rising. Coming his way. Cold sweat coated him. It was not a comforting sound. Louder and louder it rose, ominously. Covering some vast distance towards him. As it did he began to hear more clearly. Closer now, its resonance was more apparent. It was no hum. It was a shriek. It was a shriek, and it was approaching. At tremendous speed.

He turned and ran. With nothing around, no markers to guide him, he had no idea where he was going, except that it was *away*. Away from the source of that hideous shriek. His feet pounded silently against the nothing below. His panting breaths, fearful, heaved in his chest. He ran. Ran and ran. As fast as he could.

The shrieking was becoming unbearable. It blistered in his ears, and burrowed deep into his mind. *Get away. Get away. Get away.* He could barely tell if the words he heard were the cries of his own mind, or the cries of the wailing thing that pursued him. As he fled, the noise became all encompassing. So close now that he could feel it reverberating against him, its high pitched horror the wind behind his sprint.

With a *whoosh* he felt something fire past his head, close enough to ripple his hair in its wake. The shriek followed it, out in front of him now – out in front and streaking around. Following its cry, he could tell it was sweeping in an arc. Turning back for a second try. Taking aim.

Deep below he could hear more hums rising. Setting out towards him. More shrieks, following their brother. He kept his breakneck pace, boots slapping on hard ground, into the black nothing ahead.

Whoosh.

The shriek passed him again, this time headed back, at his other side. In his panic he almost fell, but, after a flailing skip, he managed to keep his footing and continue, though to what end he could not fathom. Where was he going? Where *could* he go? Those rational thoughts blinked through his frenzied mind, but were immaterial right now. All that mattered was the running. All that mattered was *away*.

As the *whoosh* of the shriek passed him a third time, a dreadful thought occurred. These were not what he had to fear here. Not *all* he had to fear. They were not trying to harm him. They would not miss so often if they were. They were marking him. Their shrieks were no war cry. They were a signal. Letting something know. Letting something know he was here. He was here, and he wasn't supposed to be.

As the fourth and fifth *whoosh*ing passes rang through his head like an electric charge, disorienting him, he stepped wildly and felt his footfall err. Where the unseen ground had supported him, now the unseen drop did not. Terror smiled ruthlessly at him through the dark, gripping him in its clammy fist. He began to fall from the invisible path, feeling the elevator-drop in his stomach as his body careened over the edge. He flipped himself around, trying in vain to catch a hold of whatever lip there was, flailing his hands out wildly.

He caught nothing, but something caught him. Some*one* caught him. A hand. A thick shovel of a hand. It snapped around his wrist as he fell, and Eli cried out as the weight of his body jolted against his arm. Pain ripped up from his wrist to his torso and smashed through his whole upper body. He felt the arm would rip clean off his shoulder, but he hung, suspended in the black. Nothing but the wild shrieks around him to give any sense of space.

He could hear one, closer than the others, directly in front of him. Audibly stationary, in contrast to the others which whipped and flew, speeding around crazed in the dark. For a second, all thought of his precarious position disappeared as he waited for it to pounce. To do whatever these things desired to do to any dumb, oblivious fucks who strayed into their lair. Then, a crack rang out above the shrieks, and in the moment of the flash, he saw the awful creature.

A daemonic, spectral face, with pincers in its shelled head. Insectoid and horrid, like a giant malicious wasp, with a trail of misty vapour seeping behind it. The flash caught it mid gawp as it dropped from the air, felled by whatever the source of the sound had been. Its image remained suspended in the black space after the flash of light had dissipated and it had spiralled down into the void.

"Come on!" growled a voice from above him, under considerable strain. The voice of his saviour, pulling at his painfully torn triceps.

"I'm not doing this on my own, kid!"

Eli snapped out of the trance his horror had trapped him in. Twisting, gritting his teeth against the violent pain in his arm, he flailed around, finally getting a hold of the edge of the path in his fingers. He strained and pulled himself up, with the help of this mystery guardian.

In the pitch dark, a second hand, this one female, grabbed a hold of his, and a voice – a familiar voice, raised over the din – cried out to him.

"Run!" it bade.

He needed no further coaxing. Clenching her hand in the dark, he followed her lead, sprinting a half-step behind. At their rear he could hear the huffing breaths of whoever it was whose thick hand had caught him, chugging behind like a steam engine.

The insect things whipped and swirled above them, their mewling screeches unbearable. The sound grated on his mind – on his *soul* – like a rusty saw on bone. It was awful. A second crack-flash and a third from the mystery man's pistol revealed his surroundings, in photo-flash strobe-light stills. A long, stone pathway, ten feet across, cut right out of rock, perfectly. At pristine, square angles. Nothing but endless black void either side. The flash of the gunfire chased down its abyss valiantly, but was no match for its appalling depth.

In his wild sprint, he could not see his guardian, the source of the gunfire that warded off the shrieking things, but to his left he saw a man. A boy, really. He couldn't have been more than a teenager. His dress was shabby and worn, but modern – jeans and a hooded sweatshirt. In his hand he carried a long silver blade. A rapier. An antique looking thing.

To his right, clasping his hand, was Deborah. Clear as life and dressed for business. Exactly as he recalled her. Exactly as she looked that fateful night. His last in employment and her last in life. Her face was a cold picture of purpose as she ran with him.

He could not tell where she was taking him. He could not tell where they were. In the awful din of the screaming things, he could barely hold on to a single thought. But he knew that was her. They ran on through the shrieking into the black beyond.

Lena and Whitman sat with Zephon on the stone ground beside the truck while Zotiel busied himself checking the state of their vehicle.

It had been about four hours, Lena thought, since Deborah and Raymond ventured in through the green door with Mark. The time was dragging already.

"Isn't this too long?" she asked Zephon, worry creeping into her voice. "I thought you said it wouldn't seem like too much time?"

"Actually, he said that," Zephon replied with an amused smirk, nodding his head towards Zotiel at the truck.

"Oh. Sorry. You guys… are very similar." Lena replied. She was not sure if this was a faux-pas or not. She had been about to say that they 'all looked the same to her', but had, at least, caught herself before that one. They *did* look awfully similar. Just two collegiate-looking white boys. The *whitest* of white boys.

But who knew what kind of earthly etiquette was required here?

"Hasn't it been too long though?"

Zephon shook his head.

"He meant it wouldn't *seem* as long - won't *be* as long – for us. As it will be for them, that is. Using the doors knocks the timelines a little. So I'm told, anyway."

"So," Whitman asked with a curious beard stroke, "they could be in there for years? Years to them?"

"Not quite. The clocks are still connected, but a little speed up and slowdown is possible. Likely, actually. After we're done, it'll correct. Over time. The timelines wax and wane a little – in pockets, here and there – but they right themselves. They *have* to. They were in sync at the beginning. And they will be at the end."

"The end?" asked Lena.

"The end of all things."

Lena looked at Whitman who remained quietly contemplative, then back at Zephon where he sat.

"Do you know?"

"Know what?"

"When the end is? *What* the end is?"

Zephon smiled.

"No."

"Does anyone?"

"If they do, they haven't told the rest of us."

"But it *will* happen? The end. It's inevitable?"

"The universe, life, everything; it's not a circle. It's a spiral. One end does not connect to the other. There are cycles, revolutions within certainly, but there is a final strand. Beyond which there is no more."

Zephon looked at her, seeing the sorrowful fear in her.

"That something will end? That is what grants it its beauty, my dear. The inevitably of eventual death is what gives life its miracle." He smiled again, comfortingly.

"I would think a mortal would understand that. It's why your kind," he gained a wistful, faraway air, "it's why you are the favoured ones. Why we are not."

Lena looked less than comforted.

"I worked in a hospital. Not a maternity ward I'll grant you, but over the course of my career I saw a lot of new-borns. Minutes old. A wonderful sight. There's nothing so beautiful, so perfect. Not in my world."

Zephon nodded at this with curiosity, beckoning her to continue.

"Are you telling me that the beauty I saw, I *felt* – the miracle of seeing those little eyes open for the very first time, so full of hope and wonder – that its beauty stems from my knowledge that someday that child will *die*?"

Zephon smiled, comprehending now.

"No, my dear." He rested his pristine white hand on the knee of her crossed leg with reassuring compassion. "It stems from your knowledge that someday *you* will."

Lena said nothing, but she did smile a little. A strange, sad smile.

Whitman stood up, looking at the door.

"Do you hear that?" he asked.

His eyes were locked on the green wood. Staring pointedly. The three looked to him, then to the door, quieting.

A distant crack of gunfire, and something else behind it. Humming. Or… screaming? Zotiel dropped his current task at the truck's engine and strode with purpose to the cab.

"Something is happening," Whitman said warily, stepping forward.

༺✦༻

Swinging the door open, Whitman stared into the abyss. He saw only black, but deep within it he could hear an unholy cacophony. Shrieks. Terrible shrieks, rising out of the dark.

"Oh my God, what *is* that?" Lena asked him from behind.

Whitman said nothing. He didn't know what he would say if he did. He could see only black. All he knew was that the screams were getting closer.

A distant flash broke the mystery. A *crack* of a gun shot rang out, and illuminated for a moment a still image – Deborah running towards him, maybe a couple of hundred yards beyond the door, with someone he did not recognise in tow. The Paraclete. At his side the image of the kid, Mark, mid-swing. The sword Zephon had granted him in his hand, swiping up at some ungodly thing, hovering above. Raymond was behind, his pistol raised in the air, taking aim at something Whitman could not see.

The scene was like the sketched image in some swashbuckling children's adventure novel. In this case though, the art would likely have been rejected by the publisher. 'I like the poses m'boy, very exciting. But the creatures they're fighting? Too frightening. The kids'll have nightmares.'

At another flash, and another, the posed mannequins of his new friends jumped closer. The floating things that followed them did too, along with their shrill, cutting screams. And something else. Whitman couldn't make out what it was, the thing behind them, but it was massive. And it was awful. And it was gaining on them fast.

"This way!" he yelled into the abyss, swinging his arm.

A hundred yards now. They could not hear, but were sprinting in the right direction regardless. His voice had no chance against the din. The only sound that could compete, could dwarf it in fact, was the thunderous, wet smacks of the grotesque creature behind them. It lumbered along the walkway at their rear. Its movements seemed slow, but what it lacked in speed it made up for in sheer size and length of gait. Every putrid slap closed the gap.

☯︎

The awful splatting was gaining on them. Through his painful, panting breaths, Eli shouted to Deborah.

"What. Is. Behind?!"

"Keep running!" was her only response.

Their sprint through the endless black continued, tearing at his muscles and lungs. Suddenly, in the blank nothing ahead, something broke the darkness. A rectangular box of grey opened, maybe two hundred yards ahead of them. Within it, the silhouette of a man.

Raymond fired a few more shots and Eli thought he could make out a few less shrieks in the cacophony, but at this point that was akin to removing two stones from a pebble beach. Another grotesque splat shook the ground beneath them. Ahead, the silhouette was waving. Eli's breath was ripping through the sides of his throat as he ran, the cold air of the abyss churning in his lungs. Tearing at his chest. Another hundred yards.

They were going to make it. They were going to make it. They were... *SPLAT*... going to make it. They were... *SPLAT*... going to make... *SPLAT*. Fifty yards from the door. The thing behind was picking up speed. Making a last-ditch, sliming sprint. Eli made the worst mistake he had ever made.

"Don't look!" Deborah yelled, but it was too late.

He turned his head, and in the gloomy light cast from the doorway he beheld the face of the monstrosity. Its enormous, pulsating octopus head. Its flapping tendrils, swinging and dripping below its bulbous cranium. Its upwards protruding tusks and its flopping, wet, catfish body. Those were grotesque enough. But its eyes – its blood-clot purple eyes – they were a nightmare beyond what he could fathom. They were sickness. They were madness. They were *disease*.

Eli's eyes widened and he stumbled. his hand loosed from Deborah's and he splayed across the rock floor, ten feet from the door that would be his salvation. Pain smashed through his head as it hit the solid ground, and a dizzying concussion brought the dark world to its knees around him.

He felt a frantic clawing at his clothes as a thick hand – the hand that had saved him minutes ago – tried in vain to grip at him as its owner passed in his own huffing, puffing sprint. Failing to get a hold, it followed its owner onward to the door. He saw, through dizzied eyes, Deborah, spinning around right at the cusp of the door. She looked his way. Did she mean to turn back?!

"N*nnn*!" He cried out, trying to stop her.

She ran back anyway, but stopped at the midpoint between him and the door, terror striking a claim across her face. She looked up behind him in fearful horror. Whatever the octopus-faced creature was, it had him now. A dismal groan slipped from his lips. He closed his eyes tight, waiting for whatever grotesquery was to be his punishment.

A guttural, triumphant roar bellowed from behind. It shook the world, and splattered his body and the back of his head and neck with some putrid, liquid filth. He felt it plummet down towards him. Right as he should have felt the crush, however, the roar's pitch heightened, and it morphed into a thunderous squeal. A squeal of anguish. A squeal of surprised pain. She lifted him.

As Deborah pulled him to his feet, gunfire rang out from the doorway. Over and over and over. The guardian man, firing a volley at the octopus creature. In its light Eli caught sight of the teenage kid, standing at his back. He was holding his rapier high above his head, the point straight up into the air. Behind him the octopus creature, swaying back in its deafening mewl, clawed at the underside of its tendrils with gruesome, fish-scaled tentacles.

Deborah shoved him violently towards the door. Eli stumbled through, taking the big shooter with him, and fell onto hard stone beyond. He flopped round just in time to see Deborah burst through the door behind him, pushing the kid with the rapier at her front. The silhouette – now a bearded old guy with a bowtie – slammed the door shut, and a muscular blonde man in a white T-shirt and jeans swung a fireman's axe, brutally smashing the pristine golden doorknob from the wood with one heavy, crunching swing.

The door, the green wooden door, identical to the one he had entered in the alley beside Furey's, seemed to age in an instant. Its bright emerald paintwork faded to a flaking, rotted grey. Its golden hinges became a rusted mass. He stared down at the doorknob as it rolled across the stone floor, coming to a stop against his splayed leg. It was ancient, tarnished brass. Dull and lifeless.

As the eclectic mix of oddballs huffed and panted around him, Eli tried as best he could to focus, and to stop his pained head from lolling around. The figures around him kept swimming in and out of focus.

One stepped towards him, out of the blur into clear space in front. She looked down at him with a smile as he strained to focus his lenses.

"Hi Eli," she said. "You look different than I pictured."

The group sat, all together in the back of the truck this time, as Zotiel sped down the spiralling road of doors.

"You need to slow down!" Lena shouted to him tensely, as she struggled to apply a bandage to the sizeable lesion on Eli's forehead. The centrifugal force in the van was impeding her attempts. "This isn't helping!"

"No can do, m'love," Zotiel called back over his shoulder. "This isn't a pleasure tour any longer. Now he's here, things are gonna get a little rough."

"They weren't rough before?!"

"Rougher," Zotiel grimaced.

"Why now?" Deborah called to him.

"Those things out there took an interest in what life you guys have left, and – no offense – but that ain't much. Imagine what they'll think of an actual living soul?"

He kept the truck's pace breakneck.

"Where are we?" asked Eli. Groggy, trying to regain composure.

"Don't worry about it now, Gorgeous," Deborah replied, smiling as best she could through the alarm and the chaos. "We'll have plenty time for that."

It felt odd to call him that now. Now that she actually knew what he looked like. Eli was a good looking guy, it wasn't that it was ill fitting. Tall and dark haired, with a disheveled look that gelled easily with his don't-give-a-shit brand of cool. It just seemed strange after so long spent using the moniker ironically. In the face of not knowing.

"I was..." Eli squinted as he attempted to order his jumbled thoughts. "Looking for you. I was meant to look for you."

"I know," Deborah replied. "You wanted to, right?"

"I chose... I think..."

"Yes." She smiled again. "Thanks for that."

"How's his head?" grunted Raymond.

"He'll live," Lena replied. "Better, if I can get this *bloody* dressing on it."

She struggled a little longer, holding lengths of gauze and safety pins in her lips as she rocked back and forth with the jolts of the truck, but did eventually get it suitably wrapped. She set to work checking the arm that he cradled.

"Why... did you turn?" Eli asked with an odd frown on his face.

"What?" asked Deborah.

"At the door... when I fell. Tried to tell you not to. That thing..."

"We got out, Eli. We got out and now we're here."

"Was stupid..." he croaked.

"Well, I'm stupid." She grasped his hand supportively. "Besides, when did I ever let you tell me what to do?"

"Just the once," he replied with groggy regret. Deborah cocked her head, first in confused sympathy, then in glum comprehension.

"Rest Eli," she sighed, letting go of his hand.

"What was that thing?" asked Mark. He had been silent since emerging from the door. He sat now, staring at the rapier Zephon had entrusted to him when he had insisted on going with Deborah and Raymond.

"Something bad," Zephon replied to him. "I don't know what it was. But there are things that live in the spaces in between. Things that don't care for any of the stakes of this world or the other. Things that just want to live. Like anything else."

Mark continued to stare at the ornate hilt of the rapier, but said nothing more.

"There will be trouble, mein freund? Outside?" Whitman addressed Zotiel at the wheel, though Zephon answered.

"I'm amazed they haven't reached us already." His face was a grim contortion.

"So what is our plan?" Whitman asked.

"Speed," Zotiel growled. His eyes never straying from the road ahead.

∽∾

Zephon's amazement did not hold for long. As the road's cyclical path began to decrease in circumference and the more obvious doors yielded in favour of rough stone outlines, the rumbling howl of the congregation below rose loud above the engine's whir. Here and there they could see grey, spectral figures bolting up the road, or clambering up over its edge. Zotiel made no attempt to avoid them. He battered their pale, sickly bodies aside with the vehicle.

The group said nothing to this. They had seen it before, and seen what could happen if one of those creatures got a grip of the truck. The hole in the roof that Zotiel had affixed a wooden board to as a temporary repair was reminder enough to elicit their tacit approval. The only one who lacked bitter experience to dull their distaste was Eli, and he was in no state to comment. His head would be a little fuzzy, Lena had told them that. He shouldn't be *this* out of it though, thought Deborah with concern. Should he?

He lay flat, his head raised up into Lena's crossed legged lap, staring at the ceiling with wide, fearful eyes.

"That's not normal is it?" Deborah asked her.

"For a head wound like his? No. But what else about this situation is normal?" Lena asked, looking just as concerned. Another slam rocked them as the truck bowled through another Lost soul.

"Whhha…" Eli moaned, staring questioningly up into nothing. There was something seriously wrong with him. Raymond and Whitman looked to each other, unsettled.

Suddenly he sat bolt upright, shocking Lena. She had been gently stroking his head in comfort.

"What is that?!" he cried, staring into middle distance at the air. Deborah glanced around, along with the others.

"What is what?"

"The goat! The goat! What is that?! What *is* that?" he babbled, his cry dripping to a whine.

Deborah turned to glance at the members of her group. Nothing in their eyes but disquiet confusion. Except in the front of the cab. Deborah saw Zephon and Zotiel glance at each other with bitter comprehension.

"You know don't you?!" she called to them. Rage was building in her. "You know what he's seeing?! Tell me!"

"We don't *know*! Not for sure!" Zephon yelled back over the roaring engine and the cacophonous din outside. Another thump rattled the van as they tore another face-painted Void Lost to shreds under the wheels.

"*Fuck you* you don't! You know! You knew before! Tell me!" she yelled.

"I think this land... I think it is claimed!" Zephon yelled back.

"What?! What does that mean? Claimed by who!?"

Thump. Splat.

"The goat skulls... The markers! The painted faces!" Zephon cried back.

"By who?!" she screamed.

The van tore down the last stretch of curve, and as the wide basin opened ahead of them the group beheld a sight that struck fear into their hearts. It was filled, end to end, with grey figures. They stood, they climbed, they scuttled and jumped, milling in every inch of the great cavern. Grotesque, hungry, naked men, their legs caked in filth. Painted-faced, harlot women, their sunken, sallow breasts swinging this way and that. Grey, vicious children, scuttling the ground like animals, gnashing little fangs. Live hunger in every pair of yellow eyes. Every tooth bared.

"Azazel!" Zotiel cried, flooring the accelerator and roaring the engine to full speed.

The group braced against the impending smash, Lena holding Eli's head tight against her. The truck ploughed through the mad crowd, crushing them beneath it as they made for the mouth of the cave.

Fracture Nine
ACTS

"Sounds to me like you think I should do it."

Rain battered off the hotel window. Real rain. Seattle rain. Just like Scottish rain, she thought nostalgically.

"I don't tell you what to do darlin'. It's up to you."

Deborah rolled her eyes. Eli was rarely so evasive. He obviously felt it was too good to be true as well, on some level at least. She looked to her side, at the sleeping figure in the bed. What had he said his name was again? Had she asked? She couldn't remember.

"Come on, Gorgeous, I'm asking you." She kept her voice low. Her bedfellow didn't stir. "You think it's legit?"

She stood from the bed, and paced, naked, out the door to the lounge section. Whatever his name, he had money. A suite in the Four Seasons on business? That was high-society business. Probably a banker of some kind. They always had more money than personality. She glanced around. Where had she left her smokes?

"It's a contract, and it came in through the secure system. It pays. A huge *amount actually."*

He paused, clearly re-reading something, clarifying. *"Yeah. Way more than it's worth, and it can be done easily with just the two of us. No split. Got a pretty quick timeframe though. Only a week to prepare, but I think we can do it."*

Deborah tut-tut'ed down the line, shaking her head to the dark hotel room.

"You're not answering me…"

"It's a contract darlin'. In case you hadn't noticed, they're getting rarer. These Chinese outfits, and the Russians? They're choking the market. Something this simple? With this kind of pay? It looks pretty good to me. I'm not the swing vote though. I just write the words. You're the one who has to act 'em out."

"Gorgeous?" Deborah was losing her patience with this runaround.

"*Yeah?*"

"Follow along with me now. Do. You. Think. It. Is. Legit?"

"*…Yes.*"

Deborah nodded quietly. She felt some relief at actually pulling an answer from him, but this job…? She wasn't convinced.

For starters, she hadn't been back to the UK for fifteen years. Not once had The Orchard offered her a contract for back home. Operatives never returned to any country they had visited prior to their career. That was *their* rule. They rarely – if ever – broke their own rules. Not without good reason. Having said that, she thought with a sigh, The Orchard wasn't what it once was. Eli wasn't wrong. These foreign outfits, with their half-mad, half-psycho trigger men? They *were* choking the market. Flooding it. Diluting the pay, diluting the art. Pissing all over the whole thing. When you don't give a fuck, it's easy to charge less. When every operative is a desperate, expendable criminal? No one cares to take care.

"You're sure?"

"*I know the system. I built parts of it. You'd need to be God Himself to get through without tripping some kind of alarm. It's legit.*"

"Maybe."

"*You don't think I know what I'm doing?*"

"I *know* that you do. I just don't think we're this lucky."

"*We've been lucky before.*"

"Not lately." She sighed.

"*So we're due?*"

Deborah smiled. Spotting her pack of slims, she grabbed them from the sofa.

"Maybe so."

She could hear Eli smile through the phone line as she lit one.

"*You know this place?*"

"No."

The photographs in the dossier hadn't looked familiar. And the name, Glen Neamh? She had never even heard of it. Though thinking about it now, that might just be the name of the estate, as opposed to the area. It was certainly big enough to warrant its own name. It was big enough to warrant its own area code.

"Why? Should I?"

"It's in Scotland is all. I thought it was a small country?"

"Yes, thank you Rand McNally. It's not *that* small. We don't all know each other. I grew up in the city. I've never been to the countryside."

"Place looks pretty huge. Guy must be rich. You see the statues in the back? And the tennis court?"

"I saw. Probably our way in," she said distractedly, thinking now.

"So we're accepting?"

"...Okay. Yeah. You can tell the client my partner convinced me."

"Thank fuck. I could do with the cash."

Deborah glanced back through the door to the bed, checking her latest, nameless dalliance was still in the arms of sleep. He was snoring softly.

"Gumbo prices rising again, Gorgeous?"

Eli laughed.

"Yeah. That's it."

Chapter Fifteen

TITAN

Grey bodies flew like spittle from the mouth of the mountain as it belched the truck out into the electric mist. Around them, great swathes of the Lost still crowded, but as they burst through the choke point like a bowling ball, sending them careening outwards, they passed the thickest crop and sped on out into the less densely packed desert. Figures swirled in throngs, shrieking and hollering behind. Cannibal natives, chanting and crying, pursuing their invaders' escape vessel.

"Who the fuck is Azazel?!" Deborah yelled to Zotiel. His white hands gripped the wheel like knuckled vices.

"The goat daemon!" Zephon shouted back, answering for him. "The second!"

The truck bumped and scraped, skidding this way and that on the powdery dust beneath its treads.

"The second what?!" Deborah shouted. Try as she might to glance at Zotiel's movements, she was having trouble anticipating the jolts of their transport. It was throwing them around wildly.

"The second in command! The second Fallen!" Zotiel bellowed, spinning the wheel violently as he did, avoiding more grey figures and a goat skull marker rising out of the dusty plain. The group went skidding to one side in the back. Deborah clung to the sides hard.

Eli looked terrible. As his limp body slid across the van, Lena tried to keep his head steady, but his horrified stare into the dead space above him was unfaltering and sickly. The bandage she had hastily applied to the gash in his forehead was slipping in the chaos, and thick viscous blood dribbled over a dislodged clot at the side of it. Deborah caught Lena's eye, and the look she returned was not comforting. A glance of anxious fear.

"Is he dead?" Mark asked as he looked down at his pale, unblinking face.

"No," Lena replied frantically, "but he's not good. Whatever is doing this to him, it isn't the cut."

Another metallic thud rocked the truck as a grey little boy, no older looking than seven, caught a grip around the lip of the cab's bonnet and swung violently around struggling to gain a foothold on it. The force splintered the arm he grabbed with, sending a yellowed bone bursting horribly through the waxy skin at his bicep, but his grip held. With his other hand he grabbed the windshield rim and hoisted himself up. His eyes peered in at them with hungry malice.

"As long as they're after us we know he's alive!" Raymond grunted, rising unsteadily to his feet.

Whitman, Mark, and Deborah watched as he pulled himself up behind Zotiel. He leaned in to the side from behind the driver's seat, grabbing the window crank.

"What the hell are you doing?!" Mark cried in shock as Raymond began to revolve the handle, lowering the window.

"My job!" he barked back.

He twisted his arm, revolver in hand, around the frame. With a crack, he fired. The vicious gnashing of the grey boy ceased as a huge flap of his cranium blew out across the desert, leaving what remained of his head to splat miserably against the bonnet. It followed his naked, rag-doll body, sliding off and under the wheels, leaving a ghastly, gelatinous smear of black down the front of the vehicle. Raymond began to hurriedly wind the window back.

Mark gawped in revulsion. Deborah stared with pride at Raymond. '*His job*,' she thought. He was in it now. All the way in.

A bald, grey woman slammed against the passenger side of the cab, grabbing the rim of the door. Her toothy, triumphant grin putrid on her gaudily painted face.

"You still got that sword, kid?" Zephon shouted over the din. Mark looked down at the rapier in his hand.

"Y... Yes..." He stuttered a little, but found his bearings. "Yes!"

"Then I suggest you use it!"

He wound his window down as fast as he could. Mark stared down at the rapier once more, then, snapping to, lifted it with speed. He plunged it through the woman's body, right between her sallow, flapping breasts. Her grin contorted to pained anguish as she lost her grip and fell from view. Mark stood in shock, staring at the blade. The black filth hung on it for a moment, but then seemed to evaporate, burned away from below, by the blade itself. It left nothing but pure, glinting silver.

"Well," remarked Whitman. "That is a thing, isn't it?" He touched Mark's arm, pulling him back from whatever place his mind had taken him.

Deborah stared out the windscreen, surveying the desert beyond. The crowd of grey figures was thinning as they sped across it, but they were by no means clear of danger. The thumps and thuds of the truck bursting them beneath its tyres was a little less frequent, but continued.

"Are we getting away?" she shouted to Zotiel.

"Maybe," he called back, "but don't..."

He was cut off by a blood curdling shriek from inside the truck. Every head but his whipped around. Eli still lay prostrate, but his stare was no longer vacant. His eyes were alive with dread.

"NOOOOO!" he shrieked. "*NOOOOO!*"

He whipped his arms around in the air above, as if swatting at an invisible swarm.

Deborah stared down at Lena as she struggled to hold him still. Her eyes were saucers of confounded fear. Deborah knelt, steadying herself against the swings of the truck's movements and the periodic thumps of the Void Lost around and beneath it.

"Eli!" she shouted, touching his face. It was cold and waxy and twitched at her touch. "Eli, what are you seeing?"

His body convulsed as she tried to steady the epileptic flailing of his limbs.

"*NOOOOOO!*" he shrieked again, in a voice mad with terror. "NO NO! *DON'T!*"

Lena pulled his head into her, cradling it. Tears streamed from her closed eyes. She muttered in frantic, hushed whispers of futile comfort. Deborah looked around in desperation, but solicited nothing but disconsolate shrugs and fearful looks from the group.

A thunderous, heaving crash reverberated through the ground, bouncing the truck several feet into the air. The group fell about within it. Deborah landed facedown on Eli and Lena, scrambling as she lifted herself.

"What the fuck was that?!" she yelled.

It had felt like an earthquake. A volcano. Something more than an instrument of attack. More than an instrument of war. It felt like an instrument of nature. It shook the desert itself.

"Oh my God."

Raymond gasped as he gazed out the window. Deborah pulled herself up to meet him, following his eye-line. He was staring out at the mountain range they had fled, now lying to their left in the distance under the fizzing, purple sky. Past the thousands of grey bodies and yellow seeking eyes, past hundreds of goat skull markers sticking like gravestones out of the dusty ground, deep in the mountain line, something shifted.

"Oh my God," she repeated, caring nothing for the use of the term.

The mountain was moving.

※

"What the hell is that thing?!" cried Lena. From where she sat with Eli, she had to squint and strain to see over the backs of the cab seats.

"A titan!" Zephon yelled. He spoke not to her, but to Zotiel.

Deborah watched in awestruck horror. The mountain folded and shifted in on itself, lifting up and reforming.

Plumes of dust belched hundreds of feet into the static air. Plates of stone tore and twisted with gargantuan, tectonic beauty. It rose, higher and higher into the lightning streaked sky, a bulbous rocky mass, levitating with otherworldly force. The sight of it was dreadful and hypnotic. As she stared, she saw it happen. She saw the change. It was no longer the top of the mountain. It was the back of a great stone giant, unfolding from its kneel. It stood, tall and terrible on the plain, between its sleeping brothers. The mountain had awoken.

※

The chaotic cacophony of the Lost continued outside the speeding truck, but now, in the face of this new awesome horror, it seemed a mere aggravation. The attention of every member of the group – conscious and otherwise – was on the titan. It stood a moment, still – perhaps contemplating its newfound mobility, its newfound life. Then, with a slow, sub-sonic rumble that vibrated the world, it turned its head their way.

"Zote!" Zephon shouted, panic rising as he stared.

Zotiel spun the wheel forcing the truck to turn at speed. It listed precariously, two wheels lifting high, then bounced as it righted, pointed away from the mountain line. He no longer cared to find the easiest path through the hordes. They had bigger problems. Smashing though the grey figures, he tore in a beeline, directly away.

༺✦༻

BOOM.

The footfalls of the titan were earth shattering. Each one sent the truck bouncing and skidding across the ground, and sent grey figures flying into the air in waves as reverberations rippled across the dust plains.

"It's gaining on us!" shouted Raymond from the back of the transport.

He had given up trying to see through the dust-caked rear windows of the vehicle and had fired two shots into the glass, shattering it. A trench-coated elbow had removed the remains of the dirty glass. No one had objected. He stood, clinging to a strap on the truck's side, staring out at the mountain behind. The mountain that pursued them.

BOOM.

The titan moved slowly, but it didn't need speed. Each step was a quarter mile, and through the crowd of vicious natives, thinner now, but still considerable, the progress of the truck was not quick enough.

"What is it?" Whitman asked Zephon. He was panicked for sure, though calmer than Deborah would have expected.

"Azazel is more powerful than you could imagine!" Zephon called back to him. "He has enslaved this place! Enslaved these people! He has enslaved the mountain too!"

"It is a golem? A daemon?"

BOOM.

"Yes!"

"I mean, it is *summoned*?"

"Yes!" Zephon shouted. He made little attempt to hide the exasperation in his cries.

Whitman frowned, stroking his beard thoughtfully. His eyes flicked back and forth in rapid contemplation. Deborah and Mark glanced at each other with some confusion.

"What?" Deborah shouted to Whitman. "What is it?"

BOOM.

∽⌇∽

Lena wept as she cradled Eli's head in her lap. Whatever the reason for his current state, he was fading fast. Whatever had a hold of him was working with terrible speed.

Once again, she thought with awful anguish. Once again she was powerless to help. It cut her deep. She had barely heard the exchange above her head, between Whitman, Deborah and the kid, but as she looked up now, nothing but sad inability in her eyes, Whitman was animated. Gesticulating wildly to Deborah. He spoke to her in a hurried, frantic hush. Deborah was nodding, her eyes widening. With what? With fear? No, though Lena. With comprehension. With *hope*.

___

"You get to the door then!" Deborah yelled over the engine. "Raymond, give Whitman your pistol. He'll need to cover you."

Raymond glanced a second at the revolver in his hand, but just a second. He knew she was right. If this was going to work, they needed him doing the heavy lifting. Whitman didn't look much for the brawn side of things. He was smart though. Raymond knew that from their brief friendship. Hopefully smart enough. Hopefully his plan would work. Because if it didn't? Then they were fucked. He slapped the gun into Whitman's hand with an encouraging nod.

"You know how to shoot?"

"No..." said Whitman honestly, holding the revolver with some trepidation.

"Imagine a swastika on their shoulder. The rest'll come natural," Raymond winked. Whitman smirked a little.

"Thank you mein freund."

"Mark," Deborah continued, "Cut as many of these off as you can. Start twisting them together. You know what we need, right?" She indicated to the straps that adorned the seats of the transport. Mark nodded in compliance, taking the rapier and slicing the first neatly from the inside wall of the truck.

"Lena's got Eli." Deborah turned to her now where she sat. "You need to make sure he stays in here. This could get bumpy."

Lena nodded tensely and busied herself wrapping one of the connected straps around Eli's limp arm. The plan was crazy. It would throw them around something awful. But it *might* work. It better, she thought.

Deborah turned to the front of the truck.

"Zote?"

"Yeah?!"

He grimaced as he navigated the truck against the crowd and the thunderous footfalls.

"I need you to slow down soon."

"What?!" he yelled incredulously.

"At the next one of those markers. You need to stop."

"The hell I will! Are you fucking *crazy*?"

BOOM.

The van jumped again as the titan stepped forward.

"*Zote!*" she screamed at him. He turned in his seat to look at her, confusion in his white Angel face. "*Trust me.*"

He looked horrified, but after a moment, looking her dead in her icy eyes, he relented. Nodding, he turned back ahead.

"I hope you know what you're doing!" he shouted. "Here's one now!"

He slammed on the brakes, sending the van slip-sliding across the powder ground, knocking its inhabitants forward wildly. It skidded one way and then the other, almost toppling, but came to rest just past one of the goat skulls on its black wooden stake.

Deborah pulled in a steadying breath.

※

"Go!" she bellowed.

At her signal, Raymond slammed the rear door lock to one side, clutching the axe Zotiel had used back at the emerald door in his thick hands. He kicked the double doors open.

Two grey figures turned, surprise streaking across their faces at their apparent good fortune. Raymond lifted the axe high, ready to bury it in one of their skulls, but as they made a move to attack, their glee turned to shocked confusion as two cracks rang out and each dropped to the ground. Whitman stood holding the revolver at length as Raymond and Deborah leapt from the truck.

"Nice shooting," Raymond yelled as he barrelled forward, an axe-wielding tank. Whitman said nothing.

The titan in the closing distance filled the sky.

BOOM.

As they ran, another almighty footfall rocked across the world, bouncing them feet into the air and sending a tsunami of dust rolling towards them. They shielded their eyes from it as they made for the marker.

Raymond swung the axe with all his might. The black wood splintered and cried beneath it, and the marker listed to one side. The dust stinging his eyes, he yanked the axe back out and swung again, then a third time. On the fourth crushing blow, the marker toppled, thudding to the ashen ground with a fresh puff of dust. The goat skull that had adorned its helm shattered.

He flung the axe aside and stooped to grab the marker post. It weighed a ton, far more than either he or Deborah had expected, given its rotten look, but between the two of them – the strength and the adrenaline – they got it lifted. They shuffled back towards the truck's rear, grunting and straining as they did. Deborah heard a third crack of gunfire in the dust cloud, and felt a thud at her side as another grey body collapsed, feet from her. Whitman's a fast learner, she thought frantically. Thank fuck for that.

They huffed and strained the heavy log to the rear doors of the truck. As they stood it on its end, Whitman and Mark began strapping it to the rear axle with Raymond's help. Deborah jumped up, past Lena and the fading, whimpering body of Eli.

"You guys about done fuckin' around!?" Zotiel shouted back at her.

Deborah turned and shouted to the team.

"We ready?"

"Just about," Mark called back in a frenzy of panic and seatbelt straps. He, Raymond and Whitman had almost finished strapping the great wooden spike to the truck. Its pointed end balanced precariously on the ground below.

"Okay!" he yelled.

"Move over," Deborah told Zotiel.

"What?!" he snapped.

Two more shots rang out from behind. Deborah turned to see Raymond had retaken his pistol and was firing out the back with one hand, gripping the ceiling strap with his other. Mark and Whitman were busy strapping themselves in.

"I'm driving!" she yelled. She shoved him to the centre of the cab as she flipped over the seat-back and into the driver's seat.

"Do you even know what you're doing?!" Zotiel asked her hurriedly as he moved.

"We better hope so!" she cried. Raymond thumped the side of the van twice, signalling the group's readiness.

She roared the engine and the truck jumped forward.

∽∞∽

They tore across the landscape ahead of the titan. As Deborah floored the accelerator, she spun the wheel a little, veering a course around to the right.

"Where are you going?" Zephon shouted.

She said nothing, but sped across the desert in a great sweeping arc, the rear doors rattling and thumping as they clattered back and forth against their hinges and the wooden stake strapped to their rear. The sound of it digging and scraping into the dusty ground was a nerve-straining grate, but the group held steady. Zephon and Zotiel stared at each-other and out the open rear of the truck in confusion.

Further and further she arced the vehicle. The titan behind twisted with slow, brutal beauty, its rock head following the movements of the tiny truck below.

"You're going in a fucking circle!" Zotiel cried.

"Yes I am," she replied, staring out the side window at their incredible foe. It loomed like a skyscraper.

BOOM.

It stamped down with a colossal stone foot, missing the truck by a few hundred feet, sending them jolting up and down as the suspension yelped in pain. Deborah kept driving. In the distance, through the billowing dust, she saw the track the black stake had ripped into the ground where she first veered right. So far, so good.

"Now comes the interesting bit," she shouted.

"Now!?" cried Zotiel.

Deborah skidded and swerved, sliding the truck to face the titan head on. The group in the back held on against the movement, glancing warily at the straps that held the wooden stake. They were moaning, hurting in the strain, but they held for now. Mark had done a good job.

Lena retightened her hold on Eli's mewling, convulsing body. He made only guttural, liquid clicking sounds from his throat. His eyes rolled in his skull and his clammy body twitched violently. Thick, frothy white was seeping from the edges of his mouth and between his clenched teeth.

Deborah floored the pedal and renewed the truck's speed, driving directly at the titan's legs.

"Are you out of your..." Zotiel began, but silenced as Deborah swung the truck left then right, maintaining as straight a line as she could while avoiding its enormous stone appendages.

BOOM.

The titanic stone foot stabbed down into the earth, fifty yards too wide. She sped on, between its legs and beneath its body. As she approached the curving scar of her trail at the opposite end of the enormous circle they had drawn in the ground, she skidded and turned, back to face the angered mountain. Before anyone could argue, she fired forward.

BOOM.

Again its plummeting stomp fell wide. She spun once more then made a third pass. Each one a beeline from one side of the circle to the other.

"What are you *doing*?! Are you trying to *anger* it?!" Zotiel shouted with furious fear in his voice.

Zephon, staring out at the titan and at the trails they were making, turned to him.

"No," he said with an odd quiet. Contemplation in his panic. "She's trying to *exorcise* it."

Deborah streaked across the circle again, under the ever-angering titan. Its movements had quickened slightly. Its spinning, fruitless stomping *was* angering it. As she skidded the truck to the far side once more and aimed it forward at the titan she shouted back over her shoulder.

"I hope your Dad bought the right books Whitman!"

"Me too, Schönes Mädchen," he yelled. "Me too."

She fired forward, streaking at the titan.

BOOM.

It slammed its stone leg down into the dust right at their back, sending a thick cloud of dust billowing in through the open rear of the truck.

The world turned to painful, eye-watering particles of grey. Deborah fought in vain to keep her eyes from closing, but it was impossible. Burning tears closed them for her. It wouldn't have mattered. All they might have seen was an impenetrable wall of dust. It filled the vehicle, the world and her lungs. She kept her foot held hard against the throttle, hoping. Hoping against hope that her direction had been good. Hope was all she had left.

They sped across the plain. As the truck thumped over the lip of the circular scar it had torn in the earth, they felt a splitting squeal and a thud. The straps had finally given out, snapping and leaving the wooden stake behind them. Then, out of the chaos, a ripping whoosh rose all around them. A vacuum roar bellowed in their ears, vibrating the chassis of their transport violently. A sucking vortex-cry, ringing out from behind.

∽∞∼

Mark peered though the cloud, fighting his tearing eyes as he did. The outline of the titan slowly emerged through the thinning cloud, and for a moment he wilted. Dismay beckoned. It hadn't worked. As the dust faded though, he saw more.

The titan was there, but its posture was different. With triumphant relief, he smiled. Its head was facing up. Facing up and crying out.

"I think it worked!" he shouted.

The others joined him in their own ocular fight against the clouded air. The truck slowed as Deborah applied the brakes, turning in her seat to look out the rear.

The titan stood, staring up to the lightning skies above, bellowing in anguish. Perfectly central in the pentagram they had drawn in the powdery ground.

The roar was a world in itself. It seemed to suck all sound from the earth, channelling it into one almighty heaven-cry. As the sonic-boom thundered across the open plains, they saw rocks – great boulders that formed its head – begin to crack and tumble down its back. Slabs and massive sheets of stone began to slip from its form, scattering and tumbling around it. Plummeting to the dust below.

"It's falling apart!" Lena shouted with ecstatic glee.

Zephon grinned at Zotiel, who smiled back. As he watched the titan fall apart with the force of an avalanche though, his smile soured to a grimace.

"You need to drive," he said turning to Deborah with haste. "It's coming down uncontrolled."

Deborah said nothing. He was right. An entire mountain was collapsing at their back.

She nodded to Raymond at the rear, who in turn looked to Mark. Mark extended the rapier, handle first, to him and, taking it, he neatly sliced a few more belts from the inside seats. He wrapped them round the inside handles of the truck's rear doors. They were bent and destroyed now, but Raymond's handiwork would hold them closed for a while at least. Deborah turned back to the front windscreen and fired the engine once more.

They sped away from the rumbling rock-fall, the whole group watching the mountain crumble behind them.

Chapter Sixteen

THE QUIET AFTERLANDS

As the hours had passed, their flight across the Void plains, away from the dominion of Azazel, showed less and less evidence of his reign. The goat skull markers, once a forest, became first infrequent, then disappeared entirely. The Lost that they did see were less and less a purposeful mass and more and more sporadic, aimless wanderers. After several hours they had seen no more of the hideous gaudy make-up on the females they did pass, and, eventually, all they encountered were single shambling souls, devoid of purpose or menace. Just Lost, sad people heading across the plains. Future conscripts to Azazel's terrible chaos-army perhaps, though they did not know it.

At the moment the titan had fallen, Eli had shown no sign of change. Over time though, as their distance from the source of his torment increased, so too did his cognisance. After three hours, he had focussed his stare back within the truck and around at the group. After six he had spoken. A plead for water.

Deborah had not thought to bring any. In her plans, she had neglected that he, unlike the rest of their troupe, would still require sustenance of an earthly variety. It had pained her to realise that this oversight could cost him his recovery, or at least slow it, but Zephon had stepped from the front of the cab where he sat alongside Zotiel, once again at the helm, and furnished them with a canteen.

"Not much in the way of wells round these parts," he had told her, "but this should suffice. And then some."

She had thanked him and asked him what it was. With a smile, he had answered. Holy water. Of course.

After twelve hours he was sitting up, and introductions had been made. All the group had been warm. Deborah had been gladdened to see that. After the dangers they had encountered, far beyond what Cassiel and the others had warned them of, she had worried that acceptance of their newest member would be sour at best. Even Mark, while remaining somewhat stand-offish, had shaken the hand that was offered. Eli's admiring gratitude for his act of courage with the octopus-faced nightmare had been contagious.

Deborah had remained relatively quiet with him during the journey, allowing the whys and wherefores of the others to distract from her own. They had much to discuss, much old business, but it could wait. It would have to.

She could not deny her own feelings. The anger she felt at his part in her death. It had been his conviction that the apparent ease of that fateful job was well founded that had helped her to set aside her own judgement. Given her licence to rush in, where she should have been cautious. In the end though, she knew, she had made the decision. *She* was at fault. She could not deny that the temptation of the easy prey, the low hanging fruit, had been her undoing. All Eli had done was point to it.

She knew the guilt he felt. She had read it in the Scroll, and even if she hadn't, she knew Eli. She had known him half her life. Even if it had taken her death to see his face.

The whole affair was a mess. This crack in their trust could heal, but it could just as easily shatter. She didn't want that, and didn't think he did either, but in matters of the heart, the wants of the actors tended not to matter in the face of the whims of the script. That much her life had taught her, over and over. So she would wait.

~

They had, after what may have been days – certainly after many hours of seeing nothing but dust in the barren wasteland – arrived back where they began their flight across The Void. The tunnel entrance lay open, as they had left it. Zotiel pulled the truck to a crawl at its entrance.

"Here we are," he told them, edging inside the wide tunnel and bringing their transport to a stop.

He opened the cab door. Zephon opened his also, making to hop from the cab. To close the gate.

"Wait up a minute," Mark said as they did.

They turned to look back at him.

"I've been a decade and a half under a black sky. Let me stretch my legs under a purple one. A moment at least."

Zotiel looked ready to object, but as he glanced at Deborah she nodded, and he held fire.

"We can take a minute. We've seen nothing for hours."

Zotiel paused then nodded back.

"Thank fuck for that," Raymond sighed. He untied the straps around the bent and distorted rear doors, swung them open and hopped to the damp tunnel floor. The group followed, Eli helped down by Deborah and Lena, bringing up the rear.

Under the purple sky a few minutes became an hour or so, but in The Void, what was an hour between friends?

In an eternal storm, what was an hour?

∽⚬∼

"So you're all dead?"

Eli lay on the powdery ground, his back propped up on his elbows.

"We all *died*," Deborah replied, smirking at Zotiel as she quoted him. The speed with which the student had become the teacher tickled her.

"You all died…" Eli repeated thoughtfully.

"Yeah," Raymond replied. He sat cross-legged across from him, inspecting his pistol scrupulously as he spoke.

"Well, *we* did. Those boys – they didn't." He cocked his head towards the tunnel where Zephon and Zotiel were tinkering at the truck. "They're not really alive though either. Being Angels an' all."

Deborah suspected that Raymond was trying to elicit some kind of shock or awe from his newest ally, but if he was, he was left wanting. Eli simply nodded. She supposed that after all he had seen since he had chosen to leave his previous life behind, hearing that two of his travelling companions were Angels would be among the least difficult concepts to fathom.

"And now you're all on this crazy…" He groped around for a word. "*Quest*. To save the world. From God."

"*For* God," Lena corrected.

Deborah frowned a little. She wondered if this was really true, but chose to hold her tongue.

"*For* God," Eli repeated dreamily. "God is dead, long live God. That it?"

"Something like that," Raymond growled as he clicked the hammer of the revolver back and forth, testing the action.

"And you want me, why? Because I know how to programme a *computer*? Write code? Hack a database?" He raised an eyebrow skeptically. "You got a lot of websites you need access to? You need a fake passport for Heaven? God has cameras?"

Deborah, happy to let her companions do the talking for the most part, stepped in here.

"No one here has any *actual* experience of this, Gorg… Eli. There *is* no experience that could prepare for it. Raymond was a cop. Lena's a trauma nurse. Whitman plays games. Mark knows the con game. There's no *experience* of what we're going to do, because no has ever *attempted* what we're going to do. But we all have a starting point."

"Sounds like you have an ending point too," Eli replied with a misty look.

"How so?"

Eli gave her a cynical glance.

"You really think you'll succeed? This isn't some kind of… suicide?"

"I know I'll try," she replied. Looking around, at the group she raised her voice a little.

"Which brings up an important question. Is everybody in?"

They looked back at her.

"Before, it was all theoretical. All talk. Agreeing was easy then. *Easier*, anyway. But we've got skin in the game now, and this will just be a taster. Pretty soon – pretty *fucking* soon, I think – we're going to step past the point of no return. So I need to know… is everybod…"

"I am." Whitman cut in before she could finish.

Deborah looked to him with credulous, amused respect.

"I don't want to sit playing games for the rest of time Schönes Mädchen. I am in."

"Me too," replied Raymond, clicking the spinner into his revolver.

She smiled a little.

"That's two."

Deborah turned to Mark and Lena who sat together.

"I already told you I was coming with you," Mark said. He sat with the rapier resting on his crossed legs, toying with it. Lena sat beside him. She looked doubtful.

"I…" She wavered.

"It's your choice Caroline." Deborah spoke softly, sadly.

"I don't think so."

She sounded dejected. Her head was bowed, eyes cast to the ground. Mark, Whitman and Raymond exchanged some dismayed glances.

Zephon emerged from the tunnel with Zotiel, and they stooped and sat with the silent group. They were careful, Deborah noted, not to *join* their circle. They planted themselves just outside its edge. Respectful maybe, or perhaps simply stepping back. Knowing their time as chaperones was now closer to its end than its beginning.

"I was no use," Lena said quietly, talking almost to herself. "Everybody was working together. Mr Czapski had the plan, Ray did his thing of course, and Mark," she turned to him with a prideful sorrow-smile, "you were so brave behind that door. Like a valiant knight."

She looked down at her own lap.

"All I could do was hold onto you, Eli." She turned to him with doleful eyes. "There was nothing I could do to help you."

Deborah knew the look in her eyes. She said nothing. There was nothing to say.

Zotiel, who had listened staring out across the electric desert, spoke up softly.

"This place wasn't always called The Void."

They glanced around at him with dispirit interest.

"It didn't always crack and fire with the lightning. It was a peaceful place. Folks came here – your folks I mean – they came here for solitude. In their penance. Not to cross, you understand. Just to *be*. To take stock of themselves, I suppose."

He spoke in the same wistful melancholy that Zephon had, Deborah recalled. When he had discussed the fate of The Purgs, back at the vista where they had shared a smoke. Back in her own moment of doubt.

"The sky wasn't like this then. It was a sunset. Orange. A sunset that never ended. Like a painting. A still image of the glory of God. Guiding souls during their crises of absolution."

"The Quiet Afterlands," Zephon said quietly. The voice of long memory.

"That's right," Zotiel replied.

"I never saw it then," Zephon told him. Once again, for a moment, Zephon seemed very much younger than Zotiel.

Lena, watching their exchange, glanced bitterly at Zotiel for a moment, then withered.

"I *am* taking stock," she told him sorrowfully. "I don't see what I could offer. I want you to succeed." She turned to Deborah as she spoke. "I just don't see what I could *do*, other than hold you all back."

The group sat gazing across the Void Plains. The lightning cracked and clawed at the mountains in the distance. One tremendous, thick streak of lighting fired down, cutting at the crest of a high peak in the horizon. As they watched its light hang – longer it seemed than any bolt before or after it – it seemed to stab right into the peak, shattering it. Crunching the top like a ice-pick into an enormous, decayed tooth.

"Not so quiet any more," Mark mused. He stared at the mountain peak with awe. Awe and, Deborah noticed, some vague suspicion.

"Who is Dawn?" Eli piped up, leaning over onto one elbow and glancing at Lena. Lena looked up at him with surprise in her glassy eyes.

"And Harold?" Eli continued. "Who are they?"

She stared dumbfounded at him. Her eyes narrowed in suspicion, but her mouth sat ajar.

"When I was in that place... with the Goat-Head Man? With the dead eyes? My body was in the truck, I suppose, but my *mind* was with him... He was cutting me. Flaying me. It was awful. They pulled me. Pulled me away a little. Who are they?"

"They're... They're my..." Lena stared at him. Her vulnerable eyes strained, looking for the punch-line to this cruel joke, but they found none. Just honest curiosity.

"I have a niece and a nephew. Dawn and Harold junior. My brother is Harold."

"Hmm," he nodded. "They saved me, you know. From whatever the Goat-Head Man was doing. They pulled me from his final strike. More than once."

"I..." Lena's mouth made to speak, but with no words, it simply opened and closed in her puzzled face.

"You were praying, my dear?" Whitman asked her, touching a gentle hand to her knee.

"I... I suppose I was. Ironic in the circumstances, no?"

"No," Zephon replied categorically.

She glanced up with an anguished, desperate look.

"There are aspects of prayer that have little to do with The Office. Little to do with anything of grandeur. Just between you and the Divine. The *true* Divine. What remains of it."

Lena appeared to take great comfort in this cryptic explanation. Funny, Deborah thought. She would likely have rolled her eyes. She would have been irritated or flat out angry at Zephon's confounding vagueness, but to Lena, it seemed answer enough. Part of Deborah wished, in that moment, that she could be a little more like Lena. Take a little more comfort in the ethereal nature of hope. Have a little more faith.

"Well," Eli leaned back, staring back up at the purple sky. "Thanks for that. *Whatever* you did for me, it's really not so different than what he did for me."

He smiled at Mark, who nodded back.

Deborah watched as Lena continued to ponder this new revelation. Her silence heavy with thought.

"It's your choice Caroline," she repeated.

Lena watched her a moment, then nodded. A simple nod, but volumes behind it.

Eli watched this exchange with interest, then grimaced a little as he unfolded his painful body and lifted himself to his feet.

"Can I talk to you?" he asked Deborah, gesturing away from the group. She glanced around at their faces, then back to him and nodded, standing.

"Mark," Zotiel spoke up. Mark looked up from the rapier once more and looked his way.

"Come over here a minute, kid. There's something I wanna talk with you about."

Mark stood as Deborah and Eli paced away from the group, and headed in the opposite direction with Zotiel.

Lena, Whitman and Raymond sat in silence, watching the lightening crack in the distance. Lena held Whitman's hand gently.

◦◦◦

"You've been pretty quiet," Eli told her.

"There's a lot of talking to come," she replied.

"Sure." He nodded.

"You didn't force me Eli," she sighed.

"I did. Well, I pushed you at least."

"No. You talked me to the cliff. I'm the one who jumped. I know that." She squinted into middle distance. Tension furrowed her brow. "I forced *you* though."

"What, to come here?"

"Yes."

"No. You showed me the cliff. I jumped."

"You didn't know what was at the bottom though."

"Neither did you," Eli replied. "It was stupid of me to think that job would be so easy. Stupid to think we didn't need to plan more, but it's not like it would have necessarily made a difference. It's not like it was an *ambush*. Just a bad plan. You... do know that, right?"

Deborah scanned the horizon.

"So you jumped. Because you felt guilty? You were trying to... What? To absolve yourself?" She smiled grimly at him. "You had *no* idea what you were in for."

"I *still* don't. Neither do you, far as I can tell." He curled an eyebrow as he scanned her face. "I'd do it again though, I think. I still '*want to know more*'."

Deborah smiled.

"Like what?" she asked.

"Like why you're doing this."

His tone was conversational, but there was insight in it. She could tell he was pressing.

"You don't think it's a worthy cause?" she asked evasively.

"Saving the universe?" he mused with a smile. "Sure. But that's not why *you're* doing it."

"I'd like it to be," she replied, keeping her sullen tone level.

"I'm sure. But it's not."

She stared out at the mountains in the distance. Something about that peak, the peak that the lightning had struck, gave her an uneasy feel.

"You don't want to kill a God because it will help people."

She stared a long time, but it wasn't going to make a difference. Eli knew her as well as anyone. As well as she knew herself, most likely.

"No," she replied finally. "But I can help people while I do."

"Sure," he replied with a cynical edge. Insightful to the end. "You can save the world *and* get what you want."

He touched her arm, coaxing her round to face him.

"They can't know your reasons, Deborah."

"I know."

"If they find out? It'll finish the whole thing. It'll end *any* hope of your little group surviving. For good."

She stared at his serious face.

"*Our* little group," he added.

"You're coming then?"

He grinned again, a cocky half-smirk. One she had heard a thousand times on the other end of a phone line, now given a real-life picture to match. It fit perfectly.

"Where else am I gonna go?"

"Even knowing what I want? What I need?"

Eli seemed to think about this carefully.

"I've been there at every kill. I know what you get from them. And I know how addiction works. Keep chasing the hit, until it's not good enough. Until you need more."

"Killing a person is a hell of a thing," Deborah mused.

"Quite the smack hit," Eli replied, with cynicism in place of judgement. "But killing a *God?*..."

Deborah said nothing. She turned back to the open skies. To the mountain peak.

⁂

When they returned to the group, Mark was standing. The rapier he had carried before was now strapped in an ornate scabbard by his side.

"You keeping that?" Deborah asked him, looking to Zotiel.

"No use for it in my current line of work," Zotiel told her. "If you crazy kids succeed, I'll take it back. If you fail..." He drifted off a little, morose, then sighed. "Then it won't matter anyway."

Whitman and Lena looked at each other with an odd parental pride. Mark stood, hand on the hilt at his side. Raymond nodded at him in stoic brotherhood. A soldier's nod.

"We should get out of here," Zotiel told them. "It's quiet now, but The Goat knows we're here. We don't know where his allegiances lie."

"You mean..." Lena began, but drifted off. Zotiel nodded.

"He was his lieutenant. He lead a mighty charge on Mount Hermon. During the Fall. Defeated, yes, Lord Michael saw to that, but not slain. He fell alongside The Morning Star."

"How would he know what we mean to do?" Lena asked.

"He was a Grigori. A Watcher. Still is, I assume. He will have his ways."

"And you think he will report... Below?" Lena asked with morbid curiosity.

"Who knows? He may yet serve his old Master. Your *intentions* may align with the Morning Star, but your *reasons* certainly will not. Neither will the goals of the Revolution, that's for damn sure. Who could fathom His thoughts on the subject? You may have more than the Celestials to worry about on your journey."

Deborah noticed Mark peering as Zotiel spoke. Peering up at the same mountain peak that played on her mind.

"Who knows what may pursue you now?" Zotiel added, ominous in his hushed voice.

Who knew indeed?

"That's tomorrow's problem," Deborah replied. "For now? We made it. That makes today a pretty good day in my book."

"Amen," said Zephon.

She watched as her band of heroes stood, gathering themselves. They stepped back through the great iron door of the tunnel, and into the waiting vehicle. The Boys followed, taking their positions at the side of the door. With a nod, they pulled the levers. The chains rumbled and squealed, pulling the mighty metal shutter closed. The group watched the lightning crack and fizzle through the narrowing slat above the door, smaller and smaller, until with a deep thud the door closed, sealing the Void behind it.

The Void was the past. The past was the past.

The team was assembled.

Heaven waited.

Nothing

NOWHERE

//// ////
////So would we have continued?////
//// ////
////Would we have complied?////
////If we had known the truth then?////
//// ////
////Had I known the truth then?////
//// ////
//// ////
////Perhaps////
//// ////
////Perhaps I had known it all along////
//// ////

//// ////
////THE ODDS WERE SO AGAINST US////
//// ////
//// ////
////BUT THE GROUP?////
////IT FELT RIGHT////
//// ////
////OF COURSE WE WERE BLIND////
////WE ALL WERE////
//// ////
////FRIENDSHIP BLINDS EVERYONE TO THE TROUBLES AHEAD////
//// ////
////BUT I TRULY BELIEVE THAT…////
//// ////
//// ////
//// ////
////THAT WE WOULD HAVE CARRIED ON REGARDLESS////
//// ////
////I THINK////
//// ////
//// ////
////IF THEY HAD JUST TOLD THE TRUTH////
//// ////
////RIGHT THEN////
////BEFORE IT WAS TOO LATE////
//// ////
////BEFORE IT MEANT NOTHING////
//// ////
//// ////
////I SUPPOSE IT WILL NOT MATTER TO YOU////

Fracture Ten

REVELATIONS

Yahoel watched as the girl lay on the grass beneath him.

For a moment, she had glanced right at him, but in his motionless, statuesque form, hidden among the lifeless figures around him, her gaze had simply scanned past his. Unknowing.

He watched with curiosity as she spoke. At first he thought to him, but the context was wrong. She spoke to no one. No one present anyway. These mortals had their methods. No All-Mind to contend with, no thought projection, but what they lacked in natural ability they made up for with their relentless harnessing of the materials of their world. Technology. Their new guiding force.

The girl scanned across the grounds of the estate Cassiel had constructed. Spying through a long-eye that she carried. She continued to address her invisible friend, who appeared to guide her hand and eye. After some back and forth, she jumped to her haunches at his side. She made her way back through the night.

She is here.

Yes.

Cassiel acknowledged, closing his black eyes for a moment. He watched the blue flicker of the television set. Watching the scenes play out.

The girl, she entered the mansion as they had predicted. From the rear. She was making her way through the lower floors. Cassiel had been thorough. The whole estate was crafted meticulously, but his sense of foreboding still grated. Guarding from the All-Mind was tiring, even for him. Guarding also against his own trepidation? His own fearful self-loathing? That was apparently a step too far.

This had to be done. She had to die. Who knew when another opportunity would arise? It was wrong. It was abhorrent. But Lord Gabriel was right. It was necessary.

He watched as Raziel, cloaked in the trappings of their kind now, stepped into the hallway.

No, he strained. *Not yet. She must succeed. The kill must happen.*

Raziel ceased his search with the light-rod and stepped back through the hall.

Cassiel watched as she stood outside the door. The meticulous way she prepared. The slow silent analysis, followed by the speed of the act. In *every* action, she was not like them. She did things differently.

She was what they needed. She could make it work. The Revolution *could* succeed. Providing they did. Here. Providing it seemed natural. To her. Provided it seemed... *unguided*.

The man in the bed? That did strike at his heart. Cassiel wished there were some other way. He had searched the texts, scoured them long, but there was none. It had to be a mortal. He could create a whole city if need be, the materials of the Earthly plains were simple. But he was not The Office. He could not create a life. None of them could. Not even Lord Gabriel could do that.

So he had plucked this one from his slumber. An evil man for sure, he had seen the Scroll. He knew. This man deserved no less. He deserved *more*. He deserved *worse*. But the act itself? The deception? That pained him.

The girl's face, as she snuffed out the fire of his life, it was terrible. Impure. Grotesque to his eyes. Her sickness was abhorrent. Necessary, of course, but a foul thing regardless. In one so pure? In a Scion? Such an act, such a *look*, was cancer.

He watched the screen with fascination.

Such odd, contradictory creatures these mortals. Free will was a concept, a pure ideal. Beautiful. The acts it permitted, though? They were atrocious. Antithetical to its beauty. To the very nature of its children.

It is done.

Raziel paced the halls. It had to be him. It *had* to be.

The mortals they had brought, these 'Orchard' men? They could no doubt complete the task, but he would not allow it. He *wanted* to do it himself.

Fifteen years he had watched the girl as she moved through the dark places of her world. She was so different than the others. Fifteen years he had watched her brutality. Fifteen years he had wondered at its repellent beauty. It had to be him. He would *know*. He would know what she *felt*.

He approached behind the mortal, as it closed the door silently behind it. He heard it pace across the library Cassiel had built. She would not fall to such a creature. She was too good for that. Raziel knew that much. Fifteen years had taught him that much.

He waited at the door. This thing that they used? This instrument of death? It was a great weight in his hand. He could feel his own purity fight its weight, but he held it steady. Steady in his pristine, white hand.

He would know.

He felt her presence beyond the door. He pushed it open and stood at her back, watching as she turned towards him.

He would know.

EPILOGUE

From atop the smoking remnants of the mountain's peak, they looked like insects.

They *were* insects. Scuttling little creatures. Milling about in their pathetic little purposes, striking their little circle in the dust. Such trivial little insects, causing so *very* much trouble. Enough even to anger Him.

So they took down a titan? So be it. They could outsmart a thing of rock and earth. A lumbering nothing. Thoughtless and witless.

Fine. That was of no concern. They might have the scurrying teamwork of insects, but they would be no match for a foe with a mind. The Master knew that. It was why He had sent her. Why He had sent her back up from the fires. The Goat Man might have fucked up his shot, but at least he knew as much. At least he had sent word.

She eyed them with disgust. These little ants. They had made it across the Void. They sat now at its edge. Clever little ants. This would not be their battlefield, that much was clear.

There would be a battle though. There would be a *bloodbath*. Every step they took, was a step towards the killing floor. The sweet, beautiful killing floor. She would be there. She would be there to greet them. Every last scurrying one of them. The little blonde cunt most of all.

That little blonde cunt would feel her wrathful vengeance. That little blonde cunt would know her, at the last. That little blonde cunt would die in agony.

That fucking little blonde *cunt*.

As the ants scuttled into the tunnel, she watched them go. Scuttle away insects, she thought from the mountain top. The rocks around her still smouldered from their assault by the lightning strike that had carried her here from the fires. She stood among them, caressing the scar at her throat with mad, gleeful hatred. Scuttle away, scuttle away. It doesn't matter. I'll find you. I'll find you and I'll *show* you what it means to scuttle. I'll show you what it means to *fear*.

Lucille smiled wide.

I'll show them fear, she thought with murderous delight.

The little blonde cunt will scream.

To be continued in…

SPLINTERS

The Divine Revolution: Book II

Coming soon

ABOUT THE AUTHOR

Will James began writing down stories and ideas at the age of fourteen, and managed to thoroughly and decisively *not* finish about a dozen books over the course of his life, before finally concluding that writing 'The End' was something done by other people.

After the introduction of a son to his household created a sudden wealth of enforced, wakeful silent-time, however, he renewed his efforts and rekindled his dormant passion, finally managing to see a story through to its completion.

He lives in Aberdeenshire, Scotland with his wife Sarah, his son Elliot and a cat named Ferris – who is his when he's good, and his wife's when he's not.

Printed in Great Britain
by Amazon